SOUL
OF THE
WITCH

ROBERT SANBORN

I0563594

VINCI
BOOKS

BY ROBERT SANBORN

League of the Moon

Vinci Books

vinci-books.com

Published by Vinci Books Ltd in 2026

1

Copyright © Robert Sanborn 2024

The author has asserted their moral right to be identified as the author of this work in accordance with the Copyright, Designs and Patents Act 1988. This work is a work of fiction. Names, characters, places and incidents are the product of the author's imagination or are used fictitiously. Any resemblance to actual persons, living or dead, places and incidents is entirely coincidental.

All rights reserved. No part of this publication may be copied, reproduced, distributed, stored in any retrieval system, or transmitted in any form or by any means, including photocopying, recording, or other electronic or mechanical methods, nor used as a source for any form of machine learning including AI datasets, without the prior written permission of the publisher.

The publisher and the author have made every effort to obtain permissions for any third party material used in this book and to comply with copyright law. Any queries in this respect should be brought to the attention of the publisher and any omissions will be corrected in future editions.

A CIP catalogue record for this book is available from the British Library.

Paperback ISBN: 9781036705749

The EU GPSR authorised representative is Logos Europe, 9 rue Nicolas Poussion, 17000 La Rochelle, France contact@logoseurope.eu

CHAPTER I

BAD HAIR DAY

March 15, 1992

Armand Moreland woke up on the floor in the attic of his home. His head throbbed as if he'd drunk an entire bottle of vodka and passed out. The last time he'd tasted vodka, however, was hundreds of years in the past, when he'd been a living, breathing, mortal human. A hangover was out of the question, yet the throb in his head persisted. With great care, he sat up and surveyed the area.

The room was a disaster. Chairs lay on their sides. Books and papers once neatly stacked and organized on the shelves lining the attic walls were strewn about. The candle at the center of a gold-flaked pentacle in the middle of the room lay on its side, the wax having spilled and hardened into an amorphous blob.

"What in the hell happened here?" he asked the room, but it held its secret.

Moreland closed his eyes, then pinched the bridge of his nose. He tried desperately to remember anything from the night before but couldn't pull a single memory forth. The

1

pounding in his head didn't help, but it made him wonder about its origin. With that, he decided logic and investigation might prove more effective than memory at piecing together the mystery of his ruined attic.

The chairs were the first, most obvious clue. They were turned on their sides but had fallen adjacent to the points of the pentacle. So there'd been a meeting. Including himself, there'd been five attendees. That was a start. There'd been witches, obviously. Why else would the fallen chairs be gathered around a pentacle? But what they'd spoken of, and who they'd been, remained the question of the day.

Moreland surveyed the room once more, deciding a search around each chair was in order. He started at his own, picking up the chair and moving it a few feet back from where it fell, then getting down on one knee and observing the floor. There was nothing of note. He moved on to the chair closest to his left, repeating the process and achieving the same result. The next two yielded nothing. At the final chair in the circle, however, he found something. It was a single silver hair. It was long, suggesting but not proving it came from an older female. Moreland pinched it between his thumb and index finger, then placed it in the breast pocket of his suit.

Once more he eyed the room, deciding there was little to be learned from the mess. He was ready to leave when a flicker of light drew his eye toward the window overlooking the Atlantic. Three of the seven votive candles lining the sill remained burning from the night before, their stores of wax almost spent. As he drew closer, something flashed in his mind. It was brief, and he closed his eyes quickly in a desperate attempt to capture the memory before it vanished.

Was it a memory? he wondered.

An image of a young man and an older woman floating on the other side of the window painted the insides of his eyelids. The young man didn't ring any bells, but the older woman certainly did. He knew of the white witch, and knew how powerful she was. The woman in *this* brief flashback was much older, and that was something worth noting since he'd no doubt it was Wanda Heinze.

The Council had been watching her for some time now —without her knowledge, of course—because Wanda Heinze was protecting Armand Moreland's eventual successor as leader of the Council of the Realms. Maybe he'd glimpsed that successor tonight?

Time would tell.

When he next opened his eyes, the vampire reached into his pocket once more and removed the lone silver hair he'd found on the floor. He wondered if the hair had come from Ms. Heinze, but when he placed it in the palm of his left hand, then covered it over with his right, he knew it didn't. It radiated evil, something nowhere to be found in the soul of the white witch. No, this had come from the scalp of a dark magick practitioner.

And he knew just what needed to be done with it.

CHAPTER 2
THE ONE THAT GOT AWAY

September 17, 2004. Almost sixteen years before. Salem seemed so long ago. So far away. He both dreaded and looked forward to returning.

Artemis Davies was dying to relive the moment. When the woman's soul had left her body that night, and he *saw* it, he'd almost fainted from excitement. What had happened was the culmination of years of study, with a fair amount of blood, sweat, and tears thrown in. Until that night, he'd had mixed results.

He'd lived alone then, and he still did now, which was how he liked it. He didn't need much, didn't want much, and didn't have much. Too much shit weighed you down, made you less nimble. Artemis *needed* to be nimble. His passion project required it.

When you were a professor of neuroscience by day, and dabbled in parapsychology and dark magick at night, your shelf-life at whatever university of the moment you happened to be working in was short.

At the time he'd filmed her, he'd been at the University of Maine in Orono for just under eighteen months. Making it to nineteen had seemed unlikely, and he hadn't liked his chances. But he'd survived, despite widespread faculty disapproval of him and his field of study.

Screw those short-sighted assholes, he thought.

Artemis stood in the middle of his dingy apartment. A small lamp with a battered red shade sat atop an antique corner table. Next to it was a beat-up, blue La-Z-Boy recliner with duct tape holding together its tattered foot rest.

The lamp was lit—he rarely shut it off—and was the sole source of illumination for the entire place, save for a compact fluorescent hung from a wire in the bathroom. When he needed light elsewhere, he simply dragged the lamp from its spot and placed it where required.

Aside from a single sized bed with a mattress so thin it might as well be a blanket, and a battered and drool-stained pillow resting against a metal headboard, it was the only furniture in the place. Well, almost. If you considered a VHS tape player and a Sony nineteen-inch color TV furniture, then the latter rounded things out.

Artemis reached into the pocket of a stained, white lab coat and pulled a pack of Marlboro reds and a Zippo from it. He lit one, dragged deeply, and blew out the smoke as he reached for the lamp. A blueish cloud engulfed his light source, then swirled wildly as he whisked it through to the opposite side of the room. He placed the lamp on the floor next to the TV. The VCR was perched atop the Sony.

Artemis sat cross-legged on the floor, flicked ash into an overflowing ashtray resting on the VCR, then pulled the tape from the inside pocket of his lab coat. He held it close to the floor and under the cone of light the lamp provided. Neatly printed on the tape's label was: Subject 16 - J. Love. Salem, Massachusetts. TOD 3:13 a.m.

"Ahh. Sweet sixteen," he muttered.

Artemis popped the tape in, then waited.

As the first images appeared, he felt his pulse quicken. The recording was grainy. Filming in the dark wasn't ideal, but he'd wanted to document the *entire* event—including his approach from the moment he'd parked behind her black BMW, until he'd met her at the front door of the old lady's house.

The memories from that night flooded back in a rush.

He'd had to play it cool. The redhead hadn't wanted to be on camera, and he hadn't wanted to think about what she might do if she found out it was running. Artemis had taped over the camera's red 'record' light. When he'd exited his car, he'd tucked the camera under his arm, but with the lens facing forward.

Artemis drew deep on his cigarette, pushed aside the foreplay of memories past, and watched.

"Where the hell have you been?" whispered Mondra Tibbets.

"What do you mean?" he asked, looking at his watch.

"You were supposed to be here by three o'clock," she said, crossing her arms.

He looked down at his watch once more. "It's 3:05 a.m.," he complained.

"Is that three o'clock?"

"It was probably close to that when I opened the door of my car. What's the big deal?" asked Artemis.

"The big deal, professor, is I told you to be here, on this

stoop, no later than three. Timing is everything with this stuff. Seconds could make all the difference in the world."

"Okay, okay. I'm sorry. I'll be on time next—"

Artemis paused the tape. On the night of the recording, he'd not seen where the skinny young man with the top hat appeared from. One moment, it was just himself and the Red Witch on the stoop, the next, there'd been three of them.

He rewound it a fraction, cursing himself for not buying one of those fancy new DVD players. The camera he'd used back then required a full sized VHS tape, and the convenience of simply popping it into the VCR straight from his camera was nice, but the image quality was average at best. Then he reminded himself how much handheld digital recorders cost, even back then. Add that to a DVD player and you were talking serious cash; something he'd always lacked.

"Beggars, choosers," he whispered to the room.

He lit a fresh cigarette then pressed play, focusing on the area directly behind her left shoulder. The video resumed at the point where he'd said, "Okay, okay. I'm sorry. I'll be on time next—"

On the second 'okay,' he saw the first glint of moonlight reflecting off something shiny; it was a black silk top hat. It didn't ease into the picture from behind the Red Witch, nor did it slide into focus from either her left or her right. It *materialized*. One moment there was nothing there, the next, the skinny little psycho appeared.

"Shall we proceed, professor?" asked the skinny man.

"Who the hell are you?" asked Artemis.

"That's nothing you need to know, professor," said Mondra.

"The hell it isn't. This is supposed to be a secret. Just between us, witch."

The skinny young man stepped around the Red Witch, descended the three steps to the walk, and stood six inches from Artemis. "My name is Jagger Corey, professor. What I'm doing here is of no concern to you. You'll get what you need out of this little gathering, and so will I. If you mention seeing me here tonight... so much as breathe a word or utter the slightest syllable regarding my appearance in any way, I'll remove your testicles, stuff them down your throat, and then duct tape your mouth and nose shut. I don't know about you, sir, but I wouldn't want to leave this glorious world suffocating on my own balls. It seems a tough way to go. Do we understand each other?"

Though he couldn't see himself on the tape, he recalled how his mouth had hung open and words failed him.

The onscreen image of Jagger rose and fell slightly as Artemis nodded from behind the camera. Shortly after, Jagger smiled and said, "Great! Now that we're all on the same page, let's head inside."

Jagger turned to face Mondra. She was smiling at Corey, then reached for his hand. He took hers in his, and as she turned to head into Jenny Love's home, Jagger cupped the left side of her ass and gave it a squeeze.

"They deserve each other," Artemis whispered to the TV.

He fast-forwarded the tape. There was no point in watching the next few minutes. The only things he'd noticed, the first time through, was the green glow of the clock on the stove as they'd made their way through the kitchen, and the lumpy silhouettes of furniture resting in muted moonlight in the living room to the left.

He hit play.

To the right was the staircase, and he followed Jagger and Mondra to the second floor. As they reached the first landing, the staircase bent to the right. Mondra was directly in front of him. When she stepped from the landing and to her right, a framed picture of Jesus was revealed.

Though not religious, he'd always believed death was *not* the end of existence; organized religion simply held no attraction for him.

It came down to hypocrisy. Legions of so-called believers *claimed* righteousness, and in the name of the very man pictured in front of him. But so many had dirty little secrets. They pretended to be caring, upright, and holier-than-thou, only to come home from Sunday services, drink themselves blind, and beat the shit out of their wives and kids. In some instances, their *husbands* and kids.

These hypocrites talked of Hell and damnation for those who strayed from the path, then stepped happily off that path the moment they got the chance. As if God was some inattentive deity only concerned with taking attendance and filling the collection baskets.

Somehow, it seemed, they had the strange notion *He* was all powerful, but *His* power didn't reach beyond the brick and mortar of the church walls. Curiously, *His* power seemed to reassert itself when it suited their needs. Just ask any televangelist begging for 'love offerings' to fund a private jet for tending to his flock.

The guy in the frozen image on his screen got it. If he correctly remembered his Bible teaching, Jesus had gone into the church and flipped the tables of the money changers. The Son of God wasn't too pleased with people buying and selling in his Father's house.

Something about that, back then, had tugged at his

conscience, but it was a conscience buried under years of rot and neglect. There *had* been a time in his life when he'd been honest with himself. Younger Artemis would have blanched at what he was about to do. *And* those he'd chosen to do it with.

But the lies we tell ourselves are bound by the most complicated knots. Artemis had not been the exception that proved the rule. On that night, when his conscience had sniffed the vapors of immorality, the man he'd grown into slammed the lid on them.

In the here and now, he felt a vague sense of shame. Pushing it way down deep once more was less of a problem. And so, he did. When he resumed the tape, shame was nowhere to be found.

The video version of Artemis turned from Jesus, choosing instead to follow the Red Witch and her psycho companion up the stairs and into the room of Jenny Love.

The path was set—its pull irresistible. He *needed* to see.

And he needed another soul.

As he entered the room, Jagger Corey was poised with the pillow, holding it a few inches above the sleeping and peaceful face of the old woman. The redhead stood at the foot of the bed, an ornate silver and crystal flask in her right hand.

Places everyone! Artemis remembered thinking, fancying himself some morbid director. Keeping to the theme, he made his way over to the make-up mirror and grabbed the dainty chair from in front of it, then rested the camera on it, setting it so it only captured the old woman from the waist up. Confirming neither Jagger's nor Mondra's face would make it into the shot, he made a show of pressing 'record' on the camera. It was probably unnecessary, but it had to look good. Getting killed this close to a breakthrough would royally suck. He'd also gotten used to his balls where they were.

"Are we ready?" whispered Mondra.

Artemis nodded.

Jagger gave her a toothy smile.

The Red Witch jabbed Jenny's toe with a hypodermic needle with one hand, then uncapped the flask with the other. A blue mist floated lazily from its top, and the entire room shimmered like a lit swimming pool at night.

Jenny Love stirred. Her eyes shot open. She looked from Mondra to Jagger to Artemis, and then back to Mondra.

"You!" she said. Jenny instantly recognized her nephew Archie's crazy, redheaded, bitch of a girlfriend.

Mondra smiled, raising her right hand and giving Jenny a pinched, crab-like wave. "Bet you never thought I'd be the last thing you saw in this world. Am I right?"

Jenny had an answer for that, but words failed her. Her lips were numb. Suddenly, her eyes felt heavy. When she went to throw the blanket from her body, her arms betrayed her.

"Wow. That worked fast," said Jagger.

"Thank God," said Mondra. "This old bat *always* had to have the last word. Isn't that right, *Jenny?* No one was ever good enough for her little *Archie.*"

Her body was stilled, and her speech silenced. But Jenny Love was alive with terror.

Mondra the Red Witch had lots of *Friends in Low Places.* She'd acquired this particular potion from a bokor—voodoo sorcerer—ages ago. It had languished in the vial for years. The bokor had called it the 'zombie maker.' Its main ingredient was the poison of the pufferfish—tetrodotoxin. When

Artemis had disclosed his plan to her, the potion sprung to mind. She couldn't wait to use it on Jenny Love.

The Red Witch stepped around the foot of the bed, strode down its left side, and stood opposite Jagger. He eagerly awaited her permission, all too happy to snuff out the old woman's life. Mondra stilled him with a hand.

"I just want you to know, Jenny, Archie's going to find out about this tomorrow morning. And that man," she pointed to Jagger, "the one who's about to suffocate you? He's going to tell him, and be released from the custody of your nephew early because of it. So, you see? You're not going to die in vain after all."

Jenny stared daggers at Mondra. It was all she could do.

Mondra made a show of turning away. Then, like a horror movie version of Lieutenant Columbo, the forgetful detective from the old TV series, she stole his most famous line. "Just one more thing, Jenny." Mondra held up the flask. "There's not going to be any visit to the 'Pearly Gates' or a nice chat with 'The Lord' tonight. This," she pinged the flask with a long, black fingernail, "is going to be your new home for a while."

Jenny's eyes went wide with horror.

Mondra held up both hands, palms out and fingers splayed. "I know. It doesn't look like much. Not a lot of room. But I assure you, there's *plenty* of space inside, lots of new friends, and more on the way. It's like a nursing home for the dearly departed."

She nodded at Jagger. The pillow came down swiftly. Jenny Love died quickly and quietly. When Jagger removed the pillow, Artemis reached over and drew his hand down over Jenny's eyes, closing them forever.

He paused the tape, breathed deeply, and tried to

remember how he'd felt that night. It came back to him with surprising clarity.

A small part of him, still capable of guilt, had felt compelled to allow her that one final dignity. But as he'd pulled away, he felt a bump on the skin of her eyelid and remembered standing to check it out. It was a strange birthmark shaped like the number eight but lying sideways. *Odd*, he remembered thinking, but like the guilt he'd felt earlier in the night, in front of the picture of Jesus, he'd banished *that* memory too.

He hit play. The camera was now solely focused on the crystal flask.

He had watched the tape several times since that long ago night. Every time the luminous silver filament of the old woman's soul slipped silently from her chest, he was awestruck anew. And every time the blueish mist of the witch's potion seized that silver filament, then returned to the flask with it, he wondered about the destiny of his own soul.

Tonight was no different.

When he looked down once more he saw the VCR had paused all on its own. Artemis pointed the remote at it and hit play. It wouldn't budge. He leaned forward, ready to give the manual controls a shot, when he saw it.

The Red Witch was still in frame from the neck down. In her left hand was the flask, in her right, the stopper. On the flask's shiny glass front, his reflection stared back at him. That was a bit unsettling. Far worse, however, was a streak of silver light exiting the frame just above Mondra's right hand. In all the times he'd watched it since that night, this was the first time he'd ever seen *this*.

Jennifer Love's soul had escaped into the ether. They'd failed.

His eyes flashed to the flask resting atop his VCR. He couldn't remember how it had come to be in his possession. And he didn't much care. Having it was all that mattered now. It was just one soul lighter than he'd assumed.

So why does that bother me so much? he thought.

His eyes were drawn to the TV again. He stabbed the off button on the remote, then flung it across the room.

CHAPTER 3
VISIONS

March 12, 2020

Wanda Heinze gazed out her shop window, feeling sad. It had been a busy day at the Emporium, especially for a Monday. The weather had been gloriously warm, close to a record for the day, and Salem's witches had reveled in Mother Nature's largesse. Not a one suspected the changes the entire world would undergo a few short days later. Wanda's Wicca'd Emporium, along with just about every other business in the free and oppressed worlds, was about to shutter its doors indefinitely.

Wanda, however, *knew* something was coming. Henry Trank had told her so just an hour ago, and she believed him.

When Jagger Corey, an insane dark witch from an alternate reality, had been forced from this world, he'd left Henry with a gift. Though, if you'd asked Henry, '*gift*' was the last thing in the world he would've called it.

'The Asshole's Curse' was the phrase he'd coined. But, like it or not, it was proving useful.

On the night he'd been reunited with Joanne and

Delilah, and after some *alone* time with Jo to 'get his mind right,' he'd felt the first inklings of this 'gift' twang the strings of intuition. The Google headline about Covid leaped out at him like a neon sign, and he simply *knew*. Knowing, however, wasn't enough. If there was anything he'd learned in the short time he'd surrendered to all things magical, it was this: Talk to Wanda!

So, he had. By the end of their talk, he'd wished he hadn't.

Wanda doused the lights at the front of the store, then waited as her eyes adjusted to the gloom. Chamomile tea's welcoming scent beckoned her across the floor and through a swinging door next to an antique cash register. She raised a hand, parting the beaded door leading to her sigil-bound hallway.

Sigils glowed sublimely from matte black walls, each brightening as she passed, then resuming their fixed states. Wanda had recently reinforced *and* added to these protections, and with good reason; the Devil himself had been in this hallway and exited unscathed. Up until then, she'd thought the protections adequate.

The sigils and protection symbols, on that day, had covered the walls and the ceiling... but not the floor. When the *'witches'* Luci and Fermina had written a letter to the League of the Moon, confessing their true identity, Wanda realized they'd traveled this hallway and left through the front door. This was an unacceptable oversight on her part. A week later she'd remedied the situation. Jazz, Mercy, and Jo added their own touches, and Armand Moreland sealed it with a blessing.

"So mote it be," she whispered to the hallway. At her words every symbol flared, including the newest on the floor. By the time she made it through beaded door number two, she was smiling.

Wanda shuffled across the gleaming obsidian floor of her safe room, crossing directly over the gold-flaked pentacle and coming to a stop at the bar. She poured herself a steaming mug of tea, grabbed a graham cracker from the tin next to the teapot, and settled into a black leather beanbag chair. She placed her mug on the floor to her left, then rested the cracker across its rim so the steam could soften it. She closed her eyes, breathed deeply, then let it out slowly. As her mind calmed and her body settled, her thoughts drifted toward her conversation with Henry.

"I've had a vision, Wanda," said Henry.

"Okay. Tell me about it, sweetie."

Henry had closed his eyes and breathed deeply, just as Wanda was doing in the here and now.

When he'd next spoken, his voice was dreamy and far away.

"I'm in a dark room. There's a man in a bed, except it doesn't look like any bed I've ever seen. more like a metal slab with a blanket, and there's a digital readout along the bottom. Blue numbers. They read 0.00313."

"Okay," she'd reassured him. "You're doing good, honey. Keep going."

"There's a blanket covering him. He's old. Thin as a rail. His breathing's shallow... phlegmy sounding. Death is close. I see vague shapes around him. They're moving. One of them reaches out and strokes his head. I can see the energy transfer between the man and whoever is reaching from that *beautiful* light. It's gold. Sparkly. Part of me wants to jump into that light. *Bathe in it!* I know if I did, I might wanna stay."

Wanda remembered buttery yellow candlelight reflected in a tear running down Henry's cheek. "Do you need to take a break, sweetie?"

Henry swiped absently at the tear. "No. I'm okay. It's just *so beautiful*. Almost Irresistible. If I didn't have Jo and DeeDee—"

Henry knew full well he was the reincarnation of a witch named Madeleine, and that he and Jo were together in that previous lifetime. It was still, however, something he only understood on an intellectual level. He had no memory of the transition from one life to the next, and didn't know there was choice involved.

Most souls wanted and *chose* to travel together, learning and growing over time with each other. Some were 'younger' souls. Or, put a better way, less mature. While others were older, more experienced, or most accurately, had overcome karmic challenges. Wanda was one of the latter. It fell to her to teach and guide the less matured souls in her group, gradually exposing them to the mysteries of their soul's journey. That included what happened between lives. And, sometimes, what happened *within* a life.

"Yes, honey. It's the beginning of the next phase. Death is not the end, just a new beginning. We get to *choose* what comes next. It's why you're with Jo and also why DeeDee chose you as parents. Things seem random when you're in the middle of an incarnation, but our souls understand our needs. And we almost always resume the journey with those we love most. Entering the light is just the first stage of transition. Living or dead, you will always want to be part of that light, whether you realize it or not. That's how I see it. I won't presume to speak for others."

Wanda paused in her recollection as something occurred

to her. Jagger Corey had been evil, but sometimes evil brought about the greater good. The gift Henry was using now was something he didn't want. It came from Jagger, and he'd told Wanda on many occasions it felt dirty... tainted. However, Wanda suspected it might end up serving them well. Her job, at least in that moment, was to help Henry see its value. Henry's vision was all the proof she needed that, despite its source, Jagger's gift *was* a good thing.

Henry was silent, and appeared uncomfortable. Wanda suspected he was trying to reconcile the 'gift' with feelings of guilt for using it. When he next spoke, she couldn't tell if he'd worked it out or not.

He shook his head gently, as if trying to regain focus. It seemed to work. "He's only got a few seconds left, now. The breaths are farther apart. The sparkly stuff between him and the others is growing thicker. He's about to become part of the light, Wanda."

Wanda held her breath. The time for talk was over. *Something* was coming, and it was more than just a strange new virus.

Henry's voice was a whisper now. "My God! I didn't see it the first time, but there's... a silvery mist rising from the man's chest. It's heading toward the light but—"

"What, Henry? What is it?" asked Wanda.

Henry looked confused. "This isn't what I saw before. It ended differently last time. When the numbers on the scale changed, he said *'It's true! One three-thousandth!'* That's the last thing I saw. I don't know how it's possible, but the vision is longer, and changed somehow. *It's still going!* "

"Just tell me what you see. Keep calm, sweetie."

Henry breathed deeply, then blew it out. "Okay. He's moving fast now. It's tough to see. The room is dark. Where he was standing before—there's a chair there now. He must have been standing in front of it. There's a small red light glowing on the chair. I think the sick bastard *recorded* this. Now he's pulling something from the pocket of... a lab coat?"

"Can you see his face, Henry?"

"No. Not yet. He's had his back to me the whole time, and for some strange reason, I can't change my vantage point. It's like I'm stuck. There's some kind of container below me. It's long and silver. There are latch hinges along its sides. Something about it won't allow me closer."

"Okay, honey. You're doing good," said Wanda.

"The thing he pulled from his coat—it's the brightest thing in the room. Wait. I see it now. It's a vial. No, a flask. It's crystal. Whatever's in it, it's wicked bright blue." He paused. "No!"

Wanda had jumped in her beanbag chair then, and once again in the here and now. "What's the matter, Henry?"

"You son of a bitch! He's pulling the guy's soul away from the light. The others are screaming, Wanda. The flask in his hand is turning bright silver, and he's forcing the stopper back into the top. Now the silver is fading, it's becoming part of the blue. The visiting souls have left. The room's dark again, except for the scale. I can *taste* the sadness in the room. It has no effect on him at all." Henry's face grew crimson. "He's fucking *happy*."

His hands rested in his lap, balled into fists. Wanda gently covered them with her tiny, cool hands, making him jump a little. Until that moment, he'd been oblivious of his own anger. Wanda's healing touch melted his clenched fists into hands once more, and he turned them so his palms faced the ceiling. Wanda saw red crescents where his nails dug into the flesh of his palms, and she rubbed the tension away.

Through it all, he'd kept his eyes closed. This had impressed Wanda. He'd tamed his temper—a sign of spiritual maturity— and remained calm enough to see the vision through. She'd asked, "Is there more?"

Henry breathed deeply, held it, then let it out, settling deeper into the beanbag chair. He scrunched his already closed eyes, as if searching the room in his vision. Archie's mantra, *'remain detached,'* came to him. He followed it, but with great difficulty, for the vision did not end with something he saw. Instead, it was something he heard.

"What is it, sweetie?" Wanda had asked.

"He's in the hallway now. I can see him, but only the back of his cotton ball head. He's talking to someone, but the person is out of sight. It's a man. Young-sounding. Maybe a teenager?"

Henry had paused at that point. He didn't want to tell her. And in that pause, she knew.

"Say it, sweetie. I'm a big girl."

"The voice tells him, 'Heinze is next.'"

Wanda opened her eyes. She reached for her tea and brought it up to sip, then paused as she saw the graham cracker had collapsed. After a moment's deliberation, she shrugged and took a sip of cracker-flavored tea, pondering Henry's revelations.

She smiled. "I think I know who you are, monsieur Cotton Ball."

CHAPTER 4
ARRIVALS AND DEPARTURES

On the other side of Salem, Doctor Archibald Love stood behind the podium in his lecture hall. Above his right shoulder, an image of what appeared to be a tunnel in outer space glowed softly on the projection screen. He looked from one young face to the next, awaiting an answer to his question.

"Anyone? Come on, you must have some thoughts about it?"

A young man seated halfway up the lecture hall took a shot. "The view from the Millennium Falcon's cockpit in hyperspace?"

Archie turned to look at the image. "You know, it kinda does, Jenkins. But that's not what I'm going for here."

He looked down at the front row and caught Mercy Glass's eye, then raised a questioning eyebrow. Mercy shook her head slightly. She'd had a near-death experience and was quite familiar with the image at the front of the room, but she wanted to let the others in the room guess at it.

Archie understood her reluctance to answer; she wanted

to see if anyone had experienced the same thing. Something like an NDE could make you feel alone... different. He suspected Mercy might be on a quest to find a kindred soul, and he didn't blame her one bit.

Mercy was very much a part of the League of the Moon now. She'd found a home. But none of them had ever *died* and come back to life. Well, not in the *same* incarnation, and he suspected it was a lonely feeling. When a voice floated down from the back of the hall, and Mercy's head snapped around to listen, Archie's suspicions were confirmed.

"Professor?" asked the voice.

Archie squinted. The voice came from high up, and the room was too dark to see all the way to the top. "Yes?"

"I've seen that before. And it wasn't in a movie theater, either."

"Under what circumstances, mister—?" asked Archie.

"Sorry, sir. My name's Jamal Khalid. I saw that when I drowned. Last summer."

Archie heard Mercy draw in a sharp breath. Not only had she found a kindred soul, but they'd died in *exactly* the same way.

"Then you'll have no trouble telling me what you think this image depicts?"

"I won't presume to speak for others, sir, but I saw that on the way to the light. I died for over nine minutes, and traveled most of the way through something similar to that."

Mercy wasn't the only one facing the back of the lecture hall now. Jamal Khalid had everyone's attention. He spoke to Archie, but his eyes held Mercy's.

Mercy, despite the darkness enveloping the back row, saw his eyes. She only took hers from his long enough to confirm she wasn't seeing things. The students to his left and right were indiscernible silhouettes. Their eyes, like the totality of their bodies, were dark. Jamal's eyes, to Mercy, were the sole visible pair in the back row. They glowed softly. Their hue she recognized instantly, for it was the light of the other side, visible only to those who'd been to the undiscovered country. It had a quality unlike anything on earth. She knew he was telling the truth. Jamal had been there, and she wanted to know more.

Jamal was poised to elaborate when a door at the side of the lecture hall banged open. A tall, thin woman with curly black hair and big, round eyeglasses approached Archie. She stopped at his left side. Archie put a hand over the microphone as the woman leaned in and whispered something into his ear.

Mercy heard Archie whisper, "You've got to be shitting me." He looked at Annie, his receptionist, for a few seconds, wondering if she was pulling his leg. The look on her face told Mercy she wasn't. Archie looked stunned.

"I'm afraid I have some bad news," said Doctor Archibald Love. "Classes are cancelled for the foreseeable future. The governor has declared a shelter-in-place order for the next two weeks. I'll post any further information I find out on my website. That's all I have for you, at the moment. Be well."

As the lecture hall emptied, Mercy scanned the top row. Jamal, and his ethereal eyes, were gone.

∽

"You've got to be fucking kidding me," said Joanne Trank. "I have to shut down my shop for two weeks?"

Chief Byron Miller of the Salem Police Department put up both hands. "I know. I know. I think it's ridiculous, too.

24

But people much higher up the food chain decided this, Jo. They sit in their offices and call the shots, but guys like me take the bullets. Apparently, everyone but those shitheads are 'non-essential,' as the saying goes."

"I'm not blaming you, Byron. I know it's not your call." She blew out the frustration. "We'll be fine for a while. But I've got employees. Kids that need their jobs to pay off-campus rent. What are they supposed to do?"

Byron shrugged helplessly. He was looking at the ground, feeling like shit for delivering bad news per the mayor's orders. Then, he remembered what Henry did for a living. "What's Henry going to do? Is he gonna stay on at MGH? From what I hear, this thing is pretty serious, Jo."

"He didn't tell you?" asked Jo.

Byron looked surprised, and a bit apprehensive. "Tell me what?"

"He's known this was coming for a long time now. Remember what Luci and Fermina said about the world changing?" asked Jo.

Byron nodded. "I do."

"Well, Henry put two and two together. What they said in the note and what he read in the papers seemed *way* too coincidental. He knew it had to be a disease of *some* kind on its way. So, he got out in front of it and took a leave of absence. He was against the idea, at first. Said he wanted to be there on the front lines if they needed him."

"What changed his mind?" asked Byron.

"He had a vision," said Jo.

In the not-too-distant past, a statement of that nature would have earned Jo a condescending smirk from Byron. Today, it snapped him to full attention. "Shit. What did he see?"

Jo gave him the CliffsNotes version.

"No better description of the guy? Or where this might have happened?" asked Byron.

"If *only* it were that easy," said Jo.

Byron thought it over for a moment. "Well, the guy probably has some kind of medical background. And if Henry's having visions of this schmuck, it probably means he's headed here. Maybe he's here already."

"What are you thinking of doing?" asked Jo. The hint of worry in her voice touched Byron.

Smiling, Byron said, "Nothing crazy. After I make the rounds, I'll head over to Salem Hospital and see if there's anyone new on staff. Probably won't amount to much, but it's a good place to start."

"Okay, Sherlock. But just remember something..."

"What's that?" asked Byron.

"If Henry is having visions of this guy, and what he's doing, it's probably not as simple as some doctor going off the rails. You pickin' up what I'm puttin' down?"

"What're you gettin' at, Jo?"

"Whoever this asshole is, he's probably connected to some really bad people. And I'm not talking shoplifters or drunk drivers, Chiefy." She fixed him with a serious look. "You can bet your ass there's dark magick involved here."

"Point taken. I'll be careful."

Jo smirked. "You better be. I don't want to have to save your sorry ass again."

Byron laughed as he turned and made his way to the police issue Ford Explorer. As he reached for the door handle, Jo called over to him. "Byron?"

He raised a questioning eyebrow.

"I'm serious. Be careful. Don't let this guy get a sniff you're looking into him. Okay?"

The look in her eyes scared him to the bone. Was she being overly cautious? Who knew? But he took her concern seriously. Jo could be a monumental wise-ass, but when it came down to stuff like this, and she got *that* look in her eye, he knew to heed the warning. He nodded gravely, got behind the wheel, and headed for the Salem Hospital.

Jo stepped back inside the Cracked Cauldron, closed the door behind her, then flipped the sign on the door from 'Open' to 'Closed.' She leaned her back against the door and let out a long breath. Closing her eyes, she sent a prayer of protection Byron's way. With that done, she prepared herself to dole out the bad news to her employees.

"At least it's only two weeks," she whispered, knowing it was a lie.

It all just felt... bigger.

~

ARTEMIS DAVIES PUT the last of his few belongings into the trunk of the rental car, then closed the lid. He stepped from behind the white Nissan Sentra and was about to slip into the driver's seat when he suddenly stopped. Something was missing.

Artemis slapped at the pockets of his lab coat. They were empty. He shoved both hands into the pockets of his tan khakis, front and back, and came away with two dimes, three pennies, keys, and a gum wrapper flecked with lint. To be on the safe side, he reopened the trunk. TV, DVD player, digital camera, a bag of dirty laundry, half a carton of Marlboro reds, a dirty black ashtray, and the suitcase containing his "soul" tapes—all his worldly possessions—were accounted for. The trusty lamp belonged to his landlord and the drool-stained, lifeless pillow had outlived its usefulness. The scale he used for his "soul work" had been sent ahead from the University of Maine, where he had miraculously remained on staff since 2003, to his next workplace. Artemis never understood why they hadn't canned him back in 2004 after numerous warnings about his conduct, but he suspected forces beyond his understanding might have played a role.

He'd received new instructions last night, as he slept. They were always, out of necessity, vague, in code, and written on an index card stuffed in an envelope and slid under his door. Excited by this newest prospect, he hastily tore the envelope open and tossed it in the trash, then focused like a laser on the first clue.

His father was killed by a cannon ball.

Artemis had minored in history. The writer of the index cards knew this. He was fairly certain the clue referred to a French aristocrat who'd volunteered for and fought in the American Revolutionary War. General Lafayette, many historians believed, wanted revenge against the British for killing his father by cannon ball during the Seven Years' War.

The second line read: *The answer to everything. Times 100.*

Artemis had laughed out loud at that. One of his favorite books was "The Hitchhiker's Guide to the Galaxy" by Douglas Adams. A fictional supercomputer's answer to "the Ultimate Question of Life, the Universe, and Everything" was a number: Forty-Two.

4200 Lafayette Street.

He committed it to memory.

The final line read: *Beauty eternal will guide you from the shadows.*

This referred to his newest contact. It was always cryptic and frustrated the hell out of him every time. Just before things came to a head, he usually deciphered it, but it was never easy. The need for complexity was understandable; someone was about to die. Concealing the contact's identity was of paramount importance. No one wanted to be an accessory to murder if things went sideways.

When he'd learned of the Red Witch's demise, he'd often wondered who'd taken over the task of sending the index cards. It *had* to be an associate of hers. In the end, he'd chosen not to give it much thought. What mattered was they kept coming, and his work continued. Now, with the end in sight, he wasn't about to delve any deeper.

With his hand poised on the Nissan's door handle, he shook the doubts. Meeting the messenger in the hallway after the old guy on the scale croaked had rattled him. Hearing Wanda Heinze's name had driven him to deeper distraction. His mind was in a million places.

One final time he ran through a mental checklist of everything needed for the trip to Salem, finally convincing himself the feeling of forgetting something was just nerves. With that, he hopped into the driver's seat, closed the door, and put the idling car into drive.

Later, he'd regret not making one more trip into his apartment.

CHAPTER 5
IN THE CARDS

A rmand Moreland was deep in meditation when his phone began playing "Witchy Woman" by the Eagles. He'd assigned each of his friends in the League of the Moon coven their own personal ringtone. "Witchy Woman" was Wanda's, and he smiled as he drew it from his pocket and tapped the green *answer* icon.

"Hello?"

"Hi, Armand. How are you, sweetie?" asked Wanda.

"Excellent. I've just finished a wonderful guided meditation. Have you ever used the "Calm" app?"

"No. But I'm always up for something new," said Wanda.

"You *really* should try it sometime. Now, to what do I owe the pleasure?"

"It's starting, Armand. Henry's visions are expanding, and the man in his latest is on the way."

Armand closed his eyes and pinched the bridge of his nose. He'd known this was coming, but he'd hoped for more time. Things in the magical world, however, worked on their own schedule. "Has Henry identified him?"

"No. I think his original intent was to relay the vision as he'd first seen it. He wanted my opinion. But something changed. Henry said it originally ended with someone's soul leaving their body. It's progressed to the point of that poor soul being captured."

Moreland gasped. "So it might be possible? I mean, I know it's possible to house a *piece* of a soul, or a fragment, but a soul in its entirety?"

"You're talking about what you did for Jo. Right?" asked Wanda.

"Yes. That was a simple memory, albeit a critical one. That's a far cry from housing a soul outside its body," said Moreland.

"Let's not forget Inanis," warned Wanda. "He captured a soul and inhabited its body for centuries. We know it can be done."

"True. But he was—is—a demon. Possession and black magick were involved."

Wanda waited before answering. "From everything Henry has seen, which isn't much, he appears to be a normal man. He's yet to see the guy's face, however. Henry said in the vision it felt like being held in place. 'Stuck in the wall' was how he put it."

Now it was Moreland's turn to be silent. After a few moments, he said, "I wonder if there's more involved than just this man?"

"Henry overheard Cotton Ball—that's what we're calling him—talking to someone else after the abduction. My name was brought up in the conversation."

Moreland waited a beat. Wanda knew him well enough to know what his silence meant; he was switching into protective mode. In a deadly serious tone, the vampire

31

asked, "What was said?"

"Cotton Ball asked this mystery person who's next. The reply was 'Heinze is next.'"

"Really, now?" asked Moreland. Only, to Wanda, it came out sounding more like a threat than a question. "Well, we'll just have to see about that, won't we?"

"I need you to do something for me, Armand. This won't be easy, but I beg you do as I ask. I might have a bead on this guy, but I need to check some things."

"What do you want from me?" he asked, warily.

"Let him, or them, come for me. And you can't breathe a word of it to anyone."

Moreland drew in a sharp breath. After a long pause, long enough that Wanda pulled the phone away to see if they were still connected, he said, "I know you well enough, now, to know your request isn't without solid reasoning. But given this man's particular stock-in-trade, i.e. *soul stealing*, and given you are most likely his next target, do you think it wise?"

"No. And it scares the hell out of me. It might not be him who comes for me. We know he's not working alone. That means somebody in Salem, or a *few somebodies*, might already be watching. I need to draw them out. There's more than just *my* ass on the line here, Armand."

"What do you mean?" asked the vampire-priest.

"Henry said he saw Cotton Ball pull the old man's soul into a crystal flask. I don't think it's this guy's first rodeo. I suspect there's a lot more than *one* soul in that flask. If we spook him, he might run. I couldn't live with myself if those souls were lost forever because I got a little scared."

Moreland sighed. "I understand, Wanda. I don't like it. I think it's risky... but I'll honor your wishes."

"Thank you, Armand."

"I hope you know what you're doing."

"Me too, sweetie. Me too."

When Wanda hung up, Armand Moreland resumed the lotus pose, re-inserted his ear buds, and took a deep breath. He tapped the phone's screen and the "Calm" app picked up where he'd stopped it. As his mind slowed, he immediately placed one thought at its center. He knew *exactly* what she was doing, and why—even if she hadn't figured it out yet. And he knew something about Henry Trank he couldn't tell a soul. His omission of these truths troubled him deeply. *'I hope they can forgive me.'*

The guided meditation ended and Armand Moreland opened his eyes. The time was now. The mirror called to him.

But first, there was one thing he needed to do. He crossed the room to the fireplace, stopping at the point where brick met hardwood floor. The vampire tapped the planks with the toe of his right shoe. When he tapped a hollow one, he scuffed that plank with the black sole of his loafer first one way, then the other.

X marked the spot. He just hoped it got noticed by the right person.

Jasmine Miso-Johnson had gotten *her* bad news visit from Byron shortly after he'd been to see Jo at the Cracked Cauldron. She knew, by the look on his face, he'd just come from Jo's place, so she refrained from giving him too much crap about it. The poor bastard was just doing his job, after all.

"When's the official shutdown date?" asked Jazz.

Byron blew out a frustrated breath. "March thirteenth. Tomorrow. I'm really sorry about this, Jazz."

"It's okay, Chief. Scott and I are okay for money. I could use the break, actually."

Byron's shoulders sagged with relief.

"Let me guess, you just came from the Cauldron?"

The question surprised him, but not as much as it would have a few months earlier. "How'd you guess?"

Jazz shrugged. "I figured you were making the rounds. Jo's shop is on the way. No magic, just a guess. She give it to you with both barrels?" asked Jazz.

He filled her in on the conversation with Jo.

"Yeah. Those kids are kinda screwed," she said.

"The whole friggin' country is kinda screwed right now. Don't know where this is all heading, but it ain't good."

Jazz nodded, then asked, "What else is on your mind, By?"

Now Byron was well and truly surprised, and it showed.

Jazz crossed her arms. "Come on, Chief. Spill it. Your aura's a mess. I see your usual colors, but there's a lotta dark shit in there with it."

Byron looked from one end of the street to the other. "I think we should talk inside, Jazz."

She thought he seemed spooked, and that wasn't like him. "That bad?"

He raised his right hand, then tilted it back and forth. "Maybe. I'd rather talk inside."

Jazz turned on her heel, pushed open the purple door to her shop, and held it open for Byron. He removed his hat, then stepped inside.

Byron had never set foot in her shop before, and he slowly took in the layout. It was much smaller than Wanda's

Wicca'd Emporium. The display area was roughly half the size of Wanda's. Two glass cases, separated for behind-counter access, ran the length of the back wall. The left and right walls were floor to ceiling shelves painted a matte black and dotted with silver and gold glitter. Similar to Wanda's shop, Jazz's shelves held spell kits, books on spells, tarot decks, and magical artifacts. Glass jars held items he mostly didn't recognize, and the investigator in him made a mental note to ask her about them later. The calming, powdery-spice scent of Dragon's Blood hung in the air.

"Chief?"

Byron snapped out of curious mode. "Sorry, just taking in your wares. Interesting stuff."

Jazz smirked. "You don't know the half of it." She tilted her head toward the counter. "This way."

Byron followed her through a separation between glass cases, and then to the right. Where the counter met the wall on the right-hand side was a doorway he hadn't noticed upon entering. It was slightly inset into the wall. Byron stopped short. "*Another* beaded door? What is it with all of you and the beaded doors? Were you all part of some 1970s cult?"

"Yes! Didn't you know? The beads were a signal to throw off *The Man*. All us hippies had to stick together."

Byron laughed, then held up both hands in surrender. "Okay."

Jazz smiled. "It's really just a coincidence. I had this before I ever knew Wanda, and I'm pretty sure Jo had hers before she met Wanda, too. There *is* a little more to them than meets the eye, though."

"Oh?"

Jazz flashed him a wicked grin. "Before we pass through

them, think of the most negative thing you can come up with."

Byron looked toward the ceiling, thoughtful. "Okay."

"Now, hold on to that thought and follow me through the beads. Copy?"

"Copy," said Byron.

Jazz walked through the beaded doorway, turned, and waited for Byron on the other side.

Byron strode through, letting the beads slide up, over, and around. When he reached Jazz, he stopped and asked, "What?"

"What were you thinking of before you came through the beads?"

Byron frowned. Concentration creased his face. He turned to look back through the beaded doorway, as if the beads might give up the answer. Then, the fog cleared. He snapped his fingers. "I was thinking of that night in Wanda's shop. When that piece of shit demon planted one on my mug."

Jazz laughed and asked, "Pretty sweet, huh?"

"What just happened? Why couldn't I remember it right away?"

"The beads are enchanted. Negativity is not only prohibited from this room, it's stripped away from anyone that passes through the beads. I'm pretty sure Wanda and Jo have them set up the same way."

"So how was I able to remember the thought on this side?" asked Byron.

"It strips *negativity*, not memory. How do you feel about that memory now?"

He took a second to answer, then said, "Now that you mention it, it scares me a lot less."

"And it will from now on, Chief. The effects are mild but permanent. It jump-starts the spiritual healing process. You're welcome." Jazz smiled.

She turned from him and headed toward a table at the center of the room. It was ringed with padded chocolate leather and had a black felt surface. Gold symbols of the zodiac were stenciled on the felt in a circular pattern, enclosed in a stenciled gold circle. A deck of cards sat on the spot marked 'Pisces.'

"We having a game of Texas Hold 'Em, Jazz?"

"Texas what?"

Byron nodded toward the deck as Jazz reached for them. "Not playing poker, I assume."

"You assume correctly. Now, what did you *really* come here for?"

"Joanne tell you about Henry's vision?" asked Byron. "I mean, the most recent one."

"In a way," said Jazz. "I found out right before you showed up. Through Wanda."

"How—wait, never mind. The telepathy thing. Right?"

Jazz tapped her temple twice and then pointed at Byron. "You got it, Chiefy. After that, though, she clammed up."

"What do you mean?"

"I can't read her right now. Our telepathy only works when we *both* open up. Which is to say, we're both usually ready to receive. If I reach out and there's nothing there, like now, it means Wanda wants her privacy. I have to respect that."

Byron nodded. "I get that."

Jazz closed her eyes and began shuffling the tarot deck. On the last shuffle, one card popped from the deck, twirled on its edge, then landed face-down.

Jazz placed the deck on the table, then flipped the card. "Death," she said.

"That can't be good," said Byron.

"It can be good *or* bad. You can never take the cards at face value, Chief. The death card *can* mean literal death. But it can also mean the end of something in your life. Put another way, a new beginning."

"You mean like giving up a bad habit? Like smoking?" asked Byron. For some reason, Henry came to his mind unbidden. Byron pushed the thought away.

"Sure. It could mean that. It could be anything. The end of a bad relationship. Changing careers. Moving outta state. You name it. So, before I turn over another card, why don't you tell me what's on your mind."

Byron rubbed his hand down the length of his face, blew out a breath, and said, "I told Jo I was gonna see if I could get a lead on the guy in Henry's vision. You know, check him out?"

Jazz nodded. Her hand rested on the tarot deck.

"Well, Jo seemed really worried about it. More than usual, I mean. You know her, always bustin' my onions. Seeing *her* that worried has *me* worried. Like maybe I'm walking into something above my pay grade, you know?"

"If this was six months ago, I'd agree. You've come a long way, though. Half the battle is believing this crazy shit is real," said Jazz.

"Having a demon-possessed witch jam her tongue down your throat's a pretty good convincer."

Jazz nodded. "No doubt." She shuffled the deck, fanned it out on the table, and told Byron to pick a card.

"Me?" asked Byron as he leaned back defensively from the table.

"What do you think we're in here for? You wanted to talk about what's going on. This is how I do it." With a long, glittered purple fingernail, she tapped the deck.

Byron hesitated. He leaned forward, his hands tucked into his lap as he studied the deck.

Jazz was about to tell him to get it over with, but held back. Tarot readings were personal. However long he needed to pick a card was however long she would wait.

Byron brought his right hand forward from his lap, then held it a few inches above the fanned out deck and splayed his fingers. With his eyes closed, he hovered his hand over the deck and moved it slowly back and forth a few times. When it stopped, he made a fist, but with his index finger pointing out. He jabbed the finger at the deck, opened his eyes, and slid one card out.

"You been doing tarot at home with Penny?" asked Jazz, surprised.

"Nah. It's just a poker thing. I do this with the guys to see who deals first. Low card wins. Closing my *eyes* is kinda new, though. *That* you can blame on Penny and meditation," said Byron. "I actually felt a little something before I picked it. It felt like a cold breeze."

Jazz's eyebrows shot up. "Really? Interesting. Flip that bad boy over."

The card bore the image of a man holding five swords. Two were in his right hand, three were in his left, and two more were planted in the ground behind him. There were seven swords in total. The man was running in the opposite direction of the two on the ground and looking back at them.

"Seven of Swords," said Jazz. "No wonder you felt a cold breeze."

"What do you mean?" asked Byron.

"In tarot, sword cards represent the element of air."

"That a good thing, Jazz?"

"Same answer as before; it can be both. Pick one more. You can do your poker thingy again. Then we'll go from there."

Byron repeated the process, jabbing down and sliding one out. When it cleared the deck, Byron yanked his finger away. "Ouch!"

"What's the matter?" asked Jazz

The Chief looked spooked. "If I didn't know any better, I'd say that card just fuckin' bit me!"

Jazz, her eye's wide, pointed at his index finger. "I'd say you got a point, Chief."

Byron turned his hand palm up. The pad at the end of his index finger had a crescent-shaped slice in it. Blood bloomed and beaded. Gravity and viscosity pulled it into a band surrounding his finger. The trails converged. A crimson droplet stretched out slowly, then dripped from Byron's finger, landing with a soft splat on the card he'd drawn. It sizzled, smoked, then flipped over all on its own.

"The Devil," whispered Jazz.

CHAPTER 6
FISHING

At the exact moment a tarot card attacked Byron, Raul Martinez was patrolling the streets of Salem. The two-way radio on his passenger seat crackled to life. "Dispatch to closest unit for the Willows."

Salem Willows is a park on a peninsula in the northeast corner of the Witch City. Raul was already close to Fort Avenue, the last street before the double-sided parking lot at the entrance to the Willows. As he swung a left onto Fort, he ripped the two-way mic from its cradle in the middle of the dashboard.

"Looks like I ain't eating anytime soon," he said, just before he keyed the mic. "Dispatch, this is 94. I'm right at Fort Ave. What's up?"

"Hey, 94. Someone from a boat near Juniper Beach just called in. Said there might be a body in the water. Copy?"

Not again, he thought. A flashback of bright white high-top sneakers jutting from behind a tombstone in the Salem cemetery rose unbidden in his mind. "Why do I always get the friggin' body calls?" Raul grumbled. He keyed the mic once more. "Copy, dispatch. You sending EMTs? Just in case?"

"Already on the way, 94. Call when you know something. Copy?"

"Ten-four."

Raul tossed the mic onto the passenger's seat. He piloted the cruiser toward the far end of the parking lot, passing first an arcade, then a Chinese food place. A green wrought-iron gate at the entrance to the footpath of the Willows stood closed. At its middle, between white letters spelling out *Salem Willows* along the gate's top, was a chain coiled in and around the bars. The heavy padlock holding the coil together declared the park closed for the night.

He slowed the cruiser and steered it left, up and over the curb, then drove across the lawn until he reached the other side. Raul pulled onto the footpath, followed it toward the beach, parked on the grass, and stepped out.

Tangy salt air filled his nostrils, and he smiled; he'd always loved the smell. Couples and singles out for a stroll in the twilight now lined the beach's edge. A few of them were pointing to a boat bobbing in the water roughly thirty yards from shore. Two silhouettes on the boat's deck stood motionless above a bright spotlight pointed into the silvery depths of the Atlantic. In the beam's path, something stark, white, and with a zippered leather ankle boot attached rose and fell in harmony with the tide.

Raul made a letter C with the thumb and forefinger of his right hand. He put the digits in his mouth and whistled loudly toward the boat. A figure behind the spotlight moved, and the light hit Raul full force in the eyes. He waved them toward shore, then walked out onto a stone jetty to get as close as possible. When they were within earshot, he asked, "That what I think it is floating out there?"

"I guess that depends on what you think it *is*," said one silhouette.

"I'm guessing it's a body," said Raul.

"Then you'd be wrong... officer?"

Relieved, Raul answered, "Martinez. Salem Police. So it's not a body?"

"Oh, it's a body alright. But you're only half wrong, Officer Martinez," said silhouette number two.

"Not sure I understand."

"There's two of them, sir. Looks like two women. Kinda youngish. Seen 'em around town before. I think they're twins."

Twins.

It's possible the bodies aren't Luci and Fermina's, he thought. If this had been a few months earlier, he'd be speechless with grief at the loss of Mercy's friends. But he knew, if these bodies *were* the twins, they were no friends of Mercy's now.

Raul dreaded what came next, because he knew before the night was over he'd be at the morgue. The last thing in the world he wanted to deal with was the ghoulish sense of humor of Mickey Schmidt, the morgue pathologist.

He headed back to his cruiser, leaned in through the open window, and yanked the mic from beneath the dashboard. "94 to dispatch. Cancel the EMTs. We need a meat wagon."

"Copy, 94. Body, eh?"

"Make it a double," said Raul.

"No kidding? Two?"

"I shit you not, dispatch."

Twenty minutes later, two divers from the Salem Police Department met Raul at the shore. They'd dragged the seaweed laced corpses onto the beach, then stepped aside so he could have a look.

One diver pulled his mask up, resting it on his head. "You know them, Martinez?"

Identifying the girls seemed just a formality now. Duty was duty, however, and he pulled the flashlight from his utility belt. He shone its beam on one of their faces, then jumped back, almost dropping the flashlight.

"Aye! Dios Mio!" yelped Raul.

Both divers staggered backward and whispered, "What the fuck?" at the same time.

After the three men recovered, they leaned back in for a closer look. Raul moved the flashlight from one dead face to the other. They were identical in every way—right down to the gaping black sockets where dead and glazed eyes *should* have been.

~

HE WATCHED them from the beach, amused. When the cop had shone the flashlight on Luci's face, and all three had jumped back like they'd seen a ghost, he'd forced the laughter back down his throat.

He wished he could follow the cop back to the morgue and hear *that* conversation.

This was going to be so much fun! And it was *just starting!*

Being twins had been fun too, of course. It was the first time since the garden and the apple he'd allowed his essence to be divided, and it had been completely fascinating! It had also taken a long time to get used to. It wasn't something you got to do every day—or millennia, for that matter.

He had the witch and the psycho to thank for all of it. When you call into the darkness, sometimes the darkness hears.

Sometimes, it shows up.

Too bad they weren't around to see what came next. Especially the redhead. Oh, what fun he could have had with her!

A couple standing a few feet to his left was staring at him. The man was tall, well muscled, drowning in cheap cologne, and wearing a black t-shirt at least three sizes too small. The woman wore tight fitting, black yoga pants and an orange '*Fit!* Salem' tank top. At first, their stares puzzled him, then he realized, from the ache forming on either side of his new face, he was still smiling.

Captain Steroids approached, his fists balled at his sides and his very hot girlfriend trying desperately to hold him back. "Something funny, asshole?"

The smile dropped from his face, he gave the couple his full attention. "Funny?"

"There's two dead girls on that beach down there, and you're standing here smiling. What the fuck are you smiling about?" The man stepped closer. The woman had both hands clamped around her boyfriend's left forearm, trying to reel him in. "Did you kill them?"

He couldn't hold it back any longer, and burst out laughing. The being who was once Luci and Fermina held up a hand. "Wait. There's been a misunderstanding. I was laughing at *you*, not those poor, unfortunate girls."

That stopped Captain Steroids in his tracks. "What the hell's so funny about me?"

"I'll show you," said the man.

Anthony Cavalieri's mouth dropped open, and he let out a soft whimper. The fists balled at his sides slowly unfolded. His shoulders and arms, tense with rage moments before, sagged suddenly, as if the bones supporting the muscle were removed by magical means.

Yoga pants yanked her hands back, startled, then took a tentative step toward him. "Tony?" She stepped around then in front of him, jumping back and clamping a hand over her mouth to stifle a scream. "Babe? What's the matter with you?" she squeaked.

"He's just in the middle of learning a valuable lesson, Jennifer."

Yoga pants whirled on the stranger. "How do you know my name?"

The stranger shrugged. "I know lots of names. You could say I know most people better than they know themselves, Jenny cakes."

Now it was Jennifer's turn. Her mouth dropped open, but unlike Tony she was fully aware of the reason. "No one calls me that except my grandmother, and that's *our secret!*"

He winked, then held up his right hand with the middle and index fingers crossed. "I won't tell a soul. Scout's honor."

From behind Jennifer, Tony's eyes remained rolled back in his head. His arms still hung limply at his sides. In a faraway voice, he said, "It's okay, Denise. Jennifer will *never* know. Half the time she's too busy looking at herself in the mirror, anyway. We could screw right in *front* of her and she probably wouldn't notice."

"Denise? That's my—"

"Your sister. Yes. Apparently, Tony's gotten to know her

in the biblical sense. I mean, you can never be *too* sure about these things. But—" He shrugged.

"Who *are* you?" whispered Jennifer.

His eyes flashed crimson. His lips parted. A grin crawled across his bright white teeth—crooked and mischievous.

Jennifer flushed, stirring in places Tony never came close to touching. It felt *nice*. He *looked* nice. *Come to think of it*, she thought, *he's kinda hot*.

"I'm the one who's always there, Jenny cakes. I'm the shadow in the corner. The chill after a nightmare. The cold breeze in an empty room. I'm what you think about when you're alone at night, climbing the walls with desire. I'm the *pleasure* in the pain. Are you tired of the pain yet, Jennifer?"

He was next to her now. Jennifer couldn't remember if she'd moved closer to him, or vice versa. At that moment, she could not have cared less. He leaned in close. She shuddered. His breath was in her ear now, and she felt his lips close around her earlobe, felt a gentle tug as he bit and pulled on it. Hard, but not too hard. Just right. He put a hand on her hip, and her skin buzzed; yoga pants be damned. The hand slid lower, down her thigh, and then toward her center. It was like he knew exactly how to touch her. Exactly how she *wanted* to be touched. Part of her was dimly aware she was on a public beach, and that there were two bodies on the sand, and that her boyfriend seemed to be on another planet confessing a dark secret to someone unseen. It was a small part. The rest of her wanted this man, this beautiful *creature*, doing things to her she'd only read about in spicy romance books. The kinds of books covered with man-chest —or chests. She laughed and moaned at the same time, thinking how nice two of *this* man would be.

Then it was over. He was gone. Jennifer whirled, looking

left and right, spinning in a circle and taking in the scene on the beach. Emptiness and carnal longing filled her as she swept her eyes in all directions at once, desperate to reconnect with the stranger.

She saw the bodies. Police stood over the dead women, flashlights in hand. Couples still stood and pointed. Some were filming the scene with their phones, others were staring in her direction, but not exactly at *her*. Their stares went slightly beyond, focused on something behind her. Jennifer turned to follow their gazes, then understood. Her boyfriend was crawling on all fours toward her. He got slowly to his feet, shook his head, and put a hand on her shoulder to steady himself. His eyes had regained some focus.

A gust of wind blew gently toward the ocean, and as Jennifer caught the stench in her nose, Tony reached behind himself and cupped a hand against his jeans. He looked at her, shocked, disbelieving, and red-faced. "I think I shit myself, babe."

Jennifer put a hand on his shoulder, then kneed him with everything she had squarely in the balls. "I always knew you were full of shit. Get *Denise* to clean it up."

As the wind died, Jennifer heard laughter. She followed it.

CHAPTER 7
WARNING SHOTS

"Well, we knew it was coming, Jo," said Henry.

"I know, but I didn't think they'd shut down everything so fast. It seems a bit... extreme."

"Government? Overreact? Get out!"

Jo laughed. "I know, I know. But even for the powers that be, this seems a bit fucking much. Where you at now, Band-Aid boy?"

"Heading home from Wanda's. You?"

"I'm leaving in a few," said Jo. "See you soon."

"Not if I see you first."

"Clever."

When he heard the phone go dead, he smiled. It blew him away how much life had changed since he'd moved to Salem in July of 2018. Every time he talked to Jo, it never failed to bring him back to the days he'd been *terrified* to talk to her. It was just so *easy* now—so natural. Her beauty had intimidated him, but the pull he'd felt the moment he'd laid eyes on her was irresistible.

Back then, they'd felt foolish for thinking it was love at first sight, only to acknowledge later it was *exactly that*. The attraction *was* instant, but the reason went deeper than anything physical or psychological. Theirs was a connection forged over eons through time and incarnations, welded together by life and death and the constant longing of their souls to find each other. In their most intimate moments, they marveled at the near impossibility of it all. Even in their present incarnations, the odds seemed stacked against them.

In her current life, Jo had flirted with suicide. Drugs, alcohol, and the succession of filth she'd had for foster fathers almost drove her over the edge. Henry wholeheartedly believed the story she'd told him about the stranger in the deli and his book of quotes on happiness, but he'd always suspected there was something more to the story. Something deep within Jo keeping her afloat until the stranger had thrown her that life preserver. There was *depth* to her soul.

Henry wasn't sure of the... mechanics, for want of a better word, of how souls became entwined, but he suspected Jo's soul reached further back in time. Or, if that wasn't how it worked, and if souls were eternal, somehow hers had more experience—had somehow *seen* more.

He was at the wrong end of a line waiting for a red light to change, and as he sat in the Camry, a conversation he'd had with Jo sprung to mind. They'd been talking the morning after he'd had his first vision of Cotton Ball, and Jo was trying to help him sort it out.

"...and he actually said the words one three-thousandth?" asked Jo.

"Yeah. It's supposedly the weight of the soul. At least, that's what I found when I Googled it."

"Why would someone do that, Henry?"

"What? Weigh a soul?"

"No. I kinda get that. If there's a way to prove to the world the soul is real, that'd be it. Other than video of one actually leaving the body, that is. Prove something like that and your name goes up there with Einstein and E=MC squared. I think if we want to find out who this whack job is, we need to understand what drives him."

Henry hadn't considered this angle. The shock of what the guy was doing rattled him. At the time of the conversation with Jo, he hadn't yet viewed the extended-play version he'd seen with Wanda. And they hadn't yet had the chance to talk about these newest revelations.

Considering the new information, Jo's earlier suggestion of figuring out what drove the guy made more sense. Cotton Ball was on a mission; that much seemed clear. His motive, however, might provide a clue to his identity. If he was going to protect Wanda from the guy, Cotton Ball needed to be identified. But there was almost nothing to go on. He hadn't even seen the guy's face.

The light turned green, and as it did, Henry's car radio turned on by itself, making him jump in his seat. "Sympathy for the Devil" by The Rolling Stones was already playing. The intro of bongos and piano had already passed, and Mick Jagger crooned out the song's first lines, introducing himself as a man of wealth and taste.

Henry stared at the radio. Gooseflesh exploded upward from his wrists to the top of his head. A chill crawled down his spine. He froze. This was something he'd dreamed about.

51

Recently. And he knew, when he next looked up, there would be a man on the corner of Lafayette and Harbor streets.

Everything in him screamed to stay put and keep his eyes fixed on the radio until the feeling passed. A horn blared from behind him; another notoriously impatient New England driver heard from. When he looked up and hit the gas, his traitorous eyes went right to the spot. The breath he'd been holding exploded from his lungs in a rush of relief.

No one stood on the corner of Lafayette and Harbor.

As he passed that corner, he peeked at his side-view mirror, reassuring himself the man from his latest recurring dream didn't appear out of thin air behind him. In the corner of his right eye, he caught movement in front of the Camry and slammed on the brakes. A man and a woman jumped backward, narrowly avoiding Henry's front bumper. Tires squealed behind him, and Henry closed his eyes and leaned forward, anticipating a blast from behind that never came. When he dared to open them, the couple he'd almost run down stood to the right of the Camry. The woman was closest to the car, a questioning look on her face. Henry grimaced, held a hand up in apology, then waved her forward. She smiled and waved thanks.

As she crossed in front of the Camry, she shot Henry a crooked grin. A grin strikingly similar to Jo's. That grin twinkled beneath emerald-green eyes, causing him to study her more closely. She was gorgeous, with straight, jet-black hair tied back in a tight ponytail. A tanned and tone arm, bare from the shoulder-hole of an orange tank top, swung carelessly at her side. Her legs looked strong, shapely, and muscular. *Just like Jo's*, he thought. *She could be Jo's sister*, was his next thought. When he looked up again, she'd already turned forward. Her profile was almost identical to Jo's. Even her *stride* resembled his wife's.

For the second time in the last three minutes, Henry was holding up traffic. This time, he ignored the blaring horns. He tracked the couple. Once past his car, they veered left... toward Lafayette and Harbor. As they reached the corner, time became thick and dreamlike. Henry heard his heart pounding in his ears.

The man walking with Jo... *It's not Jo!* was tall. Wavy black hair hung loosely down the back of his head, swaying in time with an effortless stride. An immaculate black suit hung perfectly from broad and powerful shoulders. With liquid grace, the man's left hand slid from his side, caressing the woman's lower back. In one fluid motion, it dove lower, grabbing a handful of Jo's—*It's not Jo's!*—right butt cheek, giving it a firm squeeze. A surge of inexplicable jealousy swept over Henry, and he fought an insane urge to jump from the car and beat the shit out of the guy. Instead, he looked from the man's hand and into his eyes. As the couple disappeared around the corner, the man in the perfect suit caught Henry's eye, and winked.

BYRON HELD HIS HAND OUT, fingers splayed. "It's nothing, Jazz. Just a paper cut. It'll heal on its own."

"Bullshit, Chiefy. You realize I was *in the room* with you when this happened, right?"

He rolled his eyes. "Okay. You *also* witnessed me getting a paper cut. Satisfied?"

"No. Just hold still. Let me put this stuff on it. If it doesn't make *you* feel better, it'll at least make *me* feel better."

"Fine. What is that stuff, anyway?" asked Byron.

"It's just a little healing balm—with a side-order of protection," said Jazz.

"Protection from *what*? The god of paper cuts?"

Jazz ignored him, removing a dropper from a small, blue glass bottle. She dabbed the cut with a purple cloth, then turned it face up on the table. The offending tarot card with the image of the Devil sat beside it. Jazz picked up the card, turned it face down, and dropped it onto the purple swatch holding Byron's blood. She pressed down on the back of the card with her left hand, then carefully peeled it away from the swatch.

"Hold your finger steady. I need to drip this into the wound."

Byron pulled his finger back, then opened his mouth, ready to protest. Jazz fixed him with a stare, then asked, "Did you enjoy having a demon jam its tongue down your throat? Because whatever's connected to this card is a thousand times worse than that. You didn't get a paper cut, Chief. That tarot card *attacked* you! In my book, that only means one thing. There's something terrible in town. Right. Now. And it's strong. Strong enough to animate a damned tarot card in a protected room."

Byron gulped. "You think it's got to do with the letter at Wanda's? The Luci and Fermina thing?"

She shot him a look that asked the question, 'Are you really that dense?'

Jazz and Byron jumped as his cell phone went off in his pocket. With his good hand, he pulled out the phone and thumbed the green answer button, then put it to his ear.

"Miller."

As Byron listened to Raul, his eyes slowly rose to meet Jazz's.

"And you're sure it's them, Raul?"

"Does the pope shit in the woods?" Jazz heard Raul ask as he ended the call.

Byron's face went pale, realizing he'd just mentioned them moments before Raul's call. He nodded at his injured finger. Jazz got the hint. She held the blood-smeared tarot card over the cut at a forty-five degree angle. With her left hand, she raised the dropper and gently squeezed the rubber bulb at its top. The first gold-tinged drop swelled at the glass pipette's tip, reflecting the mellow candlelight filling the room. The drop ballooned until the fat, golden drop of magick lost its battle with gravity and hit the card with a sizzle. Tiny silver sparks lit a trail down its face, and the drop rolled into the cut on Byron's finger. He grimaced with pain, but held it in place.

"Two more, Byron. They're going to hurt just as much as the first."

They came as advertised. As Jazz stoppered the blue bottle, the crescent-shaped wound on Byron's finger glowed silver at its edges. He gritted his teeth, hissing pain from between his pearly whites. The wound curled in on itself, and the potion worked its way under the skin. As the cut closed, the pain disappeared.

"It's... cold," said Byron. There was a trace of awe in his voice.

"Give it a minute."

Byron stared at the finger, fascinated. It glowed from within, reminding him of when he was a boy and he'd put his hand over a powerful flashlight. He remembered how he could see the vague grey outline of the bones in his fingers, surrounded by glowing red flesh. With his other arm, he reached behind his back until his fingers caught the top of the chair. His legs gave way, and he plopped down in the purple velvet cushion.

The coldness around the cut faded. Warmth took its place, working slowly up his finger, into his hand, then up his arm. It wound a soothing path into his chest, then around his heart. The potion's journey seemed to end between his eyes, in the middle of his forehead.

Jazz saw the faint glow emanating from Byron's third eye. His aura bloomed bright gold. "Your ajna chakra is opening, Byron."

The pain vanished. Images flashed before his eyes— memories old and buried—things which terrified him as a child: the dark, bees, his first bus ride to school, the first time he'd confronted a bully.

One by one, the memories marched across his consciousness. Fear swelled at the beginning of each, only to be surrounded by an envelope of healing golden light. As they passed, Byron felt their weight dropping from his soul, as if each was a stone he'd been carrying without his knowledge.

Moment by moment, he felt lighter. *Stronger.* Whatever cumulative power these boulders of fright once held seemed trivial now. As the last of them faded, his vision cleared.

Jazz was in her seat, where she'd been before the tarot card went rogue.

"What was *that*?" asked Byron.

"First, tell me what the phone call was about. I think I know, but I wanna hear it from you."

"It was Raul. They pulled Luci's and Fermina's bodies from the water at Juniper Beach."

"Then it's really begun. Those girls, if they were ever

really girls, are gone. He's here. I don't know *why*, but I guess we're gonna find out."

"Who's here? And what just happened to me?" asked Byron.

"It's just like the letter said. Gemini have become one. Lucifer is in Salem. His power flows through the town as we speak. Tarot cards don't usually just go off and bite people, Byron."

Byron looked down at his finger. It was completely healed. "What about this?" He held it up for Jazz to see.

"That healed nicely." Jazz blew on her fingernails, then rubbed them against her blouse. "I still got it."

"Jazz?"

"Okay. Okay. That potion doesn't just heal physical wounds, Chief. It heals wounds of the *soul*. I took the liberty of shoring up your courage."

Byron gave her the Spock eyebrow. Jo was rubbing off on him. "Courage for what, exactly?"

Jazz shrugged. "Can't say for sure, Chiefy. But the Devil's always in the details. And that seemed an awful lot like a warning to me."

As the last word left her mouth, the tarot card marked 'Devil' burst into flame.

CHAPTER 8

THREATS

Compared to his last place, this was a palace. Artemis Davies lugged the case containing his 'soul tapes' up the stairs and then into his second-floor apartment. They were the last of the items from his trunk, and this was the third trip up through the entrance hall and the long flight of stairs. Despite breathlessness, he patted his jacket in search of a smoke.

Artemis had memories, good and bad, of the Witch City and was ambivalent about his return. Aside from the night at Jenny Love's, he hadn't been here since the early nineties. The place had changed, no doubt about *that*.

"What place hasn't?" he whispered.

There was a more commercial feel to it. No, *commercial* wasn't the right word. Salem, at its heart, still had the same aura. He felt it from the moment he crossed the Beverly-Salem Bridge. *Modernized*, he thought. *Changing with the times*. He guessed he could live with that.

He laughed. "Like I have a say in the matter?"

As he pulled the Marlboro reds from his pocket, he

pushed back the nicotine-stained shade of the window overlooking the street. *At least the place allows smoking*; a minor miracle in this day and age, he felt.

Artemis surveyed the neighborhood as he puffed away. There was a Wendy's directly across the street, flanked by multi-story, multi-unit apartment complexes. To his left was a very crowded, very busy intersection. Some asshole in a red Camry was holding up traffic as a couple passed in front of his car. Angry drivers honked behind him.

Beyond the intersection, he noticed the neighborhood changed drastically, as if some magical border separated one part of Salem from the other. The buildings were a few stories tall at their highest. Most were shops of one kind or another. "Diagon Alley it ain't," he quipped.

As the memories returned, his mood darkened.

Salem. This was where it happened.

"Mother," he whispered.

Artemis swallowed hard, trying to keep his emotions in check. It was no use. Salem's night lights swirled as tears filled his eyes in a kaleidoscope of pain. He squeezed them shut, and bitterness spilled, warm and wet, down his cheeks.

He closed his eyes. The memory from the other day played once more in his mind. When the new messenger had delivered the next subject's name, Artemis played dumb. Part of him knew the day would come, just not so soon. But he was always on guard, knowing it might come at any time.

Still, at the mention of her name, a bolt of dread shot through him. It took every ounce of restraint he had not to react. He was sure, on that night, he'd betrayed nothing to the messenger.

Wanda Heinze had a lot to answer for.

"Time to pay, witch."

~

Byron left Jazz's shop and headed straight to the Salem Hospital. He was friendly with the receptionist; he was her most frequent customer, given his line of work. Linda Halsey smiled as the Chief approached the newly erected glass partition, then covered her smile with a mask.

"Hi Byron! What brings you to Salem's newest shop of horrors?"

"Hi Lin. I need a favor."

"*That's* nothing new. What is it *this* time?" she asked, then pointed to the box of masks on Byron's side of the partition.

"You serious?" asked Byron, looking at the box as if it contained a fresh turd.

"As a heart attack. We don't know what we're dealing with when it comes to this Covid stuff."

Byron shrugged. He was used to using them, but only at the morgue, where he was heading once he left the hospital.

Masks killed some of the smell of cadavers—always a good thing. More importantly, it hid his face from Mickey Schmidt, the morgue's forensic pathologist and resident ball buster. Mickey knew viewing stiffs gave Byron the heebie-jeebies. The mask helped hide some of his discomfort from Mick. Not enough to suit Byron, but you took what you could get. Mickey always walked right up to the line, but rarely stepped over it. When he did, Byron usually put him in his place. For now, he shoved *that* impending unpleasantness out of mind.

Once he masked up, Linda asked, "Now, what can I do you for, handsome?"

"You know, Lin, I'm not really sure. I'm kinda casting my line into a big lake on this one. Just hoping to get a nibble."

She raised an eyebrow, but said nothing.

"I'm looking for anyone who's recently come on staff here. Could be a doc. Maybe a mortician. I'd lean toward the latter. A photo ID would be the prize at the bottom of the box, but that's probably asking too much."

Before he'd finished the sentence, Linda Halsey's fingers were flying over the keys.

"Bingo!" said Linda.

Byron felt his pulse quicken. It always did with a breakthrough. "You have a photo ID?"

Linda nodded. "Come around the desk. I can't swivel the monitor with this new spit barrier."

The Chief sprinted for the door at the left side of the desk. Linda hit the buzzer, and Byron almost yanked it from its hinges. Three strides later, he was at Linda's side. One *second* later, his shoulders slumped in defeat.

"Not what you're looking for?" asked Linda.

"Nope. I'm looking for an older *guy*. My nephew Henry calls him 'Cotton Ball.' Carroll Kent M.D.," Byron said, pointing at the monitor, "ain't even in the ballpark."

"You never mentioned it was a man, Chief. Sorry I got you all excited."

"Nah, it's okay, Lin. It was a shot in the—"

Byron's words died in his throat. At the front entrance, Joanne Trank staggered through the revolving door. On its last turn, her hands slid down the glass, streaking it with blood. She took two wobbly steps into the foyer, then collapsed, face first, onto the rubber traffic mat. Byron flew from behind the desk, closing the distance in three quick strides.

Panic consumed him. The woman he'd come to love like a daughter looked close to death. *God, please! Not Jo!*

When he reached her, time slowed. Linda Halsey's calm, professional voice echoed from the walls. "Code Blue, main entrance. Code Blue, main entrance." To his ears, it sounded slow and far away. Then he heard Jo moan, and breathed a sigh of relief. "She's conscious, Lin! Where are the fucking ER guys?"

On cue, the doors at the far right of the main entrance burst open. A huge black man with a spinal board tucked under one arm, and an equally huge white man with a trauma kit at his right side, stepped around Byron. The Chief recognized both of them.

Jason Miggs, the man carrying the spinal board, said, "Chief Miller, you need to give us some room."

Byron didn't acknowledge him—didn't seem to notice either man. Instead, he slowly reached a hand toward Jo's head, intending to brush the hair from her face. Kenny Rhett —he of the trauma case—grabbed the Chief's wrist. "I wouldn't do that, Chief. She could have hurt her neck."

Red with rage, Byron whirled on him, coming within an inch of decking the EMT before getting a hold of himself. Kenny held his gaze. Recognizing the man's distress, he spoke with calm deliberation. "Let us do our jobs, Chief Miller."

Byron calmed, patted Kenny's shoulder, and reluctantly backed a few feet away. The EMTs went to work.

What took place next reminded Byron of too many scenes he'd witnessed watching pro football on TV. When someone on the field was injured, the standard protocol was to brace the neck first. The EMTs followed that procedure to the letter.

Kenny Rhett placed a brace carefully on the back of Jo's neck, then slowly secured it. Jason Miggs slid the spinal board so it was snugged right up against her hip, then stepped around to the opposite side of Jo and knelt.

"On three," said Jason to Kenny. Kenny nodded, but kept his eyes on Jo and a hand either side of the brace. When Jason hit three, they slowly rolled her over.

Byron stepped forward to watch. He was just in time to see something all three men would never forget.

The woman he'd assumed was Joanne opened her eyes, and as she did, the emerald green irises faded to a dark brown. The woman's hair, a jet-black clone of Joanne Trank's, suddenly morphed to a deep auburn, and waves of reddish-brown replaced Jo's straight locks.

"What in the...?" gasped Jason.

"Did you guys see what I just saw?" asked Kenny.

Byron answered for all of them. "Yeah. Not too sure what it was, but it happened."

Conflicting emotions roiled his mind. He was overjoyed the woman on the board wasn't Joanne, but felt horrible for whoever this poor girl was. In the next moment, rage and vengeance swept through him. Whoever did this had a room waiting at the Graybar Hotel.

When Byron looked down, the woman's lips were moving. She was trying to talk, but having a tough time. By the cast of her eyes, her words were meant for Byron. Kenny Rhett saw what was happening, and stepped away so Byron could kneel next to her head. When he bent low, she swallowed and whispered, "Closer."

Byron, already kneeling, leaned as close as he could. He turned his head so his left ear rested a few inches above her mouth. "What's your name, sweetheart?" asked Byron, head still turned to one side. There was no way he was going to miss a word.

"Jennifer," croaked the woman. She took a deep breath, then blew it out. Jennifer was marshalling what strength she could. "I have a message for you, Chief."

"Okay, Jennifer. You can tell me later. You need to go with these men and—"

"No," said Jennifer. "He said you need to know right now."

Byron knew the EMTs wanted her in the ER pronto, so he sped things up. "Okay. Tell me."

Jennifer took another deep breath, followed by a yelp of pain and a coughing fit that spattered more blood onto her orange, '*Fit!* Salem' tank top. When it ebbed, she spoke. "He said you need to back off or next time, it'll be the real thing. What does that mean?"

Byron donned his best poker face. "Nothing, Jennifer. Don't worry about a thing. Just get well. I'll come back and talk to you when you're feeling better."

He nodded to the EMTs.

With that, she passed out.

Byron stepped back. Jason and Kenny stepped in and whisked her away.

Linda Halsey spoke from behind Byron. "I'd say that was some nibble, Chief."

CHAPTER 9
MIRROR, MIRROR

Armand Moreland was on his knees in prayer. The vampire-priest had finished his meditations and begun planning how to best protect Wanda, the white witch—and in turn, the child of the prophecy.

The mirror hung on the wall before him. Though Henry had applied shotgun justice to it, the frame remained intact. Armand was of two minds with the mirror.

On the one hand, he knew there might be residual magick attached to it.

Black magick.

There was danger in that. The spirits and spells used to forge such a piece often lingered. He believed, however, those things were attached to the actual *glass*, not the frame. He wasn't one hundred percent *sure* of it, but felt it was a risk worth taking.

On the other, it had the potential to be a valuable tool—especially considering new developments in the world. This new virus had the entire globe in a panic.

"Justifiably so," he whispered.

Things were shutting down. The streets of Salem and the surrounding towns—really, the entire world—were about to empty. For a vampire, that was bad news.

When he walked the streets of Salem, the traffic of daily life provided cover. Though travel by supernatural means was preferable, there were times it simply wasn't practical. Portals in Salem were plentiful, but not omnipresent. It was simpler, and far less risky, to walk or ride from point A to point B, especially during the day.

Without the cover of the masses, however, the subtle differences in his appearance would stick out like a sore thumb. They weren't blatant: paler than normal skin, light grey sclera versus normal eye whites, hair that never changed or grew. But in a world with cameras *everywhere,* someone was bound to notice and question. He'd once ended up in a video on a YouTube channel called "Slapped Ham." Though he wasn't the focus of the video, one of the commenters beneath the video had remarked, "Anyone notice the pasty white dude? Vampire? LOL."

Not funny... *Dude.*

Now, all things considered, the portals were far more likely to get noticed. He was up the proverbial stinky creek without a paddle.

There had to be another way.

When news of the virus hit, he'd known intuitively things for him, and most magical beings within Salem's borders, would change drastically. For several days, he'd racked his brains for a solution to the problem of covert travel.

Then came the call from Wanda. When she'd sworn him to secrecy, it hadn't sat well with him. His entire relationship with the witches in the League of the Moon coven had *begun* on just such a premise, and he'd worked hard to gain their trust. The last thing he wanted to do was hide something from them.

Especially the green witch.

Joanne Trank had only recently begun to trust him. Likewise, Chief Byron Miller. Henry, Mercy, and Jazz had shown slightly more tolerance for his initial shortcomings, but were quicker to forgive. The trust he'd built would be at risk. He prayed Wanda would set things right in the end. If he survived.

Wanda's recent call was serendipitous. Up to that point, he'd wrestled with his conscience about the mirror. Now, in light of present circumstances, his promise to a higher authority to protect the League of the Moon took precedence over how they might feel about the mirror, and his possession of it. And failing to protect the coven, by any means necessary, could cost him his coveted reunion with his wife and daughter.

Forever.

He took heart in this: the new glass was blessed by a priest, and spellbound by the very witches he'd grown to love. Though they'd questioned the wisdom of keeping the mirror instead of destroying it, they had, literally, given it their blessings.

When he'd put in the order for new glass, he'd shipped it directly to Saint Theresa's in Salem. In the shipping details window on the website, he'd left instructions for it to be delivered to the back of the church—where there was a small receiving platform—and also for Father O'Bryan to perform the blessing. A few days later, he'd gone to the church to retrieve it.

When his knock went unanswered, he'd tried the knob,

finding it unlocked. This had struck him as odd, especially considering the vampire attack of the 1990s. Once inside, he'd made his way through storage, down a short hallway, and through a doorway at the side of the altar.

Father O'Bryan had been preparing the sacrament for the next mass. When Armand quietly called to him, the priest had almost jumped out of his cassock.

"I'm sorry to have startled you, Father," said Moreland.

The priest had stared, open-mouthed, at the vampire, then seemed to gather himself. Before he'd approached Moreland, he shot a look over his shoulder. Two altar boys, with their backs to them, had been busily polishing the brass holders of the votive candles. Moreland remembered they'd sported ponytails and longed for the days when short hair was a requirement.

"What can I do for you, Armand?"

The question had confused the vampire. "Have you forgotten? I've come to see about the mirror. Have you blessed it?"

O'Bryan had paused before answering, then said, "It's ready to be taken."

"Is everything alright, Father?" asked Moreland. He'd noticed beads of sweat on the priest's forehead.

"Yes. Yes. Just my perfectionism. Always want things to go perfectly. The *Devil* is in the details, as they say."

Moreland was concerned and considered prying, but there'd been little time and the movers had needed to be called. He'd thanked O'Bryan for the blessing.

O'Bryan had waved it away. "I did nothing."

With that done, he'd stepped outside, called the moving company, and waited.

They took the glass to Wanda's Wicca'd Emporium,

where Wanda, Jazz, Joanne, and Mercy had been shoring up the protections in and around Wanda's store. The movers had placed the glass, wrapped in a padded shipping blanket, on the pentacle in the safe room as instructed, then stepped outside.

Armand had unfurled the blanket, then asked his friends to apply the necessary protections.

"What's this for, exactly?" Jo had asked.

"I'm replacing the glass in the mirror from Jagger Corey's shop," was Moreland's reply.

"And you think that's a good idea?" asked Jazz.

"I don't see the harm in it. The frame is exquisite, and it would be a shame to destroy something so beautiful. Besides, I have four powerful witches applying protection spells." He'd smiled at them.

Jazz had simply shrugged. "Whatever floats your boat. I still think it's a bad idea."

He'd bowed "Duly noted."

And with that, the matter was forgotten.

Armand Moreland stood before the mirror in the here and now—prayers offered and protections in place. The only thing left was the incantation. He opened his mouth to speak it into life, then stopped. Sage! The mirror and frame needed to be cleansed before he broke the barrier.

"You old fool," he whispered. "It's witchcraft 101, for God's sake!"

The vampire retreated to his living room.

Soon after the events at Jagger's Magical Treasures, Wanda had prepared a bundle for him. It contained basic tools and ingredients for the wiccan neophyte. The vampire took the black velvet case down from the mantle above his fireplace, placed it on the meditation mat, and removed a bundle of sage and a box of wooden matches.

With the lid almost lowered, he paused. A glint of gold caught his eye. He pushed the lid back. Several bottles of essential oils lay in a neat row: frankincense, rosemary, cedarwood, and peppermint. He removed the bottles, exposing the flash of gold's source. It was a black velveteen bag with a gold cinch-tie. When he picked it up, it made a light clacking sound.

Crystals.

Moreland smiled, recalling how Wanda had schooled him on their use.

"The dark one is black tourmaline. It's useful in protection, especially from psychic attacks. I carry one with me at all times."

"And the other?"

Wanda held the beautiful green stone up to the light. "Malachite. It's a crystal related to the heart chakra. Very helpful in guiding you toward your higher self and, ultimately, your purpose in life. I've always found they work hand-in-hand, sweetie."

He'd believed her without question—on all of it. Later, he would realize just how important trusting her judgment was.

With the items needed to proceed, he replaced the oils, save the frankincense, then closed the lid and headed for his meditation room.

Armand put the bag containing the crystals in his pants pocket, then thought better of it. He slid them under his suit coat, then dropped the bag into the breast pocket of his dress shirt. Next, he cracked the seal on the frankincense, touched the top of the bottle to his thumb, then smeared the sign of the cross atop his forehead, then over his mouth, and finally across his heart. It symbolized understanding the gospel, proclaiming it, and taking it to heart.

Sage was his final piece of spiritual armor. Armand withdrew a wooden match from the box, then scraped it ablaze with his thumbnail. He placed the sage above it, held it in place until it caught, then shook out the match. It didn't take long for a healthy trail of smoke to build.

He bathed the entire frame in the smoke, then let the sage bundle smolder itself out in a small cauldron. The last step was the incantation, which would allow him to enter the mirror.

The world you show us
Our lives reversed. I beg to enter
Devoid of curse."

Armand Moreland watched in amazement as the candlelit reflection of his meditation room faded, and the mirror's surface glowed a soft white. Moments later, the surface dissolved into an undulating mass resembling fog. Though nothing in the room surrounding him changed, the space felt larger. But larger was the wrong word.

"Infinite," he whispered.

The feeling overwhelmed him, and he hesitated at the threshold.

What if I can't find my way?

Doubt paralyzed him, rooting him to the spot. He looked down and to his left and saw the X he'd scuffed into the plank at the fireplace. It gave him some comfort. The vampire peered once more into the vaporous opening of the mirror, as if expecting divine guidance. The mirror was silent.

He closed his eyes, breathed deeply, and whispered, "Protect me, Lord." He made the sign of the cross, then stepped into the mist.

As he disappeared from this world, the cloud of vapor within the frame turned silvery-white. The frame's edge crackled with energy. At the very top, a burst of red light appeared. It spread in both directions, arcing slowly left and right, until it reached the center where the stand holding the mirror supported the frame. At the same time, green light flashed, spreading upward in perfect reflection of the red. When they connected, red and green light flooded Armand Moreland's meditation space.

In its wake, quiet laughter filled the empty room.

Then, the mirror was a mirror once more.

CHAPTER 10
EYES OF A STRANGER

As Byron drove toward the morgue his mind was on Jennifer. After the EMTs had taken her from the hospital entrance to the Emergency Room, he'd taken time to gather his thoughts before visiting.

Everything seemed connected: Henry's vision of Cotton Ball, the rabid tarot card, the bodies at the morgue, and Jennifer. It was all happening too fast. As if something spawned within the city limits, igniting mayhem. Something evil. He could feel it in the air.

Jazz was right.

Byron, in moments like this, longed for his former ignorance. "Gimme a bad guy with a gun on a B and E any day over this wacky shit," he mumbled to the Explorer.

Earlier, when he'd gone into the ER, Jennifer was hanging on to consciousness by a thread.

He let the memory roll through his mind as he drove.

Byron had asked the nurse if the woman was up for questioning, which earned him a stern look.

"I only need to find out a few things, Lorraine. I promise I won't push too hard."

Head Nurse Lorraine Fox had crossed her arms and poked her tongue into her cheek. She stared Byron down for a long moment before saying, "Five minutes, no longer, Byron. She looks like she just got hit by a bus."

He'd let out a long, grateful breath he hadn't realized he was holding. "I probably won't need that long." In days long past, he would have pecked Lorraine on the cheek, and started to do just that when he pulled up short.

Lorraine had flushed. A grin pulled at the corners of her mouth. She'd looked left and right, then said, "Go ahead, you dinosaur."

Byron had given her a quick peck and a hug, thanked her, and headed for Jennifer.

"Tell Penny to call me sometime. We need to catch up. It's been too long."

Byron, already halfway down the hall, had raised an arm over his shoulder. "Will do. Thanks again, Lorraine."

When he'd arrived at Jennifer's bay, the white shoes of an ER nurse were shuffling beneath the hem of the privacy curtain. He'd pulled it aside and peeked in.

"Hey, Chief."

"Hiya, Ronnie. How's she doing?"

"Not great. But it could be worse, I guess. It's weird, though. You'd think with all this blood, there'd be a fair amount of trauma. You know, more cuts... a contusion here or there. But there's really only one wound site. Hell of a lot of blood, but scalp cuts tend to bleed a lot."

That had raised Byron's eyebrows. "Just *one* wound?"

"Yep. Strange. And there's a shape to it. Like a symbol.

Not sure what it is, but I know I've seen it somewhere before."

"Can I look, Ronnie?"

The nurse had been to Jennifer's right. He extended his left arm with an open palm and invited Byron to join him on the opposite side.

Byron covered the space in two strides.

Ronnie Blake had leaned toward Jennifer and gently pushed the hair back from her forehead. He'd already cleaned the wound. The symbol was small and in the middle, just shy of her hairline. It was a cross with two crossbeams sitting atop a sideways figure eight.

"You know what it means, Chief?"

Byron had shaken his head. "No. But I will before I go home tonight. I guarantee it. I need to snap a picture, so keep her hair up."

"Okay," said Ronnie.

Byron had pulled his iPhone from his breast pocket. He tapped and held the screen, taking several shots in Burst Mode while arcing the camera from left to right. The clicking sound had stirred Jennifer. Her eyes opened slowly, at first, then shot open as she unleashed a scream filled with terror.

Byron squirmed in the Explorer's seat at the memory.

Ronnie's eyes had gone wide. He bolted from the bay and returned with a syringe.

"Sedative?" he'd blurted at Byron, looking for permission he didn't need.

Byron, wide-eyed, had rolled his hand impatiently. "Do I look like a doctor? Hurry up before Lorraine comes in here and cuts my balls off!"

Ronnie had poked the needle into Jennifer's left shoulder and depressed the plunger. Within seconds her screams diminished, winding down to a whimper. Her breathing steadied. The wild beeping of the heart monitor settled.

Jennifer slowly closed her eyes. The sedative had worked fast. Too fast for Byron's liking. He'd had questions, and needed answers. As if reading his mind, Jennifer's eyes had popped open once more.

At first, she'd stared at the ceiling, her eyes far away. The next moment, malevolent clarity animated them. It had made him think of a flickering neon-red hotel sign flashing from vacant to full, and dreading the revelation of Hotel Jennifer's most recent guest.

He pulled into his reserved spot at the morgue, put the Explorer in park, closed his eyes, and let the rest of the memory wash over him.

She'd smiled a closed-mouth smile; a friendly, sly thing was that smile. Just two old friends reuniting after years apart. Only, Byron hadn't recognized its owner.

The smile had widened, and Jennifer's perfect teeth were the sole light in a crescent of dark and malicious glee.

When the thing in Jennifer had spoken, it was low. Menacing. Undeniably male.

"Hi, Byron."

Byron's mouth worked, but words had failed him.

"Cat got your tongue?"

He'd nodded, feeling stupid and scared. But not as scared as he thought he'd be, considering he'd been talking to the Devil.

As he sat in the Explorer and thought back on it, he'd been more stunned than scared. Whatever Jazz had done to him in the room with the tarot cards... it had helped.

"There's a new sheriff in town, amigo. Comprende?"

A little of the shock had worn off, and Byron found his voice. "Is that so?"

"It is. I believe you're looking for someone. You need to stop."

"Oh? Well, then. I guess I'll just call it a night," he'd quipped.

"Wow! Aren't we the brave little lad all of a sudden?"

Byron had sneered at 'Jennifer,' but said nothing.

Her eyes had flared crimson at the edge of her irises. "Did you enjoy my little show in the lobby?"

"You mean the one where you used an innocent woman? The one where you abused her to send some fucked up message?"

The thing in Jennifer had tilted its head from left to right, then nodded with satisfaction—impressed with itself. The smile grew wider. "Yeah. That one. I really think I did a fabulous job making her look like your," it put up quote fingers, then donned an earnest expression, "daughter."

Byron's face had grown red with rage.

"Sore spot?"

At that point, Byron had dropped all pretense, addressing him by name. "Is there a point in here somewhere, *Lucifer?*"

The smile had dropped from 'Jennifer's' face. With lightning speed, she was out of the bed and standing nose to nose with Byron. The Chief of the Salem Police had needed every ounce of courage—*thanks, Jazz*—to hold his ground. She leaned close, put an arm on Byron's shoulder, then whispered in his ear. "The point is, cop, we both want the same thing, but for *vastly* different reasons. I know who you're looking for, but finding him before he finishes what I need him to finish could be bad for you and yours. Comprende?"

'Jennifer' had withdrawn from Byron's ear and resumed position a few inches from his face.

Byron then leaned forward, putting his lips next to 'Jennifer's' ear. "Go fuck yourself," he whispered. He straightened and met Lucifer's eyes.

Lucifer had smiled back through her face. Byron thought he'd never seen such a humorless grin. 'Jennifer' turned and climbed back into the hospital bed. She stared at Byron for a long time.

"I think I like you, Byron. You've got stones."

Byron glared.

"But I don't think you're pickin' up what I'm puttin' down, Cheify." As he'd said this, Byron watched as Jennifer's face transformed into Joanne Trank's. Then it morphed, becoming his wife Penny's. In the next moment, he saw Wanda's face, then Jazz's, then Mercy's. All the faces Lucifer had seen when he had occupied Luci and Fermina's bodies. All *souls* he knew on a very intimate level. When he became Jennifer once more, he'd said, "There's a million ways for me to hurt you. You need to let this go."

He released his hold, and Jennifer had passed out.

Byron opened his eyes. The piss-yellow light above the morgue entrance bathed the Explorer's interior. With his left hand, he reached for the handle and opened the driver's side door. With his right, he pulled a filtered cigar from his breast pocket. He kicked the door to the Explorer closed as he lit it.

"I'll show *you* a million ways, fuckface."

He climbed three metal-framed steps to the landing in front of the morgue entrance, puffing away and thinking about Luci, Fermina, the Devil, and Mickey Schmidt.

~

MERCY SAT at the front window of her apartment. Twilight's silver curtain was now a thin strand on the horizon. She sipped hot chamomile tea—a habit she'd picked up from Wanda—as the stars grew brighter, and thought about Jamal Khalid. She'd looked for him after Archie's announcement classes would be cancelled for the foreseeable future, but he'd vanished in the throng.

Until this morning, she'd never seen him in Archie's class, and wondered if he'd been there since the start of the semester.

There's no way I'd have missed those eyes.

Curiosity got the better of her. She went to the front hall, retrieved her laptop from the backpack hanging on a wooden peg, and once more sat at the front window. She fired it up, opened Google Chrome, and navigated to the college website's student directory. When she plugged his name into the search feature, it came back with zero results. This momentarily puzzled her.

"Doh!" she said, slapping her forehead. *If you've never seen him before today, he's probably not in the system yet.*

Mercy opened another tab, then clicked the shortcut for Facebook. When she searched his name, she discovered the world had a generous share of Jamal Kahlids.

After several minutes of scrolling, clicking, and back-arrowing, she found the Jamal she was looking for, but there wasn't much on his feed. The latest post, an update of his profile picture, was dated two years in the past.

Not a fan of social media.

When she clicked on the link for Instagram, she found one post, dated more recently than his Facebook profile picture.

Jamal was in a crowd of people, so the image was probably captured by a friend or a family member. It was shot at night, and the quality was average at best. Mercy clicked it, enlarging the photo. Then she held down the 'alt' key and slid her hand upward along the mouse pad, further enlarging the image.

Jamal faced the camera, but his attention was focused downward. The people to his left and right formed a loose circle, their eyes focused similarly to Jamal's. At the very bottom of the image, tongues of flame licked upward. *A campfire?* Mercy wondered. The surrounding area suggested a forest, so it made sense.

Her initial impression of the picture was a family reunion. Even with the poor image quality, she saw resemblances among them—with one exception.

An older man knelt at the center of the circle. He was very thin, dressed in a white lab coat, and the hair atop his head was shockingly white. In his hand was a bottle of some kind.

Mercy squinted for a better look, but the zoomed-in, grainy image was of little help. Smoke, or vapor, trailed from the top of the bottle, but instead of rising from it, as one would expect, it angled downward.

Isn't that strange?

When she followed the trail of vapor, something she hadn't noticed right away caught her eye. The longer she studied it, however, the reason she'd missed it in the first place became clearer; the man in the lab coat was *blocking* most of a body lying on the ground before him. The vapor trail terminated just in front of his knee, but also above it.

Mercy tracked her eyes left, and the reason for the abrupt termination of the vapor trail made more sense. About a foot from the end of the trail was a slightly brighter splotch of color. It was almond brown, and lost in a tangle of hair.

Someone's head.

She followed back from that. The trail was connected to the prone person's chest! It wasn't leaving the bottle and drifting downward, as she'd originally assumed.

"It's moving upward and out..." whispered Mercy. "That can't be good."

She closed the laptop and sipped absently at her tea as she stared at the Moon, wondering about Jamal Khalid. She was sure she'd never seen him until today and thought it odd, given they were in the *second* semester of Archie's class.

Today's lecture wasn't the first time Archie'd lowered the lights and questioned the class. It was practically a daily thing. Yet not once, before today, had she glimpsed those very-hard-to-miss eyes.

And *one* social media post? What was up with *that*? What young kid, especially one as young as Jamal appeared to be, didn't post several times during the day? It was practically a religion now. Scratch that, it was practiced far more by the young than any religion throughout history, and you didn't have to twist arms to get them to use it. Which, in a way, made her like Jamal more.

But it didn't help solve the riddle of his sudden appearance.

Unless the post itself is some kind of message?

On the spot she decided to tell Wanda about the mysterious Jamal.

CHAPTER 11
AFFAIRS OF THE HEART(S)

Archie sat alone in his office. The lights were off. Meditation music eased from his iPhone. Dragon's Blood incense burned away in a sconce on his desk. A lone candle on a polished wood pedestal flickered silently in a corner, wavering softly in the eddies of his gentle exhalations.

Everyone, even the custodial staff, had left the building for the day. Once news of the governor's order had spread, the campus became a ghost town. It hadn't been panic, exactly—more like concerned urgency. No one wanted to get sick. Even Annie, once she'd known he was alright, yanked her collar over her mouth and bolted for the exit.

He couldn't blame her. No one knew what to expect from this mystery virus. Well, no one except his son, Henry. Not that Henry'd known what *it* was, but he'd been certain it was coming.

Part of Jagger Corey's personality, somehow, remained in Henry. It involved Jagger's practice of Scapulimancy—

divination via reading the shoulder blade bones of dead animals.

The downside, for Henry, was Jagger's residual memories. The man had done hideous evil as he'd practiced this dark art. Things Henry couldn't unsee. Memories, and the energy attached, were part of this new 'gift.' Spurts of newfound rage were the decorative bow tying it all together.

Henry, to Archie's chagrin, was a very private person. So when he'd approached Archie about it, it was both shocking and a welcomed surprise. Though he would never admit it aloud to Henry, Archie wished for deeper intimacy. There was no replacing Dominick Trank as a father figure, and zero desire to do so, but he longed to be closer to his biological son.

Several nights after the meeting at Wanda's, and the reading of Luci and Fermina's letter, his wish was granted.

"Arch, I need to ask your opinion on something."

"Sure. What's up?" he'd asked.

Henry had stalled. Archie sensed his unease. "Henry. Let's treat this like the session from 2018. We're not father and son here, we're doctor and patient."

"You wanna hypnotize me?"

"No, no. I don't think that's necessary. Just tell me what's on your mind. Something's bothering the hell out of you. Obviously."

Henry had sighed, then rubbed his temples. "It's the Jagger stuff, Arch. Whatever that asshole left behind, it's getting to me. I'm pissed off almost all the time. I can't concentrate. There are moments of pure rage. It's scaring me."

Archie's chair squealed as he'd leaned back and stroked his beard. "I have something that might help." He leaned forward, pulling open the drawer of his desk. Henry had watched with amusement as Archie rooted loudly through the contents of the drawer, cursing himself for his disorganization.

"Aha!" Archie had said in triumph. He stood from his chair and leaned over the desk's top, offering Henry a chain with a stone encased in a gold-wired mesh lattice. The stone itself was grey, with reddish blemishes covering its surface.

Henry had accepted the chain and its cargo. "What's this for?"

"That, Henry, is bloodstone. Also known as Heliotrope. Early Christians believe the red spots in the stone represent the blood of Christ. A Roman soldier stabbed him in his side, post crucifixion, to prove he'd died. The spots represent the blood on the stones beneath."

"Okay. And you're giving this to me *why*?"

Archie had pondered the question, but only briefly. Had it *actually been* the session in 2018, he would have considered his words more carefully, but Henry had come a long way.

"Because of the letter," said Archie.

"The one from Luci and Fermina?"

"The very one."

"You're going to have to give me a little more, Arch."

"I think it's quite clear, Henry. We're dealing with the Devil here. Many have dubbed that stone Christ's stone. And you just told me you're already experiencing the echoes of rage from Jagger. You need to be protected. That stone will help."

"How do you figure?"

"Remember what the letter said? It was very specific about you. '*Henry Trank will be the first of you to understand.*

Jagger is out of the picture, but he left something behind. In time, Henry, and only Henry, can control it.'"

"Holy shit, Arch," Henry had said, laughing. "You remembered it word for word?"

Archie had blushed, pleased. "Yeah, well, it's kinda my thing. But all kidding aside, Henry. They, or rather, *he,* is quite aware of what Jagger left behind. He's going to use that to manipulate you. He'll taunt you, provoke you, threaten you... maybe even *befriend* you. He's the Father of Lies, Henry. Let's not forget the other part of the letter. *'Someone is coming amidst the turmoil. He will try to take what is "ours." That must not happen. Fail, and you belong to "us."'* Whoever this someone is, he's probably already here. And if *Lucifer* is here, it would go a long way to explaining your sudden feelings of rage. The man in your vision owes him something, and Lucifer's not happy about it. We are talking about a *powerful* supernatural entity, Henry. Remember how it felt to be in the presence of Archangel Michael?"

Henry had. Although none of them had spoken aloud to each other about what happened in the church at Satan's Kingdom, they'd all felt Michael's power. Raphael's too, when he'd healed Mercy.

Archie knew he'd understood. "So make sure that stone is around your neck at all times—"

A sound in the hallway startled him from his meditative recollections. The building was supposed to be empty. He wasn't supposed to be *inside* either, but that had never stopped him before.

Archie tapped the pause button on his iPhone, quieting the barely audible meditation music, then tiptoed over to the candle pedestal, moistened his thumb and forefinger, and doused the flame. Tilting his head to one side, he listened. It came once again, followed by whispers.

Curiosity battled with fear, rooting him to the spot. Then he thought of Henry, and how bravely he was facing the coming shit storm. It shamed him into motion, and he crept toward his newly replaced office door. He uttered a silent prayer of thanks to Hecate that Eljin Black destroyed the old door, for this one opened silently.

Archie edged it open, allowing an eye-width's worth of viewing space. The corridor was dark, but he caught a glimpse of something being wheeled into a room at the far end. The door to that room closed with a soft click.

Archie crept back to his desk, grabbed his iPhone, and slipped silently into the hallway.

∿

BYRON TOOK A LONG, last pull on his cigar. He held it up, cursing the thing for not lasting longer, then pitched it into the morgue parking lot. The thought of lighting another and stalling crossed his mind. Dealing with two dead bodies, and Mickey Schmidt, could make a guy *want* a second cigar.

"Fuck it," he mumbled. "Might as well get it over with." He took a deep breath, yanked the door open, and stepped inside.

Byron pulled a mask—one of a dozen or so Linda Halsey had given him—from his inside coat pocket and hooked it over his ears. Slapping on a mask was nothing new for him *here*. He'd always put one on—when he remembered—to keep the ghosts of formaldehyde and decay at bay. Having cigar breath helped a little, too.

Once the mask was safely on, he allowed himself to

exhale. With his morgue ritual complete, he made his way toward the autopsy room, dreading each step. As he turned the corner, he saw Raul Martinez standing sentry. He held off speaking until he reached him.

"Hey, Raul. Why aren't you in there with Mick?"

Raul shook his head. "I ain't goin' back in there, Chief." The mask hid most of his face, but there was no denying the fear in the man's eyes.

"That bad?" asked Byron.

Raul nodded. "Yeah. But not in the usual way."

"Whaddaya mean?"

"It's the kinda thing you gotta see for yourself, Chief."

"I hate to ask this, but I need you to come back in with me, Raul."

"Um. I'd really rather not."

"Was Mick screwing with you again?" asked Byron. "Cuz I'll light his ass up if he did."

"No. For once, it wasn't Mick. I think he might be as scared as I am."

"Then what is it?"

"Just a feeling, jefe. It's all wrong. It feels evil."

This was no surprise to Byron, something Raul picked up on.

"You see something tonight, too?" asked Raul.

"A couple things, Raul. I'll tell you about them later. But I really need you in there with me. If for anything, just a second set of eyes. Kinda like the dog in the library thing... again."

Raul hesitated, then hung his head in defeat. He pulled down his mask. The gold crucifix was already on the outside of his uniform shirt. He raised it to his lips, closed his eyes, and whispered a prayer.

"What did you pray for?" asked Byron.

"Protection."

"Put in a good word for me. Okay?" Byron smiled. He meant it figuratively, but Raul repeated the process. *Old* Byron would have told him he was just kidding, but current Byron, especially on this night, was grateful.

"You ready?"

Raul nodded. Together, they entered the autopsy room.

Mickey Schmidt was on the far side of the examination table, bent over and studying something pinched in a set of stainless-steel clamps. Byron and Raul stopped cold when they saw the object of Mick's fascination writhe between the clamps.

"Mick?" Byron squeaked. "What in the hell is that?"

"Oh, I'd say just about the most bizarre thing I've ever seen in my life. You need to tell Raul he needs to stop bringing me cases from *The Twilight Zone*," said Mickey Schmidt.

Byron and Raul took a step closer. "What're we dealing with here, Mick?"

As Byron asked his question, the sample in Mickey's clamps started to steam. They took another step forward, and the sample flared into flames, then disappeared.

"Jesus! Same thing as before," said Mickey.

"Whaddaya mean 'as before?'" asked Byron.

Mickey pointed to Raul. "You saw it last time, right Raul?"

Raul nodded, then looked at Byron. "It started moving when I came in. He held it up to the light, and it roasted."

"Shut off the exam lights, Mick."

The pathologist stared at Byron, open-mouthed and unable to respond.

"You keep looking at me like that Mick, I'm tempted to put a hook in your mouth."

"Why do you want—"

"Just do it, Mick!" yelled Byron.

Mickey jumped. Byron saw, by the look in his eyes, Mickey's pride took a shot. He walked slump-shouldered to the switch and turned it off.

Tough shit, thought Byron.

The room's only light came from Mickey's desk lamp in the far corner of the room, turning the bodies into ill-defined lumps.

Mickey returned to the exam table. "So? Any *bright* ideas, Chief? We could use them right about now." He waved a hand over the darkened mass of bodies. Byron ignored the jab.

"Pick up another sample, Mick. Hold it up, just like before."

Mick stared at him for a moment, then sighed. "And what's the point of that?"

"Why don't you just do it, and we'll find out together," said Byron, through gritted teeth.

"So now you're a pathologist?"

Byron held his temper. Mickey was usually an upbeat guy, but he was also used to being master of his domain. For the first time Byron could remember, Mick wasn't in control. And he was scared. Working the ghoulish humor act was tough under those circumstances.

Flipping the tables on Mickey felt good, making patience easier. But that patience only went so far. Byron stared him down until Mick did as asked.

Mick unleashed an aggravated sigh, picked up his

clamps, and pulled another sample from one of the bodies. Once he did, the sample reacted in much the same way.

"Well, it *ain't* the lights, professor," snapped Mick.

Byron shot him a look, but held his tongue. "Raul. Could you step into the prep room? I wanna see something."

Raul, unlike Mickey Schmidt, didn't question Byron.

When Raul left the room, Byron made his way over to the light switch and flipped it on. Then he ordered Mick to pick up another sample and hold it under the exam lights. It didn't steam. It didn't writhe. The specimen remained still.

"Keep it just like that, Mick," said Byron. "Raul. Come back in. Leave your crucifix in the prep room."

Byron and Mick watched as Raul's eyes bugged.

"I think he just dropped a deuce," said Mickey.

Byron wheeled on him. "Could you for once, Mick, zip your fuckin' pie-hole?"

Mickey, for once, zipped his pie-hole.

The doors swung open, and Raul returned to Byron's side.

The sample remained intact.

Byron tilted his head, staring thoughtfully at the sample. "Hang tight, guys. I'll be right back."

He headed for the double doors of the prep room. Upon returning, he held the crucifix high and in front of himself, stopping a few feet into the room. He took a step closer, eyeing the specimen in Mickey's clamps. Nothing happened. He took another step forward. Same result. On the third step, steam puffed from the patch of flesh. Byron stopped, nodding to himself.

He turned back to the prep room, laid the chain and crucifix on the counter, and returned to Raul's side.

"How did you know that would happen?" asked Raul.

"That's the *rest* of the story. Like I said, I'll fill you in later."

He turned to Mick. "Give me the rundown on these two. Everything you've got so far."

"Is there something I should know, Byron?" asked Mickey in a shaky voice.

"I'll tell you what I can afterwards, Mick. Right now, time ain't on my side. Now, spill it."

Mickey nodded, shook his head like a wet dog, and got into business mode. Byron had to give him points for that; it wasn't every day you witnessed something so obviously supernatural—and evil.

"Okay. They were in the salt water for less than twenty-four hours, if I had to guess. The bloating is minimal. Some predators took a few pecks at them, but nothing serious."

"Why are their eyes missing?" asked Raul.

Mick looked up sharply. "Good catch, Martinez. I was gonna save that for last, but there's plenty of strange shit to go around. Their eyes appear to have been..." Mickey's own eyes searched the ceiling for the right term. "*Ornamental.*"

"What does that mean, exactly, Mick?" asked Byron.

"Just what I said. There are *no* optic nerves behind them —in *either* corpse, Chief. It's like they were stuck in the sockets to make them look good."

Raul crossed himself.

"What else?" asked Byron.

"Each of them has a symbol etched into their foreheads. Just below the hairline."

Chills ran the length of Byron's spine. He approached the table. "Show me."

Mickey placed the clamps on the table. They clacked against the stainless steel surface. The sample in their grasp remained still. He placed one gloved hand on Luci's forehead and pushed her hair aside. The symbol matched the one Byron had seen on Jennifer's forehead.

Mickey saw Byron's eyes widen. "This look familiar to you, Chief?"

"Yep," said Byron. Then, to thwart Mick's curiosity, he asked. "What else?"

The pathologist removed his hand, and Luci's hair fell limply back in place. He tilted his head left, motioning Byron to follow him. A blue sheet covered Luci's midsection. Mickey rolled it to her waist. "What *don't* you see?"

Raul stepped forward, taking his place at Byron's side. The pair scanned the girl's midsection for a few seconds. Raul noticed first, drawing in a sharp breath. "Where's her belly button?"

"Ding. Ding. Ding. Martinez gets the door prize. She doesn't have one. Neither does the other."

Byron was at a temporary loss for words. This seemed to please Mickey to no end; he had regained control.

"Are you ready for the cherry on the sundae, boys?" asked Mickey. The joy in his voice was unmistakable.

Byron didn't respond. Raul shook his head emphatically from side to side and barely squeaked out a "No."

Mickey ignored them, and began whistling. The tune was familiar. Somewhere, in Byron's stunned mind, he deciphered it. It was "There's No Business Like Show Business" by Irving Berlin.

Byron hadn't noticed two sets of clamps planted on either side of Luci's chest. Mick reached for them. Everything happened slowly from that point, and Byron felt the word *Stop!* forming behind clenched teeth, but the letter S never got close to leaving his lips.

Mickey raised the sawed off bones from Luci's chest cavity as Raul's legs gave way. Byron caught him as he fell, then held him in place.

Mickey held each section of ribs aloft like a proud barbecue pit master from hell. "TA DA!"

Byron dragged Raul along with him and sidled up to the autopsy table. "What is it Mick? What am I looking at?"

Mickey placed the rib sections on the table, then pulled down his mask. The glee on his face made Byron want to smack him. If he hadn't been propping up Raul, he might have.

"The question, my benevolent chief, is what are you *not* looking at?"

Byron gave Salem's Chief Pathologist a ball-shriveling stare. It did nothing to darken Mickey's mood. He was high as a kite now.

"They have no hearts, Chief."

CHAPTER 12
SPEAK OF THE DEVIL

Wanda knew what came next. She'd severed communication with the League of the Moon. Her cell phone was off, stowed in the floor safe at the front of her store. Her channel to Jazz, for the moment and by her own choice, remained dark. She'd given Mercy two weeks off with pay. Wanda's Wicca'd Emporium was locked up tight.

She sat in the small kitchenette at the back of her apartment—the point furthest from the front window. The lights were off. Wanda, on most nights, kept a candle lit in her street-facing window until she went to bed. To those in the know, it signaled a visit was welcomed. No flame flickered. The candles remained cool and dry, stored in a small end table drawer at the side of her love seat.

For a long time she sat in comfortable silence, sipping chamomile tea and nibbling honey-flavored graham crackers. On the table before her, aside from the mug and the crackers, were four items: a small LED flashlight, a battered Moleskine notebook, a gold athame dagger given to her as an apology gift from Archie, and the Dell laptop from the bar at her shop.

When Henry had visited her earlier in the day, the newest revelations of his vision tripped something inside her. She opened up Facebook and began searching, unsure what she was searching *for*, but figuring a basic search of near-death experiences was a good starting point. It turned up quite a number of hits. She had no idea there were this many active groups on Facebook. Many were public.

For the next hour, she scanned the post topics and the comments beneath them, still unsure of what she sought but letting intuition be her guide. Several minutes into her search, the sheer volume of posts and responses overwhelmed her, so she narrowed things down a bit.

Under each new post she investigated, Wanda ticked off *Top Comments*. She clicked its subheading, which read: *Show the most engaging comments first*. Immediately, it payed dividends. One name kept showing up either at the top of the comment strings, or somewhere close to the top. The username *'Soul Man'* appeared with regularity in almost every public group.

Many of the comments from 'Soul Man' gave her pause, because in a mostly positive environment—the posts were largely about the beneficial aftereffects of NDEs—his focused on what happened right *before* death. To Wanda, they seemed rude and intrusive. One exchange leaped from the screen.

ANGELA B: *Who cares what the weight of the soul may or may not be? It's the weight of the experience that counts.*

Soul Man: *It matters! If you can measure its weight, one three thousandth of an ounce, by the way...*

IT WAS the exact thing Henry had mentioned in his vision. Wanda skipped the rest. She'd seen enough of 'Soul Man's' rants to know this was the guy. The need for people to air their dirty laundry on social media always puzzled her. For once, she celebrated it.

She clicked on 'Soul Man.' When the page loaded, there was more of the same. Then, at the left side of his Facebook profile page, she saw the section headed *Photos*. There weren't many *actual* photos, and most were merely screenshots of articles about near-death experiences. Mainly, they were items he'd posted to bolster his arguments.

Wanda scrolled slowly through them. The further back she went through his history, the more the articles changed. And in a big way. Suddenly, they weren't articles at all, but obituary notices. The most recent was dated one week after Jo was attacked on the Salem Common, beginning the Jagger shit show. She clicked on the image and enlarged it. It read:

November 16, 2019
Thomas Greenfield
After a long illness. Thomas Greenfield, aged 83 years.
He is survived by his wife, Edna Banks-Greenfield, eldest son
Thomas Greenfield Junior, son James Greenfield, and
daughter Melissa Greenfield-Warner. He is also survived by
nine grandchildren.
In lieu of flowers, please send donations to:
University of Maine at Orono: Psychology Department.

University of Maine... November 16th. Wanda felt a chill run the length of her spine. *Is this the old man Henry saw on the scale?*

The more she thought about it, the more she believed it to be true. The timing of his vision and the date on the obit lined up. Even if it was a few days *after* things went down with Jagger, it was still possible. Henry's new 'gift,' after all, was glimpsing the future.

She continued through the photo section of 'Soul Man's' Facebook page. Wanda reluctantly donned her reading glasses. She hated using them, but the photo was dark, and the laptop screen small.

This was the only actual photo in the entire *Photo* section. When she clicked it, it took her to Instagram.

It was shot in the woods at night. A man with bright white hair knelt over someone on the ground. Any doubts 'Soul Man' and 'Cotton Ball' were one and the same vanished. What was happening in the photo was the same thing Henry'd reported in his vision—minus the scale, of course—right down to the silvery trail of soul disappearing into the bottle in his hand.

Wanda clicked back to Facebook and scrolled on. There were several more obituary entries in the photo section. Her eyes were getting tired, and she was about to close the laptop when she came upon a familiar name.

"My God," she whispered.

It was Archie's Aunt Jenny's obituary.

She closed the laptop, slid it across the table, then opened the Moleskine. The battered notebook was more than that; it was her diary. She'd kept it since she was a young girl growing up in Winthrop, Massachusetts. Wanda closed her eyes and tilted her head toward the ceiling.

"When was it?" she wondered aloud. She took a deep breath and blew it out slowly, flipping through memories in her mind and then the pages in the notebook. She'd first gotten sober in the mid eighties, but hadn't begun serious practice of her craft until almost 1991.

"It had to be after that," she murmured.

"Having trouble remembering, witch?"

Wanda jumped out of her chair.

The man stood in her kitchenette doorway, silhouetted by ambient light from the street lamps.

"You didn't put out the candle tonight. Very poor manners. Let me refresh your memory. Does March of 1992 ring a bell?"

Wanda settled back into her chair. Her heart slowed. She'd known the man was coming for her, but the connection to Jennifer Love was something she'd never expected. When that domino fell, it tripped something in her memory.

Now things made sense to her.

"Come to collect, Artemis?"

The man approached her kitchen table, then lowered himself into the opposite seat. He took the small LED flashlight from in front of her, frowned, then put it under his chin. "Do I really look that old?"

So much for sense, she thought.

Once Joanne had broken the news to her employees, then shuttered the Cauldron for the next two weeks—*Two weeks my ass!* she'd thought—she'd changed into her gym clothes and headed to *Fit!* Salem to let off some steam. When she'd arrived, they were already closed. She'd ripped off a litany of four-letter words on her way back to the Jeep.

Not to be denied, she'd worked out at home using her body weight in place of Nautilus equipment. Now, she sat in the bathtub, lights out, letting the near-scalding water work away the remaining tension from her body. A lone candle flickered silently in a black ceramic holder atop the toilet tank, and her orange tank top and black yoga pants lay draped over the toilet seat lid. She closed her eyes, sighed, and sent grateful thoughts toward Penny for watching Deliliah this afternoon.

The muffled rattle of keys reached her from the other room, announcing Henry's arrival.

"Jo?"

"In here. Could you grab my robe on your way in?"

"Okay."

She marked his progress by sound. Keys clinked in the bowl by the door. The bedroom closet door squealed open, then clicked closed. The soft pull of rubber souls on hardwood brought him to the bathroom door. Henry pushed it open and was swallowed by a cloud of steam, which he waved away, then tossed the robe onto the toilet seat lid. It covered Jo's workout gear. "You boiling a lobster in here?" he asked.

"One very stressed out lobster, yes. This fucking shut down's no good for anyone."

Henry shrugged. "It'll pass in two weeks. Just ask the governor."

"And if my aunt had balls, she'd be my uncle. It ain't gonna be over in two weeks, Band-Aid boy. We both know that."

Henry nodded in concession.

Jo sat up in the tub. "Can you hand me a towel?"

Henry dragged one from the rack and handed it to her. Jo stood and pulled it around herself, then stepped from the tub and onto another towel on the floor. She began drying herself off, and Henry reached for the robe. As he lifted it for Jo to ease into, the dirty workout clothes tumbled to the floor. At the sight of them, Henry froze.

Orange tank top.

Black yoga pants.

In his mind, a handsome, well-built man winked back at him.

"Sympathy for the Devil" began playing in his head. Dark clouds of jealousy blotted out reason. Anger flowed through his veins. It *had* been Jo he'd seen crossing Lafayette Street. Their phone conversation moments before had been some kind of ruse. She'd pretended she was still at the store, but she'd been with *him* the whole time.

Henry left the bathroom without another word. Jo was still drying off. As she blew out the candle and turned on the bathroom light, she heard the tinkle of keys from the front of the apartment, and then the slam of the front door. After that, something crashed to the floor.

Jo wrapped the towel around herself, cinching it at the top. Barefoot and barely dry, she scrambled across the bedroom and into the living room. She saw the cracked frame and the shattered glass by the front door. The photo was face down, but she didn't need to flip it over to know it was from their wedding day.

The sun had been shining that day. Henry held Jo suspended in his arms, as if carrying her over an imaginary threshold. Their foreheads were pressed together, and smiles of pure love and joy were plastered on their faces. From that day to this, there'd been nary a harsh word between them, and when there was, they made quick work of patching things up.

Henry was upset, of that there was no doubt. Jo racked her brains for an explanation, but nothing came. Though he'd been unusually quiet since the close call with Jagger, Jo knew, under that silence, a storm was building. Her usually cheerful husband was quick to anger lately. He'd told her, here and there, that he didn't feel like himself. That he feared too much of Jagger had been left behind. Jo had played it off. Telling him not to worry, it would pass. As she stared down at the shattered glass, she regretted her casual dismissiveness.

She ran back to the bedroom, dried herself, and threw on black jeans, a black hoodie, and black combat boots. Chesrule's knife sat in a sheath on her nightstand. The internal debate to take it or leave it lasted about two seconds, then she tucked it into the small of her back. She pulled her hair back, tied it off with a black Scrunchie, then grabbed her iPhone from the dresser. When she swiped Henry's number, it rang once, then went straight to voicemail. She didn't bother leaving a message.

Her keys were still in the same bowl Henry'd taken his from. Jo grabbed them, opened the door, and let out a surprised yelp. "God dammit! You scared the hell out of me!"

Iris Greenblatt stood in the doorway, her fist raised. "I'm sorry, Mrs. Henry. I was about to knock when you threw the door open. I heard a crash and wanted to make sure you two were okay. Is everything alright?"

Jo glared at her a moment longer, then relaxed. "Everything's fine, Mrs. G. Henry was upset about something. He slammed the door on his way out and a picture fell off the wall."

Mrs. Greenblatt gave Jo a disapproving look.

"Really. That's all it is," said Jo, defensively.

"Are you sure, Joanne? There's nothing else you want to tell me?" asked Mrs. G.

Jo's mouth hung open, then she crossed her arms. *The nerve on this woman.* "What could I possibly want to tell you? Not that I owe you any explanation... for anything."

Mrs. G shrugged. "Oh, I don't know. I thought maybe Henry might be upset about that tall, handsome fella that walked you home tonight."

Jo gave her the Spock eyebrow as her crossed arms fell. "What the hell are you talking about?"

Iris Greenblatt gave her a sad and condescending look, then turned on her heel and headed toward her own apartment. Over her shoulder, she said, "As if you didn't know!"

Jo heard her second slammed door in the last ten minutes.

CHAPTER 13
BREADCRUMBS

Mercy arrived at Wanda's place on Derby Street almost half an hour after she'd seen the strange image on Instagram. She couldn't get it out of her mind and wanted a second opinion.

Standing on the sidewalk, she noticed the candle wasn't in the window. Normally, she wouldn't ignore Wanda's passive plea for privacy, but her growing unease about Jamal's picture forced her hand. Besides, it wasn't like Wanda would chop her head off for ignoring the candle. The worst that would happen was a friendly reprimand.

Mercy stepped into the foyer and rang the buzzer. After a couple of minutes and no answer, she tried once more. Nada.

Mercy tried Wanda's phone next. It went straight to voice mail. She knew the Emporium, much like every other place in town, was shuttered due to the governor's order. She headed over anyway. When she arrived ten minutes later, she tried the front and back entrances. No sign of Wanda. Worried, Mercy threw protocol out the window. She took the keys from her coat pocket and opened the back door, then reached to her right and flipped the lights on. The safe room was empty.

Knowing it would yield nothing, Mercy chose thoroughness and checked the front of the store, getting the expected result. As she entered the protected hall leading back to the safe room, she heard soft foot steps squeaking lightly on the polished obsidian floor of the safe room.

"Hello?"

It was a man's voice. It sounded familiar, but in a town full of magic that didn't translate to safety.

Mercy tiptoed to the end of the hall. Carefully, she reached for a strand of beads in the beaded doorway, gently pulling a fistful of them aside to avoid rattling them. She leaned in and saw a man. He saw her and smiled. She breathed a sigh of relief and said, "Hi, Chief."

"I take it Wanda's not in the house?" asked Byron.

Mercy shook her head, a worried look on her face. "No. And I went to her apartment. She's either not home, or not answering for whatever reason. Oh! *And* her phone is going straight to voicemail." Mercy tilted her head. "Why are *you* here, Chief?"

"I came to ask Wanda about something on a case I'm working." He was aiming for casual, but butchered it.

Mercy frowned. "I call bullshit."

"Why do I bother? I can't get anything past you witchy types!" Byron threw his hands in the air in mock exasperation. He was smiling.

Mercy smiled back. "Okay, Chief. I'm not Wanda—no one is—but I can help. Spill it."

He told her everything, starting with Raul's discovery of Luci and Fermina's bodies, then, in succession, the tarot card incident, the woman he mistook for Jo, the possession in the ER, and ended with the encounter at the morgue.

"Dad fainted?" asked Mercy.

Byron shot her a crooked grin. "Your dad's never been too fond of the morgue. But even I felt a little woozy looking at them."

"And you say they had no hearts?" asked Mercy.

"No hearts. Their eyes were gone, and Mick said the works that are normally behind someone's eyes weren't there. *And* no belly buttons. Strangest goddamned thing I've ever seen."

"Anything else?" asked Mercy.

"Oh! I almost forgot." Byron pulled his cell phone from his back pocket, tapped the screen, then handed it to Mercy. "That symbol was on their foreheads. Jennifer's too. Ring a bell at all?"

Mercy shook her head. "No. Did you look it up on Google?"

She saw by the embarrassed look on his face he hadn't, so she did it for him. "When I bring it up on Wiki, it says it's one of the *Sulfur Crosses*. There's three of them. One for sulfur, one for phosphorous... and one for brimstone. And you said the third one, brimstone, was the one on all three of their foreheads?"

Byron nodded.

Mercy thought about it. "I wonder if it has something to do with control or possession?"

"All the more reason we need to find Wanda," said Byron. "Let's head to her place. If she doesn't answer, I'll break the door down."

They left through the back door. Mercy locked the place up tight. Five minutes later, they were back in the lobby of

Wanda's apartment building. Byron rang her buzzer, with predictable results. He tried the next one down.

An elderly female voice vibrated the tinny sounding speaker. "Who the hell is it? It's late, you know?"

"This is Chief Byron Miller of the Salem Police Department, ma'am. I need access to the building. I'm making a wellness check on a fellow resident."

"How do I know you're not some scam artist? Or a drug dealing sex pervert? We get those types around here."

Byron rolled his eyes and was about to answer when Mercy held up a hand. "Mrs. Kravitz? It's me, Mercy Glass. I asked the Chief to come with me. We're making sure Wanda's okay. Could you let us in, please?"

"Oh! Hi, Mercy. What's wrong with Wanda?"

"Nothing that we know of, Mrs. K. She's probably sleeping," said Mercy. "She's not answering her phone and—"

"She's probably still out with the handsome fella that came by earlier. Could have been a nephew, maybe? Or something better!" They heard Mrs. Kravitz giggle. "I say *good* for the old girl if she's riding *that* pony!"

"You sure it wasn't Henry Trank, Mrs. K.?" asked Mercy.

"Nope. I know what Henry looks like. And that green-eyed hellion wife of his, too. T'wasn't him."

"We need to be let in right now, Mrs. Kravitz," said Byron.

"Okay. Okay. Keep your shirt on."

She buzzed them in, and they two-stepped it to the second floor. When they arrived at Wanda's door, it was slightly ajar. Out of courtesy, Byron knocked, then pushed the door open.

"Wanda?" tried Mercy.

No answer.

They went right, down the small hallway leading to Wanda's living room. Mercy knew the place well and headed straight for the floor lamp in the corner. Once they could see, Byron asked, "Anything look out of place?"

Mercy shook her head. "Nope. There's only the kitchen and the bedroom left. I'll take the bedroom."

Byron nodded, somewhat relieved. Snooping in Wanda's bedroom would have felt a tad creepy. Byron went back into the hall and Mercy made for the bedroom entrance. She'd barely begun her search when Byron called for her. When she entered the kitchen he was huddled over a closed laptop.

"She *never* brings that home. That's the computer from her shop," said Mercy.

"You think you could find out something from it?" asked Byron.

"If it's not password protected, yes."

Mercy opened the laptop, then pressed the power button. When the screen came to life, Wanda's custom wallpaper was missing. In its place was the same symbol Byron had seen three times in the last two hours. Beneath the symbol, the standard empty white rectangle and its blinking cursor demanded a password.

"Well, would you look at that?" said Byron.

"That woman is always a step ahead," said Mercy. "But it's password protected."

"Can't get in?" asked Byron.

"I could try, but we might be here all night trying to figure—"

A buzzing sound silenced Mercy. Byron was leaning against the kitchen cabinets. It seemed to be coming from behind him. He turned, opened all three of them, and searched within for the cause of the buzz. "I can't find where it's coming from."

"Byron?"

When he turned to face Mercy, she was pointing over his left shoulder. Byron followed her finger. A box of honey-flavored Graham crackers sat atop the shelves. A pinprick of light shone through its bottom. Byron retrieved it, then placed it on the table. He tipped the box and the phone slid out. It was a cheap burner flip phone from Walmart. It's calendar was opened. An 'event' message in bright white characters read: P'word=Sulfur777.

"You gotta be shittin' me!" said Byron.

Mercy smiled and laughed.

"How the hell did she know we'd be here and need the password?" Byron wondered aloud.

Mercy picked up the phone, tapped something, then turned it so Byron could read it.

"What am I looking at?"

Mercy shook her head in amazement. "She set it to go off every ten minutes from... sixty minutes ago. So whatever she was doing, she obviously knew we'd come looking for her. And whoever she's with, she expected him."

"But why didn't she just call one of us? If she knew the guy was coming—"

"She doesn't want us to find her. Not yet," said Mercy.

"Are you saying she *wanted* to be kidnapped?"

Mercy shrugged. "Only one way to find out."

She took a seat in front of the laptop, then entered the password. It opened up to the desktop screen. Mercy waited for the machine to go through its routine, expecting something to load up and point the way.

Nothing happened. The desktop screen and its two neat rows of icons glowed stupidly back at her.

"What are you waiting for?" asked Byron.

"I was hoping, once the startup routine was over, whatever program she was running would load. Maybe show us the last thing she was looking at."

"Is there another way to find out what she did last?" asked Byron.

"Her browsing history might show it. If she's not the type that deletes stuff like that," said Mercy.

Mercy opened Google Chrome. Byron watched as she clicked something at the top right of the screen. When a window popped open, Mercy leaned closer to read the time-stamps on the most recent activity. "Yes!"

"What?"

"She was on Facebook about an hour and a half ago. It'll take me right to the last page she looked at. We can trace the history backward from there."

Mercy clicked on the topmost link. When it opened, she sucked in a surprised breath.

"What is it?" Byron asked.

"I just saw this same picture about an hour ago. But it wasn't from whoever this 'Soul Man' is. It was on the Face-book page of a guy in Archie's class."

Byron leaned in for a closer look. "What's he pouring on that person?"

"He's not *pouring* anything. He's extracting something."

"Huh?"

"I thought the same thing you did, that he was dumping something onto the person beneath him. But if you look closer, you can see the angle's all wrong, and the stuff going *into* the bottle is vapor or gas, not a liquid."

Byron squinted at the photo. "I'll be damned. And you say you saw this same picture on someone else's Facebook feed?"

Mercy nodded. "Well, Instagram. Facebook owns Instagram. Anyway, he's a new kid at the U. So new he's not even on the registry at school yet. Super young for a college kid, too. His name is Jamal Khalid. And Byron, I could tell by his eyes, he's had a near-death experience."

Byron tilted his head. "Come again?"

"There's a light I can see—especially in a dark room—that comes from the eyes of NDE experiencers. There's nothing else like it on earth. I've seen it anytime I run into someone like myself. It's part of what you bring back from the other side," said Mercy.

"That's not the only thing," said Byron. He winked at Mercy.

She blushed. "True enough. I don't know anything about this guy, but he was looking straight at *me* when he told Archie about his NDE."

"Let's see if we can find anything else," said Byron.

Mercy dug in. She clicked one link after another, opening each in its own tab so she could shuffle between them. "Huh. They're all obituaries."

Byron pulled a chair from the side of the table and placed it next to Mercy's. "You never saw this," he said as he pulled a pair of reading glasses from his pocket. "Penny calls these my 'grandpa glasses.'"

Mercy laughed, then crossed her heart. "Your secret's safe with me."

"Most of the latest ones are from Maine, looks like," said Byron. "Let's skip to the most recent. Maybe we can find something useful."

Mercy clicked on the link for Thomas Greenfield's obituary. Byron read it, then pulled out his cell phone. Before he dialed, Mercy asked, "What is it?"

"It says Greenfield worked at U Maine, Orono. Maybe there's a connection. I've got a few friends in the Maine State Police. Time to call in some favors."

Byron put his iPhone on speaker and placed it on the table. It rang once.

"Maine State Police, this is a recorded line."

"That supposed to intimidate me or something, Michelle?"

There was a pause on the line, then the voice answered, "Could you please say the phrase 'park the car' sir."

Byron grinned. "Pahk the Cah! How's that?"

Michelle Estes giggled. "I thought I heard a Boston accent in there somewhere. What can I do you for, Byron?"

He told her about the Maine link in the obituary, then what he needed from her, and how fast he needed it. "The missing woman is a close friend, Michelle. I got a hunch whoever this guy is, he's connected. I just need to know who's left the faculty lately."

"I'll get the dean's info, By. Call you right back as soon as I can."

"Thanks Michelle."

Ten minutes later, Byron's phone rang. "I just talked to the dean. He wasn't a happy camper when I woke him up."

"Poor baby," said Byron.

"Fuck that guy. I've run into him at a few fundraisers. I'm glad I woke him up. Anyway, I've got two names for you. First is Camille Leonard, 80, just retired. The other is a guy named Artemis Davies. The dean didn't have good words for old Arty. Said the guy was kind of off the rails. They finally had to let him go for ethics violations. Apparently, Mr. Davies made a purchase or two of a questionable nature. I asked the dean for specifics. You won't believe what he said, By."

Byron winked at Mercy. "Try me, Mish."

"The first is a weird one. The guy was buying lots of dry ice on a regular basis. That's not uncommon, the dean told me, but Davies wouldn't provide him with a legit reason for the purchases. Just gave him the runaround. Said it was for 'patent pending research.' The other one is waaaay out there. He used his University account to buy tetrodotoxin. It's a poison, Byron. It comes from puffer fish."

Mercy gasped.

Byron saw the recognition in her eyes. "You've *heard* of it?"

"Oh yeah. It causes paralysis. It shuts down breathing and the nervous system. Bokors—that's what they call voodoo priests—use it in their potions to," Mercy raised quote fingers, "make zombies."

"Mish. Thanks. I gotta go." Byron didn't wait for an answer. "I've heard enough. I'm putting out an APB for Wanda and this Davies guy."

"I'd wait on that, Chief," said Mercy.

Byron looked at her like she'd sprouted a second nose.

"The guy she left here with *isn't* Davies. Remember what Mrs. K said? The guy was good looking. Now, I don't know about *you*, but even Mrs. K wouldn't hop in the sack with Davies. Wanda left with someone else."

Byron went pale.

CHAPTER 14
DEAR DIARY

Wanda wasn't exactly sure where they were going, or why this man had shown up at her apartment. She'd assumed 'Soul Man,' whoever *that* was, would darken her door any minute. Henry's vision had all but predicted it.

It was the reason she'd dug out her Moleskine diary.

When Henry had revealed the mention of her name in the vision, faint bells from memories distant tolled in her mind. Tonight, she'd planned to comb through the diary and confirm her suspicions. But this handsome asshole seated across from her in the back of a huge, black limousine had thrown a wrench into her plans.

"So," said the smiling man. "The famous Wanda Heinze!" He put a flattened hand on his chest. "Color me enchanted."

Wanda frowned. "Don't patronize me."

He feigned ignorance. "Whatever do you mean?"

"Cut the shit. Should I call you Gemini? Luci? Fermina? Or should we just skip the formalities?"

He put on a pouty face. "You're no fun at all."

Wanda sighed. "What do you want from me, *Lucifer?*" She was doing her best to put up a brave front. Inside, she felt as if everything had turned to Jell-O. It wasn't everyday you sat face to face in the back of a limo with The Prince of Darkness.

He clapped his hands, rubbing them together. "Right down to business. I like that. So, we have a mutual problem. Care to guess what that is?"

Wanda stared at him, but held her cards close.

Lucifer raised a hand. The Moleskine diary tucked under Wanda's left arm flew out from under it. He snagged it from thin air, then turned it this way and that, examining it. "I haven't seen one of these in years." He snapped the fingers of his free hand, then pointed at her. "You're old-school. I like that." He smiled. It was a smile she knew she *should* hate, but it warmed her all the same, and she felt a little disgusted with herself.

Lucifer opened his hand, and Wanda reached out to catch the diary before it fell to the floor, but her hands remained empty. When she looked up, the diary floated at eye level. The notebook opened on its own. The pages turned —slowly, at first, then picking up speed. Lucifer waved his left hand. The pages stopped. He leaned forward, then blew softly on the diary. It floated toward Wanda, gently descending into her lap.

"Is that supposed to impress me?" asked Wanda, secretly awestruck.

He shrugged. "What can I say? It's the simple things."

Lucifer held out his hand, palm up, motioning toward the diary. "If you please?"

Wanda held his gaze a moment longer, feigning resistance. Inside, she was at war with herself. Part of her wanted to resist him at all costs, but another part, one she was horrified to discover existed, longed to please him. Before she allowed her eyes to drop to the diary, she marshalled every resource she could to stomp that *desire to please* into dust. It worked... somewhat.

Finally, she peeled her eyes from his. It wasn't easy. She had no illusions about who she was dealing with here, but the man's gaze was *magnetic*. She recalled a line about Lucifer being God's most beautiful angel, but that his desire to be God's equal got him cast into the pit. Whether or not the line was true, she did not know. Looking at him, she felt it could be.

Wanda's internal debate came to a screeching halt when she saw the name on the page.

Artemis Davies.

Seeing it in print, in her own haphazard writing, brought the buried memories screaming back in a painful rush. It was one of the biggest regrets of her life, because it had almost ruined her sobriety.

All these years later, the thought of what had happened made her long for a drink. A phantom taste of whiskey filled her mouth, and she swallowed greedily. It wasn't the real thing, but at the moment she figured even the ghost of a drink might calm her nerves. With dread in her heart, she realized it did.

Her eyes widened when the words on the diary's pages moved. At first, they wavered—shimmering like the heated surface of a desert highway. From the center out, they drifted slowly apart toward the edges of the page.

She gasped and looked up at Lucifer. His eyes were closed. "Remember," he whispered.

Wanda felt her muscles slacken, and her suddenly heavy head tilted forward.

The pages came alive.

He'd come to her in the late winter of 1992 a broken man. She'd been going to Alcoholics Anonymous meetings in and around the Salem area. Artemis had been in the audience—per a court order for DUI—at one meeting, and had heard her speak from the podium. When the meeting adjourned for the evening, and the post-meeting cleanup was over, he'd approached her and introduced himself.

In those days his hair was raven-black, he was clean shaven, and hadn't yet succumbed to the need for glasses. Artemis Davies had been handsome once. He'd looked nothing like the man Henry described in his vision and the one she'd seen in the Facebook photo.

It's no wonder I couldn't place him right away, she thought as the diary unfolded before her.

"I heard your story tonight, Wanda," he'd said. "I can identify with the driving part, but luckily not the crash. Congratulations on your sobriety."

"Thank you! You know what they say, though; it's one day at a time. Yesterday's history, tomorrow's a mystery."

"True enough," was his reply. He'd smiled at her. Wanda couldn't help but notice the smile failed to reach his eyes, and that his aura was tinged with dark-blue hues of sadness.

At that point in her life, she'd had some sober time under her belt, a clear mind, and her childhood ability to read auras had returned full force. Her empathic abilities were no longer blunted by the numbing effects of alcohol. This man had been hurting badly, and she'd felt compelled to help him.

Wanda had motioned for him to follow her, leading him

through the noisy kitchen at the back of the hall and outside into the emptying parking lot. She'd come to a stop under a light post in the far corner of the lot. Sparse snow drifted sideways through the post's cone of light and was eagerly devoured by darkness. Wanda had pulled her coat tight as Artemis lit a cigarette.

"What's troubling you, Artemis?"

His eyes had gone wide with surprise. "It's that obvious?"

"Not to everyone. But I'm pretty good at telling when someone is hurting. It's a *me* thing."

He'd shaken his head, smiling sadly. "And I thought I was putting on a brave face. You know why I'm here tonight?"

"No. I mean, alcohol troubles, obviously. Is it a court thing, sweetie?"

"Yeah. DUI. No one got hurt, thankfully. I'm not even that much of a drinker. It's just—"

Wanda had waited him out, opting for patience over fear of spooking him.

Artemis's eyes had grown glassy. Tears threatened and his chin quivered. He'd dragged deeply on his cigarette, then blown out the smoke, and his story, in a long and shaky rush.

"My mother is dying, and it's killing me. We live together. Or *lived* together. I don't know if she's coming back from the hospital or not. It's stage four pancreatic cancer. They've given her two months. The oncologist pulled me aside after they admitted her and told me *two months* was optimistic. It's more likely four to six weeks."

"Oh, Artemis. I'm so sorry," Wanda had said. She had stepped forward, arms wide, and he'd gratefully accepted

117

her hug. When they separated, his tears had made good on their threat.

"When I left the hospital, mother was sedated, and I went to the closest bar to do the same. Like a total fool, I didn't call a cab. I hadn't even made it a quarter of the way home when I got pulled over." He'd grunted out a laugh. "It wasn't even my driving. I had a taillight out. Didn't even know it. When I rolled down the window, the cop asked me if I'd been drinking. I told him I'd had a couple, which was actually true, believe it or not. But it was two whiskey doubles. Not enough that I felt drunk, but enough to put me over the limit."

Wanda had sympathized. "God looks out for drunks and fools. It could have been worse. Trust me."

"Truer words, and all that."

"Maybe all of this is happening for a reason, Artemis. Did you ever consider that?"

He'd tilted his head, then wiped at his eyes. "I don't see how. The doctors say there's not much they can do for her."

"They've tried radiation and chemo?"

"Yes. And a few other non-conventional treatments. Nothing seems to work."

Wanda remembered feeling sorrow radiating from him, and wanting to ease it any way she could. It couldn't be helped; it was her nature.

As her memories unfolded in the living pages of her diary, she heard herself in the limo *and* in her thoughts back then saying, "Don't do it! Don't do it!"

But she had been, and was now, powerless to stop it.

"I might be able to heal her, Artemis."

His hand had frozen halfway to his mouth. Smoke from his cigarette drifted lazily upward through the falling snow.

"I'm not making any promises, mind you. But I've done it in the past. I've got a talent for healing and I think I can help. If you're willing to let me try."

Artemis didn't speak for a solid minute. In the silence, even back then, she remembered wishing she could take the words back.

She looked up from the diary. "What the hell was I thinking?"

"Pride goeth before the fall," said Lucifer.

"You ought to know!" Wanda shot back.

"Ouch!"

"You kinda walked into that one," said Wanda.

He nodded in concession. "True enough."

Wanda's gaze returned to the diary, and she saw the scene had shifted. The parking lot was gone, and she was in a dark room. Artemis stood at the foot of his mother's bed. He'd secured her release the previous day, despite the protestations of the medical staff. "If she's going to die, she's going to do it in a place she loves," he'd told them.

Wanda saw herself leaning over Claire Davies, her hands resting just above the woman's forehead. As she moved them down over Claire's body, she stopped at her solar plexus chakra. Wanda's hands had begun to sweat, as though with a fever. She had started with Claire's crown chakra and worked her way down. Though the problem was pancreatic cancer, there was always a chance something in one part of the body might be causing another part to shut down or become diseased. Energy flow through the human form was something few, especially western medical practitioners, focused on.

Suddenly, Wanda's fingers had begun to feel numb. In all the years she'd practiced Reiki, nothing of the sort had happened before. As if on cue, Claire Davies shook, and her face had turned blue.

Artemis had rushed around the foot of the bed, taking his place at his mother's side and opposite Wanda. "Mother! What's wrong?"

Claire had turned her head toward him. Her eyes bulged from their sockets. The only answer she'd provided was a violent shake of the head.

"What did you do to her?" Artemis had screamed.

Wanda had pulled her hands free. They'd gone numb and tingly. "I did nothing. The treatment hasn't even started."

In the limo, Wanda pulled her eyes from the diary, then covered them with her left hand. "That poor woman! All I was trying to do was help! She died because of me."

"Wanda? There's more. And you need to hear it," said Lucifer.

She felt the diary being gently pulled from her lap, and opened her watery eyes. Lucifer closed it, place it on his own lap, and folded his hands over the cover. "You won't find any more answers in here. But I can tell you this; what happened that night was *not* your fault."

"What do you mean?" asked Wanda. "I know she was close to death, but she still had time! There was still a chance her doctors could've saved her. I ruined everything!"

"No. You were in the wrong place at the wrong time. Or the right time, depending on your point of view."

Wanda thought she saw a twinkle of something in his eyes, but couldn't be sure.

"Claire Davies never died," said Lucifer. He held up his left hand, index finger pointing toward the roof of the car for emphasis. "And you're the reason why."

CHAPTER 15
ENVELOPED BY LIES

J o wasn't sure where to start, or even *why* she was starting... anything. She had no idea why Henry had stormed out. Mrs. Greenblatt's accusations made no sense.

To say Jo wasn't a fan of her nosy neighbor was an understatement; she couldn't stand her. Somewhere in the back of her mind, Jo realized much of it stemmed from a lack of privacy in her years as a foster child. Her feelings mostly centered on the men—if you could call them that—back then, but there'd also been a fair share of busybody women. Mrs. G. simply brought it all roaring back. Add to that Henry's inexplicable fondness for the woman... it was enough to drive someone nuts.

She'd never known Mrs. G. to outright *lie* about something, however. Au contraire; the woman was honest to a fault. It was why Jo felt time was of the essence. The moment she fired up her orange Jeep, she slapped her iPhone on the dashboard's magnetic stand and tapped Byron's number. He answered on the first ring.

"Miller."

"Hey, Byron. It's Jo. Have you seen Henry tonight?"

"No. Everything alright?"

"He just stormed out of our apartment. Slammed the door so hard he broke our wedding picture."

"*Henry* did that?" Jo heard the shock in his voice.

"I know. Not like him at all. But since the Jagger thing, he's been a bit fucked up. I've been trying to humor him out of it. Probably not the best strategy."

"Fucked up how, Jo?" asked Byron. He sounded genuinely concerned. It touched her.

"Mostly, he's short tempered. Which isn't like him at all. But he's been down a lot. Sad. It's kind of a bummer. He's working *my* side of the street, lately. Henry's usually the one to talk *me* out of moods like that."

"And you have no idea what set him off?" asked Byron.

"Oh, I wouldn't say that. Mrs. Greenblatt made it quite clear what *she* thinks set him off. But it makes no sense."

"What'd she say?"

Byron heard Jo huff on her end. "She accused me of walking home with, in her words, 'that tall, handsome fella.'"

Byron had the phone on speaker. Mercy drew in a surprised breath. Jo heard it. "What was that? Someone with you, Chiefy?" asked Jo.

"Mercy is. Sorry, I should have mentioned we were on speaker," said Byron.

"I don't care if Mercy hears. She's family now. I care about that *reaction*. What are you two up to?"

"Hi, Jo," said Mercy. "We just heard almost the same words from Mrs. Kravitz. She said Wanda left her apartment with some handsome stranger. How much you wanna bet we're talking about the same guy?"

"I'll keep my money," said Jo.

"What were you doing right before Henry came home?" asked Byron.

"I was in the bathtub. I'd just gotten done with a workout at home because the fucking state ordered the gym closed, too. Why?"

Byron felt excited. The question was a hunch, but a hunch based on what happened at the Salem Hospital. "You don't, by any chance, work out at *Fit!* Salem, do you?"

"As a matter of fact, I do."

"What were you wearing when you went to work out?" asked Byron, positive he knew the answer.

"Um... an orange *Fit!* Salem tank top and black yoga pants. I didn't wear a jacket or anything cuz it was so nice out today. Why?"

"Where are you now?" asked Byron.

"In the Jeep in the parking lot at home. I was about to look for Henry, then realized I don't have the foggiest fucking clue where to start."

"Hold tight. We'll be there in five," said Byron.

He hung up and turned on the Explorer's siren and flashers. He wiggled his eyebrows and smiled at Mercy. "It's good to be the Chief." Then he floored it.

BYRON PULLED into the lot on Lafayette Street. Jo stood outside of her Jeep, bouncing from one foot to the other, raring to go. She jogged to the Explorer and hopped into the backseat. "Okay. Where to first?" she asked.

"Well, let's think about what we know so far," said Byron. With each point, he raised a finger. "Wanda is missing. Henry is missing. A mysterious and, apparently, handsome stranger is related to both disappearances. That's for starters."

Mercy and Jo nodded.

Byron continued. He was on his fourth finger. "About an hour ago, a woman came into the Salem Hospital bleeding from the forehead. I would have sworn on a stack of Bibles it was you, Jo. Care to guess what she was wearing?"

Jo's mouth dropped open. "An orange tank top and yoga pants."

"You said it, not me," answered Byron. "How much you wanna bet Henry saw that same woman in the company of Mr. Handsome?"

"Again, I'll hold on to my money," said Jo. "The fucker must have walked her right up to our place before he put her in the hospital."

Byron nodded. He dropped the hand with the raised fingers, realizing he might need the other hand, and maybe a toe or two, before they hashed everything out.

Mercy chimed in. "He wanted Mrs. G. to see him. Once she did, he had no more use for that poor girl."

Byron tilted his head back and forth. "I wouldn't say that."

"Why?" asked Jo.

Byron filled Jo and Mercy in on what happened at the hospital. And then what happened at the morgue.

"Wait," said Jo. "So, the corpses had that symbol on their heads, and Jennifer had the same thing?"

"Yep," answered Byron. "I think it has something to do

with how he controls people. Directly, I mean. With that mark on their heads, he can somehow make them do what he wants."

"Maybe," said Mercy. "But maybe it's more than that."

"How so?" asked Jo.

Mercy gave it some thought. "With Jennifer, he was able to make her appear as he wanted for both Byron *and* Henry. But the effect lasted only so long. By the time Byron left the hospital, Jennifer was herself."

Byron squirmed. "Yeah. But before that, her face changed several times. All people I'm close to."

"He was threatening you. Through us," said Mercy. "Remember, this bastard paraded around as Luci and Fermina. They were around each one of us, and they—*he*—learned what would push our buttons. No. He knows what you're capable of, Chief. Lucifer is hiding something. He's afraid you'll put it together."

Jo nodded emphatically. "She's right. He wants you nowhere near this thing. So, what's he trying to hide?" asked Jo. "What's his endgame?"

Mercy tilted her head. "Didn't you say Luci and Fermina were missing a few things, Chief?"

"Yeah. Their eyes, when they still had them, were fake. *Ornamental* was how Mick put it. They had no hearts. They had no belly buttons. Everything else was there, but there's no way they should have existed."

"And yet they did. Sounds like they were never born. At least, not in the normal sense," said Jo.

Byron nodded. "It's pretty messed up."

Mercy chewed a thumbnail as she thought on it. She said, "They were never born, but yet they existed as flesh and bone. Not complete, obviously, but you *do* have two decaying... somethings in the morgue. And, let's not forget, Jennifer had the same mark on her forehead as Luci and Fermina. But he could only control her—a whole, flesh and bone human being with free will and feelings—for so long."

Byron turned to face Mercy. Jo leaned forward and hung her arms over the back seat. Neither said a word because the lady was on a roll.

"When you left the hospital, Chief, was her face back to normal?" asked Mercy.

"Yes."

Mercy considered this for a moment. "Why were you at the hospital?"

Jo snapped her fingers. "That's right! At the Cauldron, you said you were going there to check up on the guy from Henry's vision!"

Byron's mouth hung open.

Mercy smiled. "Do we really think Jennifer showing up at the hospital was a coincidence?"

"He doesn't want me anywhere near the guy from Henry's vision, it seems," said Byron. "But why?"

"I'd have to guess whoever 'Cotton Ball' is, he's got something Lucifer wants. You put him in jail..." she trailed off, leaving it for Byron to draw the conclusion.

Byron slapped his forehead. "Or something he wants back! I can't freakin' believe I didn't see it!"

"What do you mean?" asked Jo.

"Think about it. Luci and Fermina were just vessels, right?" asked Byron.

Jo and Mercy nodded.

"They have *almost* everything you need to be human,

save the hearts, functioning eyes," Byron slapped the steering wheel, "and belly buttons!"

Jo and Mercy exchanged confused and amused looks. Jo said, "A little clarification is in order here, Chiefy."

"Don't you see? Luci and Fermina were never born, which we've established already, but maybe they were *supposed* to be born. That's why they exist in flesh and bone form. They *have* souls, but those souls never reached their intended bodies."

"So where are they?" asked Jo.

"Damned if I know," said Byron. "But I'll bet 'Cotton Ball' could point us in the right direction."

Byron pulled his iPhone from the front pocket of his uniform shirt. He tapped the screen and the phone rang out through the speakers of the Explorer. After one ring, a voice said, "Maine State Police. This line is being recorded."

"Hi, Michelle. It's Byron Miller again."

"Two calls in one night! I should play Powerball tomorrow. What can I do for you?"

"Mish, that guy you tracked down for us earlier, Artemis Davies... could you send someone to check out his last known residence?"

"You got it, By. Let me see if I got a unit close. Gimme a few seconds."

After what was, literally, a few seconds, Michelle came back on the line. "You lucky devil. There's a unit about two miles from his old place. What should I tell them to look for?"

"Well, provided we don't need a warrant, and the landlord is home, I'd say something out of the ordinary. It'll probably be fairly obvious to your guys."

"Can't be more specific?" asked Michelle.

"The guy's a whack job. I'm rolling the dice here, Mish," said Byron.

"Call you back in ten," said Michelle.

Truer than her word, the phone rang in the Explorer nine minutes later.

"Find anything?" asked Byron before Michelle could say a word.

"Yeah. Lucky for you, the guy had something against furniture. The place was empty except for a grody pillow, a beat-to-shit La-Z-Boy, and a lamp. The lamp was still on the floor next to a pile of ashes. My guys said the place wreaked of butts. When they moved the lamp, they found an envelope torn open and folded in half. I had them text it to you about a minute ago."

On cue, Byron's phone chirped. He tapped the notification, opening the text app, then tapped the attachment. He turned the phone sideways. The image was crystal clear. "Thanks, Mish."

"Let me know if it helped. Talk to you later."

Michelle hung up.

Byron held the phone so Mercy and Jo could see it. "Anything here rock the boat for either of you?"

"Does nothing for me," said Mercy.

Jo took the phone from Byron. She spread the photo with her fingers. "I thought you said this guy's last name was Davies"

"It is," said Byron.

Jo handed the phone back to him. "Not according to this. It's probably a typo, but it's a strange coincidence if it is."

Byron looked at the blown up image and back to Jo. He shook his head. "Afraid I don't follow."

"Look a little closer, Chiefy," said Jo.

"Davis instead of Davies." Byron shrugged. "So?"

Jo stared and waited. When Byron still didn't get it, she let out a sigh of exasperation. "Some detective you are. Davis should have been Henry's real last name. His biological mom's maiden name was Davis."

"Oh shit," said Mercy.

CHAPTER 16
THE PUZZLE OF INTUITION

Henry was in the Camry, aimlessly roaming the streets of Salem. When he'd left the apartment, he'd been in a blind rage. It scared him. Knowing a large part of it was a remnant of Jagger's invasion of his mind didn't make it easier.

As he drove, the scene from earlier in the night played on a loop in his mind. Every time he closed his eyes and saw them walking across the street, he felt red-hot jealousy coursing through his veins. When he calmed down and saw it clearly, however, he was almost sure the woman hadn't been Jo.

But he was doubting his own mind now. An alien feeling of insecurity plagued him.

Leaving the apartment had been the right thing to do. Given Jo's past, the last thing he wanted to do was outright accuse her of infidelity. Though the lust-fueled incident with Mercy had been forced on them by the Red Witch, Henry still harbored guilty feelings about it. It might have come up had he stayed and argued, which would have made things worse. Jo had been a complete adult about the whole thing, and forgiveness had never been an issue. All the more reason he loathed himself in this moment.

He pounded the steering wheel with a flattened hand. "What the hell is wrong with me?"

He needed answers.

Henry breathed deeply and calmed himself. The radio was off. After "Sympathy for the Devil" had played all on its own earlier in the night, he'd actually considered disconnecting the speakers; it had spooked him that badly. But it was also a good thing, he suddenly realized. If the radio could begin playing on its own, and in that instant he'd seen a woman he'd mistaken for his wife, could it be the entire incident had been supernatural? Was he being deliberately provoked? And if so, why?

A red light brought him to a stop. Closing his eyes, he let the scene play in his mind, focusing on the last thing he saw. The wink. The smile. The hand on her ass. Could it have all been a ruse?

"Of course it was, you idiot," he scolded.

Henry breathed easier, thankful he'd fled the apartment and spared Jo his misguided wrath. He was about to turn around and pilot the Camry back home when he paused. Jagger's Magical Treasures loomed at the left of the intersection. The huge picture window was front and center, still boarded up after Byron's assault on it with a stuffed wolf.

He drove the Camry around the corner, then parked where a narrow alley led to the back of Jagger's shop. Sudden unease filled him when he thought about the last time he'd been inside this building. Jagger, psycho that he was, had almost taken over his life. Even worse, he would have been forced to live out the existence Jagger had so desperately sought to escape. It made him shudder.

But it also pissed him off.

A sudden desire to purge the remnants of Jagger's psyche consumed him, and all at once he *needed* to be inside this building.

Henry scanned the structure from one end to the other, looking for a way in. At the far end of the alley, he noticed a low granite border jutting from the side of the building. He walked the alley's length to it, then saw it was open at one end. Seven stairs led down to a landing. There was a bright red door at the bottom and on the right. It was slightly ajar. Either luck was on his side, or someone was expecting him. It didn't matter either way. Intuition brought him here on autopilot. There *had* to be a reason for it.

In the blink of an eye, Henry found himself pushing through the red door. It was pitch black inside. He pulled out his phone and tapped the flashlight app, muted the sound, then squeezed the button on the side to extinguish the screen.

Before moving, he swept the room to get the lay of the land. The first thing he saw was a shovel lying face up. Spent coal sat atop it and also ringed the surrounding area. Square lumps of ash dotted the floor, perfectly preserved and so fragile a slight breeze might dissolve them. Henry realized this was the spot Byron had freed himself from Jagger's dungeon.

He noticed trails through the ash led away from the shovel.

Byron's chains, he reminded himself.

He followed their path through the dungeon, where they terminated at the foot of the stairs leading to the first floor. He put a hand against the cool granite wall, then crept quietly upward. Intuition might have led him here, but advertising his arrival seemed foolish.

Henry stopped and chanced a look up. A dim, grey rectangle awaited, seeming to float in the air above. Light from the street leaked in, and he was relieved to douse the iPhone's flashlight.

One less thing to worry about.

Before he knew it, he was standing in the doorway, breathing as quietly as possible and giving his eyes a chance to adjust. When they did, he had a rough layout of the place. A counter to the right ran the length of the wall. The middle of the room was wide open, and directly across the floor were stacks of boxes lining the wall beneath a staircase leading to the second floor. He squinted, tracing the line of the dusty, moonlit staircase railing upward, following its path as it twisted its way around the upper level. Grey rectangles of light glowed softly, just beyond and slightly above the railing.

A second set of stairs awaited.

When they'd left this place on the night they'd battled Jagger, he'd taken little notice of the shop's layout. He'd been happy to escape with his life. Now, with every step closer to the staircase, things felt familiar, though none of it was clear. These were emotional shadows—more feelings than actual memory. He'd come into the building through a mirror, after all. But when Jagger had last entered this place, he'd mostly taken over Henry's body and mind. This, Henry figured, accounted for the unreliability of recall.

At least until what came next.

When he reached the top of the stairs, he felt dizzy with recognition. To his right, the floor trailed off in a gentle arc following the curve of the room below. Dust motes swirled lazily in the moonlight cast through the huge reading nook windows. As he turned to the left, he felt faint. Henry staggered to the closest nook and sat down hard. Dust from its seldom used cushions flew up in angry swirls, and he absently waved them away.

When he felt stronger, he peered into the room. At the threshold was a line of dark powder with glints of silver and gold scattered throughout. *A barrier?* It reminded him of something Wanda might use. Traces of it led further into the room in the shape of footprints.

The memories were there, he knew, but they remained trapped in a maddening haze. In his mind's eye, he saw the same room, but from *both* sides. Music played. The Beatles were singing "I am the Walrus," but the lyrics were wrong.

He stopped once more. Closing his eyes, he breathed deeply in and out for several moments until the tangled memories subsided. When he opened them, the room was just a room, and he saw it solely from his own eyes.

As he stepped forward, something crunched under his feet. Glass shards, some shiny-side up, some dull grey, formed an almost perfect oval. Bordering the shards, also in a near-perfect oval, was a clear space, and beyond that, a lesser ring of shards. The empty space, he realized, belonged to the missing frame of the mirror he'd blasted with Byron's shotgun.

He studied the destroyed mirror for a long time, thinking about how he'd come to be in this building tonight... how he'd been *led* here.

"There are *no* coincidences," he whispered to the room.

Henry bent low, taking care to keep his feet in the area of the oval devoid of shards. He started flipping the dull grey pieces of mirror shiny-side up, then began matching edges.

High up, in the corner of the room closest to the entrance, watching eyes glowed.

CHAPTER 17
WHAT'S IN THE BOX?

"We're here," said Lucifer to Wanda.

Wanda nodded.

"Do you understand now?" he asked.

She shot him a stern look. "I do."

"And you're okay with this?"

She laughed. "Does it matter? You're forcing me to do this whether I want to or not. Or am I mistaken?"

He tilted his head back and forth. "That's more or less the case."

Wanda frowned. "No surprise there. How do I know I can trust you'll hold up your end of the deal?"

"You don't. I am not to be trusted. Don't you read the history books, dear witch?" he asked, grinning.

"Then what's the point?" she fired back. "Why should I help you at all?"

"Because if you don't, I will be forced to take drastic measures. Artemis and his mother made a deal with me. One way or the other, I intend to collect. *You* must end their lives. When I know that's happened, I'll spare Henry Trank."

"Why don't you just take them yourself?" demanded Wanda.

Lucifer shook his head slowly from side to side, mock pouting. "Now, where's the fun in that? Besides, if things go wrong, the sapphire witch is my insurance. I'm down two souls—" he paused. "Correction, two *witch's* souls. Do I have to explain the difference?"

It came down to control of Salem. Magical souls went a long way toward that. But there was something more to it this time, and she still needed to figure that part out. Wanda slammed the door to the limo. As it sped away, Lucifer kept his eyes on her, a stupid and knowing grin plastered on his face.

Wanda flipped him the bird. "Fuckstick!"

A sly smile crept across her lips as she turned toward the building. Scenes from the last hour replayed through her mind, and she prayed she hadn't tipped her hand. Satisfied Lucifer had bought her performance, she made for the door. "Father of lies my ass," she said.

Wanda giggled to herself as she walked toward the entrance to Salem University. When she caught sight of Artemis waiting behind the glass doors, the smile vanished.

There would be death tonight. Souls would change hands. But not in the manner Lucifer expected.

LUCIFER SMILED as the limo pulled away and the witch dwindled in his sight. He patted the right side of his suit, feeling the reassuring shape of the gold athame. The witch had been too busy with the diary to notice he'd taken it. Now that he'd convinced her he would spare Henry Trank's life if she did as he asked, killing him with the golden dagger, *her* athame, would be that much sweeter.

~

ARCHIE WAS HALFWAY down the hall when the door at the other end suddenly swung open. He looked left, saw no escape, then pivoted right and dashed through the open mailroom door. Two quick and quiet steps found him inside. Breathing heavily, he fought to quiet it, but the adrenaline pumping through his veins made it tough. As two pairs of footsteps headed in his direction, he opted for holding it.

In the dim hallway, their silhouettes passed. One was a tall, thin man. Even in the muted light, Archie saw he had a full head of bright white hair. The second was a few inches shorter, athletically built, with dark hair. As they passed the entrance to the mailroom, Archie saw only their backs, but the shorter man seemed somehow familiar. As the echoes of their footfalls diminished, he let his breath out in a rush.

It took a few seconds to calm his nerves—and regain his courage—before he stepped into the hallway once more. Like a Saturday morning cartoon character, Archie took an exaggerated step over the threshold and slowly lowered his right foot, then leaned out just enough so his right eye could scan the hallway's length. Somewhere, in the back of his mind, he knew he must look ridiculous, but he didn't care.

Something was going down.

Convinced for the moment he was safe, he tiptoed into the hallway, moving toward the room the two men had just vacated. When he reached the door, Archie put a hand on the knob, took a deep breath, checked the hallway in both directions, then twisted. It gave easily. He stepped inside and eased the door shut.

The room was dark. Archie pulled his iPhone out and used the muted glow of the screen to navigate.

Wary of tripping over something or bumping into things and making noise, he scanned the room first. It was neat as a pin. Two rows of black, epoxy resin tables lined the walls on either side of him. A microscope sat in the middle of each table. Small, stainless steel sinks with arched fixtures were inset into each table at the sides closest to the walls. The light from Archie's phone caught the fixtures and he quickly tilted the phone toward the floor to minimize reflections. Inching forward, he closed on the professor's desk. As he passed the last row of tables, he chanced raising the phone. In its light, the object of his curiosity loomed.

A long, rectangular, brushed aluminum box, at least six feet long and three feet wide, hung a few inches lengthwise over either side of the professor's desk. Archie stared at it, trying to wrap his head around what he was seeing.

Using the phone's light, he circled to the side of the desk closest to the chalkboard, then stopped to examine the box. A rounded swell ran the middle of the box's length. Squared cuts divided the swell at even intervals, and Archie realized he was looking at one long hinge. Curious, he shuffled back to what he now realized was the front of the box.

On his first pass, he hadn't noticed the latches at each end. They reminded him of the draw latches on his guitar case, though he doubted *this* one protected a Gibson Les Paul Goldtop.

Archie peered over his shoulder. There was no telling how long the two men would be gone, or if they were coming back at all tonight. He stalled. Part of him was dying to know what was in the box. Another part, the part that usually won out, wanted to get the hell out of this office and forget what he'd seen.

Don't be such a chickenshit! he chastised himself. His next thought was of how bravely Henry was facing things, and he felt his face flush with shame.

There was no doubt in his mind the white haired man he'd just seen leaving this office was the same man from Henry's vision. Whatever was in this box—*casket*, he corrected—might be something which could help Henry figure things out. His son had made it quite clear the guy was an evil, soul-stealing bastard.

"Bah! Fuck it!" said Archie. Before he could talk himself out of it, he flipped the latch on the left, then shuffled right and unsnapped the other. Archie shoved the lid upward, but overestimated its weight. Before he could slow its momentum, the brushed aluminum cover slipped from the grasp of his shaking and sweaty hands and boomed against the back side of the desk. He cringed, then hissed "Jarsus Murphy!"

He prayed they hadn't heard the crash, but knew in the deathly silence of the empty university, it was highly unlikely. Sensing time was short, Archie raised his phone, tapped the camera app, and snapped off a quick burst of shots without looking into the container. He fired them off to Henry in a text with the caption "At SSU."

With that done, he raised the phone once more, then turned on the flashlight app. In the rush to get the text to Henry, he hadn't wasted time looking at the images. He'd soon wish he had.

In the glow of the phone's light, mist crawled from inside the metal box. It was thick and cold. Archie reached out with his phone hand and waved the cloud of frost away, instantly regretting it. Any lingering question of the case being a casket vanished. He slapped a hand over his mouth, stifling a scream. A moment later, as his heart rate slowed and the shock wore off, he whispered aloud. "What in the actual fuck?"

As if answering his question, the overhead fluorescents sprang to life, momentarily blinding him.

"Watch your language around Mother, professor."

Archie whirled toward the voice. Two figures stood in the doorway, but only one was who he expected. He tilted his head in total confusion as next to Artemis stood his best friend in the world, Wanda Heinze.

Artemis held a hand by Wanda's neck. From Archie's vantage point, it looked like he was pointing a finger gun at her jugular. As they approached, it became horrifyingly clear what it was. Fluorescent light twinkled from the rounded glass tube of the syringe pressed to Wanda's neck.

Archie, out of pure reflex, brought his phone up and started to call Byron.

"Put the phone down, professor," said Artemis, sounding almost bored. He nodded toward Wanda. "Tetrodotoxin. One full squeeze and she'll be dead before she hits the floor."

Archie looked to Wanda. She gave him the slightest of nods, and he complied. It pained him, but knowing he'd sent the text to Henry gave him hope. Doing as this loon wanted would buy some time, and in that time he prayed Henry would figure something out.

"This is between myself and the witch. I have to ask you to leave now. Please douse the lights on your way out. My associate is in the hallway. He'll escort you from the building... or kill you, if need be."

141

Archie didn't move. Artemis turned toward Wanda, flexing the thumb on the syringe's plunger ever so slightly.

"No! I'm going." He started back up the aisle, returning the way he'd come in.

"Use the other entrance, Dr. Love."

Archie cursed the crazy bastard, but only in his mind. He'd had visions of getting close enough to do something to disarm the whack-job, but the guy was nobody's fool. With that, Archie held up both hands, fingers splayed, and backed away from them, maintaining eye contact with Artemis the entire time. The expression on his face conveying the message, *if you hurt her, you're as good as dead.*

When he reached the entrance at the front of the room, the door swung silently open. Archie felt a hand lock around his arm at the crook of his elbow and pull him through. The door closed in front of him with a soft click. In his stunned silence, it was the loudest sound in the world.

He turned to face the man who'd pulled him through the door and away from his best friend. The second loudest sound in the world was Archie's quick and sharp bark of surprise.

CHAPTER 18
BEAUTY AND THE BEAST

Byron, moments after they'd confirmed Artemis's identity, ran down his address. The building, in a twist of irony, was owned by one Solomon Dobson, who'd gone missing in 2018. Leonard Shrumm was designated first caretaker and also listed as missing. Delilah Davis was listed as second caretaker, with the same designation as Leonard. Joanne, being Delilah's legal daughter-in-law, superseded the need for a warrant and the building supervisor granted them access.

Mercy spotted the index card sitting atop an ancient Sony VCR. They all sat down on the floor in Artemis's living room.

"What's this guy got against furniture?" asked Jo.

Byron shrugged. He turned to Mercy, noticing the puzzled look on her face. "What is it?"

"It's this last clue. I *think* I know what it means—or, more correctly, *who* it means."

"Read the quote to me again," said Byron.

"*Beauty eternal will help you from the shadows,*" read Mercy.

"And you think that refers to a specific person?" asked Jo.

Mercy winked at her. "I'd be willing to bet Byron's life on it!"

Jo laughed out loud.

"Hey!" said Byron.

Mercy squeezed his shoulder. "Just kidding." Then she turned serious. "I saw something today, in Archie's class. He put up a slide for the whole class to see. It looked like a tunnel, but—"

"You mean like the Sumner Tunnel in Boston?" asked Byron

"She didn't say it showed a nightmare," said Jo.

"Good point," said Byron.

"The image reminded me of my near-death experience. Tunnels are a common theme in NDEs. It can be different for everyone, but similar. There's usually this beautiful, irresistible light at the other end."

"Is that what you saw when you died?" asked Byron.

Mercy nodded emphatically. "It's the kind of thing that makes you want to stay. Forever. But the intelligence in that light *knows* whether or not it's truly your time. The choice, however, is still yours."

Byron tilted his head. "The choice? You mean to stay there or return to life?"

"Yes."

He considered it for a moment. "Okay, I'll buy that. But what's it got to do with the index card?"

"Sorry. I got a little off track. When Archie asked the class what they thought the slide represented, no one answered, at first. He knew I'd get it, but I begged off. The fewer who know I've been there, especially in this town, the better. One guy *did* answer, but wasn't close. Then, someone else spoke up." Mercy leaned forward for emphasis. "*From the shadows* at the back of the lecture hall. The clue reminded me of it. Of *him*."

"Like Wanda says, 'no coincidences,'" added Jo.

Mercy snapped her fingers and pointed at Jo. "Exactly! When I meet someone like me, who's come back from the other side, I know it right away. It's something in their aura, and I can *see* it. Day or night. This guy was *different*, though. I saw it coming from his *eyes*. There's something about the light over there unlike anything on earth. It's ethereal. I see traces of it in me when I look in the mirror. But this guy is like a freakin' lighthouse. I've never seen it so bright."

"So what's he got to do with the line from the index card?" asked Byron with a trace of impatience.

"When I tracked him down on Facebook earlier today, I saw this." Mercy tapped her phone twice, then pinched and expanded something on the screen. She handed it to Byron. "You can see Jamal Khalid—that's the kid from my class—in the line of people in the background. He's behind the guy with the bright white hair. That would be Artemis Davies."

Byron nodded. "Okay. There's a connection. I'll give you that. But Cotton Ball, apparently, goes all over the place doing this shit."

"Yep," said Mercy. "The post was, originally, in Arabic. I was lucky to find anything. Jamal isn't exactly Mr. Social Media. He has hardly any posts. And like I said before, that *'from the shadows'* line jogged my memory. So, just now, I turned on translation in Facebook's settings. Jamal's name is bold. The translation is underneath."

Byron squinted but couldn't make it out. He reached into

his coat and pulled out a pair of reading glasses, then shot Mercy and Jo a stern look. "You never saw this."

"No need to be embarrassed, gramps," said Jo with a shit-eating grin on her face.

Byron paused with the glasses raised halfway to his face. He gave Jo a death stare. She stuck her tongue out at him. He fought a smile and lost. When he finally donned the glasses, his eyes grew wide. Whipping the glasses off, he stared at Mercy.

She nodded. "In Arabic, Jamal means *beauty*. Khalid means *eternal*."

"Holy shit!" said Jo.

"Do you know where this guy is, Mercy?" asked Byron.

Mercy's shoulders dropped. "No."

Byron hung his head, squinted, and pinched the bridge of his nose. After a few moments, he snapped his head up. There was only one guy in his department he trusted with this kind of thing. Raul Martinez was, very reluctantly, becoming a believer.

Byron put the phone on speaker.

"Martinez."

"Hey, Raul. Where you at?"

"Just finishing up at the Willows. Came back to see if I'd missed anything."

"Find anything useful?" asked Byron.

"Nada."

"Okay. When you're clear, I need you to do me a favor. Well, two favors, now that I think of it," said Byron.

"Name it."

"I need you to run a name for me. It's a long shot, but I need info on this guy. The name is Jamal Khalid. I doubt you'll find much, but anything might help."

Byron heard the scratch of Raul's pen on paper. When he was finished, Raul said, "What's the second thing?"

"I need you to keep an eye out for Henry Trank's vehicle. Jo's worried about him. He left home a little while ago and she hasn't heard from him."

"He drives a Camry, right? Red?" asked Raul.

"That's the one. Call me when you find him. The tag is 031-320."

"Huh. That's weird."

"What's weird, Raul?" asked Byron.

"Henry's license plate number. That's tomorrow's date."

Byron killed the line, then looked at Jo. "I'm a little less worried about Henry, at the moment. I don't know what's up with him, but he's a big boy. I'm a lot more worried about Artemis, Jamal, and Wanda missing. And since I'm not exactly the witchy type, I think I might need you two with me if that kind of shit's gonna go down."

Jo glared at him for a brief moment, then conceded. She wanted badly to chase down Henry. But she had to admit to herself the more immediate danger was Artemis, Jamal, and the mysteriously disappearing Wanda. Thinking along those lines, she asked, "So, where do you think they are?"

Mercy spoke up. "I'd start at the U, since Cotton Ball's last place of employment was another university."

Byron cursed and jumped up. They flew down the stairs, out of the building, and into the cruiser. Byron yanked the Explorer into drive. "I can't believe I wasted time looking for him at the hospital."

Jo shook her head. "I wouldn't beat yourself up over that, Chiefy. You found out he worked at U Maine like, what? Twenty minutes ago? You were *meant* to be at the hospital tonight. That was no accident."

He shot her a brief look, then pinned his eyes back on the road. "You think so?"

"No coincidences. Remember?" As she said it, she thought about Raul's comment on Henry's license plate.

Suddenly, Jo felt very cold.

~

HENRY SPENT the last hour in a daze. He'd flipped every single piece of the mirror shiny-side up. As he'd done so, more and more of the night he'd spent in this place came back to him. Instead of vague feelings and hazy memories, intact moments roared to the surface like hungry sharks in dark water—complete with teeth.

Archie's mantra to *'remain detached'* played over and over in his head, but as the mirror took shape, he found it increasingly harder to follow his father's sage advice. It felt to Henry as if something was coming for him, and he was powerless to stop it.

No, that's not it, he thought. Abandoning the mirror *was* an option. He realized he could put the pieces down right now and walk away. Nothing, at least physically, kept him here. It was something... bigger. He felt *driven* to reassemble the mirror—he just didn't understand why.

Moments later, he would.

With the last shard placed, he stood, breathed deeply, then let it out slowly. Unsure what came next, he spied a chair just inside what was either a closet or a coat room. Rounding the mirror, careful not to displace his handiwork, he crossed the room and brought it back, placing it a few feet behind the final shard.

No sooner had he put bottom to chair top, the mirror

began to glow—faintly, at first—and he almost mistook it for a reflection of the streetlights. The problem with that, he realized, was the light hadn't been there before he'd gotten the chair. Secondly—the room was windowless once you got past the reading nooks just beyond the entrance. The lights came from *within* the mirror.

Green light bloomed lazily from the edge closest to him. Red light suffused the edges at the far side of the ragged oval. Henry stared at them, hypnotized.

A voice from behind broke his trance.

"Tomorrow is three-thirteen, Henry. Your time has come."

Henry's heart leaped in his chest at the sound of that voice, but his body did not betray him. Instead, he turned calmly toward its source. The familiar figure of Eljin Black stood before him. The shapeshifter had chosen its human form to speak with Henry, and in his eyes, Henry saw compassion. But he also saw knowledge. A knowledge of things to come, and an understanding of Henry's role in them. He shared what knowledge he could with Henry, though no words were spoken.

In his mind, when the shifter finished, Henry saw one word.

Destiny.

～

THE LIMO ROLLED TO A STOP. Lucifer stepped out and strode toward the driver's side door. "Wait for me. This might take a while."

"Yes sir."

Yes sir. He liked that. Whoever this guy was, he was efficient as hell. Probably retired military—he'd seen it before. Whatever the case, the guy was gonna get a nice tip.

Per Lucifer's instructions, they'd parked around the corner from his destination. Despite liking his driver, he'd decided discretion was best.

As he rounded the corner onto Essex Street, Lucifer smiled. Wanda's Wicca'd Emporium was dark, as was every other business in Salem. The shutdown of commerce couldn't have come at a better time. Even if he kinda knew it was coming.

"One less thing to deal with," he told the empty street.

The shop of the white witch was behind him now. Lucifer crossed Essex Street on a diagonal, his heels echoing from the walls of empty shops, and headed straight for Jagger's Magical Treasures. He paused at the boarded up window, wondering how it ended up like that, then continued on toward the front of the store.

He reached for the ornate handle on the front door and pulled. It didn't budge. "Perfect," he said, smiling. "One more thing to check."

Lucifer strolled down the alley at the side of the building. As expected, the red Camry was there. He traced a finger down the driver's side, across the trunk, and halfway up the passenger's side until he reached the stairs. Just as his foot touched the first step, a strobing blue light at the end of the alley caught his eye. Martinez, the cop from the beach, stepped from the cruiser. Lucifer cursed Byron Miller under his breath.

ONCE HIS 'CLIENT' turned the corner, the limo driver drew the cell phone from his front pocket. He tapped her number. It rang once. When he'd told her about his latest client earlier in the night, she'd had her suspicions. It was simple math, when you got right down to it—his was the only limo operating in Salem after the governor's shut down order. The GPS tracker on the driver's phone told her the rest.

"What's he doing?" she asked.

"He made me park around the corner, but he's on Essex Street. He's checking the Jagger place out."

"I wonder why he went *there*?" asked the woman.

"Didn't you say Henry Trank drives a red Camry?"

"Yes. Is it there?" she asked.

"It is. Is Henry in trouble? You need me to do anything?"

There was a long pause on the other end. The driver began to wonder if she'd hung up. "Jazz, you there?"

"I am. Just thinking things through. Knowing where he is for now should be good enough."

"Okay. I love you. Be careful," said Scott Johnson.

"Love you, too. Now get out of there."

Jazz's husband hung up and drove away.

CHAPTER 19
THE EYES HAVE IT

The elevator stopped at the top floor. Artemis had taken the syringe from Wanda's neck and stood behind her with it.

"Where are we going?" asked Wanda.

Artemis chose silence. The only sound was the clacking of his shoes on the glossy black linoleum. Soon enough, Wanda had her answer.

The Astronomy department at the university had its own observatory. Wanda had been there a few times in the not-too-distant past. The stars and the heavens awed her, and Archie never missed a chance to invite her when his schedule allowed.

Artemis pulled aside the door on his left, then ushered Wanda inside. When he flicked on the fluorescents, Wanda saw the room was cleared. Chairs normally laid out in four rows of five were pushed haphazardly aside. At the center of the room was a gurney covered in black vinyl. It looked like a cheap version of the Reiki table she kept at the Emporium.

Artemis held up the syringe, then motioned for her to mount the gurney. Wanda took a deep breath, then did as instructed. She laid down without a fight and without a word. Artemis put the syringe up to his mouth, clamped his teeth around the length of the tube, and commenced strapping Wanda down. When finished, he strode to a corner of the room. With a click, the overhead lighting winked out, plunging the observatory into darkness.

A low hum rattled the room. Seconds later, a silvery slit spawned several feet directly above Wanda's head, like the eye of some monstrous cyclops waking from deep slumber.

The hum suddenly stopped, and the Moon became its iris. It was almost full. There had been a Supermoon four days earlier, on March 9th. Supermoons, Wanda remembered, were a combination of the full Moon occurring as it was closest to Earth. The energy she felt flowing from it was comparable to a normal full Moon, though it was actually in its waning gibbous phase. It calmed her.

Artemis approached the gurney. Wanda watched in silence. He placed a black bag at her feet. Moonlight painted it a luminescent grey, and the bag's chrome trimmings glinted silver slashes across Artemis's face, making him appear insane.

Well, more insane, thought Wanda.

She strained her head forward, watching as Artemis flipped the clasp holding the top of the bag together. It snapped open with a loud click. Bright blue light, *the shade of a lit swimming pool at night,* thought Wanda, flooded the observatory.

When Artemis brought his right hand out of the bag, the light's intensity doubled. Wanda squinted and saw its source was a crystal flask framed in silver with a glass stopper at its top. Artemis moved the flask over her body and placed it a few inches above the left side of her chest. Right above her heart. With his left hand, he removed the syringe from between his teeth, then inserted it into the median cubital vein of Wanda's right arm. Wanda laughed.

"Something funny?" asked Artemis.

"I was just thinking you look like the phlebotomist from Hell. Given what's going to happen to you tonight, it seemed appropriate."

Artemis didn't respond. Instead, he applied a fraction of pressure to the plunger. Not enough to kill her. Not yet. Just enough to put her on the border between life and death. And to shut her up.

~

"Why are you doing this, Jamal?" asked Archie.

Jamal had ignored all of Archie's questions since yanking him through the lab door.

"Left," said Jamal.

"I don't know what Davies has promised you, but he'll never deliver on it," tried Archie.

They walked another twenty feet.

"Left."

"There are better ways to get what you want, Jamal. But your best chance was back in the lab with a syringe stuck in her neck."

Archie walked on, then noticed his footsteps were now the only ones echoing from the basement's walls. When he turned, Jamal was stopped in the middle of the corridor. A blank expression crossed his face, and his head was turned slightly upward.

"Jamal?"

Jamal held up his right hand, shushing Archie. A dagger in his left glinted in the light from the overheads. When he looked back down, his eyes blazed with blueish-white light. He smiled at Archie. There was no malice in it, but rather sympathy. "The witch has entered the in-between."

Archie's legs turned to rubber. He swayed, reaching for the closest wall. Blood thundered in his ears, and he felt on the verge of passing out. Dazed, he fought to remain upright.

"Breath, Professor Love. There's nothing to fear."

"But... my best friend is... dead. You... you helped kill her."

To Archie's surprise, Jamal lowered the dagger and slid it into his belt. He made his way over to Archie, then offered him his hand. Archie looked down at the offered hand as if it were covered in dog shit. "Are you out of your fucking mind?"

Jamal smiled at him like a parent might at a confused child.

"The vampire warned me this is how you might react. It's understandable. From what he's told me, you're her best friend in the world. Is this so, professor?" asked Jamal in an oddly gentle tone.

Archie began to wonder if he might be asleep and having the strangest goddamned dream he'd ever had. He reached for his right hand with his left, then pinched the skin on its back so hard he winced.

"I assure you, professor, you are wide awake. Though I understand your confusion."

"That makes one of us." Archie flattened his hands against the wall and pushed himself upright.

Jamal nodded to his left. "Let's go in here. We need to talk."

Archie had regained his composure, and with it came anger and urgency. He shoved Jamal aside and started to run back the way they'd come.

"Professor! Stop!" urged Jamal.

Without slowing, Archie shot him the bird over his right shoulder.

"If you interrupt what's started, your friend will die!"

It was probably the only thing Jamal could have said to stop him, mostly because it made zero sense. Archie, his chest heaving from exertion, turned to face him. "What the hell are you talking about? I thought you said she's in the in-between."

Jamal held up both hands as he approached his professor. "She is. And, for all intents and purposes, she *is* dead. But there is a reason for that, and you need to know about it. I have something to tell you, and you must hear it. Right now."

"Why in the world would I trust you after you forced me down here at knifepoint, Jamal?"

"Because, as crazy as it sounds, professor, your best friend in the world is in the process of *saving* souls." Jamal pulled the dagger from his belt once more. He spun it in his hand so the point faced his own stomach, then held it between his thumb and index finger and offered it to Archie.

At first, Archie assumed it was a trust offering, and he was reluctant to take it. They were separated by twenty feet, but Jamal was slowly closing the distance. Archie was wary, but sensed nothing malicious or dangerous in Jamal's eyes.

As his student drew closer, Archie focused on the knife, realizing it wasn't a knife at all. It was a dagger. More correctly, it was an athame. Despite minor alterations, it looked very familiar.

With three feet separating them Jamal stopped, the athame still held before him as an offering. Archie plucked it from his hand. In an offer of good faith, Jamal took three steps backwards, raised both arms, and held his hands by his head—palms out, fingers splayed.

Archie, out of an abundance of caution, also took three steps back. When he felt safe, he held the athame up to the light. On the blade was an ornate engraving he instantly recognized, because he was responsible for its existence. Three words were scrawled on the blade at the point closest to the thick black leather comprising its handle.

Wanda Grace Heinze.

"How on earth did you come by this?" asked a stunned Archie.

"From your desk, professor. The vampire put it there, and told me where to get it," said Jamal.

Archie peeled his eyes from the athame. He tilted his head in confusion. "What the hell is going on here?"

"Many things at once, professor." Jamal nodded toward a grease-smeared, light-blue door. *Maintenance* was stenciled in black across its front. "Let's talk. You can hold on to the athame until I've explained myself. But we must be quick."

Archie stared at his mystery student for a moment. When he thought hard about it, other than earlier in the day, he was pretty sure he'd never met Jamal Khalid, yet there was something undeniably familiar about him. It had nothing to do with the young man's physical appearance; he would swear on a stack of Bibles he'd never seen him until this morning. But when he spent more than a few seconds gazing into the young man's eyes, it felt like looking at an old friend.

Jamal flashed him a knowing grin, then reached for the knob to the maintenance door, turned it, and stepped into the room.

Without a word, Archie followed.

CHAPTER 20
DISCONNECTED CONNECTIONS

Byron drove over the sidewalk and then straight up to the glass double doors of Salem U. He slammed on the brakes, ripping up chunks of manicured lawn in the process. The Explorer slid to a stop less than four feet from the entrance. Mercy and Jo jumped out before it came to a complete stop. Jo reached the doors first, ripping them open and ushering Mercy through.

"Let's go, gramps!" said Jo as Byron slammed the driver's side door.

Byron hobbled a little on his bad knee as he strode for the doors. Between breaths, he said, "I'll give you gramps."

"Blah, blah, blah," said Jo.

Mercy had already disappeared around the corner. "Where'd she go so fast?" asked Byron.

"Archie's office would be my guess."

Byron nodded and Jo took off after Mercy. "I'll meet up with you two. This running shit ain't cuttin' it for me."

When he reached the office, Jo was on the far side of

Archie's desk, standing over Mercy, who was slumped and slack-jawed in Archie's leather chair.

"What happened?" asked Byron.

Jo whipped her head around, a worried look plastered on her face. "I don't know. As soon as we got in here, Mercy headed straight for Archie's desk. She sat down and started to go through it, but as soon as she hit the chair..." Jo motioned toward Mercy, then shrugged helplessly.

Byron stepped to the side opposite Jo. He leaned forward, then took Mercy's left wrist in his hand. "Her pulse is slow and steady. Breathing is too. Did she say anything before this happened?"

"Not a fucking word. I was checking Archie's white board for anything helpful. I turned around and saw her like that. She didn't make a sound. It's like someone pulled her plug, Byron."

At that moment, Mercy's eyes flew open, then rolled back to the whites. Her body spasmed, and she sat bolt upright in Archie's chair as if tasered by an invisible enemy. A low moan rolled from the back of her throat, then she spoke. "Wanda's reached the in-between. I can feel it."

Mercy tilted her head to the right, a curious look on her face. She looked like someone listening in on a secret.

"She says it's beginning."

Byron gave Jo a look, then a shrug.

"What's beginning, Mercy?" asked Jo.

"What's always been meant to happen. Henry must take his place, but he must also pay a price."

Jo's eyes went wide with alarm, and she reached for Mercy. Byron saw she meant to shake Mercy out of whatever trance she was in, and he held up a hand to stop her.

"Mercy," said Byron. "What do you mean when you say Henry must take his place and pay a price?"

The young witch sat still for a long time, so long Byron was tempted to repeat the question. Then she said, "Wanda is there to guide him, that's why she's dead now."

Jo's hand flew to her mouth. Byron's eyes went wide. "How do you know Wanda's dead?" asked Byron.

"She told me," was Mercy's reply.

"You're talking to her right now, Mercy?" asked Jo.

"Yes."

"How?" asked Byron.

"Beauty Eternal is in this building," said Mercy. "Somehow, he's making it possible. He's been to the other side, too. He's—" Mercy's eyebrows rose in surprise, "—*helping* me. From the shadows..."

"Who's place is Henry supposed to take, Mercy?" demanded Jo.

Mercy tilted forward, as if straining to hear. Jo chewed a thumbnail, if only to keep from grabbing Mercy and shaking the answer out of her. Byron held his breath.

Mercy gasped. "She doesn't know, but she keeps saying *three-thirteen*. Wanda says everything comes down to three-thirteen."

"Raul mentioned that was Henry's license plate. And it's also tomorrow's date—" said Byron.

Jo cut him off. "Every time something meaningful happens to Henry, it has to do with those numbers. Every time he's had a dream or a premonition, he's always woken up at 3:13 in the morning. When he dreamed of someone dying out at Satan's Kingdom, he told me he woke up at 3:13. When I went into labor with Delilah, we both woke up at 3:13 a.m. When he first got to Salem, and we started to talk, he'd told me more than once the dreams always ended at that time."

With all the talk of time, Byron looked at his watch. "Oh shit."

"What's the matter?" asked Jo. Her voice cracked a little.

After swiping numerous missed call notifications from Raul aside, Byron turned his phone so Jo could read its face.

"That's not possible," she said. "How could it be that late?"

She pulled out her phone, positive there must be something wrong with Byron's. The times matched. "It's two-fucking-fifty-three in the morning?"

"Time is different over here," whispered Mercy. "Minutes pass like seconds. Eternities are lived in a single moment. Jamal is directly beneath me, Wanda is directly above. You and Byron are within that vortex. Time as you know it, though you can't feel it, has been altered. Wanda says you two need to go." Mercy leveled her eyes at them. "Now!"

Byron and Jo jumped at Mercy's last word. They backed away from her and toward the opened door to Archie's office. Out of an abundance of caution, and a sudden intuitive urge, Jo locked Mercy in.

To be sure he hadn't dreamed the whole thing, Byron looked at his phone once more. There'd been at least ten attempts by Raul to get a hold of him, after the last attempt, there was a notification at the bottom. A voicemail from the same number. Byron tapped that.

"I've been trying to call you all night, Chief! I found Henry Trank's car. It's parked down the alley next to that whacko Jagger's old shop. I got news for you on that Artemis guy, too. You need to call me, pronto! His mother—"

There was a loud clatter on the other end, causing Byron

to yank the phone from his ear. "Jesus! What the hell was that?" When he put it back, he heard a scraping sound, like plastic on concrete. And then breathing. A familiar voice, one he'd heard just hours ago, came across the line. "Jesus can't help you, Chief Miller. I warned you to stay away. You should've listened."

~

ARCHIE WATCHED JAMAL IN SILENCE. When they'd entered the room Jamal had doused the lights, save for a small desk lamp next to which sat a soiled red recliner. He'd offered the seat to Archie. Archie had chosen to stand.

Jamal pulled a wooden stool from its place next to a tool-strewn workbench, placed it a few feet from the recliner, then straddled it with his feet resting on the crossbeams.

"This is Carl from maintenance's domain. My apologies for the accommodations. With the statewide shelter-in-place order we needn't fear interruption from Carl, however." Jamal extended a hand. "The athame, please."

Archie looked down at the gold-plated dagger of his friend, then back at Jamal.

Jamal said, "You must realize I mean you no harm, professor. Why else would I have given that to you?"

Archie pondered the question, but not for long. He'd reasoned that the kid might be full of shit, and handing it back to him might end up with his insides on the outside, but intuition told him otherwise. Well, that and the fact he was still alive. Jamal could have killed him at any time on the way down here.

"I need it to strengthen the bond with the white witch,

and also Mercy Glass, who at this very moment is directly above us."

Archie's eyes went wide. "How could you *possibly* know that?"

Jamal gave him an understanding smile. "We are both travelers to the undiscovered country, professor. We've been to and returned from the land of the dead. I can feel it when one of my kind is near. The feeling is even stronger when the Moon is so close."

"But how could you know she'd be here, and at the exact moment you needed her?"

Jamal laughed softly. "You credit me with too much. The vampire has orchestrated much of this. I am but a helper."

"Armand Moreland did all this?"

"You seem surprised."

Archie was at a loss for words.

Jamal closed his eyes, then began taking deep breaths.

"What are you doing?" asked Archie.

"You have trusted me, proving I can trust you. I'm going to connect with Mercy and Wanda. You can hold on to the athame and see what transpires, or you can let it go and wait until we've finished. The choice is yours. But be warned, professor. This is not, as the saying goes, a 'done deal.'"

Archie sat in the recliner, took a deep breath of his own, and held on tight.

CHAPTER 21
XTREME MEASURES

It was all coming together now, and Jazz had to act fast. Wanda had cut off their telepathic link the moment the Moon had turned into a super moon back on March 9th. It was only the second time in their entire friendship Wanda had ever done such a thing. The other was when Henry Trank had been four and they'd needed to hide him from the Order Immortalis. Wanda had kept things from Jazz until she couldn't anymore for her own safety back then, even though Jazz's husband had been involved in hiding Henry.

Scott was involved once more. Jazz had been against it, at first. But once Scott caught wind of it, he couldn't be talked out of helping. Though he wasn't magical in any way, he'd seen enough to know it was realer than real. His intuition and instincts were as sharp, maybe even sharper, than those of some magical beings. It had kept him, and the men in his charge, alive in Iraq and Afghanistan. And true to his military bearing, he would die to protect his wife, her friends, and Salem.

Landing the job driving Lucifer had been a snap. Byron hadn't bothered telling Scott he was shut down, he figured Jazz would give him the message. The only other limo company in town had been one of Byron's first stops. Transportation, in all its forms, was a guaranteed spreader of infectious disease, and therefore a top priority. With the competition closed, Scott had been the only game in town.

No coincidences.

Her thoughts circled back to Henry. Jo had mentioned he wasn't himself lately, and Jazz suspected something akin to an emotional and spiritual hangover from basically *becoming* Jagger. And she wondered why that might be.

The night she'd left Wanda's Wicca'd Emporium, she'd snapped a photo of the letter from Luci and Fermina. Since that night, she'd made a point of going over it at least once a day until it was burned into her memory. As she thought about it now, one passage stood out loud and clear: *When you call on the darkness, the darkness listens. When you think you control it, it controls you. And when you use it to take what you want, you are taken.*

This passage, of course, referred to Jagger and the Red Witch. Mondra was dead and gone—Jo had seen to that—but Jagger, as far as Jazz was concerned, was an unknown. He'd been banished from this world when Byron knocked his teeth out and then handed the shotgun to Henry to destroy the mirror. She'd watch him get knocked cold, saw him sink below the surface of the mirror, then saw its surface harden. Henry then blew it to pieces.

"We don't know if he's dead," whispered Jazz to her dark and empty shop. This simple fact worried her most. Because if Jagger *wasn't* dead, and if what Henry said about breaking the mirror in Jagger's room in the alternate universe was true, then Jagger was trapped. It might be his *corpse* trapped between worlds, but what if it was more than that?

He might find a way out.

If *she* saw this, she knew *Wanda* did, too.

Jazz reached out again, desperate to connect with her old friend. The channel remained dark, but there was something different about *this* darkness. It reminded her of the difference between turning the lights out in your apartment versus a power outage.

When you turned the lights out, there were still other things running in the background. You'd hear the sound of your refrigerator running, or the heat ticking its way through the baseboards. A power outage, however, was a big zero. No sounds. No suggestion of normalcy within that darkness. Nada, zip, zero. That's how *this* felt, and it scared the hell out of her.

Jazz jumped up from the purple velvet chair in her safe room and grabbed her phone from the tarot table. She tapped the contact for Armand Moreland. It rang once, then picked up. She seized the moment with a rapid-fire burst. "Armand, it's Jazz. I can't get a hold of Wanda—"

Three tones rang out, stopping her mid sentence, followed by a very efficient digital female voice. "The caller you are trying to reach is out of the network coverage area. Please try again later."

Jazz wasted no time. She grabbed her satchel, slung it over her shoulder, and dropped her phone into it. Her safe room, much like Wanda's, had a back entrance to the parking lot. Jazz bolted through the door, locked it behind her, and was in her purple Lexus SUV in three quick strides.

Five minutes later, she was walking up a flagstone path bordered by high shrubs. Ornate gas lamps stood sentry at staggered intervals on either side of the path. Thick ocean fog hung halos of gold around the tops of the lamps, obscuring the path and the estate at its end.

When she reached the stairs she took them two at a time, then shuffled quickly across the veranda to a massive mahogany front door.

Intricate carvings, *most likely some form of protection,* thought Jazz, surrounded a gleaming gold gargoyle knocker. Jazz grabbed the ball at the end of the knocker arm and gave it three quick, hard slams. When the third one landed, the door creaked inward. It was already open.

"That can't be good," she whispered.

Jazz looked left, right, and behind. Thick fog surrounded her on all sides. If anyone *had* been waiting to ambush her on the veranda, it would have already happened. This gave her scant comfort. The opened door gave her less. If Armand Moreland *was* home, something must've happened to him. Though she didn't know him well on a personal level, everything about him told her he wasn't the kind of guy who forgot to lock his front door.

When she stepped inside, her heels clacked loudly against the floor. Jazz slipped out of them, picked them up, and slid them into her satchel, retrieving her phone at the same time. She gave her eyes a few moments to adjust to the gloom.

Upon entering, she'd thought the place was completely dark. Though the fog outside was thick, the walkway lamps seemed like the Sun compared to the interior of the house.

Golden light, faint and wavering, glowed at the top of the stairs to her left, and she headed for it. Any worries about creaky stairs vanished as her bare feet sank into plush carpet. She took advantage of it and flew up to the second floor, stopping short at the top.

The light was brightest to her right. She leaned only her head into the hallway, then tilted it in both directions. The left side was almost completely bathed in shadow, save for a table covered in white cloth with a vase of red roses on it. They appeared black in the sparse light.

Beyond the table was a window overlooking the Atlantic. Jazz saw the warning light of a lone boat bobbing lazily in the fog. Knowing her left flank was covered, she bolted right. In the pin-drop quiet, she heard her bare feet *shooshing* across the carpet.

She considered turning on her phone's flashlight but held off. The house *seemed* empty, but this was the home of a vampire. The place would seem dead and empty even if the next room was filled with them.

Soulless bastards. I don't trust vampires, she thought.

Even Armand Moreland, after all they'd been through together, hadn't gained one hundred percent of her trust. She liked him, respected him, and forgave him for past transgressions, but the dude was still a vampire. A line from some long-dead politician came to mind: "Trust, but verify." It fit the moment.

When she reached the room from which the candle glowed, she stepped to the right of the door's frame. The door itself was three-quarters opened. Instead of walking into the room unprepared, Jazz tapped her phone, opened the camera app, and hit record. Reaching around the frame on the opened side, she slowly tilted the camera back and forth, sweeping the room.

When this was finished, she retreated a few steps, then

tapped play. The room appeared empty, but something on the video made her heart skip a beat.

"I told you not to mess with that mirror, Jeevesy," she whispered.

Jazz dropped the phone in her satchel, then scampered back. She pushed the door the rest of the way open, stepped inside, closed it, and locked it.

The mirror took up most of the wall to the right of the fireplace. The frame's restoration was impressive. Jazz saw the protection spells they'd placed on the frame remained active.

On the day Moreland brought the frame to Wanda's place, he'd mentioned it had recently been shipped there from Saint Theresa's church. The priest in residence was *supposed* to have blessed it. Other than her's, Wanda's, and Jo's spells, she detected nothing.

At first glance, and to the novice eye, it *appeared* as a holy blessing. It explained why she, Jo, and Wanda had willfully added their own protections to the frame. They'd never thought to question it. Armand Moreland was a priest, after all. If the blessing was suspect, he would surely know. Unless he'd been fooled himself... or he'd had some other agenda.

Jazz stepped closer to the mirror. Its surface rippled. She took another step, and had to clap a hand over her mouth to stifle a scream. Her mirror twin's long, luxurious, shiny black hair turned at first green, then red, then a wilted and limp silver, finally ending in a stark, cotton ball white. Along with each, Jazz's face in the mirror began to melt, then morph, then change into the faces of each distinctive hairdo's owner.

She immediately recognized the first two, and the auras

surrounding them. Jagger's snide face and puke-green aura kicked off the festivities, followed by the smug face and sparkling and deadly crimson energy of Mondra the Red Witch. Next, the haggard face of an older man slowly replaced that of Mondra's. Jazz gasped when she saw he had no aura. In the next instant, wrinkles dug deep into the flesh of the old man, and a scary and inexplicably familiar face stared back at her. A blackened aura, twice the size it should have been, surrounded the old crone. She knew she was looking at a dark witch, but she didn't know *how* she knew. There was a memory of... something, but it was gone almost as soon as it came.

She slammed her eyelids closed and prayed. When she opened them, the old woman had vanished.

At the end of her prayers, something warmed in her satchel. At first, she thought it might be her cell phone's battery. She'd heard about the damned things bursting into flame, and remembered a YouTube video of a guy's leg catching fire from his phone. With that in mind, she threw the satchel from her body. When it hit the floor, she pushed it open with her foot. The cell phone was still in one piece and nothing, at first, seemed out of the ordinary.

"What in the hell?" she whispered.

Jazz bent, then carefully withdrew one item after the other. The satchel was almost emptied when she saw it. She looked from the item, to the mirror, then back. Instead of touching it, she lifted the satchel by its straps, then dumped out what remained. Like some weird, slow motion shot from a movie, items tumbled slowly to the carpet, the last of which trailed crimson smoke.

Jazz watched, dumbfounded, as its ashy surface took on color. It was *unburning* itself! It scared her badly, at first.

Then, she saw it for what it was; a sign she was on the right track. Whatever might be at the other end of this mirror, she knew the card was telling her where to go. It was her personal deck, after all. She had to trust it.

And hadn't the cards prepared Byron for the night ahead?

"Yes, indeed," she whispered.

When it reached the floor, smoke trailed lazily upward, unveiling the tarot card marked "Devil." It was face up. A low whoosh sounded in front of her, and she watched as the remaining smoke was quickly sucked away. When she looked up, the mirror's surface was gone. The black and beckoning hole within its frame seemed to call her forward, and the frame itself glowed red at the top and green at the bottom. Jazz recognized their auric shades instantly. That they still existed scared the hell out of her, and she realized Armand Moreland might be in real trouble.

She was kneeling and absently dropping her scattered belongings back into her bag when she noticed the X scuffed into the hardwood.

"What are you up to, Jeevesy?"

She rapped the plank with a knuckle. It sounded hollow. Just to be sure, she tapped a plank on either side of the one marked X. They sounded solid. Jazz rummaged through her newly organized bag, looking for something to pry the plank from its spot. "Yes!" she hissed. It was a silver nail file.

She stuck its point between the bricks at the foot of the hearth and the plank marked X. It came away easily. Then she took her phone from the satchel and tapped the flash-light app. When she shone it into the recess, she saw a plain paper lunch bag wrapped around something rectangular. There was a note taped to the top left corner.

Jazz retrieved the package, placed it on the floor next to her satchel, then dropped the plank back in place. In a moment of intuitive inspiration, she used her sleeve to erase the X.

When she picked up the package, she gave it a shake. It had a familiar plastic rattle to it and Jazz knew instantly it was an old VHS cassette.

"This better not be some kinky vampire shit, Jeevesy," said Jazz.

She turned the tape back over to the side with the note, then drew in a sharp breath when she saw the salutation printed in small, neat block letters.

dear Jazz.

The shock of seeing her name on the package knocked her off her game, but only momentarily. She stowed it in her satchel, prayed once more to Hecate for protection, and entered the mirror.

CHAPTER 22

3:13

Henry was deep in meditation. After Eljin Black confirmed for him what he'd known in his heart must happen, he needed every ounce of strength and courage he could muster.

In meditation, he found reserves he'd never imagined possible. In a lot of ways, it was like working out. The more you did it, the stronger you got. Though both required discipline and dedication, physical exercise demanded adding more and more to get stronger. Meditation, paradoxically, required you to *release* everything. Its strength came from what you *didn't* reach for. Letting go was the key. It was a surrendering of the ego. A realization that a power greater than yourself ran the universe.

When the next step on your path included death, ego kinda went out the window.

Over the past few months, Henry had been a man at war with himself. Jagger Corey wasn't part of this world anymore, but the remnants—*stains*, Henry thought—of his personality remained. They leached into the core of his spirit, tainting everything.

He'd been short-tempered with Jo and impatient with friends, family, and coworkers. Lately, violence as a solution to normal life situations seemed attractive.

He could not stand for that, and never would.

Meditation somewhat tamed the alien beast within, but he knew he was fighting a losing battle. Jagger Corey needed to be removed by the roots if peace was to be had. There was only one way that was possible.

Henry had reached the delta wave state of meditation, a state second only to gamma, which was largely the province of monks. When the phone in his pocket buzzed, he barely noticed. He tried to ignore it, and found himself wishing he'd turned the damned thing off. It persisted, and was enough to drag him out of delta wave bliss and toward the beta wave state of normal consciousness.

Calmly pulling the phone from his pocket, he fought a sudden urge to hurl it at the brick fireplace across the room. *Thanks, Jagger!* Instead, he placed a finger on the biometric fingerprint icon and unlocked the phone. He tapped the messaging icon, then found the most recent text. It was from Archie. There were several images attached, but the thumbnails were too small. Henry jabbed one with his finger and the image filled his screen.

At first, he wasn't sure what he was looking at. An elderly woman, her head propped on a white satin pillow, seemed to be sleeping—or dead. A swirl of smoke or mist surrounded her head, frozen in time by Archie's cell phone camera. There were several more pictures included in the text. Henry swiped through them quickly, then swiped in reverse order. He did this a few more times. The effect was like watching a short, choppy film. The mist swirled around her head, but in the last picture the swirl seemed slightly disturbed, as if by the slightest of breaths.

Henry ran through the images forward and backward one more time. He left the first image on his screen and stared at it for a few moments. Something about it seemed familiar, but he couldn't place it. He drew the screen closer to his eyes, so close his breath fogged it. Then he held it at arm's length, hoping distance might solve the riddle. Tilting the screen one way or another also proved fruitless.

Exasperated, he let out a long sigh and dropped the phone in his lap. There was something important in these shots from Archie, aside from his father's urgent text message. Henry found himself wishing Wanda was with him. She was as sharp eyed as they—

Wanda!

He snatched the phone from his lap, double tapped the image on the screen to enlarge it, then traced a finger along the bottom of the photo. A long line of dull, reflective aluminum ran across its length.

"Where have I seen that?" he whispered, then pounded his forehead with the heel of his hand.

And then it hit him.

The thing in his vision of Cotton Ball. It was the item in the room he'd told Wanda he could not pass. The item preventing him from a better look at the white-haired mystery man of his visions. The woman in these images sent from Archie's phone had somehow managed to hold Henry's astral body in place during the visions.

But how was that possible?

If she was dead she could, in theory, do something like that.

Maybe.

But the dead resided on a different plane. They could visit the astral realm, he knew, to ease the suffering of loved ones, but usually did this in dreams. They were called visits or visitations. He doubted the dead were capable of *actually* altering the actions of a living soul in the astral realm. In all his travels to that ethereal plane, and there were many, he'd never once seen it happen. They could influence. They could *suggest* actions or ideas to the living; so he had to allow for that. But they couldn't directly alter the course of events. Free will was still free will.

This meant, as strange as it seemed, the woman might be *alive*.

So why is a living woman being kept in a casket? Henry wondered.

It made him think of Solomon Dobson. They'd all assumed he was human, and he'd somehow managed to keep himself alive by consuming the life essence of the living. An ethereal vampire of a sort. In reality, he'd trapped a soul in a flask for almost a thousand years in order to keep the flesh he'd stolen intact. By keeping that soul close, the demon Inanis freely roamed the earth inside the soldier's body.

Questions swirled in his mind. Was something like that happening now? Had the old woman in the silver casket been straddling the borderlands between life and death? Kept alive by Cotton Ball and the stolen souls of others? And what did the fucker want with Wanda?

A cold chill ran down Henry's spine. The vision he'd relayed to Wanda began playing in his mind. The mysterious stranger in the hallway had asked Cotton Ball what came next. "Heinze, the witch," was the response.

In that moment, Henry realized he'd been played. This entire night had been one big set up. The radio playing "Sympathy for the Devil" at just the right moment. The woman who looked *too* much like Joanne crossing in front of his car.

"She looked *exactly* like her," he whispered to himself.

The handsome guy grabbing her ass, then turning to him and winking.

He was winding me up. He knows exactly how much Jagger still affects me, Henry thought.

He rose from his seat, cell phone in hand, then headed for the exit. Again, he whispered aloud. "The whole thing was to keep me from protecting Wanda!"

"Close, Henry. But no cigar. I need you right here."

Surprised, Henry stumbled backwards. In the doorway between the mirror room and the reading nooks stood the man in black. Behind him, dust swirled in the moonlight slanting through the nook windows, casting him in silhouette. Two crimson eyes glowed with cheery menace, lighting a grin that made Henry think of Heath Ledger's Joker.

As if reading Henry's mind, Lucifer darted forward and shoved Wanda's dagger deep into Henry's belly, then stole the Joker's line. "TA DA!"

Henry's upper body folded over the golden dagger's impact. He caught a glimpse of his own blood as it leaked around it. *No,* he thought. *It's not a dagger. That's an athame. And it looks like Wanda's!* His next thought was, *it can't be hers, there's a crystal on the handle.*

Lucifer placed his left hand on Henry's right shoulder to keep him from toppling backwards, then laid him gently on the floor next to the mirror.

As the shock of the swift attack and the initial burst of

pain subsided, he was surprised by how little it hurt. As the man lowered him to the floor, Henry's head lolled to the right. His cell phone was still in his hand. In glowing white numbers on a black background, Henry saw the time and date.

3-13-2020
3:13 a.m.

∿

WANDA WAS, for all intents and purposes, dead. The moment the tetrodotoxin entered her system, her breathing had ceased. There'd been a moment of disorientation, and then an all-encompassing darkness. It reminded her of how it felt to be anesthetized during surgery, only without the clinical amnesia.

When she'd been much younger, the absence of memory from her appendix operation, combined with darkness and a loss of the sense of time, had caused her to question her beliefs about life and death. It had scared her badly, that loss of time and memory, until the doctor informed her that anesthesia actually activated memory-loss receptors in the brain, so patients wouldn't recall traumatic events from surgery.

This felt nothing like that, for the darkness was short lived. It ended in a spectacularly bright but gentle light.

Thanks to Mercy, she understood The Light. She knew it would draw her. Call to her. And the desire to be one with The Light would be almost insurmountable. Mercy strongly emphasized the choice to stay or go had still been hers, however. Knowing this, Wanda kept Henry's face front and center in her thoughts, making sure he was the *only* thing on her mind. She was his only way back.

As she slipped from her body, her spirit rose into the moonlit night. The freedom of movement was exhilarating, but for a few brief moments it was also terrifying. In short order, she realized how flighty the human mind could be. Artemis's current thoughts and memories assaulted her. She glimpsed them quickly, and in full, then shoved them aside. Though she'd made a supreme effort to keep Henry front and center, her very next thought upon crossing over was an earthly one. She thought about her store, and was instantly transported smack dab into the middle of the pentacle in her safe room.

What she saw amazed her.

Time meant nothing in her current state. Everything and nothing could happen at once. She saw the League of the Moon sitting around the pentacle, talking and laughing. In the next instant, she saw the demon Inanis circling the pentacle, looking for a way through its barrier so he could kill them all. The scene morphed once more, and the Red Witch was casting a spell to claim the demon Inanis from baby Delilah.

The memories came fast and furious, but they didn't *feel* like memories. It all felt real. It felt ... *Now*. What she'd always sensed during meditation—that time was an illusion —was now reality. Alive, it had *felt* like a truth. Dead, it was stone-cold fact.

In the instant she understood this, much as Henry had learned at his mother's house when travelling the astral plane, she knew this *power of thought* must be tamed immediately. Henry's life was in the balance. As was the future of the magical beings of Salem.

His destiny was *Salem's* destiny. From the moment she'd taken responsibility for protecting him since he was a boy, Wanda had been tasked with making sure that destiny came to pass. Nothing was guaranteed, however. And the things that must happen on this night, before all was said and done, had to happen just right.

With the arrival of Lucifer, all the players were present and accounted for. His sudden appearance at her apartment had been a severe curve ball. *Artemis* was who she'd expected to darken her door earlier in the evening. The result, in the end, was the same. The only thing changed was the method of deliverance.

No coincidences.

The limo ride with Lucifer provided an edge she'd not expected. When he'd pulled the trick with the diary, she saw her opportunity... and took full advantage. The pages had shown only what Wanda *wanted* him to see, but even better, what she needed him to believe; that she still thought Claire Davies was dead and that the death had been her fault.

It was something she'd believed until the moment she discovered Artemis on Facebook. After that, the old witch's spell was undone, and the memories flooded back.

So she'd entered the limo armed with new facts, but she'd put on a show for Lucifer as if the facts in the diary were still the truth as she knew it.

When she saw the smug look on his face through the rear window as his limo pulled away, she knew he'd bought everything. And even better, Lucifer believed she was doing his bidding—that they'd somehow struck a bargain.

Leaving the athame behind in the limo had been the cherry on the sundae. She knew Lucifer would never be able to resist the irony of ending Henry's life with it.

Wanda shifted her thoughts back to Henry. In the next instant, she was in Jagger's Magical Treasures. Henry's body glowed bright blue, but parts of his aura were tinged with the green stains of ethereal envy from the corrupt essence of Jagger Corey. An essence which drew closer with every passing moment.

CHAPTER 23
OUT OF TIME

"What time is it?" asked Byron as he swung the Explorer around the corner and onto Essex Street.

Jo glanced down at her phone. "3:11 a.m."

As he straightened out the SUV, Byron shot a quick look toward Jo. Her face was tear-streaked but determined.

"He's going to be okay, Jo," said Byron.

At that moment, Jo's eyes widened. She shot her right arm up and pointed toward the windshield. "Look out!"

Byron turned his head just in time to see Raul Martinez walking down the middle of Essex Street in a daze. The front of his uniform was streaked with blood. Byron yanked the steering wheel hard to the right, then snapped it back to the left. They zoomed past Raul, who didn't so much as blink.

The Explorer's left side came off the street for the briefest moment. Byron overcompensated by whipping the steering wheel back to the right. When he slammed on the brakes, his front wheels weren't straight. They hit the curb hard. There was a loud bang, followed by a metallic popping sound as both axles snapped. The cruiser rolled onto its side, and then onto its roof. It slid across the sidewalk, the roof's metal screeching like an outraged eagle. With a thunderous bang, the eagle was silenced by the sturdy granite walls of Jagger's Magical Treasures.

Inside the Explorer, all went white. Byron and Jo hung upside down, suspended by their seat belts in a cloud of deployed airbags.

"You okay?" asked Jo.

"Yeah. You?"

Jo didn't answer. Instead, Byron heard the click of her seat belt, then saw her jet-black hair as her head slammed into the roof of the Explorer. It barely slowed her. Two seconds later, he saw the rugged soles of her combat boots as she scrambled through the shattered passenger's side window.

"Jo! Wait!" yelled Byron.

She yelled something back, but Byron didn't catch it. The Explorer rocked slightly as Joanne hauled herself up, onto, and across the cruiser's prone belly.

"What the hell are you doing?" demanded Byron.

He was answered with a loud, cracking sound and a flash of brilliant emerald light as Jo obliterated the boards covering the window. The very window he'd shattered a few months earlier.

"I'm gettin' too old for this shit!" said Byron. He braced himself, placing his right hand flat against the roof of the Explorer, then releasing the latch on his seat belt with the left. He crashed down onto his right shoulder. Pain exploded through it, followed by a stream of obscenities directed at someone's anonymous sister's ass. "At least it wasn't my goddamned head," he finished.

The driver's side of the Explorer was dark, save for the reflective flecks of mica in the granite walls of Jagger's shop. Byron made for the passenger's side, following Jo's route out of the cruiser. When he stood, he saw the damage Jo had inflicted on the boards. As he pulled himself up and over the carcass of his ride, he peered through the maw of splintered wood and couldn't shake the feeling he was entering the mouth of a huge and terrible beast.

Ahead, he saw a flare of emerald light at the top of the stairs near the reading nooks. He'd seen what happened to the poor bastards who'd ended up on the receiving end of that light. Smiling, he made for the stairs.

JAZZ CREPT through the ethereal mist, her phone's flashlight app the sole source of illumination. In the upper right corner of her phone's screen it read 'no service.' The robotic female voice from earlier replayed in her head. "...out of the service area? Ya think!" she said out loud.

The mist was thick, that was bad enough, but it also had a reflective property which slightly blinded her. Tiny particles floated in the mist, bouncing light back into her eyes when she held her phone forward. They seemed strangely attracted to the light—sparkling moths to the synthetic flame. She pitched the screen down and away from her, lighting the spot just in front of her feet.

Sound had an odd quality in this land inside the looking glass. Her footsteps made muted crunching sounds, like walking through leaves covered in cotton. It was barely audible. Still, it was better to be safe than sorry, and she decided to keep her boots in the satchel.

There was no telling how far she'd come, or how far she had to go. She wasn't even sure *where* she was going. Armand had gone into the mirror, and had also known she'd follow him. It was now down to a matter of trust.

The colors and faces she'd seen earlier told her the vampire was most likely not alone, and probably headed for trouble. Whether he was aware of it or not was, to her thinking, still up for debate. She desperately wished she could watch the tape she'd found in the vampire's floor.

Jazz looked up from the light and into the sparkling gloom, then stopped dead in her tracks. Green light flickered briefly in the distance, followed by a flash of red. She killed the light on her phone. Darkness swallowed her, and she waited.

All was quiet for a few seconds, then came a distant wail of pain with the unmistakable tinge of Armand Moreland's voice wrapped inside. In the next moment, she heard a peel of familiar, wicked female laughter. Goosebumps sprang on every surface of her skin, and her mouth flooded with the electric taste of fear. Jazz shook it off quickly, then shot into the mist toward light, laughter... and pain.

ARTEMIS KEPT one eye on Wanda Heinze, and one eye on his watch. 3:13 a.m. was the time he'd been instructed to release her. It went perfectly. Claire's warning, all those years ago, echoed from the walls of his guilt-ridden mind. "The white witch must die when the child of the prophecy dies. Then, neither can help the other."

Wanda dipped into the thoughts and memories she'd snagged from Artemis as she'd left her body, exploring them fully. They'd been brief—quick flashes of consciousness, reminiscent of the way she communicated with Jazz, but without Artemis's permission. In that moment, she got her first taste of how time and thought functioned in the in-between. Thoughts carried a payload of memories with them. In a millisecond, the blank spots in her memory became filled.

This is what she saw:

At first, he'd had reservations. Even though he'd loved Mother with all his heart, he'd had a hard time believing something supposed to happen thirty-two years in the future could have any bearing on the present. The he remembered it was never supposed to have taken this long in the first place.

March 13, 1992 had been a long time ago. Heinze had been there. At first, he thought the witch had killed his mother, and he almost threw her out of the apartment. Just as he crossed the foot of the bed and reached for Wanda, his mother had stirred.

"Artemis? Where are you?"

Artemis had stopped in his tracks, then bolted back to the head of the bed. "I'm here, Mother."

"Don't blame the white witch. I summoned her. She only answered my call."

"You what?" asked Artemis.

"Come now, Arty. We both know you aren't the type who drinks and drives. But I needed the white witch. I'm sorry you had to go through that."

Artemis remembered how his jaw had hit the floor with that. "You... you caused my arrest?"

"I had to. I'd learned something new. I needed to know if it was true," said Claire Davies.

"Learned something?" asked Artemis.

Claire had nodded weakly. "When I was at the hospital, and they told me how long I had to live, they assumed I would be devastated. When I assured them I was fine, and that I'd suspected the end was near... well, they naturally assumed I was in shock. You can't blame them, really. It's their job to look out for their patients, especially those at death's door."

Wanda had kept silent. She'd suspected something... *off* when her fingers went numb and Claire had begun to shudder violently. Just what that something *was* remained to be seen.

Claire continued. "So, they made me wait. Said they wanted me to talk to someone. I tried once more to tell them I was fine, but they wouldn't have it. After a few minutes, in walks this man. He was an odd looking fellow. Not dressed like a doctor at all—more like a sixties hippie. Said his name was Archibald something."

Wanda had frozen, praying to Hecate her face hid her surprise. *What the hell was Archie doing at the hospital?*

"What did he say?"

"Well, he was very forthcoming. Wanted me to know, right up front, that he wasn't a medical doctor. Nor was he a psychologist. Well, not a normal psychologist, anyway. He dealt with parapsychology. You know, the study of the paranormal and such?"

Artemis had nodded. "But why would they call on someone like that, Mother?"

"You have to remember, Arty, it was around the holidays. They were short-staffed. From what the man told me, he was the only one remotely qualified in the building that day to handle a situation like mine."

Claire had become winded, and held up a hand. Artemis poured water from a pitcher into a plastic cup, then held it to her lips. After a moment's rest, she'd continued.

"They'd obviously briefed him about my situation. He was so kind. Walked right up to me and took my hands in his. That's when I knew... when I saw!"

Wanda recalled something dark had crossed Claire's face. The woman smiled, and it had made Wanda think of a raven slowly spreading its wings.

"What did you see?" Artemis had asked, his voice high and tight.

"I read him like a book. The white witch," Claire had nodded toward Wanda, "is his friend. I knew at once I needed her. She's a healer, you see."

Wanda's blood had run cold. The numbness she'd felt in her fingers, as she'd tried to heal Claire, hadn't *been* a failure of her Reiki healing. Claire Davies had been *using* her. *She's a dark witch!* And, from what she now remembered, a powerful one indeed.

"The doctor is also a witch, though he doesn't seem to realize it. His young son is a *very* powerful witch. Possibly the one from the prophecy. The doctor knows nothing about him. I believe the child is the one Lucifer fears most!" She'd gripped him tight at the wrist. "Fortune has smiled on us, Artemis. If you can keep me alive, I believe a bargain can be made!"

"Well, why don't we just pick him up and offer the child to him straight away, then?"

"A valid question, dearest. As I said, the hippie doctor is unaware of his child's existence. The mother, at this time, is unknown. When I touched him, I saw the white witch also has no knowledge of the child."

In that moment, Wanda remembered thanking her higher power. The blocking spell she'd put on herself, and several others, when it came to knowledge of Henry Trank and all that surrounded him, had worked.

"She knows too much now. Shouldn't we... dispose of the threat?" Artemis had pled.

Claire had waived a shaky hand in the air, dismissing the notion. "By the time she leaves this room, she'll have forgotten our names and just about everything to do with us, dear one. I made sure of it when she laid hands on me. When the child is found, the proposal to the dark one will commence." She paused. It had seemed to Wanda, at the time, overly dramatic. "Unless I die before that day. Should that happen... I fear we are both lost."

"Is there an inkling as to the child's whereabouts?"

"At the moment, no. A powerful man in Salem searches high and low for him as we speak. Solomon Dobson seeks him. For what reason? I do not know. I believe Dobson is on the Board of Trustees at the hospital. Your connections there may serve us well. Should Dobson find the child, we would be among the first to know. Should the child elude him, you'll need to procure souls to sustain me until he's found, and thus keep Lucifer from consummating the deal."

"How will I do that?" Artemis had asked.

Claire had pointed a gnarled finger at the wall opposite her bed. A crimson velveteen curtain stretched from one wall to the other. Artemis moved toward it, then to the right of the curtain. There was a soft click as he slid the dimmer switch slowly upward, shedding just enough light on the curtain to bring it to the shade of dried blood. When Claire had nodded, Artemis pulled down on a gold rope sash. With a soft *whoosh!* the curtain parted, revealing a large, oval mirror. It had gleamed dully in the soft light like the eye of a dead dragon.

The lights in the room had flickered, and Wanda watched as the eyes of the dark witch rolled back, exposing bloodshot whites. As Claire had begun her incantation, the whites faded to a lightless black. Though the windows were closed on that cold March thirteenth night, a sudden and violent vortex blew papers around the room, rattled the curtains at either side of the mirror, and had sent a chill through Wanda's bones.

> **"Souls of tomorrow**
> **Souls of today**
> *Let the spirits of the mirror out for a stay."*

On the last word, the mirror's surface had swirled. At first, the patterns seemed random, like wind-whipped waves on a stormy pond. Wanda had watched, horrified, as agonized faces breached the dark storm of the mirror's surface, screaming silently beneath terrified and pleading eyes. One by one, they'd begged for release, but she couldn't move. At first, she'd believed fear rooted her to the spot, but that wasn't it. Claire's dark magick had bound her. She hadn't been able to move a muscle.

The air in the room shifted then, sucked toward the maelstrom on the mirror's surface. Then, with a loud pop, all had become still. The mirror's surface morphed into a black and infinite maw out of which had floated a glowing crystal flask framed in sterling silver. It had come to rest on the hardwood floor, turning the polished wood the glittering blue of a swimming pool at night. An eerie silence had filled the room. Papers caught up in the furious wind seesawed silently to the floor. "Take it, Artemis," Claire had commanded.

Artemis had failed to respond right away, and Wanda couldn't tell if he was too terrified to move, or too awestruck.

"Artemis!"

That had snapped him to it. He bent and retrieved the flask, then moved toward his mother's bed.

"What is this?" Artemis had asked, mystified.

"Our salvation, dearest. The more souls you collect, the stronger I become, and the longer I—we—live."

"But how do I do that?"

"Seek the Red Witch, for she is the mirror's owner. And remember one thing above all else, my son."

"Yes?"

"Wherever you are, and whatever takes place, 3:13 in the morning and March thirteenth of the given year is when it will happen."

Wanda carried Artemis's thoughts, and the revelations within, to her rendezvous with Henry in the in-between.

CHAPTER 24
NO SYMPATHY FOR THE DEVIL

When Jo reached the top of the stairs at Jagger's Magical Treasures, she saw a man in an immaculate black suit standing in the doorway to the mirror room. *He's handsome*, she thought. *Beautiful.* Jo looked beyond him, and saw her husband lying motionless on the floor. Blood pooled around his midsection.

The man in black opened his mouth, but nary a syllable escaped before Jo flashed her hand and emerald fire blasted him in the midsection. Lucifer was flung backward, over Henry, and over the shards of mirror neatly laid out in the middle of the room. He crashed into the wall opposite the mirror room's entrance, leaving a man-shaped imprint in the plaster. When he picked himself up from the floor, he was laughing.

"Now *that*," said Lucifer, "was impressive!" Then, in tandem, he spoke with the voices of Luci and Fermina. "I—we—should have seen that coming, though. You were always a hothead, Jo."

Jo ignored every word. She knelt next to Henry, her knees

sliding a little in his blood. Tears welled in her eyes, and she placed her index and middle fingers at the pulse point of his neck.

Nothing.

The phone rested in his unnaturally still left hand. The display was black, save for bright white digits showing the time. Jo wiped away her tears and saw it was 3:14 a.m.

One minute too late.

Her husband was dead.

"I warned him. I warned all of you. Artemis has taken what is ours. Henry was supposed to stop him, and he failed. But like I—we—said in the letter. Fail, and you belong to us."

Rage quickly replaced grief, and Jo stood and faced him. "That's bullshit!" She took a step closer. "Why kill Henry if you need him to recover something from this Artemis asshole? The guy only showed himself today. That makes zero sense!" Jo tilted her head, as if considering something for the first time. "But you know that already, don't you?"

The smile on his face slipped. It was brief, a slight tremor. But Jo knew she'd hit on something.

"Was it Jagger?" she prodded.

Again, Lucifer twitched.

She nodded, then took another step closer. "It was, wasn't it? You *need* Henry for something, but figured if you could replace him with Jagger, that would have been just as good. That ship sailed when your little puppet Jagger got whacked by us. So what is it? What are you *really* after?"

She never saw him move. One moment, he was across the room, the next, his hand was on her throat.

"You know what one of my favorite movies is, Jo?" asked Lucifer.

When she didn't answer, he lifted her slightly from the floor, then shook her a little. Jo grabbed for his forearm with both hands, trying to relieve the strain on her neck. She could only answer with a shake of her head.

"Christopher Walken was in it. He played the angel Gabriel. I liked his version a lot better than the real thing. Gabie get's on my nerves. Anyway, it's called *Prophecy*. You'd love it. *Movie* Gabriel loved to refer to human beings as 'talking monkeys.' I liked that. So let me be clear, *Joanne*. Watch your tongue with me, you talking fucking monkey." He clamped down harder, smiling viciously. "You're right though, I *do* need something—your husband's soul. I just needed a way to get him here. Henry's little visions of Artemis and *Mommy Dearest* were a clever bit of theater though, if I do say so myself. They don't call me the *Father of Lies* for nothing."

Lucifer got a far away look in his eye then, like being lost in the warmth of a fond memory. As if he'd forgotten Jo's neck was in his hands, he refocused. "I'm a collector. Did you know that?" he asked, as if sharing a secret with an old friend. "Souls are my thing, as you might have heard. You'd do just as nicely as Artemis or his mother. I'd prefer to have *them*, since they kinda owe me, but I'm not that picky." With his free hand, he snapped his fingers, then pointed a finger gun at her like he'd just come up with the most amazing idea. "Or, I could take *Delilah*. Like I said, I'm not that picky. I know she's with Penny right now. Come to think of it, they'd both do n..."

At the mention of her baby's name, Jo kicked at him wildly. Her boots connected, but to little effect. Lucifer yawned, then squeezed her neck until her legs slowed and her struggles weakened. Her grip on his arm loosened. Her left hand fell away, then her right. The room grayed, and stars swirled in her eyes. She was on the verge of passing out when she heard a loud bang. The iron clamp on her throat was gone in an instant. Cool, blessed air flooded her lungs, and color rushed back into the world.

Lucifer stood a few feet away from her now, hunched over and holding his left side with his right hand. He stood slowly, taking the hand from his side and holding it up at eye level. The dark one stared at it in disbelief, mesmerized by the drops of crimson as they slowly dotted the floor. In the silence following the boom of Byron's gun, they sounded like the beats of a bass drum.

"That's not supposed to happen, now, is it?" asked Lucifer. More to himself than Byron or Joanne.

Byron kept his gun and his eyes pointed at Lucifer. He sidestepped slowly toward Jo, taking his left hand from the butt of his gun and offering it to her. Jo took it with both hands, and Byron pulled her up. As Jo rose to full height, so did Lucifer. Cop and witch faced the Prince of Darkness in what Byron thought was probably the strangest stand-off in human history. Little did he, Jo, or Lucifer realize the strangeness factor was about to rise by several degrees.

Lucifer advanced on them slowly. Jo and Byron stepped backwards, matching his pace.

"I should lay both of you out right now. Send you to your eternal *reward*," mocked Lucifer.

Byron stopped where he was, taking his left hand back from Jo and placing it once again on the butt of his gun to keep it steady. He spread his feet in a shooter's stance.

Lucifer stopped, then laughed. "Is this the part where you say 'Go ahead. Make my day?'"

Byron tilted his head from side to side. "Works for me, asshole. I'm a bit tired of you beatin' on women tonight."

"How chivalrous!" taunted Lucifer. "I think I've had enough of *you* for one night."

Byron felt a tickle at the middle of his forehead, like something had crawled inside his skull, looking for a place to settle down. It was a weird sensation. It reminded him of what Wanda mentioned about the demon Inanis's power. How when he tried to crawl around inside your head, it felt like you might have eaten an overly sweet piece of cake. Wanda had called it 'brain puckers.' This was a first-hand demonstration.

Lucifer's eyes bored in on Byron's, and the dark one expected the cop to fold like the jock on the beach had, but the cop was... *resisting* him. Lucifer probed his mind, looking for weakness. It was a trick and a tactic as old as time. He'd been using it to control the talking monkeys all the way back to the Garden of Eden—and even further back than *that*.

But when he saw the landscape of the cop's mind, the usual fears weren't there. *No, that isn't quite right*, thought Lucifer. *They are there—but severely muted.*

Everyone had core fears: death, poverty, loneliness, illness, rejection. They were staples in the vast menu of emotions he'd always been able to pluck from. Whenever he probed someone's mind, the subject always presented as a landscape of memories both beautiful and terrifying. The beautiful ones, the *cherished* memories, spawned images of sunny open fields, or calm peaceful lakes, accompanied by happy smiling faces and warm feelings. He didn't give a rat's ass about those.

He was after the burning houses and mangled bodies, the bee stings and broken bones, the betrayal of adultery and the rage of revenge. *The good stuff!* In the minds of those he sought to control, *that* part of the landscape showed up barren or burnt—scabs dotting the terrain between the happy crap. These weren't there with the cop, but they weren't totally gone either. In their place, the land had... healed somehow. Purple flowers grew where parched land belonged, and in the spots where the land should have smoked with the fire of fear, hopeful green grass sprouted.

Witchcraft! Or Magick. Someone had done something to the cop, because the cop didn't fear him—and that was bad. Real bad. Because there was no way the cop's bullets should have had any effect on him. It wasn't a Superman kind of thing; bullets didn't bounce off of him. It was more like, well, a magic thing or a spiritual thing. They simply never reached him.

He'd always controlled *any* potential threat by pulling the strings of fear like those of a puppet. That included things like making the jock at the beach crap his pants, or making a smoke show like Jennifer want to screw his brains out.

Or making a cop with a gun twitch just enough to miss.

This? This was something new. The hole in his side proved it.

"Your little mind thing not working?" taunted Byron.

A crooked grin sprang on Lucifer's face. With his free hand, he shook a finger and nodded at Byron. "I could tell there was something different about you. At the hospital. Most people would have left that room running. I mistook your lack of fear as foolish bravado. But that's not it at all. You're not afraid right now because you can't be. Can you?"

Byron shrugged. "Whatever works, right?"

Lucifer's crooked grin turned into a full smile. "Hey!

Thanks for the idea! I just wished I'd thought of it before you put a hole in this magnificent body. Do you know how hard it was to find this guy?"

Byron caught Jo's movement out of the corner of his eye just in time. Her hands flew to her head, and she screamed. "No!" A second later, she was on him in a flash, reaching for his gun. He pulled it up and away, Jo's hands swiped at empty air and she tumbled past him. She quickly righted herself, and was getting ready for another try.

Byron knew he was no match for Jo. Maybe if he were twenty years younger, thirty pounds lighter, and didn't have a bum knee he could have fought her off. He was none of those things, now. It made his next decision easy.

From where he stood, he glimpsed a sliver of moonlight in the reading nook window, visible through the mirror room's entrance. Byron reared back, then hurled the gun toward it. The black pistol clipped the frame of the door, chipping the white paint. A round discharged with the impact.

Two things happened next.

The force of the blast sent the gun spinning wildly through the opened doorway like a metallic crow on crack. It crashed through the brittle, antique glass of the multi-paned nook window, then clattered lightly two floors below on the bricks of Essex Street.

Secondly, the discharged round struck Lucifer in the knee, sending him crashing to the floor.

Lucifer's hold on Joanne's mind lifted, just as she'd raised two hands pulsing with emerald light in Byron's direction. Once started, however, the energy had to go some-where. Jo moved her hands away from Byron and aimed them at the floor—directly at the shards Henry had arranged in a loose approximation of the original mirror. A brilliant flash of emerald fire swept across the room.

Lucifer, still clutching his knee and writhing in pain, saw what was happening. With little time to react, he quickly rolled from the path of the green witch's magic and pressed himself tightly to the wall. Nausea consumed him as the purity of her magic grazed him, and he crossed his fingers none of it entered his wounds. For the first time in eons, he knew *real* fear.

Something had gone terribly wrong tonight, and he hadn't the foggiest idea where and when it had happened.

As the fiery magic of the green witch dissipated, he saw the cop and Joanne suddenly shuffle backwards toward the far wall. There was a faint gritty sound coming from the room's center, followed by a single click.

Then came another.

And another.

Soon, they merged into a cacophonous roar.

The shards of the mirror, spurred somehow by Jo's magic, were becoming one.

Oh shit! thought Lucifer.

CHAPTER 25
STORM OF TRUTH

Wanda was back in Wanda's Wicca'd Emporium. Henry was with her. It took a few moments for both of them to regain control of their thoughts. Henry was enormously confused; Wanda was prepared for it. What she had to tell him next would only confuse him further, but it had to be said. Once he seemed settled enough, she began.

"We're both dead, Henry. Do you understand that?"

Henry looked around the room, puzzled. "I don't feel dead. But I'm not quite sure how I got here."

"You remember Luci and Fermina?" asked Wanda.

"Yes."

"Their bodies were found earlier tonight. Well, technically yesterday. Lucifer returned, in the flesh... well, some poor soul's flesh. You probably saw him at some point. He—"

"There was a guy. Good looking. I saw him on the way home. He was with Jo. At least I thought it was Jo. He groped her, Wanda. I think he was taunting me—"

"It's not important right now. It was all an illusion. Lucifer knows there's a lot of Jagger left in you. He was pushing you the way he wanted you to go. For a long time now, I've suspected you might die on this night. And he's made sure of that. He *thinks* it's what he wants, but he is sorely mistaken."

"What? You knew this was going to happen?"

Wanda felt his anger, amplified by the emotional and spiritual remnants of Jagger Corey. It was in her nature to be empathetic, and her first instinct was to calm him. But Wanda pushed that empathy way down deep. If they were to come out of this alive, Henry's feelings had to take a back seat.

"No, not until tonight. I told you before, after the business with Inanis, that I would never do that again. And I haven't. But when you had visions of a man stealing souls, I began to wonder—and prepare. Just in case. I think Armand did, too. The letter from Gemini was part of it—and 313. When numbers attached to significant events keep coming up like that, I can't ignore it. I think you knew it, too. Something deep down *had* to be screaming at you from inside. Or am I wrong?"

That last question hit a sore spot. Red flared in Henry's aura, dark and dangerous.

It was clear to Wanda part of him remained unconvinced. But if she lost him now, they might never return to their current bodies and lives. She took off the kid gloves. "Now you listen to me, Henry Trank." Wanda pointed an ethereal finger at him. "If you ever want to see Joanne and Delilah in a living, breathing body again, you need to get a hold of yourself. Right now!"

Auric red ballooned, followed by tinges of Jagger Corey's green. He was on the verge of outright rage. Then, to Wanda's relief, calm blue suffused his entire being. His emotional control was, at least on this side of the veil, impressive.

He said, "Okay. Tell me what I need to know."

"It's better if we find out together." Wanda offered her hands. Henry took them.

This is what they saw...

A house. It was set high on a bluff overlooking the ocean. The night was dark and the Atlantic boiled with the energy of a Nor'easter. Wind blew the rain in all directions.

They moved closer, flying up and over foamy rocks at the foot of a bluff, then higher, over sea grass whipsawed by shifting winds. They crested the bluff and sailed over a white picket fence marking the border of an enormous and immaculate lawn. A flagstone patio glowed wet and darkly golden at far end of the lawn, lit from somewhere above. Henry traced the light's source. Rain assaulted a huge, multi-pained window on the highest floor, smearing the light and making the human shapes within appear to dance. As they drifted closer, Henry heard fat drops of rain smacking the glass so hard they sounded like pebbles being flung by the handful.

They stopped, floating a few feet from the window.

He sent a thought to Wanda. "Where are we?"

Wanda responded with a shake of the head, then returned the thought. "You'll figure it out pretty quickly."

They moved closer, stopping just short of the window. At first, Henry couldn't make out a thing. The rain was ferocious, smearing the human beings inside into melting and moving wax shadows. Then, there was a brief lull in the storm. Gravity smeared rain in small waves down the face of the window. A figure inside approached. White votive candles dotted the sill in front of him. Passing from shadow and into the candlelight was the face of Armand Moreland. He stared straight at Henry. When their eyes met, Armand smiled. There was no humor in the vampire's smile, but only sadness and, if he read him correctly, regret.

"He *sees* me, Wanda. How is that possible?"

"Remember what you told me about the rooms of the in-between, Henry? And the door marked Madeleine? This is the same thing, only this is one of *my* doors. History is a two-way street."

Henry wanted more answers. He pulled his eyes from the window and the vampire, but Wanda only stared forward. When he turned back, the vampire was moving toward the middle of the room.

"That's our cue to enter, Henry."

Without a word, they slipped through the window. The candles on the sill fluttered briefly, and a cloaked figure sitting in the circle shot a curious glance in their direction.

Armand Moreland saw this, and quickly covered. "Drafts!" he complained to his companions. "Black and Blue House is going to be the death of me. Or my bank account. Now, where were we?"

Henry studied the cloaked figure, whose gaze lingered on the sill. After a moment, the figure's attention returned to the circle. Moreland's explanation seemed to satisfy whoever it was.

The vampire took his place in the circle at the far end of the room. They floated after him. Henry noticed the room beyond the candles was very dark. A lone candle burned at the center of a gold pentacle painted on a black floor. The space was eerily reminiscent of the safe room at Wanda's Wicca'd Emporium. He considered asking Wanda about it, but stopped short.

At each point of the pentacle sat a cloaked figure in a chair. The one who'd noticed Henry and Wanda's arrival—or at least *suspected* something—sat to Moreland's left. She was first to speak.

"What of this prophecy, vampire? Who is this supposed 'heir' to this home?"

Moreland cleared his throat. "I've heard rumors, but nothing concrete, Mistress Davies."

Claire Davies cackled. "Do you think me a fool, Moreland? I have as much right to this house as this *alleged* heir. We don't even know if he exists. Where is he? Who is he? I demand to know his identity!"

Moreland deliberated for a few seconds, then gave in. "Fine! If you must know, the heir lives but the individual's identity is unknown. However, your claim of 'rights' to this property are superseded by the lineage of the heir's soul." Moreland shot back. "Said individual will remain anonymous until their safety is secured. There are forces at work, at this very moment, seeking the child's destruction. This dwelling will remain the Council's until the heir can safely take control."

"He's been protecting me all along?" Henry asked Wanda.

"Us, sweetie. He's been doing this for all of us. I wish we knew sooner," said Wanda.

"The Council of the Realms only controls this land

because it is protected by white magic," the dark witch shot back. "As a vampire, you know nothing of magic—light or dark. Yet they entrust you with its care. Why is that?"

"The Council," said Moreland, struggling to remain patient, "is comprised of magical beings from *both* sides. For balance. As a vampire, one with an abundance of self control, I might add, I'm seen as neutral. Salem's very existence depends upon that balance. *You* seek control of Black and Blue for very different reasons than you present. Reasons that would directly alter that balance."

"Nonsense!" she growled. "I'm entitled to this property by blood. You know nothing of which you speak." As she said this, she shot a quick, guilty look around the room.

"Doesn't he, though?" asked the figure to Moreland's right. "How is your health these days, dear witch?"

Henry realized this figure, almost since they'd entered the room, had kept her head bowed—as if deep in meditation. When she removed the hood of her cloak, Henry's ethereal jaw hit the floor.

"What the hell is Jazz doing here?" asked Henry.

Again, Wanda chose silence, and Henry turned back to listen.

"My health isn't at issue here, gypsy. I—"

Jazz cut her short. "Oh, but it is. You're dying. Pancreatic cancer, I believe?"

With that truth exposed, Claire's eyes narrowed to hate-filled slits.

Jazz continued. "You duped a certain doctor when you were at the hospital, only he has *no idea* he's been duped. You used what you learned from him to lure a good friend of mine to your home, used her healing powers to save your sorry ass, then blocked her memory. How am I doing so far?"

The dark witch fumed, but said nothing.

"I've got a news flash for you, lady. I saw the whole thing. You see, Wanda and I have a special connection. If I let her, she can see my thoughts. And vice versa. We were in contact that night. You, your pathetic son Artemis, and a certain mirror belonging to a certain redhead were all part of it. And I believe something came from that mirror, if I'm not mistaken. Something used to collect souls. Am I warm?" Jazz nodded. "I think I am."

"Is this true, Mistress Davies?" asked Moreland, his tone reproachful.

"It is," said another figure next to Jazz. A much younger Wanda Heinze drew her hood back. "Though I've no recollection of what happened. I still don't, aside from what Jazz just told us, but we *were* linked that night. Of that I'm sure. Claire's reaction says it all."

Henry's mind reeled. Another version of Wanda sat, alive and kicking, mere feet from where he stood. For the last time, he turned to the Wanda at his side. "What in the hell is going on here?"

Finally, she turned to him. "We're both about to find out."

The last figure drew his cloak back. It was Archie, but he looked strange. A reddish glow surrounded his irises, and the unvarnished malice on his face looked alien. The Archie-thing leaped up from his chair, and Claire Davies rose with him. They joined hands. Before Moreland, Wanda, or Jazz could react, Claire Davies and a possessed Archibald Love raised their hands in unison. Red and fiery magic burst from their hands. Chairs toppled. Witches tumbled. Some of the candles on the sill and the candle at the pentacle's center blew out, and along with them went the consciousness of everyone else.

Silence reigned.

"Shall I kill them now, master?"

The thing inside Archie turned toward her. "Kill them? Are you insane?"

"We can seize the property now. I thought that's why we—"

He shook his head, then looked at her with disappointment on his face. "Have you learned nothing, witch? This place is protected by white magic. Try a killing spell in here and you'll be dead before you hit the floor. The only reason you're even *in* here is because the vampire allowed it. *Thankfully*, he's far too trusting. At least we know now why blood alone won't put the house in your hands."

"We do?" asked Claire.

Lucifer waited a beat, allowing her time to figure it out. When she didn't, he sighed. "The heir is not entitled by *blood* alone, but by the *legacy* of its soul." He stopped to think, then said, "Make them forget. The child will be found soon. Solomon Dobson—" he shook his head, corrected himself "—*Inanis the demon* believes himself safe. And he is, for now. Once the child is found, I'll deal with the demon's betrayal. When the time is right, the heir must die, and this house... and Salem, belong to me once more."

"As it was in 1692, master!" Claire exalted.

He smiled broadly through Archie. "Good times. Now, get me out of this monkey suit."

Claire began the incantation:

Dark dwells in light...
Like night wrapped in day.

May all trace be lost...
Of revelations this day.
So mote it be!

When Claire Davies finished, Archie crumpled to the floor. Lucifer shot from his body, through the window on the top floor, and into the stormy night.

"Well, that was enlightening," said Wanda.

CHAPTER 26
THREADS

Lucifer stood at one end of the room, near the entrance to the hallway and the reading nooks. Jo and Byron stood diagonally across from him, as far away as they could possibly get.

The last pieces of the mirror were clicking together. When the final piece slid into place, there was a blinding, reddish-green flash of light. It caught Jo and Byron by surprise, rendering them momentarily sightless. It had the same effect on Lucifer, for he was still bound to a human body. When all three regained their sight, the middle of the room was empty.

The mirror had moved of its own accord. It was suspended in midair, shiny side out, and slowly, silently floating toward the back wall of the room. As it closed on the wall it slowed even more. A *whoosh* of air and dust puffed from its sides as it connected. The heavy silence that followed was short-lived.

At the mirror's apex, a ball of sparkling red light sizzled. At the same time, a murky-green twin of sparkling light sprang to life at the bottom. Each spread out, running slowly along the sides of the mirror and then meeting in the middle. Brilliant light burst forth with their collision. Smoke billowed along the circumference of the mirror, and the room became filled with it.

Byron kept one eye on the mirror and one trained on Lucifer. Given the circumstances, it was no easy feat. He decided to give the dark one all of his attention, but as the smoke cleared, he saw Lucifer was dumbfounded.

"Byron. Look," whispered Jo.

"Ho-ly shit!" he whispered back.

The smoke cleared from the room quickly, thanks to the hole his gun had made in the nook window. Even through the cloud that remained, there was no mistaking what he saw. The mirror had fused neatly with the wall, as if the most talented interior decorator had surveyed the room and found the perfect spot for it. And in the place where a few short moments ago red and green magick sizzled along its sides, a beautifully ornate stone frame had formed.

Byron thought it was the most astonishing thing he'd ever seen, and that included the smelly, canine-at-the-library incident. But in the magical world he now fully embraced, it quickly became the *second* most astonishing thing—because Armand Moreland suddenly appeared dead center in the middle of the mirror. He was screaming in agony as his left hand breached its surface.

The clock on the iPhone in Henry's dead hand read 3:17 a.m.

~

Wanda released Henry's hands, and they were back in her safe room.

"I'm part of some prophecy, now? Did I understand that correctly?" asked Henry.

Wanda's answer was simple and, to Henry, incomprehensible. "Apparently so."

Henry's eyes went wide. "Apparently so? You mean to tell me you were unaware of what we just heard?"

"Didn't you see what I just saw? Claire Davies made us *forget*, Henry."

"So how did you know to go there *now*?"

Wanda put her left elbow in her right palm, then pulled at her lip. It was how she did her best thinking—in this world or the next. She said, "When someone puts a strong spell on you, like Claire Davies did, it's almost unbreakable. Almost. An event can trigger a memory, and that memory is like a loose thread in a sweater. Most of the time, you just yank the loose thread, it snaps, and that's the end of it. But sometimes the thread doesn't snap. You keep pulling and pulling, and the fabric starts to bunch up. The loose thread becomes a problem. Or, sweetie, put a better way, it becomes quite noticeable. You with me?"

Henry nodded.

"When you started talking about Cotton Ball, and then my name was brought up, the thread started to show. I pulled. When it didn't snap right away, I noticed. That's when I started digging. I checked out a few things on Facebook, chased down a few leads, and almost all of it came back to me in a flood. Cotton Ball's real name is Artemis Davies. I met him way back when, at an AA meeting. Claire is his mother. And, as you just learned, she had a chance meeting with Archie. Although, the longer I exist, I'm starting to wonder if there's any such thing as *chance*. That's how she got to me. *And* she hit me with that damned spell twice! But by the time Artemis got me to the observatory and injected me, the memories were almost all intact. I snagged the last of it from him on the way here to meet you."

"You said she got to you through Archie. Does he remember any of this?" asked Henry.

Wanda tilted her head. "I'm not sure, sweetie. Why?"

Henry reached for his chest, then remembered he was dead. "He gave me something the other day. It was a stone. Heliotrope."

Wanda's eyes went wide. "The Bloodstone. The stone of Christ."

"Archie filled me in on the history," said Henry. "He said to keep it around my neck at all times for protection. He gave it to me a couple of days after we got the letter from Luci and Fermina. Doesn't seem to have protected me all that well."

Wanda shook her head. The look on her face was part amazement, part amusement. "Thank God you have a scatterbrain for a father."

Henry tilted his head. "What's that got to do with anything?"

"Do you know *where* your father got that stone?" asked Wanda.

"That would be a big fat no," said Henry.

"Armand Moreland asked him to have it examined. Archie was supposed to turn it over to the Archaeology Department at the university. They were going to do carbon dating on the piece." Wanda practically glowed as she said this.

"I'm still not following you, Wanda."

"What vampire-priest do we both know who used to work at The Vatican?" asked Wanda.

"You're not saying—" Words suddenly failed Henry.

Wanda nodded. "That is not 'A' bloodstone, Henry. That is *THE Bloodstone*."

~

THE GOLD-PLATED athame in Archie's hand became warm. When he looked down at it, it glowed white at the edges. Suddenly, the room filled with familiar scents. They seemed to be everywhere. It was a mixture of many smells: lavender, sage, Dragon's Blood, and White Rain shampoo. They all combined to form the aromatic tapestry of his best friend in the world—Wanda Heinze.

"Do you smell that?" Archie asked Jamal.

"Yes. You're friend is preparing to return. But you need to hold firm to the athame. It is where she'll be safest, if only for a few moments."

"Safest? I'm not sure I understand," said Archie.

"The dark one seeks souls, professor. But not just any souls. In order to bring Salem under his control, he requires the souls of witches—the more powerful, the better. And one above all others. The twin athames will hide both of them long enough to evade capture."

Archie tilted his head in confusion. "Both?"

"Your son is also in the in-between, professor."

"No! What's happened to Henry?" Archie had all he could do to remain seated. Every instinct screamed at him to toss the athame aside and rush to the aid of Wanda and Henry.

Jamal anticipated his reaction. "I know your first instinct

is to go to them, professor. Should you discard the athame now, you would seal their fates. You need to trust the judgment of the vampire, for he has prepared the athames to protect them both. Failure to do so ensures Salem will fall under control of Lucifer, and he will work his will through the Obsidian Witch. Dark Magick would become the dominant power in Salem once more. It would spread slowly throughout the world, affecting every enclave of magick and every coven within. With the present circumstances the world is headed for, imagine the devastation."

"So I'm supposed to just sit here?" asked Archie.

"If you ever want to see your son and your best friend in the flesh once more, then yes." Jamal caught his eyes and held them. A sympathetic and understanding smile spread wide across his face.

At first, Archie fought the urge to reach out and smack the smile from Jamal's face, but the longer he studied that face, and the smile plastered across it, the more familiar it became. Something made him want to trust this kid, he just couldn't figure out what.

MERCY SAT ALONE in Archie's office. With Jo and Byron gone from the room, she found herself able to concentrate, and thus better able to perform the task which had been thrust upon her.

With Wanda lying dead above her, and Archie and Jamal holding the fort directly beneath her, she was free to observe everything from a unique perspective.

She felt power radiating from Wanda's athame, and through her connection with Jamal and Archie, realized its purpose, though she felt she only had half of the equation. Wanda would use it to protect her soul from Lucifer, that much was clear. What she didn't understand was how her good friend and mentor was going to come back from the dead.

As if Wanda could read her mind, she heard the voice of the white witch speaking softly to her. It felt like she was standing right next to her, whispering in her ear. "Be prepared, Mercy. Keep the connection open, no matter what you hear or feel. The shit's about to hit the fan."

Mercy smiled. It didn't matter if Wanda was alive, dead, or somewhere in-between. She was always just *Wanda*.

"What about Henry?" asked Mercy.

"He's with me, he's—"

Mercy sat up sharply, almost losing her composure. "Henry's dead!?" Wanda's warning to maintain their connection no matter what she heard or felt replayed almost instantly in her mind, and she quickly got a hold of her emotions.

"It's okay, Mercy. He's with me. Lucifer means to have our souls, among others, but that's not going to happen. Well, at least not to Henry and I. I can't speak for the other two. You know about the athame Archie's holding, correct?"

"Yes," said Mercy. "From what I can tell, it's beginning to glow."

"It's preparing for my return. There's a pair of athames, honey. The other is, presently, buried in Henry's belly, and most likely doing the same thing. When we leave here, our souls will attach to them."

Wanda was saying this for Henry's benefit as well as Mercy's, killing two birds with one stone. She continued.

"When the time is perfect, we'll be able to leave them and return to our bodies."

"How will you know when the time is right?" asked Mercy.

"I don't. But sometimes you have to trust in providence. Sometimes, you've got to have faith."

"You said Lucifer means to have *your* souls, but you can't speak for the *other* two," said Mercy. With a tremor in her voice, Mercy asked. "Who are the other two?"

"Claire Davies and her son, Artemis. She's known as the Obsidian Witch, and she makes your mother look like Mary Poppins."

"She wouldn't happen to be in this building tonight, would she?" asked Mercy.

"She is. Artemis has her secured in one of the labs. He's been keeping her alive all these years with the souls in the flask. Her flesh is being preserved in a bewitched cryogenic casket."

Mercy stared at the wrinkled, angry face in the window on the other side of Archie's brand new door, wishing the old door with the frosted glass was still in place. The door rattled in its frame.

"I think she's awake."

CHAPTER 27
SOUL OF THE WITCH

Armand Moreland breached the surface of the mirror. The moment he did, his silent scream transformed into a bellow of pain. He staggered forward, barely able to keep his balance. It looked like he was being pulled from one side to the other by invisible hands.

Jo and Byron rushed to his aid, each taking an arm and steadying him. It was no easy task, however. The vampire-priest fought them.

Lucifer saw the distraction as an opportunity, and made his way over to Henry's body. He knelt on his left side, wincing at the pain from the gunshot wound, then lowered an ear to Henry's chest. When he heard nothing, he smiled. It was time to claim the soul of the witch.

The smile on Lucifer's face broadened when he realized Henry Trank was a two-for-one special. Not only was he about to capture the soul of a witch powerful with light magic, but he was also claiming the heir to the Council of the Realms, thus preventing any future reincarnations. The balance of light and dark in Salem would shift back in his favor.

Just like old times, he thought.

Besides, as he saw it, the League of the Moon owed him. The Red Witch and Jagger Corey had belonged to him, and now they were gone. Henry and Joanne Trank were directly responsible for their loss.

As a bonus, Wanda Heinze would be out of the picture completely. When he'd dropped Wanda at the university, he'd all but convinced her they were on the same side. What he'd seen in her diary amazed him. What amazed him further was Wanda had no idea Claire was still alive. By delivering Wanda to Claire's son Artemis at Salem University, he believed he was solving two problems in one shot.

He'd known Wanda was a bleeding-heart type. In the limo, when he'd revealed that Claire still lived, he figured she would jump at the chance to set things right. He also wagered Wanda might *actually* believe doing so would spark a change of heart in Artemis, and that Claire's soul-stealing, scumbag son would change his ways.

That wouldn't be the worst thing in the world, either. But Artemis had grown to love his work—had begun having delusions of grandeur. He'd begun to entertain thoughts of a Nobel Prize in his future, and so *Mother* had taken a back seat somewhere along the way. He hadn't lost total sight of the picture, however. Artemis was well aware his own soul was already spoken for, even if it was his own mother who'd done the speaking.

As Lucifer prepared to capture Henry's soul, he paused, wondering why his thoughts in the present moment were so focused on Artemis Davies and his 'soul work.' The heir to the Council was most important right now. Henry should be his sole focus, but the dark one felt something was... off. A vague sense he'd missed something. A big something.

Lucifer stood. He looked down at Henry, then over at the commotion by the mirror. The cop and the green witch were struggling with Armand Moreland. The vampire wailed in pain, but there was something else. Every so often, Moreland emitted an auric glow. One moment it was green, the next, red. Back and forth it went. Armand Moreland looked like a man possessed.

"Because he is!" whispered Lucifer.

Somehow, the souls of Jagger Corey and Mondra Tibbets were trapped in the vampire. He'd counted them lost. But was it possible they'd escaped obliteration? Things were happening at breakneck speed, and he put that question on the back burner to concentrate on the current mystery.

He looked down at Henry once more, then thought about all the times he'd watched Artemis as he claimed another soul. There'd always been a silver filament rising from the bodies before Artemis transferred them to the flask. When Lucifer had ended Henry's life, he never saw the filament leave the body. And there was no trace of it now. So where the hell was it?

Lucifer realized, in that moment, he'd been duped.

~

"Time to go, Henry," said Wanda. "You know what to do?"

"Yes. We're gonna owe Archie a big one for this. Even if he didn't realize what he was doing," said Henry.

"Things sometimes have a way of working out, sweetie. See you on the other side."

Henry winked. "You bet." And then he was gone.

Wanda thought she felt a change in him. His spirit seemed lighter—like the Henry she'd always known. It made her wonder what *had* happened to Jagger Corey as he'd slipped under the surface of the mirror when Byron knocked his teeth out.

Wanda had one thing left to do. She sent a thought to Mercy. "Keep that channel open, sweetie. Or I'm gonna be room temperature permanently."

Her message was met with silence.

"I HAVE TO GO, PROFESSOR," said Jamal Khalid. "Do not let go of the athame. Not for one second."

"What? Where are you going?" asked a stunned Archie.

"Mercy Glass is in trouble. The Obsidian Witch has risen."

"Who the hell is the Obsidian Witch?" yelled Archie as the door closed.

CLAIRE DAVIES NEEDED something to break the door's glass with. She stepped back into the corridor from the reception area outside of Archie's office, then scanned it from one end to the other. Her eyes fell upon a small fire extinguisher hanging on the wall ten feet from where she stood. The Obsidian Witch hobbled toward it, then unlatched it from its cradle. As she turned back, faint footsteps echoed from the corridor, followed by the metallic screech of a hallway door crash bar being depressed. The footsteps grew louder, and she halted at the entrance, risking a peek around the corner. When she saw Jamal Khalid heading toward her, she breathed a sigh of relief.

"Mercy Glass is in that room. The door is locked," said Claire.

"That is most unfortunate. Wanda Heinze has almost returned," was Jamal's reply.

"I'm going to kill the girl and sever the connection. Heinze won't be a problem after that."

"Not a bad strategy, but I have a better idea. Why don't you join Artemis in the observatory. I can handle Mercy Glass. I'm sure Artemis will be overjoyed when he sees all his work has finally paid off, and that his beloved mother is back. When the white witch is delivered to the dark one, you can enjoy your newfound freedom with your son."

Claire looked from Jamal, to the fire extinguisher in her hands, to the door at Archie's office, and back to Jamal once more. After a moment's deliberation, and a rueful sigh, she placed the extinguisher on the floor in front of Jamal. "Perhaps that would be best. In my current physical state, I'm not sure if I could break the glass."

On the outside, Jamal smiled warmly. Claire returned his smile and lightly tapped his cheek. Inside, he collapsed with relief, and cringed at her touch.

"The elevator to the observatory is at the end of the hall and to your left." He smiled once more. "Go. Your son and freedom await."

Claire hobbled past him and toward the corridor. She stopped at the threshold. Jamal pretended not to watch her, and made a show of picking up the fire extinguisher. When he looked up, he was greeted by a hideous smile. "Thank you for all you've done, Jamal. After Mondra passed, we didn't know who to trust."

Jamal waved it off. "It was nothing. For all she did for me, I felt I owed this to her."

Claire made her way slowly down the hallway and toward the observatory elevator. It never once dawned on her the trip to the elevator was completed in total, non-glass-breaking silence.

ONCE JAMAL HEARD the elevator begin its creaky journey upward to the observatory, he tossed the extinguisher aside, then made his way to Archie's office. When he got to the door, he tried the knob and found it locked. This he expected. They'd never officially met, and for all he knew she might still consider him a threat.

Mercy remained in her seat, fixing him with a wide-eyed stare. She looked neither frightened of him, nor brimming with trust. The last thing he wanted her doing was moving from her spot. She was the white witch's link between worlds. So, he said the only thing he could think of to set her mind at ease. "Ask the professor if I can be trusted."

Mercy tilted her head, unsure what to do next or if she could trust him. Earlier, she'd believed he was helping her. At least it had seemed that way. But Claire Davies, upon his arrival, had *willingly* left. That wreaked of cooperation.

But he *had* gotten rid of the scary old bitch, and that said a lot.

Jamal put both hands together in a pleading gesture, hoping she would understand *he* was the reason she still sat at Archie's desk and still drew breath. When she closed her eyes, he breathed a sigh of relief. When she opened them once more, he knew she'd asked Archie what he wanted her to ask. The startled expression on her face said it all.

"Once you know Wanda is safe, tell the professor to head straight to the observatory. You must come as well."

Mercy nodded and smiled, then closed her eyes once more.

Jamal turned and headed for the elevator.

~

WHILE LUCIFER WAS PREOCCUPIED with the spectacle of the possessed vampire-priest, Henry Trank's soul re-entered his body. In his moment of distraction, the dark one had missed his opportunity.

Henry's essence slipped silently into the clear quartz crystal atop the handle of the gold-plated athame jutting from his belly. The bloodstone pulsed dimly in response, as if sensing his presence. Then, like a traffic light with a frayed wire, it flashed wildly.

The serendipitously donated stone from Henry's father somehow sensed life nearby, and it reached out to the spirit in the athame. Henry felt the pull.

An overwhelming sense of love, light, and forgiveness consumed him. It was the love of his parents, the love of his soulmate, Joanne, and the love of their daughter, Delilah. It was all of those and more. It was the source of all love, contained in a beautiful and fantastically bright light that was one color, and *all* colors, at the same time. Colors he'd seen with human eyes over many lifetimes, and colors he'd seen only *between* those lifetimes. And in that light, time ceased to exist.

The Light showed him all he'd ever been, and all he'd ever be. It showed him the path of his incarnations over eons, then showed him what the path looked like. Henry recognized his soul's journey traced out the lemniscate, though he'd never heard the term before. He'd always heard it called the symbol for 'infinity.' It looked like the number eight on its side.

The Light pulled him upward and outward. He felt as if he were seeing the entire universe from an impossible viewpoint, and saw the infinity symbol shape of his soul's path linked through other's like it. These belonged to the people he loved, and *theirs* linked to others. Some links in the chain gleamed, some were dull, and some were red with anger and fear. But they were all linked, and The Light somehow made him understand that all lives are connected, and in those connections, lessons are learned.

Just as quickly as he'd been shuttled by The Light to the outer edges of what he assumed was the universe, it brought him back to his body and the here and now. There was no sense of movement, no sense of being in one place and then blasted to the next, it was simply a shift in perspective.

At that moment, Henry thought of Mercy Glass. He remembered the day he met her, and how touching her hand had made him feel. There'd been power in her touch. He'd never understood the mechanics of it all; how someone who'd passed through the gates of death and returned could impart that power to others—until now. One could not travel to the undiscovered country and return unchanged.

Henry knew of stories where people with near-death experiences came back happier. They'd mentioned that the things they used to consider important—money, fame, attention, material possessions—lost their pull. They'd changed for the better. Relationships with those they loved and a deep desire for inner peace were what they now craved. And to be sure, he felt all those things too, but there was something else.

If pressed to put a name to it, he would have labeled it as

heightened perception. It was something he'd experienced when meditating, but never to *this* degree. He'd always understood that deep meditation was dipping his toe into the spiritual. This felt like *bathing* in it. He had a sneaking suspicion the magical blood coursing through his veins played a role.

As if on cue, the bloodstone flared to life on his chest. A single spot of red speckling its surface beaded up and rolled down its dark and curved side. It leached into and through the cotton of his T-shirt, contacting the blood shed by the athame. The moment it did, a bridge between life and death was created. Henry felt movement this time, but it was not the movement of a body over distance, it was the rise and fall of his chest as he breathed himself back into the three dimensional world. His heart began to beat once more, strong and true.

When he opened his eyes, a light haze of smoke hung lazily above him. Green and red light pulsed within it, reminding him of the Fourth of July fireworks display he'd gone to with Jo last summer. He was about to sit up and discover the source when he remembered there was a dagger planted firmly in his midsection. He reached for it with his left hand, grasped the hilt, and pulled it slowly free. When it was all the way out, he felt the area of the wound grow cold.

He stared down at the spot. The blood on his shirt receded, drawing itself inward and through the hole made by the gold dagger. He lifted his shirt to expose the wound, and his eyes bulged with wonder. The blood on his skin retreated into the wound, exactly as it had on his shirt, only now it glowed with flecks of healing golden light. Crimson-gold tendrils drew themselves inward, like a spider escaping danger by tucking its legs into a hole in the wall.

The wound closed, and soothing warmth spread throughout his entire being. The gash shrank to the size of a pinhead, glowed fiercely, then winked out.

No scar. No blood. No pain.

Miraculous.

Henry Trank, risen from the dead, trained his gaze on the man in black.

CHAPTER 28
MIRRORLAND

As Henry stood ready to face Lucifer, Wanda's soul entered the twin to Henry's athame on the other side of Salem. At the same moment, the door to the observatory creaked open.

Artemis turned at the sound. Light from the hallway assaulted the darkness, and he shielded his eyes until they adjusted. When they did, the wispy silhouette of his mother darkened the rectangle of light. Long, white, frizzy hair framed her head. Backlit by fluorescent light, she reminded him of Medusa, if Medusa had stuck her finger in a light socket. Claire's shadow stretched for him, bathing him in darkness. The crown of her head covered his heart.

In a shaky, awestruck voice he croaked, "Mother."

Mercy felt the awesome and sublime power of Wanda's soul approaching the observatory. It passed through her body, then shot downward toward Archie and the athame.

After it did, she decided caution was best. She'd already contacted him once telepathically tonight, proving he had some residual powers left over from their time out in Satan's Kingdom, but this was too important to leave to chance. Mercy pulled out her iPhone and tapped Archie's name. He answered on the first ring.

"Mercy?" asked a confused Archie.

"No time for chit chat. You need to get that athame up to the observatory right now. Wanda's life depends on it."

"Already on my way," said Archie.

"Be careful. The Obsidian Witch is up there. Jamal is on his way right now. I'll meet you there."

Mercy heard Archie's shoes and the huffing of his breath as he clacked his way to the elevator. In a breathy voice, he asked, "Who the hell is this Obsidian Witch? Jamal mentioned her too."

"It's Artemis's mother. She—"

Mercy stopped talking as she heard Archie draw a shocked breath. "You mean the one I just saw in the lab? That woman was practically dead!"

"I'm pretty sure she's not, anymore. Or never was. And I'm pretty sure we're talking about the same person," said Mercy. Through her phone she heard the elevator doors slide open. "I'll see you up there. Shut your phone off, Arch. I'll do the same. I'll be waiting for you up there."

"Why don't you just go up with me?" asked Archie.

"Because I'm already on the fifth floor. I took the stairs. Now kill your phone."

"Okay. See you soon."

"And Archie?"

"Yes?"

"I'll need the athame."

"Are you sure? Jamal was very clear about—"

"I need you to trust me on this one. I'm going with my gut."

After a short pause, he said, "Okay."

Before pocketing her phone, she noted the time. 3:18 a.m. Henry and Wanda had been dead for five minutes. Mercy switched it off. Thirty seconds later, she was on the eighth floor. Before she went through the door, she took off her Reebok's and set them aside, then slowly depressed the crash bar and prayed it didn't squeak.

JAZZ WORKED her way through the hazy, crystalline fog of what she would come to call *Mirrorland,* letting the green and red flashes ahead guide her. She wasn't sure what was happening to Moreland, but after the sinister laughter and his cry of pain, she made an educated guess; somehow, Mondra and Jagger were a part of this place.

Jagger's presence she understood. She'd seen him sink through its surface when Byron knocked his lights out. His corpse was either in this bizarre place somewhere... or dissolved by it.

Mondra was another matter.

Joanne had killed the Red Witch, and had watched her body shrivel to ash and collapse. Moreland had taken care of the cleanup. At least, that's what he'd told them. Jazz wondered how much of that was actually true. Even though she'd come to love and trust the vampire, she knew he kept his cards close to the vest.

"Damn you, Jeevesy," she whispered. "What have you gone and done?"

Ten more steps led to an answer. Jazz was unsure how she'd come upon it so fast—judging time and space in this alien terrain was proving next to impossible—but she stood at the end of the tunnel. An all-too-familiar oblong opening wavered before her. On the other side Jo, Byron, and Moreland looked like dance partners in a frantic underwater ballet. Beyond them, at the far end of a room she now recognized, were the shapes of two men.

On the right was Henry Trank. Despite the wavy, waterlike surface of the portal before her, she could see his aura clear as day. It was about ten times brighter blue than normal, but familiar all the same.

The other she recognized not by appearance... but by energy alone. Such a pure and powerfully evil energy permeated everything. Jazz first noticed it the moment she'd opened the door and invited Byron into her shop. Byron was as rock-steady as they came. Not much scared him. So when she'd sensed the underlying fear the Chief of the Salem Police felt, inviting him in and then guiding him to her safe room was a no-brainer.

Luci and Fermina knew about Byron—not just from his closeness to Jo, but also because *Byron* was the one who'd brought Henry to Wanda's parking lot when he was on the verge of transforming into Jagger Corey. Byron *always* figured shit out. They also knew Byron had somehow found a way out of Jagger's basement after being chained to the wall. Against all odds, he'd come through. So, naturally, they saw Byron as a formidable threat.

Jazz figured they, or now more rightly, Lucifer, would try to take Byron out of the picture early. When the tarot card gashed his finger, she saw it for what it was—a warning to keep away, of course, but it was also a vulgar display of power. Lucifer couldn't resist showing off—it was how *he'd* rolled since the book of Genesis, probably longer. Except he'd stupidly, and blatantly, done it in front of her face. Jazz took it as a disrespectful taunt. In that moment, she'd decided payback was needed.

The potion was something she used on rare occasions, and in the most serious cases. Byron was brave enough to face down just about anything on his own, including a sloppy kiss from a demon. So putting the potion into his bloodstream was like giving steroids to The Terminator. She *knew* Lucifer would try and mess with his mind, and that he'd probably use Joanne to do it. The dark one had a history, after all. Jazz just wasn't sure how it might go down, but she'd had her suspicions.

And been proved correct.

Always trust your gut, she thought as she edged closer to the mirror.

Then there was the matter of Jagger's corruption of Henry's soul. By fortifying Byron, she'd killed two birds with one stone. Jo was now protected from Henry's growing temper, *and* she had someone watching her back when it came to Lucifer—because Jazz knew from moment *one* Jo wouldn't hesitate to take on the Prince of Darkness to save her husband. Jo was tough, and she could defend herself, but the man she loved was going off the rails. Jo was too close to see it, but Jazz gambled Byron would.

At the present moment, Jazz was overwhelmed with relief. Her instincts to protect her friends had payed off in a big way.

Entering the mirror, however, had *never* been in her plans for tonight. She'd only gone to Moreland's because she knew something was seriously wrong with Wanda, and figured his connections to the Council might come in handy.

That thought made her pause. Wanda Heinze did nothing without purpose. She might fly by the seat of her pants sometimes, but there was always a solid reason behind it.

So what was it?

Jazz almost jumped out of her skin when she got an answer.

"Because I needed to die tonight, sweetie."

"Wanda?"

"It's me. And there's not much time now, so listen up."

"All ears, crazy lady."

"Lucifer came back to claim Henry Trank's soul. Henry was dead until—"

"Henry's alive. I'm looking right at him, Wanda."

"How can you be looking at him?"

"I went to Count Chocula's house tonight to see if he knew what was up with you. He wasn't home. But I found his mirror. I'm in it now."

"You're what?"

"I followed him into that mirror he had us bless at your shop. Not sure why he—"

"Oh, no!" said Wanda. *"He's trying to protect me. I knew I shouldn't have said anything, but I felt I had no choice."*

"Well, whatever he had planned, it went sideways," said Jazz.

"In what way?"

"Jagger Corey and the Red Witch have possessed him. What's left of them was hiding out here in Mirrorland. I've got to go help them, Wanda."

"No, honey. Don't. Stay where you are. Henry will take care

of it. If Armand needs to escape, the mirror is where he'll go. I'm guessing he'll be in pretty bad shape."

Jazz was about to argue and thought better of it. Wanda was genius-level smart, and her instincts were almost always spot on. She sent her thoughts back to Wanda one final time. *"Okay, I'll hang tight. Now what's this business about you having to die tonight? I leave you alone for five minutes and you up and die on me?"*

"When this is all over, you'll know everything. I have to go now, sweetie. I've got a witch to catch."

In the blink of an eye, Wanda was gone.

Jazz fought every instinct she had to plunge through the mirror. She didn't realize how close she was to the surface, however, until Henry caught her eye. From behind Lucifer, Henry put up a hand and made a back off gesture. Jazz took the hint, stepping back a few feet. Henry nodded, smiled, and winked. His calm amazed her. He mouthed the words *'be ready.'*

"You bet your sweet ass I'm ready!" thought Jazz.

For the second time in two minutes, Jazz almost jumped out of her skin. Because the next thing she heard was, *"Never doubted it."*

It was Henry Trank's voice in her mind. Just like Wanda's.

Jazz leaned forward just enough so Henry could see her shocked face through the mirror. He batted his eyebrows twice. *"How you like me now?"*

She stepped back out of site. A smile played at her lips. *"Showoff!"*

All was silent for a few moments, then Henry spoke once more in her mind.

"Shit's about to get real."

CHAPTER 29
PLAN B

Vampires are strong. Jo and Byron were finding out the hard way.

When Moreland came through the mirror he was flailing and screaming in pain. Byron and Jo's first instinct was to simply help him any way they could. The moment they approached, he went from being in pain, to being in pain *and* enraged at the site of them.

"Great!" Jo said to Byron as they advanced on Moreland. "First the Devil, now the pissed off vampire from Hell."

"Yep," said Byron. "The bonus plan. I always knew I was God's favorite." He waited a beat. Out of the side of his mouth, he asked, "Any chance you can blast him with some of that green shit?"

"Not a chance. I don't think he's alone. It might make things worse."

They were right in front of Moreland now. His flailing ceased for a moment, the muscles in his face spasmed as the man inside fought for control. He looked directly at Jo. "It's Mondra and Jagger. Get me on the ground. Now!"

His eyes clouded once more—a green and red storm.

Jo made the first move, trusting Byron to figure out it was only a diversion so he could seize one of Moreland's arms. She moved in on Armand's right side, feigning a grab at his wrist and shoulder. He lunged for her, and Jo quickly danced out his reach.

"Bitch!" screamed Moreland in Mondra's voice. "I'm gonna rip those green eyes from your head!"

The spirits controlling the vampire hadn't yet gained full control of his body. Their attempt at Jo was awkward and uncoordinated, and they stumbled. Byron moved fast. As soon as Jo was out of Moreland's reach, he made the same move as Jo, only it wasn't a feint. The Chief clamped his left hand around the vampire's left wrist, then he moved with lightning speed and slapped his right hand to the shoulder blade of the stumbling vampire.

Jagger's voice snarled out of Moreland. "I should have carved your fucking eyes out when I had the chance!"

Byron yanked the wrist violently and pulled it up and behind Armand's back as he'd done hundreds of times arresting bad guys.

Jo recovered her balance, and was turning to help Byron when something stopped her cold. At first, she couldn't believe her eyes. She knew Lucifer had been hurt, and watched as he stood up slowly. This wasn't what shocked her. She'd expected that, at some point.

Her husband standing behind the Prince of Darkness, healed, smiling, and holding a gold dagger in his hands that —moments ago—protruded from his dead body... well, that would have pretty much stopped anyone in their tracks.

Lucifer believed she was looking at *him*, and naturally assumed she was in awe of his quick recovery. He smiled and limped toward her. "You didn't actually think something as simple as a bullet would end this, did you?"

Henry put a finger to his lips. Jo kept her eyes trained on Lucifer but caught the gesture.

Byron was still wrestling with Moreland, fighting a losing battle to keep the vampire pinned. "Jo? I could use a little help here." As the last word left Byron's lips, Armand Moreland pushed himself, and the two hundred-twenty pound Chief of the Salem police, up from the floor. Byron kept Moreland's left arm pinned, then swung his right around the vampire's chest, hanging on for dear life as the vampire pushed them upright.

Jo came out of her semi trance, breaking eye contact with Lucifer. She assessed the situation in an instant. Priority one was getting the vampire under control. She whirled around, just as Moreland was preparing to rise fully. Jo took two steps forward, dropped to one knee, and swept her left leg into the calves of the vampire. There was a double grunt as over four hundred pounds of men hit the floor.

Behind them, Lucifer clapped. "Excellent. I always knew you were a badass, Jo. But that was impressive. I—"

His voice cut off so sharply it caused Jo, Byron, and even the flailing vampire to freeze on the floor. When the three looked up, they saw Henry standing directly behind Lucifer. One arm was wrapped around the dark one's chest, the other was at his neck. The dagger threatened, appropriately enough, under his Adam's apple.

Lucifer at once appeared scared, angry, and surprised. Strangest of all, he seemed physically diminished. As if something sapped the energy from the body he'd chosen to possess. Like someone had pulled the plug on him.

"Where did you get that?" asked Lucifer. The tremor of fear in his voice was unmistakable.

"From my stomach," said Henry. "Short memory, asshole?"

"No. The blood of Calvary. I can feel it. I can feel *Him!* It burns!"

"Oh, that," said Henry, looking down at the Bloodstone hanging between them. "That was a gift from my thankfully forgetful father, courtesy of Armand Moreland. Doesn't tickle, I'm guessing?"

Lucifer's breath was labored. He was rapidly weakening, and Henry tightened his grip around the man's chest. "Let me go witch. I'll grant you anything. *Just let me go!*"

"You know, you seem a lot less cocky all of a sudden," chided Henry. He tightened his grip on the athame, pulling it tighter against Lucifer's neck. A trickle of blood oozed toward the collar of his black suit. Blue fire danced in Henry's eyes, and he pushed his chest harder against Lucifer's back, grinding the Bloodstone into his spine. A legion of cries roared from the possessed man's body. Henry ignored his pain and pleas, forcing him a few steps closer to Moreland, Jo, and Byron. As he approached, he felt a sudden urge to cut the man's throat. It showed on his face.

Moreland was pinned to the floor with all of Byron's weight on his back. "Do it!" screamed Moreland with Mondra's voice. "Gut him like a fucking fish!"

Jo stood up slowly from the floor, then raised both hands, palms out. "That's not *his* body, Henry. Don't."

The image of this man cupping Jo's ass, and then winking at him, flashed through Henry's mind. Rage and jealousy roiled his insides, and he dug the athame a fraction deeper. Blood oozed across the suit's collar, staining the white shirt and matching the man's crimson tie perfectly.

In the next moment, it was Jagger's voice. "He's a pussy. He'll never do it. Henry the fucking Boy Scout!"

That made Henry stop. They were less than ten feet from Jo. She stepped slowly around Byron and Moreland on the floor, her hands still raised. "They're trying to goad you, Henry. You're not a killer. If you do it, you're giving him what he wants. This is about your soul. It's always been about *your* soul."

Henry knew something was off. The closer he got to the vampire and the polluted souls within, the brighter red his anger grew. Every inch gained pushed him toward violence, toward Jagger Corey and the pull of his malignant ego. The ego they'd once shared.

Even in his weakened state, Henry realized, Lucifer was still manipulating him.

He looked once more to his wife, and her beautiful green eyes. Eyes he'd traveled through *time* with. The only eyes on earth capable of showing him the truth about himself without a word spoken. They shattered his budding rage, stopping it, and him, where he stood.

In a lightning flash of insight, Henry saw the whole of the last few days for what they *truly* were: the baiting on the street, Lucifer grabbing his wife obscenely, the 'fight' with Jo that had forced him from the apartment and back onto the street, the draw of this place earlier tonight as he piloted the Camry aimlessly around town—a town which was, coincidentally, emptied of cars due to a budding pandemic—pulling him here like a magnet, the letter and the visions following it, resulting in the mention of Wanda's name, which had gotten the whole thing rolling.

Each event, taken separately, *seemed* random. Taken together, however, they had pointed Henry exactly where Lucifer wanted him.

It seemed improbable, if not impossible. Until he realized how deeply Luci and Fermina had been entrenched in the lives of Jo and Mercy and Jazz. When he thought about it that way, it seemed—pardon the pun—likely as Hell. They *knew* how tight Henry and Jo were. They knew what Jazz was capable of, and they understood how Mercy's power worked. Gemini, the 'twins,' were first-person puppets, controlled by him. He used their bodies as the military might use a drone to gather intel on the adversary. Much like that drone, they were expendable when the mission was complete. Given all that, and coupled with Wanda's revelation that he was part of some 'prophecy,' it made sense. Though the whole prophecy thing eluded him at the moment.

Did Lucifer know about the spirits in the mirror? Did he know they were there the whole time?

Henry decided he did.

So then what of Moreland? Why had the vampire gone into the mirror? He *had* to have known Jagger and Mondra were there. Henry knew Armand had taken the mirror to Wanda's to have it blessed, Jo had told him as much. *This shouldn't be happening.* Unless something had gone wrong, maybe?

There's no way of knowing right now, he thought.

Lucifer felt Henry's indecision. He felt the pressure of the athame lessen ever-so-slightly, and the grip around his midsection wane. This, for him, was both good and bad. The pressure and searing holiness of The Bloodstone became slightly less unbearable, but it also signaled a flagging of

Henry's resolve. He needed the witch of the prophecy to kill *this* human vessel, for if Henry spilled the blood of the innocent, he would never command the Council of the Realms. It wasn't what he'd planned for when the night's festivities began, but as a backup plan, it would do.

The only thing Lucifer was completely sure of, no matter what happened from this moment forward, was the vampire would die. No being, aside from one like himself, could house two souls at the same time. Armand Moreland would cease to exist in short order. Mondra and Jagger would tear him apart from the inside out. And then the fun would really begin.

Henry's grip loosened a bit more, and Lucifer made his move.

CHAPTER 30
THE MOON, THE STARS, AND THE DAMNED

Artemis trembled at the sight of his mother, and felt chilled in her shadow—a feeling he'd grown used to. He loved her dearly, but it was a love couched in fear. The result? Blind obedience.

In the days she'd been closest to death, he couldn't imagine life without her, but he was never quite sure which emotion drove him. In the end, he decided it was love—regardless of the deal she'd consummated with Lucifer for their souls. He'd moved heaven and earth since, supplying her with the souls needed to sustain her physical body. Never realizing, or caring, that each of those souls had a destination—and that once removed from the continuum, they would be missed.

But forces, both light and dark, *had* noticed.

Waiting for Mother to arrive in the observatory, Artemis spent his time thinking. His thoughts settled on something he'd seen earlier tonight, and it had to do with Jamal Khalid.

When he'd entered the lab classroom with Wanda Heinze in tow, the last thing he'd expected was Doctor

Archibald Love to be in the room with the barely alive body of his mother. For one ball-shriveling moment, he thought the professor might have killed her. Had that been the case, he would have dropped Heinze where she stood, then used the rest of the toxin on Love. Once he realized the professor was just snooping, he forced him from the room with the help of the ever-ready Jamal.

As Doctor Love backed out of the room, Artemis had kept pace with him, catching sight of Jamal as he'd opened the door. The kid stepped inside just enough for Artemis to see he wore only a long-sleeved T-shirt due to the unusually warm weather. Almost every time he'd seen him before tonight, the boy had worn one of those North Face jackets with the collar turned up, so he'd never noticed the strange tattoo on his neck. Until tonight.

A black number eight, lying on its side, sat roughly two inches below Jamal's left ear . Nothing *too* strange about that. Just about every young person he saw these days had some sort of tattoo or piercing.

As he'd continued to wait for Mother, Artemis closed his eyes and brought the scene to mind once more. There was something about the tattoo, upon further reflection, that just didn't sit right with him. Its borders were ragged. There was a slight non-uniformity to it, like Jamal had hired the world's worst tattoo artist.

But... that wasn't it. It wasn't the lack of artistry that bothered him. The tattoo *itself* had made him uneasy. There was a phantom familiarity in its shape, but he couldn't place it. Artemis squeezed his eyes tighter shut and pinched the bridge of his nose, as if he could wring the answer from his mind.

Where have I seen that fucking tattoo? On the heels of that question, another possibility hit him. What if it wasn't a tattoo at all? The thing *looked* like a half-assed prison tattoo. Shit, he'd seen better ones on inmate cadavers in the college morgue.

It could be a birthmark! he thought. When he allowed for *that* possibility, memories poured forth like water from a breached dam.

Jenny Love had sported the same birthmark.

When they'd killed the old woman and thought they'd captured her soul, he'd felt moved to offer her one final moment of dignity by closing her eyes, but when he'd laid his left hand on her eyelids, he'd felt something odd—a raised patch of flesh on Jenny Love's left eyelid. Stealing a glance at Mondra and Jagger to make sure they weren't watching, he'd stood quickly for a peek. It was a ragged number eight lying on its side.

Exactly like Jamal's.

The dam was gushing now, its unstoppable flow bringing another memory with it.

The video.

On the night they'd ended the old woman's life and captured her soul, they'd been too impressed with themselves to consider failure. It wasn't until Artemis watched the tape that final time that he'd realized what had happened. At the time, however, he hadn't considered the implications. Now, he did.

When the VCR malfunctioned, it froze on the *only* frame containing Jennifer Love's fleeing life force. But no matter how many times he rewound and fast-forwarded afterward, he could never make the tape stop at that exact spot again, so he'd chalked it up as an anomaly. But it wasn't.

Every ounce of intuition screamed a simple truth. Jenny Love had escaped.

The wispy silver filament of her soul had *never* entered the flask.

So what does that have to do with Jamal? he asked himself.

Beauty eternal will help you from the shadows.

The clue written on the index card! It dawned on him he'd never actually solved the riddle. Every time before this, he'd been able to uncover the identity of his contact. It had been done that way up until the night of Jenny Love, Jagger, and the Red Witch. Once Mondra Tibbets had entered the scene, she'd been his sole contact since September of 2004.

Almost sixteen years ago.

Almost.

But Mondra was dead. The green witch named Joanne had done the deed less than a year before. Artemis had captured only two more souls since Mondra's death. Both were old men at separate nursing homes. With the Red Witch gone, both captures had been set up the old way—with the index cards. Which begged the question he'd been too blinded by his soul work to ask: Who had taken over choosing and setting up the targets since her death?

He wasn't sure he wanted the answer... but he had his suspicions.

Until Jamal, he'd always worked out his contact's name *before* the meeting. Right *then*, he should have known something was up. Of all the contacts he'd ever had, including initial contact with the Red Witch, Jamal was the *only one* who'd ever revealed himself first.

When he'd been approached by the kid, it surprised him. Jamal was extremely young, for starters. The boy had mentioned being a student at the university. Artemis thought that odd, but child prodigies *were* a thing. When Artemis asked him how old he was, Jamal had said, "Almost sixteen years old."

Almost sixteen.

It had rung a faint bell at the time, but he'd let it slide because the end was in sight. Heinze would most likely be the last in a long and winding trail of souls, and orders were orders—how they were delivered, and by whom, seemed unimportant now. The translation of Jamal's name had matched the cryptic clue on the index card. It checked out. He'd dropped the matter.

Artemis's eyes popped open, and he trembled at the implications. "It can't be," he whispered, just before his mother had opened the doors to the observatory.

His mind snapped to the present. Though her eyes were hidden in shadow, he felt their probing chill. Artemis was almost sure she couldn't read minds, but he pushed thoughts of Jamal Kahlid way down deep, just to be safe.

He'd been expecting her, of course, but the meeting came much sooner than anticipated. When he croaked out her name, the silhouette of her head tilted. "You seem surprised to see me, Artemis. Is everything alright?"

A weak "Yes" was all he could manage.

"You don't sound very confident, my son. Is there something you're not telling me?"

He thought, *you don't know the half of it*, but said, "No. The white witch is dead. Her soul is in here." Artemis withdrew the crystal flask from his lab coat and held it up for her to see. It instantly bathed his body, and the stilled body of Wanda Heinze on the table next to him, in shimmering silver-blue light.

Claire's head straightened, and she uttered a satisfied "Ahhhh." She ambled forward. By rights, she shouldn't have been able to walk at all, given she hadn't used her legs since the first Clinton administration, but the rejuvenating power of stolen souls went further than skin deep; it penetrated to the bone.

Step by creaky step, she drew closer. The Obsidian Witch smiled savagely, her scraggly, too-big-for-her-mouth teeth reflected the flask's silver blue light. Fear dried Artemis's mouth. His throat clicked as he swallowed. The flask trembled slightly in his hand, and he wondered what Mother might do when she took hold of it and realized Wanda Heinze's soul was nowhere to be found.

MERCY CREPT to the elevator and waited. It didn't take long. The doors dinged softly open, and she prayed the sound hadn't carried the length of the hall and through the closing doors to the observatory. As Archie stepped through, Mercy held a finger to her lips, then beckoned him to follow.

ARTEMIS LOOKED beyond his mother and toward the doors closing behind her.

"What was that?" he asked.

Claire waived a hand dismissively. "It's the elevator. Jamal Kahlid is on his way."

Artemis's eyes went wide with fear, and Claire noticed. "There *is* something wrong. What aren't you telling me, Artemis?"

. . .

MERCY OPENED the door to the the stairwell, and waved Archie in. She extended a hand, and Archie—reluctantly—placed the athame in it.

"What comes next?" he asked.

"Is there another way into the observatory?"

Archie thought about it for a moment. "The roof. There's a maintenance entrance for the telescope, but it's most likely locked."

Mercy turned for the stairs, but Archie grabbed her arm before she could get going. "What the hell are you doing?" he shout-whispered.

"I can't very well go walking in through the front door, Arch. I'll have to find my way in from up there," she said, pointing toward the stairs leading to the roof.

"I just told you, it's locked!"

Mercy shrugged. "*Most likely*, said you. Not definitely. I'll take my chances. But I've got to go. Now!"

Archie released her, and Mercy bounded up the steps two at a time.

ARTEMIS LOOKED AT HIS SHOES, the ceiling, the opening where the telescope spied on the universe—anywhere he could to avoid his mother's gaze. She reached out, resting a hand on his cheek. Her touch was cold and dry, like a reanimated corpse fresh from the morgue drawer. Claire squeezed his chin between her thumb and forefinger, pulling his face even with hers. When he drew up enough courage, he raised his eyes. Her face glowed with the light of the flask, but her eyes were dark and malevolent pools.

In that moment, Artemis thought about something he'd heard long ago.

The eyes are the windows to the soul.

As he stared into the eyes of his mother, he realized the windows were dark because all light had long since died. Claire Davies still drew breath, but it was merely fuel for the furnace of a blackened heart.

And in the next moment, he knew he was damned. Her empty, dead soul had no room. It was filled with self. The only soul on the bargaining block was his own, and always had been.

Claire smiled.

Artemis felt like Little Red Riding Hood.

MERCY STEPPED into the open dome of the observatory. She'd already tried the maintenance shed, finding it locked as Archie'd feared. The new approach was far riskier, but she had no choice.

The moon was bright, and she hid her shadow from the floor below by keeping her body in line with the barrel of the telescope. A few feet ahead, she saw a metal staircase at the end of a short catwalk. She was glad she'd left her sneakers in the stairwell with Archie, for stealth was the watchword of the moment.

Artemis, and his living zombie of a mother, talked quietly on the floor below. Behind them, Wanda lay still on a gurney. As Mercy drew closer, the athame tucked into the small of her back grew warmer. When she reached the stairs, she heard Wanda's voice in her mind. *"Not yet."*

Mercy ducked low, then shuffled a few feet over and hid behind a file cabinet. *"What am I waiting for?"* she thought back at Wanda.

"The answer is in the stars," was Wanda's reply.

Mercy looked up, toward the opening in the dome, and waited.

CHAPTER 31
OUT OF THE BLUE

Lucifer felt the pressure from behind ease a fraction more. It was enough. His strength surged, he shot his head forward hoping the athame would do the rest of the work, mortally wounding the vessel he occupied. But it was not to be. When he lunged, he felt cool air on the warm blood of his neck... nothing more. He whirled and saw Henry had retreated, the gold dagger at the ready.

"I see there's still something of Jagger left in you after all. Saw that one coming pretty quickly, eh?"

Henry smiled.

Lucifer didn't like that smile. No, not one bit. There was *confidence* in that smile. *Knowledge*. In a witch who'd touched *The Light*, that was bad news.

"If there *is* anything left from that scumbag," said Henry, "I'd say I got the juicy bits. Whaddaya think?"

Lucifer was about to reply when he looked sharply left. From the shadows of the reading nook, two huge, gleaming yellow eyes suddenly appeared, and a screech like a giant's fingernails scraping down a chalkboard tore through the room.

Lucifer noticed Henry never moved—didn't so much as flinch. Instead, the sapphire witch spread his arms wide. The gleaming eyes streaked from the darkness. A massive Snow Owl made a beeline for Henry's chest and plucked the Bloodstone from it without slowing. The owl banked hard over the prone cop and vampire, then buzzed by Lucifer's head, causing him to dive for the floor to avoid the Bloodstone. Eljin Black's owl form streaked through the broken nook window and into the night.

Beyond the window came a screech of triumph—already echoing and distant. In that moment, Lucifer understood the only part of Jagger remaining in Henry Trank was the ability to glimpse the future, if only slightly ahead of events. He'd retained the powers from Jagger's practice of Scapulimancy —only without the need to harm a living being. Henry's encounter with The Light had burned away the darkness inherent in Jagger's ability, leaving behind only the benefit.

Lucifer realized maybe *that* had been the real point all along. And that maybe... just maybe, he was never *really* in control from the start. Maybe *he* was the one being used.

Pride goeth before the fall.

Lucifer was desperate now. His carefully laid plans were woefully off the tracks. With Henry's heightened abilities, the only advantage he had was space, and quickness. He seized the opportunity. Henry saw it coming, but realized his disadvantage instantly—distance. Before he could stop it, Lucifer dropped down on his good knee, and in an eerie echo of Jo's takedown of Moreland, he swung his damaged leg at Jo's calves. She hit the floor hard, the wind knocked from her body in a painful grunt. Lucifer, ignoring the injuries to his borrowed body, scrambled over her like Regan MacNeil, the possessed girl from *The Exorcist*, pinned her arms to the floor with his knees, and clamped a hand over her throat.

"You kill *me* or I'll kill *her*," said Lucifer. The right side of his mouth curled upward in a triumphant sneer. "Ironic, don't you think? Not even two minutes ago there was our JoJo, saving my ass from your little dagger." He looked down at Jo, mock shame on his face. "I know this may *look* like a lack of gratitude on my part—me ready to snap her neck and all—but she really should have kept her trap shut."

Lucifer squeezed. Jo fought, her legs flailing. She tried to buck him off, but her upper body was pinned hard.

Henry closed his eyes, raised the dagger, then moved forward.

Lucifer relaxed the grip on her neck, and Jo sucked in a great gasp of air.

"GIVE IT TO ME, ARTEMIS!" Claire lowered her hand from Artemis's face, turned it over, and held it out expectantly. Long, cracked fingernails glowed blue in the light from the flask. A greedy smile crossed her face like that of a spoiled child on Christmas morning, exposing teeth that were at once crooked, huge, and strangely wolf-like in her gaunt and shrunken face. A rotting soul turned inside out—the fruit of polluted soil.

In that instant, Artemis realized his only salvation was denying her the flask. Once relinquished, he was as good as dead. He took two steps backward, turned, and placed the flask on the metal table next to Wanda.

"What are you doing?" asked the Obsidian Witch.

"What I should have done a long time ago," replied Artemis.

As he had so many years ago, he put their fate in the hands of the white witch. Only this time, he knew *exactly* what he was doing.

~

MERCY KEPT a watchful eye on the openings at either side of the telescope. The night was bright, and stars twinkled fiercely. Suddenly, on the left side of the telescope, a few vanished... and then a few more. A shadow swelled.

As the heavenly eclipse grew, a shape formed within the cluster of stars. It looked birdlike, and huge. Almost all the stars were gone now. Taking their place were twin orbs of fire, growing as they headed straight for her. The owl swooped low, riffling her hair and making a beeline towards Wanda, Artemis, and the evil-looking old woman.

Remembering Wanda's words, Mercy sprang from her spot. She stood just in time to watch the biggest Snow Owl she'd ever seen pull up short, hover over Wanda, and drop something on her chest. In a moment of manic absurdity Mercy covered her mouth, stifling a laugh. It looked like the owl had dropped a massive turd on her friend.

It hadn't.

The moment it landed, brilliant sapphire light flooded the entire observation area. The jewel on the athame's hilt began pulsing in her hand... like a newly beating heart.

Mercy sprinted for the table. As she drew closer, the owl hovered between Wanda and the others. It spread its wings wide in protection, unleashing a thunderous screech, reminding Mercy of the T-Rex from *Jurassic Park*.

The force of it propelled Artemis forward, and she watched him crash into the evil-looking old witch. They were sent sprawling.

She was only a few feet from Wanda. The gemstone on the hilt beat faster. The blueish light on the far side of Wanda grew brighter with every stride. When Mercy reached her, she instinctively placed the hilt of the athame over Wanda's heart, and then stepped back. She watched as the owl's wings swooshed in time with it, beating faster with every passing moment.

All at once, the athame, the flask, and the Bloodstone burst in a dazzling display of light. Overwhelmed, Mercy fell to her knees, startled to feel tears of joy streaking her face. She cried not only for the return of her treasured friend and mentor, but for the utter and boundless love contained in the light bathing the room.

Wanda gasped deeply, and sat up. Mercy shot to her feet, and was immediately at her side undoing her bindings. When Wanda smiled at her, Mercy felt as if her heart might explode with happiness. She went to hug her friend, the glorious white witch, but Wanda held up a hand. Mercy halted as Wanda leaned to her right, then brought the crystal flask to rest on her lap and pulled the stopper from its top.

Tendrils of sparkling silver light sprang from the flask, reaching out for the light they'd been denied for years. They swirled about the room, dashing happily in all directions, like a pod of dolphins freshly released from captivity and into the wide-open sea. Much like that pod, they were attuned to imminent danger. Sensing an enemy near, they quickly closed ranks. Moving as one, they streaked toward the floor and engulfed Artemis and his mother. They coalesced into a ball of righteous fury, thrashing the bodies of the Obsidian Witch and her hapless son.

"Forgive me! Forgive me!" screamed Artemis as he flailed on the floor, his arms and legs kicking wildly at the air. His mind flashed to the picture of Jesus on the stairway in Jenny Love's house. Something deep within, on that long-ago stairway, had begged him to stop. But unlike the transformation of Paul on the road to Damascus, he'd ignored his soul's call—and now the bill had come due. Silver tendrils criss-crossed his body, dashing in and out at random points, claiming his soul piece by piece.

Claire Davies did *not* beg for forgiveness. Instead, the Obsidian Witch fought for all she was worth, uttering curses and unleashing black bolts of malignant energy in every direction. Wanda and Mercy ducked several times as Claire's dark, magick-fueled rage barely missed them, while countless other attacks were absorbed by the Snow-Owl-form of Eljin Black. The old and powerful witch fought on another level, and she meant business. Though her barrage was furious, the wrath of the wronged soon overwhelmed her. The energy drained quickly from her overtaxed and frail body.

The blue and silver and black fireworks of the previous moments winked out. The owl ceased flapping its massive wings, its talons clicking softly on the floor as it landed. Artemis and Claire were stilled, and the observatory went silent and dark. Wanda and Mercy held their breath, watched, and waited.

They felt it before seeing it. A low hum filled the room. It rattled the fillings in their teeth, and vibrated in their bones. Wanda felt goosebumps break out all over her body, and as Mercy reached for her, Wanda felt them on the back of her friend's hand.

The humming died. A ball of sparkling silver light emerged from the body of Claire first, and then Artemis. At the center of each was a black smudge that could only be the dark masses of their forsaken souls. Together, twin silver orbs moved silently towards the crystal flask. The one containing the essence of Artemis dove quickly into the flask, exiting in the same fashion. The one containing the Obsidian Witch followed in kind. Wanda dropped Mercy's hand, grabbed the flask, then jammed the stopper home. The top of the flask rattled, and the stopper almost came free as the damned and blackened souls within fought to escape. Wanda almost dropped it. Mercy moved to catch it but Wanda recovered quickly, wrapping it in her hands like a child clutching a souvenir baseball.

"Help me down please, Mercy."

Mercy stepped in front of Wanda, whose legs dangled over the edge of the metal table and a foot from the floor. She put a hand under each armpit, lifted her, then placed her on her feet.

"I better get a height upgrade in the next life," said Wanda, smiling.

Mercy laughed softly, then asked, "What comes next?"

"This," said Wanda. She pulled a black velveteen pouch from her robe pocket and laid it on the metal table. She said, "Hold this, please," then handed the blackened crystal flask to Mercy.

Mercy's eyes widened with shock. "Oh, my God! It's so cold!"

"No surprise there," said Wanda. "Those two are about as close to demons as it gets."

Mercy nodded, but said nothing. All her concentration was on the flask and Wanda.

Wanda opened the pouch, slid the athame inside, and turned to Mercy.

"Henry is at Jagger's shop. Lucifer is there. If what I think is going to happen does, he's going to need this athame." She closed the bag and set it aside, then focused on the flask. "Now, hold it steady and with both hands, sweetie. This might get interesting."

Wanda closed her eyes, and began an incantation.

"Souls once lost but now unbound,
return to The Light, your home is found."

As the last word left her lips, the sparkling spheres hovering over and guarding the flask in Mercy's hands eased apart, and individual souls swirled about the observatory. At the easternmost end of the room, a pinprick of light flared. It was intensely bright, but neither Mercy nor Wanda averted their eyes. For them, it held no pain.

The Light expanded. In its glow, the sparkling silver filaments of once captured souls cast shadows long and dark across the observatory floor, reaching toward Wanda and Mercy. When the witches looked up, the astral bodies of newly freed souls were now made whole by The Light. Untethered to their *earthly* bodies, they were radiant.

One by one they ascended. Each in turn smiled back at Wanda and Mercy, the intensity of their gratitude so thick, it felt almost physical to the two witches—like being wrapped in a warm blanket of ethereal bliss.

The opening widened from ceiling to floor. At its bottom, loved ones waited to greet them, and the souls of the freed became one with the the throng, and then one with The Light. As the last souls entered, the light faded. The old man from Henry's vision was last to leave. Wanda and Mercy caught his final thought before he crossed over.

Thank that young man Henry for me.

What only moments before was a feeling of joy so thick they could taste it began to fade, and as The Light winked out, it left the witches feeling whole and complete—but also longing. They'd both glimpsed The Source, and once experienced on this side of the veil, its pull would always remain.

Wanda now fully understood the things Mercy had known in her heart but could never put into words, and it would bind them forever.

Mercy spoke first. "What about these two?"

Wanda placed her hands over Mercy's, then began the incantation anew.

> **"Greed of life, greed of spirit**
> **Be gone from this plane,**
> *no more will we bear it."*

"So mote it be," they said in unison.

A brief flash of golden light surrounded their hands, and a feeling of pressure pushing down on all sides made both witches jump a little. "Must be the extra kick I got from, you know, dying and all," said Wanda.

Mercy smiled and nodded. "It does that."

"You can let go now, sweetie."

Mercy removed her hands, then reached for the black bag already containing the athame. She saw the jewel on its hilt was dark now. But *dark* wasn't the right word. It felt... empty. And Mercy wondered what might fill it before the night was over.

Wanda was about to put the flask in the black bag with

the athame, then thought better of it. Instead, she slipped it into her robe pocket.

Mercy shot her a questioning look, then let it go. Wanda always had her reasons.

"Pull the sash closed on it, please," said Wanda.

Mercy did, then handed the closed bag to Wanda, who strode a few short steps and stood before Eljin Black. The shifter flapped his wings and rose from the observatory floor.

"I'm not sure who this goes to next, Mr. Black, but be quick."

She placed the bag in his left talon, then stepped back. Eljin blinked twice, and Wanda took it as confirmation he understood. It took two powerful swoops of the shifter's massive wings and he was up and through the opening to the left of the telescope and into the night.

Behind them, the doors to the observatory opened. Archie and Jamal stepped into the room. When he saw Wanda alive and unharmed, Archie ran to her and threw his arms around her.

"Thank God!" whispered Archie, his voice thick with emotion. "I thought I lost you, you crazy old witch!"

After a moment, Wanda pulled back from him and placed her palms on his cheeks, then wiped his tears with her thumbs. "It's gonna take a little more than dying to get rid of me, Arch." She smiled at him, then lightly slapped his cheeks twice, fighting back tears of her own.

Jamal, who'd kept a frantic Archie waiting in the hall until things were settled, had also kept his distance during Archie and Wanda's reunion. He cleared his throat to draw everyone's attention. "I believe we need to head to Jagger's

Magical Treasures. There is much to be done, and no time to waste."

CHAPTER 32
POSSESSION IS NINE TENTHS

As Henry moved toward Lucifer, he tried to read what came next. When he came up with nothing, it scared him. Jo's neck was still in his hands, and Henry didn't doubt for an instant the dark one would follow through and take his wife from this world.

What the fuck good is this power if I can't use it to save her? he wondered.

In the next moment, he had his answer. It was a quick glimpse—a snippet of an image less than a second in the future. He took one step to the right and let it happen.

The shot rang out from behind him, and Lucifer's mouth formed a surprised 'O' matching the new hole in the middle of his forehead.

Henry whirled at the sound and saw a battered and bloody Raul Martinez holding the smoking gun. Raul swayed a little on his feet, then smiled. "I found this out on the street. It looked like Byron's."

Lucifer stood up slowly, then put a hand to his forehead. He pulled it away, held it at eye level, and studied it like a scientist might study a strange new species. "Well, Henry, I guess neither of us saw that one coming. Am I right?"

Henry shrugged, his body language and knowing smile suggesting he might have had some idea.

"Nobody likes a know-it-all, Henry." His last words uttered, Lucifer's surrogate body tottered towards the floor, a witless victim whose confused soul would arrive between lives utterly clueless.

Jo turned and scrambled as the body fell, knowing instinctively to be touched by it would be far worse than having her neck snapped. With what must have been the last of any strength left in the man's body, Lucifer shot an arm out in desperation as he fell, and clamped a hand around Jo's wrist. She was yanked backwards and down, her feet flying forward and away from her. She landed hard on her back, smacking her head against the floor in the process, then went still.

Henry dashed over to her.

Raul followed on unsteady legs.

Byron saw Jo fall and couldn't help his reaction. For a split second, he lost focus. It was all the possessed vampire needed. Moreland, or more correctly, his *guests*, pushed up from the floor with a mighty heave. The move, intended to gain freedom, instead drained the last of Moreland's physical energy. The vampire collapsed and lay still.

Byron was thrown backwards and towards the mirror, his back crashing hard into its frame. Momentarily stunned, he started to fall forward, but was suddenly yanked upright from behind. Pinpricks of pain dotted his upper arms. The pain made him focus. When he looked down, he saw glittering purple fingernails dug in deep against his biceps. His eyes took in the nails, the dark and toned arm, and its termination at the mirror's surface.

From behind him, Jazz whispered. "Stay focused. Let Henry handle Jo."

Byron leaned back and turned his head toward Jazz. "What do you mean *handle* Jo? She's out cold and—"

Joanne suddenly sat up. She looked quickly in all directions, like an evil lost toddler in search of her missing mommy. When her gaze finally settled, it was on Byron. Any resemblance to an innocent and bewildered child evaporated as a malicious, familiar, and mischievous grin spread wide across her face.

It's a replay of the hospital and Jenny, he thought. To Jazz, he said, "Let Henry handle Jo. Got it."

~

ELJIN BLACK LANDED on the underside of Byron's overturned Explorer. With one flap of his mighty wings, he flew through the wrecked boards of the front window, landing quietly in the middle of the lobby to Jagger's shop. He transformed into his human shape, then thought better of it. He tried to think how his master, Armand Moreland, would want him to play it, thinking about the time they'd met out in the graveyard. That night, he'd chosen to appear before the vampire as a wolf.

There was no way of telling what was going on upstairs in the room with the mirror, though he'd been gone for less than ten minutes. Stealth seemed the most sensible approach, and Eljin considered his options. When he settled on a form, he whispered, "I claim the earth."

The change was quick, smooth, and effortless. White

feathers darkened, morphing silently into dark fur. Huge wings shortened, rounding into muscular legs leading to paws tipped with sharp silver claws. Talons shrank, extending backward. Black and glossy fur sprung from rugged and scaly claws, and the talons of the owl became the hind legs of a panther.

The satchel he'd flown over from the university observatory fell to the floor with a soft *fwump!* Eljin slunk low, grasping the black velveteen bag in his huge mouth, making sure the braided yellow rope hooked around one of the fangs of his lower jaw. Now an apex predator, he darted low toward the staircase running along the wall.

As he reached the top, he lowered his powerful body to the floor, then hugged the railing to his right until he reached an area of complete shadow. That done, he turned and made his way back toward the room with the mirror, keeping fast to the curved wood beneath the nooks and out of extraneous light from the street lamps. At the nook closest to the mirror room, he dropped flat to the floor and assessed the situation in silence.

There was game to hunt in this room, and it didn't come much bigger than the Prince of Darkness. But the man Lucifer had possessed lay dead. With the heightened senses of an apex predator, he smelled the man's blood, and recognized his decaying scent.

Eljin was glad he'd chosen this form. In the silence and dark, he waited for his prey to peek its head up.

~

MICKEY SCHMIDT WAS ABOUT to close down the morgue for the night when he heard a noise coming from the autopsy room.

His private office was two doors down from the room where he did his best work, and he loathed every minute he spent in it doing paperwork. *Why can't I have a secretary do this shit?* he wondered for the thousandth time. And for the thousandth time, he shoved the thought aside. Now, something new battled for his waning attention.

What the hell was that noise?

Mickey stood up and came around his desk. He wasn't a superstitious guy, but something deep inside told him it might be a good idea to flick the fluorescents off. At the moment the office was plunged into darkness, there was a loud bang in the hallway, followed by the tinkling rain of shattered glass.

Mick's breath caught in his throat, and his pulse pounded loudly in his ears. But not loud enough to drown out the crunch of glass beneath footsteps. With sudden dread, the layout of the hallway flashed in his mind. The autopsy room was at the end of it. No door from outside of the building led into the back, and no one, other than himself, had passed through those doors in either direction since the Chief and Raul had left.

That left one horrifying and unbelievable possibility.

Mick tiptoed from the office door as fast as sound would allow, then crouched behind his desk chair. It was a gamer's chair—sleek, black, and tapered narrow along where one would rest his back. The headrest was rectangular, with a smaller rectangular cutout in the middle. Mick squatted down behind it and looked through the opening.

The marching crunch of glass drew closer, but dwindled in volume with each step taken. When it stopped, Mick ducked low and listened. He heard a soft, metallic rattle that repeated a few times, then suddenly ceased. Against every instinct for survival, he slowly rose to peek once more through the rectangle to see who was trying his doorknob... and felt his insides loosen.

Two female figures stared into his office through empty-socketed eyes. The symbol he'd shown Byron earlier pulsed red through hairlines of fine black hair. One of the girls smiled, then turned away from the door as the other stood her ground. When she returned, Mick saw she had a fire extinguisher. Luci or Fermina, Mick didn't know which, and at the present moment couldn't have given shit one, raised the extinguisher and brought it down hard against the wired glass of his office door. It spidered but held. She brought it down again, and the upper right corner of shattered glass tore loose from the frame like the edge of a used Band-Aid on an old wound. The girl... *thing*... holding the fire extinguisher tossed it aside. Mick heard it bonk against the tiled floor as the other one reached into the opening at the top, ready to tear the glass Band-Aid loose from its frame. It was halfway out when she suddenly stopped. The sheet of shattered glass flopped inward, slamming against the side closest to Mickey. Pieces of glass ticked off the floor as they flew in every direction.

Silence reigned.

Mickey held his breath. The girls—*if that's what they are,* thought Mickey—tilted their heads, as if concentrating on a sudden call in a Bluetooth earpiece. Without a glance back at Mickey through their sightless but somehow *seeing* eyes, they simply turned and walked away. He waited until he heard the door at the end of the hallway click closed. Mickey let the breath he'd been holding explode from his lungs, and walked toward the front of the office on rubbery legs, where he waited for a second door slam. When he heard it, he bolted for the hallway door, locked it, then retreated to his office.

Mickey dropped into his gaming chair, pulled a key ring from his lab coat pocket, and unlocked the bottom drawer of his desk. A closet alcoholic all his life, Mick kept a bottle on hand at home, at work, and in the trunk of his Honda, hidden beneath the spare tire 'doughnut' and wrapped in a pillow. With shaky hands, he unscrewed the cap on a bottle with the brand label 'Demon Rum.' He laughed loudly as he read the label, and heard the slightest fraying of his sanity in that laugh. It scared him. With shaking hands he raised the bottle to his lips, and guzzled until he felt his nerves smooth.

Once he'd calmed enough to think straight, he wondered if this kind of shit happened in other towns. *Or is it just a Salem thing?* As the booze worked its way through his system, he decided he didn't care. The thought of calling Byron Miller and letting him know what just happened crossed his mind. Mick took another swig, then thought better of it. Lately, the Chief had been bringing stranger and stranger cases to his door, then giving him the mushroom treatment—shoveling shit on top of him and keeping him in the dark. As he got drunker, he got madder.

Mick raised his bottle to the empty room. "Here's to you, *Byron.* I hope they tear you a new asshole."

～

ARCHIE'S VW MICROBUS was still in the same spot since the governor had basically closed down the state. He jumped in and fired it up. Wanda grabbed shotgun, Mercy and Jamal took the back.

Wanda closed her eyes, then reached out to Jazz.

"What's happening there, honey?"

"Wanda? Thank God you're okay!"

"I am sweetie. We're on the way. Fill me in."

Jazz described the chaotic scene before her, finishing with news of Jo's possession by Lucifer.

"Has Eljin Black returned?" asked Wanda.

"If he has, I haven't seen him. But we both know that doesn't mean anything."

"He's probably being extra cautious," said Wanda. *"Armand told me the shifter is extremely smart."*

"Speaking of Armand. Jagger and Mondra have possessed him. They were both in the mirror."

Wanda moaned, both to Jazz and out loud.

Archie shot Wanda a concerned look as he turned onto Lafayette. "What's the matter?"

Wanda, eyes still closed, held up a hand. To Jazz, she sent the thought, *"I knew he was up to something, but I never imagined it would come to this!"*

"What do you mean?" asked Jazz. *"Come to what?"*

"I hope I'm wrong, honey, but he might not survive."

"I don't follow."

Wanda went silent. Jazz knew *this* silence for what it was. The telepathic link was quiet, but she could feel the weight of her friend's thoughts... and fears. When Wanda came back to her, it wasn't in the form of words. Instead, Jazz saw a series of images. She knew Wanda chose to communicate this way when words were inadequate, and also when she was emotionally overwhelmed.

When the images finished, Jazz felt tears at the corners of her eyes. To Wanda, and out loud, Jazz said, "Oh no."

CHAPTER 33
EVICTION NOTICE

L ucifer stood, keeping his new, emerald-green eyes on Byron. There was a stutter in his step as he fought for control over Jo's body. The witch was fighting him from within, and he had a sudden, sinking feeling she might have been more than he bargained for.

But there'd been no choice. She was the closest warm body.

The body of the handsome lawyer had served him well; the deceitful were easily controlled. What he hadn't counted on was Byron Miller's ability to resist his power to manipulate hidden human fears. All *that* had gotten him was shot in the leg and an eventual hole in the head, and now he was inside the body of a witch who was turning out to be a pain in the ass to control. Still, you played the cards as they came.

One of the witches did *something* to protect the cop, and Lucifer cursed himself for not seeing *that* coming.

Even when you'd stacked the deck, things still sometimes went sideways.

What he saw *now* was the uncovering of Claire Davies's

past. A quick trip through Joanne's memories revealed the cop, Mercy, and Joanne figuring out Claire's secret. Lucifer had failed to scare Byron off at the hospital when he'd briefly taken over her body. The woman from the beach hadn't been a total waste, however; she hadn't *deterred* Byron, but she'd been supremely useful in prodding Henry's Jagger-fueled jealousy.

Jagger Corey was gone—at least in body—but his petty, envious tendencies had remained within Henry, ripe for exploitation. But now that, too, was in question. Henry's soul, the soul of the sapphire witch of the prophecy, had eluded him. Inanis the demon had failed twice to kill Henry —three times if you'd counted Madeleine. Tonight's failure was the fourth. Had they been successful in *any* attempt, the house of the vampire would then fall to the Obsidian Witch, who owed Lucifer her soul.

The evil bitch had thrown in her son's soul as a kicker. Lucifer had never asked for it. *Talk about mommy's dedication!*

Claire Davies, aka Claire Davis, was part of the same bloodline. With Henry out of the picture, and Claire living far past her expiration date thanks to her soul-stealing son, Lucifer could still install her as his puppet, giving him control over Salem.

The Witch City, in and of itself, was just the beginning. Black and Blue house would be the first of many important outposts needed; it was the starting point for a much larger game. One that would play out during the budding pandemic.

But all that would have to wait. Things weren't going as planned... but he had an ace in the hole. Well, two, actually. And they were on the way.

He moved closer to Byron.

When Lucifer smiled through Jo's face, it looked at once familiar and alien, and it made the Chief's heart ache.

Lucifer sensed zero fear from the cop, and thus couldn't exploit it. But fear wasn't the only currency in which he dealt. Anger worked just as well.

Time to fuck with Barney Fife's mind.

Lucifer reached a hand behind Jo's back, then came up with the knife she'd stolen from Chesrule in the not-too-distant past. He held it before Byron, knowing it wouldn't scare the cop. Stabbing him wouldn't, pardon the pun, get the point across. But hurting the woman the cop loved like a daughter? Now that was some premium shit right there.

"I could slice you up nice and good right now, Big Chief. But we both know you don't fear death. Am I right?"

Byron said nothing.

Lucifer smiled. "I've got a better idea, though. And you're gonna watch me." He turned his head to the side, catching Henry and Raul in his peripheral vision. "And you two need to back up, or I'll end miss greenie's life right now and take my chances."

Henry and Raul stopped in their tracks.

"What in the hell do you want?" asked Byron.

Lucifer was slicing through the right sleeve of Jo's black hoodie. "What I came for. But unfortunately, that ship has sailed."

"And what was that, exactly?" asked Byron.

The sleeve of Jo's hoodie fell to the floor. Lucifer watched it fall. When he looked up, Byron was a step closer.

Lucifer took a step back. "Uh uh uh," he said, then placed the blade flat against Jo's biceps. He ran the knife slowly down Jo's arm, stopped at her wrist, then tilted it sharp-side down. "It would be so easy to just draw this across. Like slicing butter. Now, since you asked... I came for Henry's soul. Only, you messed things up, *Chiefy*. I missed my opportunity because you couldn't take the fucking hint. So, I'm gonna take something from you. Someone you lllllloooovvvveeee!" Lucifer flicked Jo's tongue at Byron, then drew the knife across her wrist, but only deep enough that a single drop of blood welled through her skin.

Byron wanted to reach inside and yank the bastard right out of Jo. The urge to do something... anything, was almost too much to control.

Henry and Raul were directly behind Jo, holding position. Byron saw Henry holding Raul by the wrist, keeping him in place. Keeping him *still*—as if Henry sensed something was about to happen.

And then, it did.

In the corner of the room, by the entrance near the reading nooks, Byron caught faint movement. A shadow crept low across the floor. He struggled to keep his eyes forward, knowing he must keep Lucifer engaged. Byron realized instantly it was Eljin Black. He smiled, thinking to himself *Who the hell else could it be, dumb ass?*

Byron's smile caused Lucifer to pause, the knife glinting precariously over Jo's wrist. "Something funny, *jefe*?"

He hadn't realized the smile had reached his lips until Lucifer called him on it. Since any other solution to the current situation eluded him, Byron decided to play it out. "Oh, I don't know," he said, shrugging. "You amuse me, is all. I mean, you're supposedly," Byron held up quote fingers, "the 'Devil,' right? Mister King Shit ruler of the underworld?"

Lucifer's mouth dropped open, and the knife moved slightly away from Jo's wrist. Anger flashed red around Jo's green irises, but Byron saw something else in those familiar eyes. Curiosity.

The panther kept a slow, steady pace. It was less than ten feet from the collapsed vampire. Byron pressed on.

"I just find this all fuckin' hilarious," said Byron. He side-stepped slowly right, slightly changing the angle of his body. He had the dark one's attention now, and he wanted to provide a little more cover for Eljin Black.

Lucifer moved the knife from Jo's wrist, turning it toward Byron. He smiled back. "Care to elaborate?"

Byron's smile changed from amused to condescending. "You don't see it, do you? Mister King Shit ruler of the under-world is too fucking stupid to see it!" Byron unleashed a belly laugh, bending at the knees and moving ever-so-slightly to the right once more.

Lucifer stepped closer, the knife raised high.

Byron took a step backward toward the mirror, raising his arms, feigning fear that wasn't there.

This seemed to please the dark one. "See what!?" he growled.

Since time immemorial, Lucifer's biggest sin was pride. Byron had simply drawn it out of him... and bought the time he needed.

"That," said Byron, pointing behind Lucifer.

Lucifer smiled. "I'm supposed to fall for the oldest trick in the book? One that I invented, by the way..."

Byron cut him off. "Suit yourself, shithead." He took two steps backward and disappeared into the mirror.

Dread filled him then, and the dark one turned slowly around. When he did, Henry held the Bloodstone inches from his face. Behind Henry, Armand Moreland stood next to a black panther, an opened black velveteen bag at his feet. In each of his hands was a golden athame. Crystals at the top of each hilt pulsed with energy, clearly visible to Lucifer because the points of the daggers were aimed at Moreland's body.

"What are you doing?" he asked the vampire, incredulous.

Moreland jerked and spasmed, the inner conflict with the Red Witch and Jagger raged on. A battle the vampire was now clearly winning. When he spoke, it was with great effort. "I'm fulfilling the prophecy."

Armand Moreland plunged the daggers straight into his own belly. When he screamed, he screamed as three. On his left side, the dull green energy of Jagger Corey flew from his body, arcing far out into the room and then curling in on itself as the crystal atop the athame captured his essence. On his right side, sparkling crimson bolts shot in all directions. The burst was several times more powerful than the one from Jagger, reaching every corner of the room, but the white magic of Wanda's athame's proved too powerful. Moreland screamed again, and in it was the terror and frustration of Mondra Tibbets. The crimson bolts curled in on themselves, nearing the crystal on the athame and spiritual imprisonment. Several bolts, just before the crystal swallowed them, coursed over the body of the vampire. This time, the scream was *all* Moreland. The dark magick of the Red Witch lashed his body, cutting deep gashes into almost every part of him.

Almost.

As deadly energy tore at him from all sides, the bolts receded, drawing up from his feet, running the course of his legs, and then onward and upward, scorching flesh and searing the fine silk of his suit. Armand Moreland spasmed, then fell to the floor.

Mondra's point of attack shifted, bypassing the athame for one final blow. The crimson bolts drew in on themselves, then arced high above Armand's chest, forming the glittering scales of a serpent—an unintentional tip of the hat to Lucifer. The crimson snake reared back, spread its jaws wide, then tilted its head toward the vampire. It swayed from side to side, dancing like a cobra rising from a charmer's basket, only its *music* was the screaming of Moreland in place of "The Streets of Cairo."

The swaying slowed.

The serpent loomed.

The vampire's screams melted into the low moans of lingering agony, and the snake was content to drink in his pain before the kill. When Mondra had her fill, she struck down at the space above his heart with brutal speed. In the moment she did, Armand Moreland's mind flashed on his conversation with the white witch:

"The dark one is black tourmaline. It's useful in protection, especially from psychic attacks. I carry one with me at all times."

"And the other?"

Wanda held the beautiful green stone up to the light. "Malachite. It's a crystal related to the heart chakra. Very helpful in guiding you toward your higher self and, ultimately, your purpose in life. I've always found they work hand-in-hand, sweetie."

He'd taken her advice... and quite literally, for the two crystals lay in the breast pocket of his dress shirt, right above his heart. Mondra's attack backfired. The crystals from Wanda sent the crimson energy of her black magick attack screaming into the clear quartz atop the second athame. It flared red, then became still.

Henry advanced on Lucifer with the Bloodstone raised high, taking two quick steps and blocking his path to the mirror. Raul had fully recovered from his injuries and flanked Lucifer, taking the position directly behind him. Byron's second in command already had his crucifix out, and when Lucifer turned to flee from Henry, he pulled up short. The cross of Calvary glowed with holy light, and Lucifer knew without question it only meant one thing; its owner's faith was real. There was but one path left for the Prince of Darkness, and it closed instantly. The black-panther-form of Eljin Black blocked the room's exit—head low, ears pinned, haunches elevated. Lucifer saw the black of the cat's pupils swallow the yellow of its eyes. Bright white fangs accompanied a low, guttural growl. The big cat's tail wagged slowly from side to side, a sign he was ready to pounce.

"There's nowhere to go, Lucifer. You've lost." Henry stepped toward him. The beautiful green eyes of his wife were fixed only on the Bloodstone in his left hand, and they radiated fear. Seeing that fear coming from his wife's eyes hurt him deeply, but he reminded himself of its true owner. He stepped closer, keeping the Bloodstone dangling from his left hand less than an inch from Jo's nose. With his right arm, he reached around Jo's back. In one fluid motion, his hand dipped low, grabbing his wife's behind. He gave it a good squeeze, then smiled and winked. "Now... get the *Hell* out of my wife."

Lucifer nodded, his grudging smile formed on Jo's lips. "Touché."

When he exited Jo's body, the room grew cold. His ethereal form was not what Henry expected. Instead of something black as midnight, it was radiant. His mind flashed back to a line from Luci and Fermina's letter—*we bring light to bear*—and he understood.

But he also didn't. How could something so bright, beautiful, and regal be so utterly corrupt? Was it pride? Jealousy? Envy? All of the above?

Or maybe it was shame. Shame at having been given everything a being could ever want, and then spitting in the face of the one who'd made it possible.

A question for another day, he decided.

Jo shook her head, clearing the cobwebs from her mind. She seemed surprised to be in Henry's arms, and she gave him a suspicious look. "What are you up to, Band-Aid boy?"

"What? A guy can't hug his wife?"

Jo looked around the room. The night's memories flooded back. "Where is he?" she asked. Alarm and anger colored her voice.

Henry pointed at the bright, amorphous cloud heading toward the room's exit. It floated over and past the attack-ready form of the panther, and then out of the room.

Once it disappeared around the door's frame, Jo turned to Henry, questions in her eyes. "Okay. Why aren't we chasing after him?"

Henry went to speak, but Jo held a finger to his lips. "And what the hell is a black panther doing in the doorway?"

"Are you finished?" asked Henry, smiling.

"Not even close," said Jo.

From behind them, Raul Martinez cleared his throat. "This guy doesn't look so good."

When they turned, Raul, Byron, and Jazz stood over the vampire. Armand Moreland was still. The twin athames and their glowing crystals were the only signs of any life.

"What can we do for him?" asked Jo.

Henry thought on it for less than a second. "Can you three get him into the mirror?"

"Yes," said Jazz. "What are you thinking?"

"I'm thinking if anything can save him, it isn't in this room. But it might be at his home."

With that, Henry took Jo's hand and started for the door to the reading nooks.

"Where are you going?" asked Jazz.

"We've got a date with the Devil," said Henry.

CHAPTER 34
FOUR'S A CROWD

As Armand Moreland was plunging the twin athames into his midsection, Archie whipped the wheel left and skidded around the corner and onto Essex Street.

"Look out!" yelled Mercy.

Archie swung the wheel hard left. The VW skidded, its rear end fishtailed, and he fought to regain control. The right front fender clipped the side of a mailbox. A hollow boom followed a metal-on-brick crash as the mail container tore loose from its moorings and slapped the corner of Wanda's Wicca'd Emporium. He'd barely missed the two women walking down the middle of Essex.

"Well, you don't see that every day," said Wanda, pointing back through the rear window.

"Is that who I think it is?" asked Archie with one eye on the road and one in his rear-view mirror.

Mercy drew in a sharp breath. "Luci and Fermina? How is that possible?"

"Lucifer must need them," said Wanda. Her voice was calm. "That's a good sign."

"On what planet are walking corpses a good sign?" asked Archie.

"Wanda is correct," said Jamal. "It means he's lost. Otherwise, there would be no use for them." Jamal nodded in the direction of the twins.

"He means to escape through them, doesn't he?" asked Mercy.

Wanda nodded, then smiled at Mercy.

Worry on her face, Mercy asked, "What are we gonna do about it?"

"Let's find out."

LESS THAN A MINUTE later Archie pulled the VW into the alley at the side of Jagger's shop. He parked nose to nose with Henry's car. All four of them jumped out and scrambled down the steps and through the red door leading to Jagger's basement. Archie tapped the flashlight app on his phone, leading the way through the basement, up the stairs, and into the first floor of Jagger's shop. The basement door opened into the area near the counter, and they quickly settled behind it and out of sight of the approaching twins.

Seconds after Wanda and company dropped below counter level, Luci and Fermina mounted the Explorer carcass and dropped through the remnants of the boarded up window. Wanda risked peeking over the top of the counter. Thanks to Mercy, she knew the girls were found dead in the water at Juniper Beach, and assumed they'd been to the coroner's office and examined right away. So when they looked as they had a few months earlier, she was slightly surprised. The only thing different was their eyes; the sockets were dark, as if waiting for something to fill them.

Once the twins passed by, Wanda stood and turned to the other three. She held a finger to her lips, then mouthed the words *follow me*. As they crept from behind the counter, each kept an eye on Luci and Fermina, but they needn't have worried. Once the twins reached the bottom of the steps leading to the reading nooks they stopped, becoming eerily still. Luci and Fermina tilted their heads upward—twin prom queens from Hell awaiting their dates.

Wanda guided the others toward the entrance to the shop. Once there, they took position, two to a side. Mercy was on the outer left-hand side, Wanda the outer right. Jamal stood next to Mercy, Archie next to Wanda. They joined hands.

Three of four in this last line of defense had died and come back to life. Two of four were witches. It was more than enough to ward off any dark magick attack, especially for those whose magical abilities were fueled by contact with The Light.

The white witch leaned forward, catching the eyes of each of her friends, making sure they were ready. Making sure they all *believed*. Faith, in these next few moments, meant everything.

She liked what she saw. Even *Archie* looked unafraid.

The room suddenly grew bright. At the top of the stairs, a brilliant cloud appeared. At the bottom, red light pulsed from the symbols on the foreheads of Luci and Fermina. Wanda recognized the markings immediately. "Leviathan Crosses," she whispered.

Both Archie and Jamal nodded. Mercy leaned close to Jamal. "What's a Leviathan Cross?"

"It's the alchemical symbol for the fire and brimstone of Hell. Also called the Satanic Cross. It's how he controls them."

Mercy thought of the woman at the hospital Byron had mentioned, and hoped her days of being controlled were over.

The cloud of light at the top of the stairs moved silently downward. It hung briefly before the twins, illuminating the dead sockets of their eyes. Lucifer's essence split, and twin serpents of light rose from the main cloud. They slithered silently through the air, then connected with the symbols on Luci and Fermina's foreheads.

"Talk about the third eye from Hell," whispered Archie.

Lucifer, Latin for 'bearer of light,' brought it to bear once more into the flesh shells of the twins. Skin glowed crimson. Bones shone through skin, as if suspended in deep red, female-shaped Jell-O molds. Each of the girls moaned, and the sound was a combination of agony and ecstasy. The last trace of Lucifer's essence split, passing through the Leviathan Crosses. Once complete, the symbols vanished.

Luci and Fermina, whole and unmarked, turned to face the four blocking their path. The eyes of the twins were closed. When they opened, the empty sockets were filled. Once more, they glowed a brilliant hazel, identical to those of Mondra, the dark witch responsible for their creation. And, once more, those familiar hazel eyes focused with hatred on Wanda Heinze.

When they spoke, it was as one. "You don't expect me to leave here empty handed tonight, do you?"

Even now, when she knew the exact nature of the

twins, it was strange to think of them as one entity. It was the same feeling she'd gotten when reading the letter they'd—*he'd*—sent back in November of 2019. It had only been a matter of hours since she'd spoken to him in the limo, but it felt like a lifetime ago. And, since she'd died between that conversation and this one, she realized it was.

"No," said Wanda. "But we both know you're not leaving here with what you came for."

They smiled. "That remains to be seen."

~

Jazz stood over Armand Moreland. The vampire looked bad, but showed faint signs of... *what? Life? Existence?* She wasn't sure what it was called, exactly, when it came to a vampire, and now wasn't the time for internal semantic debate.

"Jo. Henry. You're going to need these." She pointed to the athames protruding from Armand's belly. She gripped the hilts and carefully extracted them. Moreland let out a low, almost imperceptible groan.

"What do we do with these?" asked Jo.

"They're for Luci and Fermina," said Henry. "Right, Jazz?"

"Yes. I'm pretty sure Armand knew that, too. There's more, I'm sure. I have a tape from him. I found it in the house. But he needs to be moved from here if he has any chance of surviving."

Jazz offered the athames to Henry and Jo, taking care to offer Henry the one holding the Red Witch and not Jagger. It probably didn't matter anymore. *But why take chances*, she thought.

Without another word, Henry and Jo accepted the daggers, turned, and headed for the stairs.

Byron and Jazz took Armand Moreland under the arms, Raul grabbed his legs.

Before they got moving, Byron asked Raul if he was okay with going through the mirror.

Raul nodded. "After what I just saw, I ain't worried about the mirror, jefe. I don't think I wanna be around what just went down the stairs before Henry and Jo."

"Okay, Raul. I know this is a lot, but we're gonna be okay." He looked to Jazz. "We ready?"

"As we'll ever be, Chiefy."

"Where's that mirror lead to?" Raul asked Jazz.

"His home. Only, I don't think it's his anymore. And we gotta move right now."

Without another word, Jazz and Byron backed through the mirror. Raul, a vampire leg tucked under each arm, followed.

HENRY AND Jo reached the top of the stairs. When they looked down, Luci and Fermina were at the center of the room, slowly advancing toward Wanda and the others. Neither Henry nor Jo heard what Wanda said to the twins—she was too far from them—but they heard the reply of the twins. "That remains to be seen."

They moved with stealth and quickness to the bottom of the stairs. Henry spoke from behind them. "What remains to be seen?"

Luci and Fermina whirled toward his voice, only momentarily startled—they'd been expecting him. "Who ultimately controls Salem. It would have been easier, of course, if you could have just died like you were supposed to. But Black and Blue House is still very much in play."

"Is it now?" asked Henry. He held the athame before him. The top pulsed with red energy. Jo did the same, hers pulsed a dirty green. Together, they stepped toward the twins. Luci and Fermina's newly occupied eye sockets went wide, and they took an involuntary step backwards.

Henry smiled. "To paraphrase Jagger, *'Sometimes when you call to the darkness, it answers back.'* Since I know everything he ever did, I know Jagger and Mondra created those bodies for you. Conjured them, if I'm not mistaken?"

Their silence was confirmation.

Henry took another step forward, lifting the athame to eye level. He stared at it in mock wonder. "Funny thing, conjuring whole bodies; they don't just simply pop into existence. Well, I guess technically they do... but they have to come from somewhere." With a smile, he looked up from the glittering dagger to the twins. "You've been around a while, so I'm sure this isn't news to you."

When they—*he*—didn't answer, Henry continued. "Those bodies were always meant for *someone*. Weren't they?"

He turned to Jo. "What did Byron say they found out about them in the morgue, Jo?"

Jo looked to the ceiling with one eye opened and the other closed, feigning concentration. "Umm—" She dragged it out a few seconds more. Then, she snapped her head down as she snapped her fingers in a *Eureka!* moment. "No belly buttons! No hearts! Yeah, that was it."

Henry smiled. "Johnny! Tell this lovely lady what she's won!"

Wanda and the others moved a step closer. Luci and Fermina shifted position, back to back, assuming a defensive posture.

Wanda picked up where Henry left off. "Those bodies were *meant* to be born. They exist, and you occupy them, but they belong to someone else. They *would* have been real people. You stole their legacies—the only chance they had to change the paths of their souls. Am I right so far?"

Fermina faced Wanda. A smile played at her lips, but she said nothing.

"I never should have *met* Artemis," continued Wanda. "He never should have been at that AA meeting. He was destined to die in a drunk driving accident, but you made sure he got arrested instead. Claire didn't arrange that. It was you, wasn't it?"

Fermina's smile got wider; the cat that ate the canary. "I might have had a teensy part in that."

Wanda was nodding. She was piecing things together on the fly, but knew she had most of the picture now. And she also knew pride, above all else, fueled this fallen angel; he couldn't resist having his grand plan laid out for all to see, and she was more than willing to oblige. "He survives instead of dying. Claire is on death's door, but she meets Archie—*touches* Archie—and sees he's the father of the child of the prophecy. But she also sees Archie and I are friends, and that I can heal her."

"Yes," said Fermina. "But she *didn't* see you were the one protecting Henry. She knew the child of the prophecy was Archie's son, but couldn't get past your defenses, obviously." Fermina sighed. "Regrettable. This business could have been solved long ago."

"So, you had to keep Claire alive," said Wanda. "She

already owed you her soul, and she sweetened the deal by throwing in her son's. Sadly, for him, I don't think he realized the full implications until tonight."

"Poor, misguided Artemis," said Fermina, donning a mock pouty face. "He's very useful, though. As you know, I'm in the business of souls. The more I keep from Him," she pointed upward, "the better. So Artemis's collection will do nicely. There must be twenty-five or thirty-something in his little flask. When I see him later tonight I—what are you smiling about?"

Wanda feigned shock. "You haven't heard? All *powerful* Lucifer is in the dark?"

Fermina's eyelids narrowed into suspicious slits. Red ringed her hazel irises. In an angry whisper, she asked, "What have you done?"

Henry and Jo, sensing the shit was about to hit the fan, moved closer, athames at the ready.

Wanda, Jamal, Archie, and Mercy, hands locked, stepped forward as one. Wanda said, "I believe Artemis, right before he *died*, said it best. *'What I should have done a long time ago.'*" She released Archie's hand then pulled the crystal flask from her robe pocket, cupping its bottom with her left hand and grasping the stopper between the thumb and forefinger of her right.

Fermina focused closely on the flask, noticing for the first time it wasn't glowing its usual bright blue, but instead contained a swirling dark mass. "What have you *done?*" she repeated.

"Oh," said Wanda. "I think you know."

Wanda pulled the stopper from the flask.

Dark energy exploded from its top. The glass of the flask disintegrated in Wanda's hand, leaving only the silver frame.

She tossed it aside in disgust, as if suddenly realizing she was holding a dead fish.

The blackened souls of the Obsidian Witch and her doomed son rose high in the room, swirling toward the ceiling, as if sensing Lucifer's presence and attempting to flee.

Luci and Fermina reached for the ceiling. Crimson energy burst from their fingers, clawing high and wrapping around the fleeing souls of Artemis and Claire. Moans of agony filled every space of the huge room as Luci and Fermina pulled them lower, toward bodies Artemis and Claire were once destined to occupy, but now never would. Lucifer bellowed with triumph as he absorbed their souls.

His victory was short lived.

Henry moved quickly and without mercy, driving his dagger deep into Fermina. Jo followed his lead, plunging hers into Luci. Lucifer fled their bodies, shooting upward and out.

The effect of the daggers was immediate. Everything holding the twins together suddenly unwound as the architects of their creation tried desperately to inhabit the bodies. Energy, green and red, crawled over the twins. They jerked wildly, as if strapped to the magical and spiritual equivalent of an electric chair. Screams of pain, of rage, of sadness, and of triumph caused the walls of Jagger's Magical Treasures to tremble. The flesh forms of Luci and Fermina began to break down. The skin covering their bodies strobed green then red then green again, cycling faster by the moment.

Just as suddenly as it began, it stopped. The twins stilled like dual versions of Lot's wife when she looked back at the destruction of Sodom and Gomorrah, only instead of becoming pillars of salt as mentioned in the Bible, their flesh turned to ash. They collapsed into twin piles of dust.

In the silence, the crimson essence of Mondra the Red Witch, and the puke-green spirit of Jagger Corey floated above the remains. They were idle, as if confused by the sudden collapse of the bodies they desperately fought to possess, but would now never occupy.

The luminous form of Lucifer descended from the ceiling, where he'd waited them out, biding his time until he could claim them. When he did, it was like watching a spider gather the corpses of flies.

Silently, Lucifer settled within the circle of witches. The glittering ethereal cloud of his essence formed first in front of Wanda. It spasmed, contorting and bending itself until it became a perfect, glowing mirror image of the white witch. Lucifer repeated this process with everyone in the circle, and they understood he was marking them.

He finished with Henry. "Congratulations, *Councilor*," he said in a mocking tone. "You've won this battle, but be ready for the war."

Henry stepped forward. As he did, The Bloodstone flared. The irises of his eyes glowed bright and blue, and Jamal Khalid couldn't help but smile, because he'd seen that shade before, at the end of his last life, when he'd been Aunt Jenny to Archibald Love.

It was the color of a lit swimming pool at night.

At Henry's advance, Lucifer retreated. Henry leaned toward him, sapphire flared in his eyes. He smiled, and it was filled with righteous anger and willing menace. "Bring it."

He took another step forward. Lucifer fled.

CHAPTER 35
IN YOUR DREAMS

As Byron and Jazz approached the back side of the mirror, they each saw the interior of the vampire's meditation room over their shoulders. They slowed, getting ready to ease him through the surface of the mirror and onto the floor. Raul slowed with them.

Byron was first to step through, placing his boot onto the hardwood. Jazz followed suit on the opposite side. They straddled the frame of the mirror, half inside it, and half in the room. Byron nodded at Jazz. "Ready?"

"Ready."

They heaved backwards, expecting to bear the weight of the vampire as they brought him through the mirror. Instead, they tumbled backwards. Byron backpedaled furiously in an effort to remain upright, but his feet tangled and he went down. Jazz was a bit more graceful and coordinated, and merely tucked into a somersault then sprung to her feet. She moved quickly and helped Byron to his.

"What in the actual fuck?" asked a confused Byron.

From inside the mirror came Raul's muffled voice. "Nice job, you two. You bounced the poor guy's head on the floor."

Jazz ignored both of them, staring at the mirror and tapping her lips with a finger. "He can't come through."

"What?" asked Byron. "Why not?"

Jazz threw out a guess. "This place is for the leader of the Council of the Realms. That's Henry now."

Byron tilted his head in confusion. "Last time I checked, neither you or I are Henry Trank. So why are we able to come through?"

Jazz had no answer.

Raul spoke up from behind the mirror. "Guys? I think you need to get back in here, and fast."

~

Once Lucifer was gone, the room went still. Everyone was silent for a few moments, then Henry tilted his head in apparent confusion.

Wanda saw the look on his face. "What's the matter, sweetie?"

He held up his hand, asking for a moment. When he put it back down he locked eyes with Wanda, his expression grim. "Armand Moreland isn't long for this world. He wants us to be there when it happens."

Without a word, they headed for the stairs to the second floor of Jagger's shop. Eljin Black, still in the form of a panther, waited in front of the mirror. When the shifter saw them coming, he turned and strode through. Henry thought he saw sorrow in the panther's yellow eyes, and realized he felt the same.

He stopped in front of the mirror and turned to look at

his friends. It was in their eyes, too. Without a word, Henry turned and lead them.

～

ARMAND MORELAND MOANED. Jazz knelt at his right side, and took his hand in hers. Byron knelt on his left, and took his other hand. Raul held his gold crucifix to his lips, stood at Armand's feet, and prayed. They knew he didn't have long, and tried to give him every ounce of energy they could until the others arrived.

His body was ravaged. Gashes in his fine suit were everywhere, and the black blood running through his veins leaked slowly from almost every part of him. It ran out along the strange floor of the place Jazz had taken to calling 'Mirrorland,' mixing with the fine crystals that seemed to be everywhere.

Moreland stirred when he heard the muted footsteps of the others approaching. He looked to Jazz. When he spoke, it was barely a whisper. "Please prop me up, Jazz."

Her eyes were wet, and her throat was clogged with emotion. She managed a sympathetic smile and a nod, then gently moved her right hand under his neck. Byron slid a hand under Armand's back. Together they lifted, and Jazz scooted behind him, kneeling once again and resting his head and shoulders on her lap.

From the gloom ahead, sapphire light bloomed. Henry's eyes glowed, lighting the way for all. The fine crystals in the air shifted in his presence, swirling in and around his body and framing it in a halo of blue. Raul moved aside, and Henry stepped into his place.

Wanda and Mercy walked around Henry. They each took

a spot next to Jazz, knelt, and took the gypsy's hands. Jo stepped up to Henry's right, Archie to his left. Together, they knelt at the vampire's feet. Jamal and Raul, each took a side, Raul next to Byron, Jamal next to Wanda. The circle was complete. Eljin Black took position behind Henry, then faced away from the circle and stood guard over his soon-to-be new responsibility.

In the silence that followed, everyone in the circle focused their energy on the vampire. He was beyond saving, but they understood he wanted, and needed, to be heard.

As the League of the Moon focused their intention, healing energy flowed into Armand Moreland. His breathing, ragged and shallow only moments before, became steady and rhythmic. He opened his eyes, smiled weakly, and said, "My friends. My beautiful friends."

Tears and smiles met his words.

"Time is short," said Armand. "There is much to tell, but that's for another time. Jazz will be able to settle that score for me."

No one spoke. No one wanted a word or a moment to be wasted. This was Armand Moreland's time, and he would have his say.

When he next spoke, it was directly to Henry. "I'm sure you have an endless list of questions, Henry. In time they will be answered." He closed his eyes, winced, then continued. "For now, know that you are, and were destined to be, Salem's protector."

Henry nodded, a sad smile on his face.

Moreland looked at each of them in turn, then back to Henry. "You will all have your roles to play in the next few years. This will not be an easy time. Chaos is on the horizon, both in the real world and the magical one."

He coughed loudly. Black blood trickled from the corner of his mouth. Jazz smoothed his hair with one hand, then dabbed the blood from his mouth with the end of a sleeve.

"Watch each other's backs. Be vigilant. And know this; the Council of the Realms has many heads, and many doors. Not all can be trusted. Exercise caution, as you did with me, and you'll come through just fine. It has been my complete honor to know and serve all of you. I love you."

Another spasm of pain wracked his body. Jazz cradled his head, Wanda and Mercy steadied his shoulders until it passed. It was quiet for several moments. Random jerks and spasms briefly animated the failing body of the vampire like the aftershock of an earthquake—until they didn't. Armand Moreland became still, and his friends thought he was gone.

Quiet sobs filled the odd terrain of the land inside the mirror, sounding muted and strange. Through closed eyes, Henry noticed a subtle change in the light behind his eyelids. It seemed to come from above. Wanda and Mercy noticed it next, quickly followed by Jamal Khalid. It was an ethereal glow they recognized instantly, for they'd once bathed in it, and returned forever changed. Soon Joanne, Byron, Raul, and Jazz sensed something different. When they opened their eyes, they saw the others looking upward, but only saw a hazy and dim glow.

Henry realized they weren't seeing what he and the others were. A brief flashback to the moment he first met Mercy came to mind, and he whispered to everyone, "Join hands."

When they did, the League of the Moon saw as one. What came next would change each of them forever.

Armand Moreland stood before them, radiant. His wounds were healed. His eyes sparkled with life. And his tears were wiped away. It reminded Wanda of an old Bible passage she'd learned as a young girl in catechism class:

"... there shall be no more death, neither sorrow, nor crying, neither shall there be any more pain: for the former things are passed away."

As she looked upward to her former adversary and now dear friend, she felt nothing but joy for him. Through their joined hands, Wanda knew her friends felt the same.

In that moment, the earthly body he'd occupied for centuries struggled briefly to hold its shape, then collapsed in on itself, sending a small plume of dust upward in its wake. The remnants of the vampire were suddenly swept up by the glittering dust permeating the land within the mirror. It was soon absorbed, becoming part of the whole. Jazz and Henry exchanged a glance, confirming what they suspected all along: the dust was alive and sentient.

The thought was quickly noted and tossed aside as the light above them glowed brighter. As if in response, the dust surrounding them swirled, rotating around the circle they'd formed with their joined hands. Armand was still at its center, but his eyes were far away. In the smile on his face, every member of the League saw wonder, joy, amazement, and love. They followed his eyes.

In the distance were three figures. On the left was a tall, beautiful woman. Her hair was long, wavy, and raven black; a striking contrast to the bluish-grey eyes fixed lovingly on her husband. On the right was a miniature version of herself, only the eyes were a deeper blue and matched the shade of her father's exactly. Behind them, the archangel Gabriel stood in flowing robes of brilliant sapphire. When he spoke, it seemed to come from every direction at once, and those in the circle realized his voice did not vibrate their eardrums, but reverberated in their hearts.

"Well done, good and faithful servant. I release you. You are whole and restored by the fruits of your deeds."

Armand Moreland bowed deeply. "Thank you, Gabriel."

Gabriel smiled warmly at the restored soul of Armand Moreland, then turned and was swallowed by billowing clouds of crystal.

The circle of friends parted then, forming two rows on either side of the former vampire. Victoria ran to him then, leaping into the arms of her father. She hugged him fiercely, sobbing with joy. Armand placed a gentle hand on the back of her head, pulling her tight. He whispered, "Shh, shh, shh. All is well once more." As he comforted his baby, his eyes were on his Katarina. She moved toward him slowly, fearful sudden movement might reveal the moment as nothing more than a dream. When she reached them, Katarina raised a tentative hand toward her husband's cheek, running her fingers along his jaw. At her touch, Armand closed his eyes, absorbing the moment. When he opened them, he whispered, "It's real, my love." He reached for the hand on his cheek, then pulled her in.

After a time, they separated. Armand held a hand out at each side, and his family took them in theirs. Together, they followed in the footsteps of the departed angel. When they reached the point of Gabriel's exit, they stopped as one and turned. Armand Moreland smiled at his friends. Henry stepped forward. "Will we ever see you again?"

Armand looked first to Katarina, then to Victoria. Returning his gaze to Henry, he smiled. "Of course you will. All of you will. In your dreams."

And then he was gone.

CHAPTER 36
THE WITCH OF ENDOR

One by one, they filed through the mirror and into what used to be Armand Moreland's meditation room. Eljin Black stood at the opened door across the room and directly opposite the mirror, where he'd shifted into his human form.

The last time they'd seen him this way, he loosely resembled Byron. Now, he wore an immaculate black suit, spitshined loafers, and a serious look. Grey hair, white at the temples, rested above a square jaw. His eyes were a perfect match for his hair.

Henry led the way, stopping in front of the shifter. "So what comes next, Mr. Black?"

"I am at your disposal, Mr. Trank. But Armand's instructions, earlier this evening, were that you follow me to the top floor."

Henry held out a hand. "Lead on."

Eljin Black turned sharply, guiding them down the same hallway Jazz had travelled earlier in the night. As he approached the table with the roses, which sat in front of the window overlooking the Atlantic Ocean, Jazz said, "Dead end."

Eljin Black turned at the sound of her voice. "Things are not what they seem at Blue house, Miss Miso." The shifter turned, then walked through a very solid, very real-looking white wall. Everyone was momentarily stunned. As the footsteps of Eljin became fainter, Henry put a hand to the wall. It disappeared up to his wrist.

"This way, Mr. Trank," said Eljin. His voice sounded impossibly far away.

Henry turned to Jo and shrugged. "The man said this way."

"Indeed he did. Lead on, Band-Aid boy."

"You know, you're gonna have to stop calling me that, Jo. I'm a big deal now." Smirking, he turned. He knew a whack on the ass would soon follow. Jo did not disappoint. "Let's go, Big Deal."

They followed Henry through the wall. Wanda brought up the rear, giggling along the way.

Once through, they followed a long corridor leading to a steep set of narrow stairs carpeted in black. Henry came to a stop, placed his hand on the rail, then looked upward. Though he'd seen the house from the outside earlier in the night in Wanda's afterlife vision, the length of the staircase seemed at odds with the size of the home.

"That makes *zero* sense," said Byron.

"You ain't lyin'," said Raul.

"I can't wait to see what's at the end of this thing," said Jo. "I feel like Alice Through the Looking Glass."

"That may be closer to the mark than any of us realize," said Wanda.

"Let's not keep Mr. Black waiting," said Henry.

What at first seemed a steep and long climb took less than a few seconds. No one felt they'd missed any of the numerous stairs, and none felt as if they'd suffered missing time—as if encountering a UFO—but the speed of the journey had them standing at the top in confusion.

"Okay. What the hell was that?" asked Jo.

"As I said, things are not what they seem at Blue House. You'll get used to the house's eccentricities in time," said Eljin.

"Why do you keep calling it Blue House?" asked Henry. "Didn't Lucifer call it *Black* and Blue House?"

"Yes," Eljin replied. "When you survived, and the Obsidian witch perished, the dual nature of this dwelling changed. Thus... Blue House."

Henry looked to Jo. She shrugged. "Works for me."

Eljin snapped around and opened the door.

Henry stepped through. "*This* looks awfully familiar."

"Indeed it does," said Wanda. She was last through the door, closing it behind her. The room looked exactly as it had in her earlier vision, right down to the rain beating on the window and the votive candles burning on the sill. The only differences were a lack of chairs surrounding the gold-flaked pentacle and the addition of a VCR and TV on a stand in the corner of the room. The candle, as in her shared vision with Henry, burned quietly at the pentacle's center.

At the opposite corner of the room Eljin opened a door, then stood to the side. He cleared his throat. "Seats for everyone."

The dimness of the room prevented a clear view into the closet. Henry followed him over, then stopped short. "I don't see any chairs."

The shifter allowed himself a quick, almost imperceptible smile. "Look closely, Mr. Trank."

Henry was about to lean in and inspect the closet, but pulled up short. He turned to Eljin Black. "What do I call you? I mean, now that you, for lack of a better term, work for me?"

"I am at your command, Mr. Trank. You may address me as you see fit."

Henry nodded, poking his tongue against his cheek, as if pondering something. "Okay. And that goes both ways?"

Eljin tilted his head. "I'm afraid I don't follow, Mr. Trank."

"You may address *me* as you see fit."

"I hardly think that's appropriate. There's an order to things, Mr. Trank, I—"

Henry held up a hand. "Never you mind, Eljin. From now on, just call me Henry."

The shifter opened his mouth to protest, but Henry stopped him.

"Uh uh uh. You're supposed to do what I say, right?"

Eljin Black looked fit to be tied. He didn't answer, but simply nodded, waving an arm toward the closet. "Look a little more closely, Henry."

Henry leaned forward, but not before catching the smallest smile of approval, or maybe it was appreciation, on the shifter's face.

"I'll be damned," said Henry. "Is this one of those places where you think about something you need and it suddenly materializes?"

Jo snapped her fingers, trying to remember the name of the room. "Ah, ah ah..."

Eljin beat her to it. "It is not a *Room of Requirement*, ala Harry Potter, if that's what you're implying."

"Then why is there suddenly a stack of black beanbag chairs in there?" asked Mercy.

"Because Mr. Moreland knew you'd be coming here tonight, and prepared accordingly," said Eljin.

"That's some serious foresight," said Byron.

Eljin Black nodded in concession. "As the saying goes, 'You ain't seen nothin' yet.'"

"Meaning?" asked Henry as he tossed beanbag chairs from the closet.

"I believe the video in Miss Miso's possession will answer that in short order," was Eljin's reply.

The beanbags were in place, forming a semicircle around the edge of the pentacle. Everyone took their seats. Eljin retrieved the tape from Jazz, slipped it into the VCR, then pressed play.

After some old-fashioned grey and white snow, the picture cleared. In the foreground was a red cherrywood table with a single white candle burning away in a gleaming gold sconce. The background was entirely covered with a black velvet curtain.

Armand Moreland strode in from the left, centering himself in the frame. As usual, he was dressed to the nines. "Is this thing on?" he asked someone off camera and slightly to his left. Barely audible, Eljin Black whispered, "Yes sir."

The vampire cleared his throat. "Hello my dear friends. If you are watching this tape, I'm no longer a part of your world. Also, you are all alive and things went as I hoped they might. Please realize, each and every one of you, nothing aside from a reunion with my wife and daughter would make me happier. I've come to love you all very much."

"We love you too, sweetie," was Wanda's hoarse reply.

"To Henry. You are now the leader of the Council of the Realms. You were *always* meant to be its leader. The Council has followed the path of your soul since Inanis the demon set foot in the New World. Before that, we were monitoring him in Germany.

"When you were Madeleine Tranch, you were the first and only witch we'd encountered with an ability to resist the demon's mind probing in, at that point, six hundred-plus years. We knew then that you, or more correctly, your soul, was the one spoken of in the prophecy."

"By now, you're asking," Armand raised quote fingers, "what *'prophecy?'* At this point, I've instructed Eljin Black to hand the remote to you, Henry."

Eljin paused the tape, left his post at the side of the VCR stand, handed the remote to Henry, then made for the door. When he opened it, Henry asked, "Where are you going?"

"What comes next, I've seen. Mr. Moreland's instructions, from this point on, were very specific. A select few individuals around the globe are privy to this information, it must be guarded jealously. I am to secure the grounds."

Eljin's words were met with stunned silence. He stood in the door and waited. Wanda spoke up from behind Henry. "He's waiting for you to tell him he can go, sweetie."

"Oh!" said Henry. "Okay. Do your thing, Eljin."

The shifter shot Wanda a thankful look, then left.

Henry pressed play.

"In the Bible, in the book of Samuel, there is mention of a witch. She is known as the witch of Endor. Long story short, the prophet Samuel dies. Saul, the king of Israel at the time, seeks direction from God when preparing to battle the Philistine army. None comes. Saul had previously driven all necromancers and magicians from the land, so he anonymously seeks the advice of a witch and hears of one living in the village of Endor."

"Endor?" asked Jo. "Isn't that the Ewok planet from *Return of the Jedi?*"

Henry paused the tape. "Forest moon. But yeah, same name. You *know* everything comes down to Star Wars, Jo."

Jo nodded. "True enough."

Henry hit play.

"Saul finds her, but she refuses to help because of the laws he's imposed. He assures her she will not be punished. Now, remember, he's there incognito. The witch summons a spirit that Saul cannot see, and in the summoning works out Saul's true identity, and is furious with him. He reassures her of no punishment and asks what the spirits says. The spirit is angry at being disturbed, chastises Saul, and predicts his downfall *and* the deaths of his sons. Sure enough, this all comes to pass, and the next day, Saul commits suicide."

"The Bible can be so cheery sometimes," cracked Byron.

Henry paused the tape. "I wonder what happened to the witch?"

When no one offered an answer, he hit play.

"So you're probably wondering what happened to the witch?" asked video Moreland.

"Gotta give it up to Jeevesy," said Jazz. It was met with nods all around.

"Truthfully," said Moreland. "Nobody really knows. Most scholars believe she died the next day. Others disagree, but offer no plausible alternatives. In truth, they may never know. But, to be quite frank, I'm glad the mystery remains. Because I know the truth. The witch of Endor is currently holding the remote to this VCR."

Henry hit pause. He looked from Jo to Wanda, Byron to Archie, Mercy to Raul, and finally to Jazz and Jamal. Each of them looked as stunned as he felt. None of them knew what to say. Henry, too, was at a loss for words, so he hit play once more.

"If I know you as I believe I do, you are all probably speechless. I would be too. So imagine my surprise when we found this," he held up a silver staff. It was roughly three feet long, the circumference of a silver half-dollar, and had a claw at its top holding a crimson sphere. "The talisman of the witch of Endor. It was found buried on the grounds of an abandoned state mental facility in Danvers, Massachusetts in 1992. As I'm sure Wanda will verify, Danvers, in 1692, was known as Salem Village. Madeleine and David's home was in Salem Village. On that very plot of land."

"Oh my God," whispered Mercy.

"The moment the talisman was removed from the ground, the closest Council of the Realms guardian sensed its magic, but was unable to retrieve it in time. Eventually it was pawned in Chelsea, Massachusetts, then subsequently sold. The owners of a home on Tremont Street in the same town purchased it, stored it in the basement, and basically forgot about it. The home was rumored to be haunted. No surprise there, really, as the witch's talisman is used for summoning the dead. The family eventually moved out. In the time between their moving and the sale of the property, we reacquired the piece. It is in the room you occupy at the present moment."

Henry tapped the remote and the video reproduction of Armand Moreland froze. He got up from his beanbag and began searching the room. The rest of them soon followed, pulling out books from the book case and looking behind them, rapping lightly on the walls, ceiling, and floor and listening for hollow spots, and even lifting their beanbag chairs and shaking them. It was nowhere to be found.

Soon they gave up and took their seats. Henry pressed play. "Don't waste time searching the room," said Armand Moreland. "You won't find it."

"Nice job, prophecy boy," said Jo. Henry gave her a smile and a helpless shrug.

Moreland continued. "When you have need of the item, enter this room, and utter the phrase, *iftaḥ yā simsim.*"

Jamal Khalid barked a laugh. Henry paused the tape. "You know what that means, Jamal?"

Jamal was smiling. "The vampire had a sense of humor. It means 'Open Sesame' in Arabic."

Smiles and laughter all around.

Henry pressed play. "Henry, the phrase will only work for you, unless you verbally delegate it to someone else. I recommend you do this rarely and only under dire circumstances. Stop the tape at this point, and summon the talisman."

He did as instructed. "*Iftaḥ yā simsim.*"

Directly above them, unnoticed until that moment, a small, crystal chandelier rattled softly. It rotated slowly clockwise. As it did, the hub cylinder of the chandelier slid open at the bottom, and the talisman of the witch of Endor floated out. It hung suspended a few feet above the candle at the center of the pentacle. The silver of its shaft glowed softly in the candlelight, and the crimson orb resting in its silver claw sparkled brightly with magic. Henry took hold of it. When he did, the orb pulsed in time with his heartbeat. He turned it over and back in his hand, and the orb trailed sparks of crimson in its wake.

"That is seriously cool," said Mercy.

"Okay, fake-ass Jedi," said Jo. "Time to put the saber down and finish the tape."

Henry laughed. He released the talisman. What happened next happened out of instinct. He repeated the phrase, knowing the talisman would return to its hiding spot. In that moment, though he could never have put it into words, he understood everything about it, as if memories from that long ago time were instantly uploaded to his head. For some strange reason, it comforted him.

The item floated upward, righted itself, then slipped soundlessly into the chandelier. The crystals rattled softly once more as it rotated and the bottom slid shut. Once the last crystal stilled, they took their seats.

Henry started the tape.

"Pretty nifty, eh?" asked Moreland with a mischievous grin. "I'm sure you felt many things once you touched the talisman, Henry. In time, it will reveal its secrets." Moreland turned serious. "Now, I believe you have many questions about Lucifer, and how we got here. And, more importantly, what comes next. If you'll indulge me—"

CHAPTER 37
LUCIFER EXPLAINED

"Many things transpired to bring us to where we are today," said Armand Moreland. "I'll be as brief as possible, but I owe it to you to fill in some of the blanks."

The vampire paused, seeming to gather his thoughts.

"When Joanne killed the Red Witch, Mondra sought refuge in the one place available—the mirror in her room. At the time, I was unaware this was even a possibility. As you know, or at least have heard, vampires are soulless entities. I've come to realize this is, at least in part, untrue. My death, if I am correct, has only confirmed my suspicions. Redemption is the only path to restoration for our kind, but one must be willing to accept the required trials of that path. I did. Mondra the Red Witch, did not."

Moreland paused, looking troubled and sad. "There is only one result possible in rejecting the path I chose, and that is darkness—or better put, absence from The Light. I fear Mondra is lost for good, claimed by the darkness and separated from The Light. I entered the mirror with hopes of

309

achieving two goals: Mondra's possible redemption, or her removal from this world. This brings me to Jagger Corey. As of this recording, I am unsure if he lived or died. Only you will know for sure, and only after I'm gone."

"Well," said Byron. "Check those two items off the list."

"When I acquired the frame of the mirror to have it restored, my interest was twofold. I wanted it for personal reasons, of course—I have a weak spot for antiques—but I also knew that as long as Jagger Corey existed in any form in this dimension, Henry and the prophecy were both in danger, which meant the balance of power in Salem and the rest of the magical world was also in danger."

Henry tapped the remote. He turned to Jo. "See? Big deal."

She snorted. "And then you woke up, sitting on the bedpost and screaming your own name."

Byron laughed so hard at Jo's comeback, he fell backwards off the beanbag. Wanda and Archie helped him back up, laughing as they did.

Henry was still laughing and shaking his head as he rewound the tape. "I fucking love you," he said to Jo.

Jo smiled broadly. "I know. Hit play, Big Deal."

Moreland continued. "What I never counted on was Mondra's *continued* existence in that realm. It was only after I entered the mirror, the day I brought it home, that I realized she still remained. Mirrors are spiritual portals, you see. But they are also portals for those adept at magic, and she figured out a way to survive beyond the simple mirror in her room. In the coming pandemic, you will be forced to use them frequently, and in a similar fashion."

"Pandemic? Is he talking about the Covid thing in the news?" asked Mercy.

Wanda answered. "Yes. It looks like the two week shelter-in-place order is just the beginning, sweetie."

"Great," said Joanne.

On screen, Moreland continued. "Since you are watching this tape, we all know the outcome of these decisions. I only hope you can forgive me for the numerous mistakes I've made along the way."

Moreland sipped some water. "Firstly, to Wanda. When you called the other night, I promised I would not intervene. I hope you realize, now, that I had no choice." He cracked a smile then. "Who am I kidding? I think you knew exactly what I intended to do. Or at least suspected. I only hope your death was painless. And I've no doubt you live once more.

"You're probably wondering how I knew you would be resurrected. And ditto for Henry. I have a confession to make; the twin athames you received as a gift from Archibald Love were sold to him by me. Only, he would never remember who sold them, as I was in disguise. The owner of the shop where he purchased them is a member of the Council, and he provided me with the opportunity.

"The Bloodstone I gave to Archibald, not too long ago, under the guise it needed precise carbon dating, making sure to stress there was no rush. I took a chance he might forget about it—no offense, Archibald, but it's been known to happen—and that knowing its true origin and power, and also the nature of the current danger, he might feel the need to protect his son. It was a longshot, but it worked."

"I'll be damned," whispered Archie.

"The items are actually Vatican artifacts. I didn't foresee Archie inscribing the athames, however. So... maybe the Vatican doesn't need to be reminded they're missing?" He winked.

"The Council of the Realms, back in the day, followed the *career* of the Red Witch quite closely. When she used a black magick love spell on Dr. Love, we decided to intervene—albeit indirectly. I believe Archie gave you the athames as an apology for all the trouble his love life with Mondra Tibbets had caused you? I could be wrong, but I suspect not. Regardless, the gold daggers were put in play because we believed you would understand exactly how they *could* be used."

"That clever bastard," said Wanda.

This caused Henry to stop the tape and ask, "He's right? You knew what they were for?"

"I did. They were inscribed, they came from Archie, but I knew there was something different about them. It was nothing I could put my finger on, at the time, but that changed last night."

"What was different?" asked Henry.

"Luci and Fermina died," said Wanda, matter-of-factly. "When Lucifer left their bodies, and before he must have possessed the lawyer, the athame began to vibrate. His energy is powerful."

Byron looked at his healed finger, then at Jazz. She gave him a wink and a smile.

Wanda continued. "I'd forgotten all about them. Funny thing was, when I opened the floor safe, there was only one there. The other was missing, and I hadn't the slightest idea what had happened to it." Wanda shrugged. "I only know that when we needed it tonight, it was there. Thank God."

"I don't think it was God, Wanda. At least not directly," said Jazz. "Hit play, Henry. I got a feeling we're about to find out."

Henry did.

"This is where things took a fortuitous turn," said Moreland. "I was approached by a young Arabic man."

Everyone turned to look at Jamal Khalid.

"It was plain to me," said Moreland, "as it was when I first met Mercy Glass, that Jamal had touched the divine, and returned to tell about it. Jamal told me about things he had no business knowing. One of those things was about the night he died. But not the night he died in his current incarnation. Instead, he told me how he died at the hands of Jagger Corey, Mondra the Red Witch... and a man named Artemis Davies. He told me about the early morning hours of September 17, 2004. The night Jenny Love, Archie's aunt, passed. You see, Jamal Khalid was Jenny. And she has returned."

"I knew it!" shouted Archie.

"Really?" asked Wanda, her tone doubtful.

Archie shook his head. "Not that he was aunt Jenny— who the hell could have figured that? But that there was something familiar about Jamal. I thought he was helping *Artemis*, at first, but he could have killed me anywhere along the way. Once I realized he was actually on our side, I started to look at him a little more closely. It was his eyes—"

"The windows to the soul," said Mercy.

"Exactly," said Archie. "I just couldn't figure out whose."

"I must apologize for all the subterfuge," said Jamal. "But in approaching Mr. Moreland, and then disclosing my identity, he advised, and I agreed, discretion was the better part of valor, as the saying goes. But we did leave a small trail of breadcrumbs in hopes one of you would figure out I was working, as the vampire put it, 'both sides of the street.'"

"The Facebook post," said Wanda and Mercy at the same time.

Jamal smiled. "Yes. We were aiming for two results from the post. The first was that you would figure out the coded name for Beauty Eternal."

"I got that from the Facebook translator," said Mercy.

"Excellent," said Jamal. "The second was a hope that through further digging, my connection to Artemis would be uncovered."

"I found his posts thanks to that, Jamal," said Wanda. "He was going by the forum name 'Soul Man.' The coincidence seemed too neat. Knowing what I know now, I think Artemis's conscience was beginning to get the better of him. I think he *wanted* to be caught."

Mercy was nodding. "That explains him turning on his mother at the last moment in the observatory at the U."

"There's something I don't understand," said Byron. "How did you get that index card to Artemis without making him suspicious?"

"That," said Jamal. "Was another stroke of luck. Or maybe coincidence—"

"No such thing," said Wanda.

Jamal was momentarily startled by the interruption. He tilted his head contemplatively. "I think you are right about that, Wanda."

"So? What happened?" asked Byron impatiently.

"Mr. Moreland informed me that the mirror he'd commissioned to be repaired, after the repairs were completed, was shipped to a church immediately after—to be blessed. When he'd arrived at the church, the priest in charge seemed to be extremely nervous. As we know all too well, not much escaped the vampire's notice. When Armand asked him about the blessing of the mirror, Father O'Bryan seemed to have forgotten about it. Another thing he noticed, or more correctly, something that irritated him, was the ponytails of the altar boys."

"They allow that now?" asked Byron. "I thought they had a dress code."

"They do not allow it. At least, not at that church. There were two more things Armand informed me of that he said, and I quote, 'Got my Spidey senses tingling.'"

"Armand Moreland used the term 'Spidey senses?'" asked a surprised Joanne.

Jamal smiled. "I had the same reaction. He then told me the priest mentioned something about the *'Devil being in the details.'* An obvious, if overlooked, clue at the time. But it was the *last* thing Father O'Bryan said to him that stuck in his mind, making him call the priest later in the day. At the church, when Moreland thanked him, O'Bryan said, *'I did nothing.'* Initially, Armand assumed Father O'Bryan was showing humility and giving the credit to God, but Armand told me the more he thought about those words, and the other things O'Bryan had said, and then adding the out-of-dress-code altar boys to the equation, he began to believe there was more than met the eye at his visit."

"So what was said in the call?" asked Byron.

"Nothing. O'Bryan refused to talk about it on the phone," said Jamal.

"And Moreland just dropped the whole thing?" asked Jo.

"No," said Jamal. "Far from it. Mr. Moreland arrived later in the night with the shifter at the rectory. When O'Bryan still refused to talk, they removed him bodily and brought him here. And that's when they discovered two very important things. The first was that the altar boys were not boys at all. They were Luci and Fermina. O'Bryan was trying to tell him that with the *'Devil in the details'* line."

"Why the hell were Luci and Fermina at the church?" asked Mercy.

Jamal pointed at her. "That's the question. It turns out they'd been hiding there all along, since they had escaped Wanda's shop."

Wanda groaned. "If I'd only protected that hallway better."

Jamal felt badly for her, but rehashing regrets would help no one. He continued. "In the time they'd spent hiding in the church, O'Bryan had been under constant threat. Luci and Fermina wanted him to deliver something for them."

"The index card with Artemis's next target," said Byron.

"Precisely," said Jamal. "Since the Red Witch was gone, Lucifer did not trust the usual method of delivery. Father O'Bryan had the index card with him at all times. Moreland simply changed the first line, coming up with the Beauty Eternal clue."

"What was the original line? Do you remember?" asked Byron.

"It had something to do with O'Bryan's last name, but I don't recall." Jamal shrugged. "It didn't matter, at that point. We found out where O'Bryan was to meet with Artemis. I took his place and told him the next target was Wanda Heinze. I remained "in the shadows" during our conversation. Armand wrote that line purposefully, and I made sure I played it to the hilt until it became unavoidable to reveal myself."

"Why were you worried about revealing yourself?" asked Byron.

Jamal pulled the collar of his shirt aside, revealing the

'infinity symbol' birthmark. "The day I made first contact with Artemis, it was quite warm. If I'd shown up in a jacket with the collar pulled up, he might have been suspicious. So I chose to remain in the shadows. It is the same mark I had on my eyelid when I was Jenny Love. Artemis might have put two and two together."

"*That's* why I couldn't see the other person in my vision!" said Henry.

Jamal nodded. "After that, when Artemis arrived in Salem and I contacted him, I explained what my name translated to. He had some misgivings, but accepted it readily enough. I don't think he really suspected anything was off until earlier tonight... or this morning, if we want to be accurate. At that point, it was already too late for him."

The room was silent for a while after that. It was a lot to swallow. Without a word, Henry tapped the remote. When Armand Moreland began speaking, he launched into a recap of most of what Jamal had laid out for everyone. It lined up perfectly.

"Before I get to what comes next for you, Henry, and for the rest of the League of the Moon, I think I need to explain myself. I hope you all find it in your hearts to forgive me for what I'm about to reveal next, but friendships not based in honesty tend to crumble, and I have no intention of hiding information behind my death so you'll think better of me. I am a man of great faults and, at times, questionable motivation. I only ask that you consider the end result when you make your final judgment. I did what I did out of love, both for you, my dear friends, and for the chance to be with my wife and daughter once more."

The tape faded to black. Snow ran on the screen for several seconds. A loud click came from the VCR, and the screen went black. In the top right corner of the screen, white digital block lettering read *'Input 1.'*

"What the hell just happened?" asked Jo. "Where's the rest of it?"

Henry shrugged helplessly. "No clue."

In the next moment, the door to the room swished quietly open. Eljin Black carried a gleaming silver tray, held aloft by the splayed fingers of his left hand. He resembled a waiter at a cocktail party. On the tray were ten shot glasses filled with a glowing green liquid. Nine of them were intended for the current occupants of Armand Moreland's—now Henry's—attic room. The tenth was for the very attractive woman who'd followed him in.

Byron gasped. "Jennifer?"

It was the woman from the hospital.

CHAPTER 38
CHECKMATE

Eljin Black made his way around the circle of beanbags, lowering the tray for each to take a shot glass.

Henry fetched Jennifer a chair. He placed it in the spot closest to the TV, completing the circle around the pentacle. When everyone was seated, Eljin placed the tray on top of the VCR, then turned to address the circle.

"Mr. Moreland felt the last part of this needed a more personal touch. In your glasses is a potion concocted by a powerful white witch who lives in London. I know this because I brought the ingredients to her two days ago, returning yesterday. For now, her name is not important. You will know it soon enough."

The shifter turned to Henry. "If you've no further need of me, I'll rejoin the protection detail."

Henry raised the shot glass. "Thanks for the drinks."

Eljin turned sharply and walked out of the room.

"I don't think he likes me," said Henry.

"It takes time," said Jo. "You're an acquired taste."

"I believe they call that *'damning with faint praise,'* " said Jamal.

Jo tapped her nose, pointed at Jamal, and winked.

Jennifer rested the shot glass on the floor, then tucked her feet up and under her legs.

"If Archie tried that move he'd have rolled over the back of that beanbag chair," said Wanda.

Archie grinned, turning slightly red. "It's true."

"At least we don't have *that* in common," said Jennifer, smiling.

Her comment was met with curious silence.

"We have something in common?" asked Archie, eyebrows raised.

"We do," she said, then dove right in. "Your aunt Jenny was my mom's stepmother. So, basically, my step-grandma. I was named after her." A wistful smile crossed her face. "She used to call me 'Jenny-cakes.' What a sweet woman. We lost touch years ago, when my mother divorced Alvin and we had to go into hiding, but I never forgot the things she taught me."

Archie was equal parts surprised by their connection, and repulsed. He looked like he'd taken a full bite of a lemon. "That's a lot at once. What did that fool cousin of mine do?"

"I was very young when it happened. Grandma Jenny sensed early on that I had some magical ability, and she began teaching me the craft. When I showed signs of true ability, your cousin Alvin—my stepfather—took notice. I don't have to tell you, Archie, what the potential outcome *there* might have been."

Archie gave her a sympathetic look. "He was always the odd one out. Didn't want to have anything to do with Penny or I. Part of it was probably him being much older than us, but he always had a mean streak. We haven't spoken in I don't know how long. No big loss. Where is he now?"

Jenny untucked her legs and sat straighter. "Until yesterday, he was in a Romanian prison for dark magick practitioners who cross the line. Apparently, he'd been there for the last fifteen years. I can only imagine what he might have done. And where he might be now."

"Wonderful," said Henry. "Another psycho family member on the loose I know nothing about."

Wanda jumped in. "We can discuss Alvin another time. Jennifer, sweetie, why are you here with us now?"

"I moved back to Salem two years ago, after my mother died. I don't know what it is about this town, but it never leaves your blood. Armand Moreland tracked me down just last week. He introduced me to Jamal, then told me who Jamal was... or still is." She shook her head. "It's still hard to wrap my head around everything. They asked for my help, then told me everything that was going on with Lucifer."

"Did he mention the small detail you might, you know, end up possessed? Then have the shit beaten out of you?" There was steel in Byron's voice.

"Not in those words, but he said it could go very wrong. He made it clear right up front that my life, and my immortal soul, might be in danger."

"And you were *still* willing to do it?" asked Archie.

Jennifer answered Archie's question while looking into the eyes of Jamal. "For Jenny? Yes. And I'd do it again. Right now, if I had to."

Jamal smiled, getting a little teary.

There was a long silence after that. Henry broke it. "I guess all that's left is to drink this and see what happens." He raised his glass, the others followed suit.

"To Armand," he said, then downed the potion.

"To Armand," they replied, raising their glasses in salute and then drinking.

After a moment, the room dimmed—only it didn't really. They were looking at the same room, but it was in complete disarray. Five chairs were toppled on their sides. Papers and books were strewn about the room. The candle at the pentacle's center had toppled. The flame was out and wax had spilled and dried. The candle in the here and now still glowed, but its light was muted, as if overlaid by a thin, invisible sheet. Armand Moreland knelt by one of the chairs, staring at something pinched between his fingers. They heard what he thought. *"I know exactly what to do with this."*

The scene shifted. They found themselves in the woods. Armand Moreland moved through the forest with liquid ease, his vampire eyes attuned to the dark. To the circle of ten under the potion's spell, the forest was a mix of silver dappled trees and undulating shadow; the hues of twilight.

In the distance, a shimmer of orange light painted a ring of trees in a small clearing. A fire burned at its center, and a lone figure cloaked in black stood waiting. At the site of him, Moreland shivered, and they all felt it. The vampire had doubts, but he was also desperate. The thought of never seeing them again was more than he could bear. And the promise of a reunion, whatever the means, was too much to resist.

Besides, the angel told him this was how it had to be. This was his trial. It didn't mean he had to like it.

Armand reached the clearing. The cloaked figure was a solid mass, darker than a moonless night. The vampire couldn't tell if he faced its back, or if he'd been watched. His answer came when Lucifer opened his eyes. Bright crimson surrounded oblong vertical slits—the eyes of the serpent. The dark one smiled, his teeth grey and his fangs long. "You showed. I didn't think you had it in you."

The circle of ten felt the vampire's self loathing, but they also felt him push it down. "I miss my family."

Lucifer laughed. "Spare me the melodrama. Did you bring it?"

Moreland reached into his pocket. He handed Lucifer a small plastic baggie with a single strand of silver hair inside. "You have one last chance to back out of this. After that, it's out of my hands."

The ten saw that outwardly, the vampire appeared angry having to rely on Lucifer. Their unique perspective, thanks to the potion, made them privy to his inner feelings. Armand Moreland was relieved. "Just do it."

Lucifer raised his right arm. From the sleeve of his cloak he extended a hand. He drew one long, daggered finger through the empty space to his right. A gash rippled in the air, and the fabric holding reality together tore. Through the opening he saw a clearing with a fire, identical to the clearing he currently stood in, but occupied by two very different people. A beautiful woman and a teenage boy knelt by the fire. They seemed to be in prayer, or chanting. Moreland recognized Mondra the Red Witch right away, for the Council had been watching her. The boy he did not know, but he looked familiar. It made him think of the vision he'd had the night before his 'hangover.' The one where the white witch and the man hovered just outside his window.

Mondra stopped. "He's here, Jagger. The dark one has answered our call."

Lucifer held up a hand to Moreland, then stepped through the opening between realities. Armand realized he could see the woman and the boy, but that they could not see him.

Lucifer spoke to the woman. "This is her essence. Use it to create the bodies." He handed her the bag with the strand of Clair Davies's hair in it. "In exchange for time, the Obsidian Witch and her son have given their souls to me. But you *both* can have what's theirs, if you want it."

"How?" asked Jagger.

"If you defeat the sapphire witch, you'll inherit what's rightfully the heir's. It's down to either you, or the Obsidian Witch. All I need is one of you for control of Black and Blue house. With the child of the prophecy dead, or replaced, Salem is once again mine."

Lucifer turned to the Red Witch. "Your estranged daughter Mercy's power would go a long way to making this possible."

"Consider it done," replied Mondra.

"When will *the heir's* life become mine?" asked Jagger.

"November 9, 2019, it begins. *If* you are successful, you will inherit powers and riches beyond your dreams. *Fail?*" Lucifer shook his head.

"How will I know when to cross into his reality?" asked Jagger. "Time is different here."

"You'll know," said Lucifer. "Why do you think she's here?" Lucifer pointed at the Red Witch.

Jagger turned to Mondra, then back to Lucifer.

But the dark one was gone.

WHEN LUCIFER APPEARED ONCE MORE in front of Moreland, he said, "It is done, vampire. If all goes well, you'll be with your wife and child again."

"How?" asked Moreland.

"I have my ways," said Lucifer.

ONCE MORE, the vision shifted. Armand Moreland was back in the very same room in which they sat, but the pentacle and chairs were missing. The debris strewn about the room from earlier in the vision was gone. Moreland sat at the room's center in the lotus position. His eyes were closed, his breathing was slow and rhythmic. When his third eye opened, all ten in the circle saw what Armand saw.

Archangel Michael appeared before him.

"It is done, Michael," said Moreland.

"Lucifer promised to deliver you to your family?" asked the angel.

"He believes that *I* believe he can reunite me with my family. Though I don't see how that's possible."

"He believes he can because he is full of himself, and considers himself equal to *Him*."

"What of the others? What of the child of the prophecy? What will become of them?" asked Moreland. He was riddled with guilt for betraying people he knew, and people he'd yet to meet.

"This I cannot tell you, because I do not know. Only *He* knows. Watch over them, vampire. Guide them. Protect them. If your heart is true, and your motives pure, you may call on us. Myself. Gabriel. Raphael. Ariel. Azrael. We can, and will help, but only when *He* allows. No more. The rest is up to you."

. . .

THE POTION'S EFFECT WANED, and reality settled on them like a warm blanket.

When they were all the way back, Joanne spoke. "So, he basically sold us down the river thinking he could get his family back. Nice."

"No. I know it seems that way," said Henry. "But I think there's more to it."

"Okay," said Byron. "I kind of agree with Jo on this. So, what's the 'more?'"

Henry stood, stretched, and began pacing the room. "I know, on the surface, it looks like Armand betrayed us. Or he at least tried to make it look that way for Lucifer. But we know Michael told him he had to do it. So it begs the question; did he actually have any choice?"

"Of course he had a choice," said Byron. "When the angel told him to do it, he could have said no. Armand might not have known about all of us, but he sure as shit knew Wanda and Jazz at that point. Archie too."

Henry shook his head. "Michael didn't *tell* him to do it. Michael told him, and I quote, 'this is how it had to be.' Now, I sure as hell don't know enough about the will of God, or Hecate, or whoever is running things, but aside from Lucifer, I know this; angels follow orders. They don't question. They don't ponder. They act. Plain and simple."

"And what about all the time in between, Henry?" asked Jo.

"Meaning?"

"Think about it. It started when I went after that hoodie guy. Moreland threatens us with a letter. Then there was that good looking vampire, Xavier... whatever-the-fuck's his name? He almost let that bastard kill us."

"Saulis," said Mercy.

"Huh?" asked Jo.

"Xavier Saulis was his name," replied Mercy, her cheeks turning crimson.

Wanda was giggling a little. "It's okay, sweetie. That was one pretty man."

"He was, wasn't he?" said Jo with a smile.

"Hey!" said Henry, smiling. "Focus!"

"Speaking of that whole shit show out in Satan's Kingdom, how is it Armand could call down angels from *On High,* but he can't take care of a half-assed demon and his perverted sidekick?" asked Jo.

Henry held up both hands. "All true. And all good points. I can't argue with any of them. I won't even try."

"So how can you sit there and defend him, Henry?" Byron asked. "I know we all felt badly about him dying, and I'm glad he's with his family again. But the shit we had to go through—" Byron suddenly stopped.

Wanda saw the look of sudden understanding on his face. She wanted desperately to say something, but she also wanted them to arrive at the same conclusion on their own.

Henry was smiling, because he saw it too. Just like Wanda, he held his tongue.

"What is it Byron?" asked Jo. "You look like you blew a gasket."

"I get it," said Byron. "I completely understand it."

"Care to enlighten us?" asked Jo. "Cuz from where I'm sitting, none of this shit should have happened."

"That's the point, though. Isn't it?" asked Byron. "Think about it. When all this shit started, Henry didn't believe any of this crap was real. Am I wrong?"

"Nope. Thought it was complete bullshit," said Henry. "And I *had* to start believing it—like *yesterday.*"

Byron was nodding, getting into the flow. "And you, Jo. I know you're a believer, but I know the hell you had to go through to get to that point. It was trial by fire. Wanda got there much the same way, from what she's told me."

Wanda closed her eyes and nodded.

"And there was no one who thought all this magic and past lives and demons and vampires was a bigger pile of shit than I did. But I've seen too much now. We all have. And I think that's probably been the point all along."

"Which is?" asked Jo.

"We were *always* going to go through what we've just gone through. If Armand Moreland hadn't stepped in when he did, think about what would have happened. Chesrule would have killed Mercy. Strike that. He *did* kill Mercy, but Moreland just happened to be able to call an angel down and heal her. Henry would have died tonight. Wanda too. Every move Armand made was designed to keep us alive, but more than that, he helped shape us into what we've become."

"Okay," said Jo. "But he had an ulterior motive, noble as it might seem. He wanted his soul back. He wanted his family back. Let's not pretend otherwise."

"*This is how it has to be*, is what Michael told him," said Byron. "I know when I first heard that, I was thinking the angel was telling him he had no choice, betrayal was his only option. We all *felt* his shame. Now... I think it was way deeper than that."

Wanda was nodding. Henry was nodding.

Byron pointed at Wanda and smiled. "No coincidences."

"No," said Wanda.

"Armand Moreland did what he did, the good *and* the bad, because just like he moved us around like pieces on a chessboard, he wasn't the actual player. He was just another piece in a much larger game. He became a vampire because he was *destined* to become a vampire. I believe his wife and daughter died so that would happen. It's an intentional chain of events, stretching back through time. It's the same for all of us."

Henry nodded. "I couldn't agree more."

In that moment, Wanda knew why Henry had been chosen to take over for Moreland. It went beyond wisdom, for wisdom alone didn't make leaders. Wisdom *and* loyalty were two of the ingredients of true leaders. And she also understood, on many levels, why Henry was allowed to die, and then come back.

Because *patience* was the third ingredient.

Jagger Corey, and his desire for a quick solution to the sad mess that was his life by stealing Henry's, was the ultimate expression of impatience, when you cut it to the bone. Henry had to experience that firsthand, and then have it burned away by dying. It was *his* trial by fire.

She didn't know what came next, but she knew he was ready.

He always had been.

CHAPTER 39
HENRY CHECKS IN

Hey! It's me again. I'm gonna try and catch you up on what's going on—as promised.

Okay... where to start with this one?

I guess I should start with the move to Blue House. Yes, we're living here now—for a whole shitload of reasons.

Neither of us wanted to move. I just want to get that out right up front. I know the "dream" is a big house, a picket fence, and lots of land. But I kinda liked the idea of coming home after work, kicking off the shoes, and not worrying about taking care of a bunch of shit. There's already enough to deal with in life. I can't speak for Jo—not *just* because it's dangerous—but, between you and me? The Cracked Cauldron takes a lot out of her, and I suspect she feels the same about it as I do.

When we all left the attic room at Blue House and went our separate ways, Eljin Black took Jo and I aside. He didn't say much—Eljin is a man... sorry, *shifter* of few words, but he makes them count.

He handed me a letter from Armand Moreland, who seems to have a hell of a lot to say for a guy that's, well, dead.

Just saying.

Eljin said, "Read this soon." That was it. He turned on his heel and left. That's his thing, I guess.

Anyhoo, when we got to our building, guess who was up and waiting for us? I'll give you three guesses, but I'm pretty sure there'll be two left on the table.

Yep. Mrs. Greenblatt.

How'd you know?

Get this! Jo greeted her with a hug. When I asked Jo about it later, she said she felt bad about scaring the living crap out of her when Jagger Corey escaped through Mrs. G's apartment on the night he tried to steal my life. Apparently, in the heat of the moment, (and with glowing emerald eyes, no doubt), Jo mentioned something to the effect they should chat sometime. She probably said it just to calm Mrs. G down, but my intrepid neighbor took her up on the offer. No surprise there. When I asked her how *said* chat went, I had my socks knocked off once again.

"She's really a sweet lady," Jo had said. "Once you get past the nosiness bullshit."

We are truly living in the age of miracles, my friends.

Jo broke the news to her about the move the night after we read the letter together. We promised to keep in touch.

Normally, I'd say it wasn't that big a deal. At forty-four thousand-plus people, the Witch City is actually just under the fifty thousand population threshold to officially make it a city. It's more like a large town. Crowded, for sure, but not overwhelmingly so. Visiting, under normal circumstances, wouldn't be a problem.

But these are strange times.

The streets are emptying. The powers that be haven't forbidden visiting... yet. But it wouldn't surprise me if that's next.

This Covid thing has blown up, as I feared it might when I read that headline a few days after we offed Jagger Corey. The two week, shelter-in-place order was the tip of the iceberg. Now, we're in lockdown. I just thank God Jo and I aren't packrats.

When we moved, we were packed and ready to go in less than a day. Since we couldn't hire a mover, due to the lockdown, Byron and Raul helped with the heavy stuff. Having the Chief of the Salem Police in your family has its advantages during this period in time. No one busted our balls about masks and gatherings and all that happy horseshit.

Enough about how we got here. Here's the good stuff.

The night we came home from the attic, and after greeting Mrs. G, Jo drove to Penny's house and picked up Delilah while I put on a pot of coffee.

"Don't you dare start reading that letter without me," she'd threatened. I didn't. I was a good boy and waited. Why get on her bad side when I don't have to?

Don't look at me like that. You would have waited too.

I didn't wait long. Jo's legendary lead foot had them back less than fifteen minutes later. While I poured coffee, Jo put Delilah to bed. By the time she came into the living room, I was sitting down with the envelope in my hand.

"Fork it over," said Jo. "I'll read it out loud."

I was about to protest. I wanted to read it silently together, but I held my tongue. I don't know what it is about having died and come back, but I've become much more of a diplomat about things. A bit more chill, if you will. I kinda like it.

So, I handed it over.

Jo tore it open, then tore into it.

"Dear Henry and Jo,

If things have gone the way I hoped, you are happy, healthy, and reading this together. Know that I'll miss all of you, but none of us is ever truly gone.

There's not too much to say here, and after the attic, you'll probably be relieved to hear that.

So, right down to it.

Blue House is yours. It is to my great relief I can call it that now. That being said, you need to know what to expect, and also what comes along with it. I think you'll be pleasantly surprised.

The first and most important thing; it is a fortress protected by powerful white magic. Now that the threat of takeover by Lucifer has been, at least for a while, thwarted the grounds are protected by guardians of the Council of the Realms. Each of them has been vetted by myself, Eljin Black, and the very same London witch who brewed the potion for me: Dame Elizabeth Bourden."

Jo lowered the letter and stared deadpan at me. "Lizzie Borden? You gotta be kidding me."

"Well, not a bad thing, necessarily. If she's on our side."

Jo raised the letter, she read the next line to herself and laughed out loud.

"What?" I'd asked.

Jo picked up where she left off.

"Whatever you do, DO NOT call her Lizzie. No one wants a nickname synonymous with an ax murderer, acquitted or not."

"Gotta give it to the guy," I'd said. "He thought of everything."

"True."

Jo read on.

"You will find no better ally than Elizabeth this side of Wanda Heinze.

"Next, when you take up residence in Blue House, it will take a while to get acclimated. The house will learn you, and you will learn it. Yes, you've read that right. The house is, for lack of a better term, alive. Now that it is one hundred percent under the protection of white magic, it will change to suit you. But not only that, it will defend you in the event of a breach. Is it any wonder Lucifer wanted the place as badly as he did?

"I told you at the start, this letter will be brief. So here is the punch line. The moment the house became yours, Henry, everything attached also became yours. I know you love your job as a nurse, but I'm afraid those days are over. And Jo's days at the Cracked Cauldron are probably numbered too. Regardless of the outcome of the budding pandemic, your needs have been considered and well provided for."

"We'll see about that," said Jo.

When she got to the next lines in the letter, her eyes bugged out. "Holy fucking *shit*," she whispered.

"What? What is it?" I'd asked.

"Read the next lines to me. I wanna make sure I didn't imagine it."

I scanned the letter up to the point where Jo left off, then read it aloud.

"The contents of my bank account were transferred into a new, joint account under both of your names. A safety deposit box, as well as a storage unit, are included in the will. The documents

await you at Blue House. All told, in both cash and property, it totals roughly seventy-seven million dollars. That should keep the lights on and the furnace full, methinks.

"*I'll leave you with this; you need never worry about earthly things again. It does my heart good to leave it to you. Disperse it as you see fit. I've no doubt you'll do wonderful things with the money.*

"*The safety deposit box and the storage unit are another matter. Items in both locations are precious, irreplaceable, and may, no probably will, save your lives and the lives of others. Use them wisely. May God, Hecate, or the Higher Power of your choice bless you and keep you.*

Your friend and servant always,

Armand J. Moreland."

Needless to say, we didn't sleep much that night. Jo and I talked into the early morning hours about what we could do with that kind of money. Jo's first thought, to her eternal credit, was for her employees. It killed her when she had to tell her "kids," that's what she calls her employees, they were laid off for the next two weeks. When it became evident two weeks was turning into something much longer, she cut all eight of her employees checks for a year's worth of salary. I wish I could have seen the looks on their faces.

Jo has zero intention of closing The Cracked Cauldron, by the way. Surprised?

Me neither.

As for me? I loved my job at Mass General, but I'm not going back. It has nothing to do with the pandemic. To be honest, I wish I could pitch in and help right now, because this thing could get ugly fast. I get a lot of satisfaction out of caring for sick people and helping them get better. It's rewarding. And I almost *did* go back. But something happened a few nights ago that changed my mind in a hurry.

It happened a few weeks after we read the letter from Armand and we were settled into Blue House. Jo had just put Delilah to bed.

She's talking now, my little girl, which is a thrill and a delight for both of us. Unfortunately, her mother has the linguistic stylings of a long-haul trucker, and my beautiful daughter's first word was, of course, *'Fuck.'*

I'd thrown my hands up. "Why am I not surprised?"

Jo had clapped a hand over her own mouth to stifle a laugh.

Since that night, Jo agreed to substitute *duck* for *fuck*. Sometimes, she's even successful.

Gotta take your victories where you can get them, right?

Anyway, Delilah's room is right next to ours. We always leave the door connecting the rooms open because some nights Delilah wakes up screaming bloody murder. You see, my daughter has epic nightmares. Jo and I suspect it might be trauma from the end of her past life.

I don't need to rehash that, you know the story there.

Researchers into past lives, reincarnation, karma—call it what you will—seem to mostly agree past life memories stay with children until as late as their seventh year. Interesting number. I'm kinda into the numbers thing since the 313 stuff. Anyway, as I said, we *thought* it might be past life memories.

After tonight's nightmare, Jo and I think there may be a bit more to it.

When we finally got her calmed down, she was trying to say something. It's truly a wonder to watch a child wrap their heads around a new word. It's the first time they'll ever use it, and it will stay with them the rest of their lives.

At that stage in life, parents are *gods* in their eyes, and they look for approval for every little thing. Her first try at the new word sounded like "*tote.*" The next attempt was a bit clearer, "*toast.*" Delilah could tell by the tilt of our heads she wasn't getting the point across. In that moment of frustration, I saw a mini version of my wife, and cupped a hand over my mouth to stifle a laugh. Exasperated, she stood up in her crib, held onto the railing with one hand, then pointed into the corner and added the new word to her vocabulary with some mustard on it.

"*Ghost!*" screamed my daughter.

Great.

Can't wait to see where this one goes.

FROM THE AUTHOR

Hi again! Thank you so much for reading *Soul of the Witch*. I hope you enjoyed the story. The ideas for Book 6 are already brewing in the cauldron. As I write this, the opening scene has pretty much formed in my mind. I'm looking forward to seeing where this one goes because this bitch is about to go international. I guess we'll all find out soon.

I have some thoughts on this one, and some fun "inside" stuff to share with you about the writing of this and the previous books.

So, I'll start with this: this was the most difficult book to write in the series to date. Not in the sense of the actual story. The ideas and the scenes came to me, as in the previous stories, pretty much the way I saw them. The characters still do shit I don't expect though, which is what makes it so much fun.

I know I've mentioned this a million times, but it bears repeating; I don't know what's going to happen next until I start writing. I wouldn't want to do it any other way.

I've toyed with the idea of writing an outline for each book, but whenever I start doing it, it bores the ever-loving shit out of me. It's like knowing the ending before you start. I don't know about you, but I wouldn't pay to see a movie if someone told me how it was going to end. I might stream it somewhere down the line, maybe, but the payoff couldn't possibly have the same impact.

I've gotten to the end of each book and had the same feeling as reading someone else's book for the first time. There's *nothing* cooler than seeing your own story end in a way you never expected.

Well, now that I think of it, there's *one* thing cooler. Hearing from a reader and having them tell you they loved the story. That NEVER gets old.

I've had my share of readers who thought a story I wrote sucked, too. And that's fine. You can't be everyone's cup of tea. I'm just grateful they at least gave it a shot. I know I've left a few books I've started, here and there, unfinished.

The difficulty with *Soul* came in working the actual writing of the story into everyday life. I still work a full time job, and the travel back and forth to that job eats up at least three hours of every day. Thankfully, I have long periods of down time and can whip out my trusty Chromebook and tickle the keys for a few hours.

Then there's the creative part.

Full disclosure: writing a novel is a challenge. If you've written a book, I'm not telling you anything new. If you haven't, it's *worth* the struggle. I don't think I fully appreciated the work that goes into it until I started *In Your Dreams*. My books are roughly seventy to eighty thousand words long. I think of a guy like George R.R. Martin and the length of his books, probably in the neighborhood of three hundred thousand words, and I'm in awe. *That* is some serious commitment. I think it might work out for him. *Wink*

I'd be full of shit if I didn't tell you there are times I feel like giving up. It usually happens, for me, somewhere in the middle of the story. I can't see the forest past the first few trees. There are plenty of times I've felt lost, or that I was losing the narrative along the way. It frustrates the hell out of me. But, like most things worth doing, you have to fight through it. And I always get to the end happier for overcoming the obstacles. It's *always* worth it.

Okay, enough of the violins. Let's get to some of the cool stuff.

Wanda's hometown is Winthrop, Massachusetts. I grew up there. So it's a tip of the hat to my old stomping grounds.

Salem State University is mentioned a lot in this book and others in the series. I went there when it was called Salem State College, many moons ago. My major was psychology, but I wasn't ready for college at that point in my life. I lasted almost two whole semesters!

My current hometown is also mentioned in the books. I won't name it here, but you've probably figured it out by now.

In *Blood, Magic & Mercy*, there is a location known as Satan's Kingdom. This is a real place. It's an unincorporated village in Northfield, Massachusetts. My wife and I drove out to see it. Nothing like some real life research to add some flavor. The church where a lot of the action takes place is completely fictional.

In *The Red Witch*, the car the Red Witch steals toward the end of the book is actually my sister Susan's car. She is always the first to read the finished book, so I laughed my ass off thinking about her reaction when she first read it. To continue with the theme, Wanda has a memory in *Blood, Magic & Mercy* where she recalls seeing the woman whose car is stolen being interviewed by a local news reporter, along with her upstairs neighbor. They are my sister and my wife, Diana. My wife usually reads the book *as* I'm writing it.

At that point, it's usually a dumpster fire, but she doesn't care. I watched her as she read that part.

In Your Dreams, when I started writing it, I had nothing to write it *on*. I suppose I could have used pen and paper, but I think the discouragement factor would have figured in quickly. The first drafts of that book were done on Microsoft Notepad, which is the modern-day equivalent of "roughing it" for a writer. I had Notepad pages all over my PC desktop. I believe it was a minor miracle Book 1 ever saw the light of day.

Those are just some fun things I wanted to share with all of you. I always like when writers give me a peek behind the scenes, so I figured I'd do my own version of it.

One other very big thing has happened between publishing *Black Magick & Envy*, and *Soul of the Witch*. I got an email in my inbox looking for submissions to a new publisher. The person I received it from is someone I had almost worked with in the past, but budgetary considerations put his excellent work just out of reach. He's worked with some big name authors in the past. One in particular hails from Maine. I think his name is Stephen something. Anyway, I figured "what the hell?" So, I gave it a shot.

I heard back from this publisher fairly quickly. They said they were interested in my series, and asked if we could set up a meeting.

I did not play "hard to get."

As you may have noticed, their publishing logo is at the front of this and my other ebooks now. So I am beyond thrilled to let you guys know I've signed on with Vinci Books. If you'd like to see who is helping me take the series to the next level, you can check them out here at Vinci-Books.com

Let me know what you think! I'd love to hear from you.
I answer every email personally.
Thanks again for reading *Soul of the Witch*.
Take care. Be safe. And happy reading!
August 11, 2024

MORE IN THE LEAGUE OF THE MOON SERIES

vinci-books.com/savingthewitch

Enter a world of witches, magic and past lives.

Henry's dreams have begun. Now, the Order Immortalis must find the boy—and the secret he carries—or silence him forever.

Turn the page for a free preview...

PREVIEW OF
SAVING THE WITCH

CHAPTER 1 — EYES IN THE SKY

August 2, 1992

Wanda Heinze was having the most beautiful dream. In it, she was walking along the shoreline at Salem Willows—a park on the upper northeast side of the Witch City of Salem, Massachusetts. The sun was shining. A cool ocean breeze blew her hair back and passed through the sheer, purple silk robe she was wearing. It felt so wonderful and real; it was a dream about the moment you never wanted to end—solemn and peaceful. At least, that's how it started.

But somewhere, a phone was ringing. The sound seemed to come from far offshore, maybe from one of the boats cruising about lazily in the harbor, or maybe from one of the few other human beings out in the Willows carrying one of those new cell phone thingies. It grew louder, more insistent, and moved closer by the moment. She looked around and tried to pinpoint the source, but it eluded her.

The sky grew dark. Swollen purple and black storm clouds blanketed the horizon, moving into the harbor at impossible speed. The warm feel of the sun fled from her skin, chased away like a rabbit fleeing a fox at the first hint of trouble. A drop of rain dotted her nose and sent a flash of cold throughout her body. Several more drops pelted down on her, a merciless onslaught of liquid daggers flung from the heavens by angry black clouds.

Then, eyes appeared in the clouds—cold, blue, and searching. They were looking for something. Or someone. She knew those eyes. And she knew, deep down inside, who they searched for. Who they'd always been searching for. Somewhere, in the depths of a once beautiful dream, reality surfaced. The phone was not on a boat in the harbor, or in the pocket of a passerby in the Willows, but ringing insistently away on her nightstand. She snapped awake, fumbled for her phone, and snatched the receiver before it could hit the floor.

"Hello."

"It's me. He's starting to remember," the voice said.

"Okay. I'm on my way. You have everything set up? Did you call them and let them know?" Wanda asked.

"It's all taken care of. Once this part is over, I have to go away for a while. I don't have a choice. You know that, right?"

"I do. I'm gonna miss you, honey."

"I'll miss you too. We must never be seen together again. Well, at least until the time comes," she said.

Wanda fought back tears. "I know."

"Make sure you watch your back. They're probably already somewhat aware of what's happening," the voice warned.

"They are. I saw him, in my dreams, right before you called. He's searching. I recommend you don't sleep at all tonight. He'll be looking everywhere and you're the closest connection."

"Don't worry, the coffee's on. I couldn't sleep if I tried, anyway. I can't believe this is happening. I prayed this day would never come, or that it could pass us by somehow. But you know the saying, wish in one hand, crap in the other, see which one fills up first."

Wanda laughed, but it was filled with sadness. "I'll see you in about three hours. Is that enough time for them to get there?"

"They'll be here, ready to take him. What about them? Won't he try searching through them?"

"I'll take care of that. By the time Henry gets where he's going, his new parents will think he *really is* their child. They'll always suspect something strange, and in the backs of their minds, they'll know something is off. It won't be enough to get Henry in trouble. Not for a good number of years, at least. I hate to do it this way, but there's really no choice."

The voice on the other end sighed. "No, there's really not."

"I'm gonna head to you soon. Stay safe." Wanda said.

"You too."

Wanda hung up, showered, dressed, and phoned her best friend in the world, Doctor Archibald Love.

"Archie, it's me. I need a favor."

A sleep-bleary voice croaked on the other end. "Wanda? It's three-thirteen in the morning. What's the matter? Are you okay?"

"I'm fine honey. I need a ride to meet up with someone.

And I need another pair of eyes watching my back on the way there."

"What's going on?" He sounded nervous.

"You remember what we discussed a few years back? About Madeleine?"

"I do." Archie said.

"Her soul has returned," Wanda said in a matter-of-fact tone.

"You're shitting me."

"I shit you not."

"Who is it?"

"You know I can't tell you that. It would put both you and him in jeopardy."

"It's a boy. Interesting."

Wanda cursed herself for letting even that much slip. She chalked it up to lack of sleep, but she would have to be more careful from here on out.

"Can you take me?"

"Of course I can. I'm throwing on my sneakers and heading out the door as soon as I hang up."

CHAPTER 2 — WANDA'S WICCA'D EMPORIUM

A gleaming, black Cadillac Brougham pulled into the streets of early morning Salem. The car was long—a living room on wheels. Chrome glinted, reflecting the piss-yellow, low-pressure sodium street lights, making the body of the car almost invisible. It was blacker than night itself.

"Where to, Mr. Dobson?" asked the driver.

"I'm not sure. Essex Street keeps popping into my head. Let's start there. And get Leonard on the phone for me."

"Yes, sir."

Solomon Dobson smiled. He liked his driver. Scott Johnson was ex-military. No bullshit. No drama. Yes sir, no sir, and get the job done.

The phone buzzed in its backseat cradle.

"Yes, Mr. Dobson?"

"She's back, Leonard."

"Madeleine?"

"Yes."

"Are you sure, Mr. Dobson?"

Solomon rolled his eyes and wished he had an army of Scott Johnsons. "For fucks sake! Of course I'm sure, Leonard."

Leonard Shrumm gulped and kept quiet.

"I want you to hit the streets. I'm heading toward Essex at this very moment. Check the Willows, then up by the University. Branch out from there. Pay attention to any cars containing more than one person. You know what the witch looks like, right?"

"Heinze? Of course," said Leonard.

"Pay attention to the passenger sides. Since the old sot quit drinking, she doesn't drive. And tell the others under your supervision to get their asses out of bed and on the road. Give them the same instructions I've just imparted to you. Understood?"

"Yes, Mr. Dobson."

Click.

As Solomon ended the call, the Caddy rolled to a stop.

"We're here, sir," said Johnson.

Solomon looked out of the left rear window. Above, a sign gleamed gold in the night—lit from within and visible only to his eyes. Wanda's Wicca'd Emporium was protected by the most powerful white magic Solomon had ever encountered. Heinze was a powerful witch, and her IQ was in the stratosphere. For someone like him, it was a deadly combination.

It did not surprise him his hunch led here. They'd done battle before, long ago, and victory had been his. It was minor consolation. She'd done her best back then to protect the others long enough to keep something precious from him. Something which could spell the end of his very existence. Tonight was a chance to nip it in the bud. If he could kill the body that housed the soul, he would be safe.

As he dwelt upon it, another option presented itself. A much more thorough and complete option. If he could tail the witch to the child's house, he could take the child, have Leonard Shrumm or one of his other followers raise it, and then turn him or her into an endless source of information. He could ferret out the entire League of the Moon, one by one, in every corner of the world. Wipe them from the face of the earth.

Madeleine was back. It scared him. But sometimes the sweetest opportunities came from the most dangerous fruit.

CHAPTER 3 — HENRY

The boy emerged from his room. His light-brown hair plastered down on the left and sticking straight up on the right. His dark-blue, sleep-wrinkled Underoos sported an image of his favorite superhero. Batman looked pissed off and ready to kick ass.

Henry balled both fists, rubbed the sleep from his eyes, and headed straight for the living room TV. He flicked the remote's on button and the Sony glowed to life. It was on Channel 2. It was always on Channel 2 because Sesame

Street, The Electric Company, and Zoom could not be found on the yucky adult channels his mom watched. Mommy always set it to Channel 2 for him before she went to bed.

He smelled bacon, which meant mommy was awake. Mommy was never awake before he was on a Sunday because she worked late on Saturday. Henry hated when mommy worked Saturdays because it meant Mrs. Andersen would babysit him. Mrs. Andersen's breath always smelled funny. The kind of funny that hurt his nose and made him want to gag. And her daughter cried a lot. She was a baby, but man did her little Jo-Jo want to be heard!

Henry had asked his mother once about his babysitter's breath.

"Well, Henry, sometimes people are sick, but it's a sickness that doesn't make them cough or sniffle. It's something inside here." She'd pointed to her heart.

Henry's mom didn't relish leaving Henry with Terry Andersen, but there was no one else in the area she could hire to watch him when she worked late. They lived in a sparsely populated area on the fringe of Salem. Most of her neighbors were either too far away, or professionals without children and working jobs that consumed massive amounts of time.

Terry lived a quarter of a mile away in the next town over at the Happy Acres trailer park. She couldn't afford a car, so there were no worries she would drive over shit-faced. And her drinking, though a problem, seemed manageable enough. Terry was what reformed drinkers would call a *functioning alcoholic*. Beggars couldn't be choosers, and Henry's mom fell squarely into the beggar category.

Henry was curious enough about his mom being awake

before him on a Sunday that he found the will to let Big Bird navigate Sesame Street without him.

"Mommy, what are you doing awake?"

She jumped at the sound of his voice. "Good morning, honey. I couldn't sleep, so I made you a big breakfast!"

Henry saw the smile on his mother's face. It looked real enough, but her eyes didn't match her smile. He thought they looked like sad eyes. Mommy's crying eyes. He pulled no punches when he asked the question. He was too young to know better. "Why were you crying, Mommy?"

She smiled again. It was filled with sadness but also pride. Henry was so perceptive and empathetic. It killed her to know she would only take part in his life, from this day forward, as a watcher from afar. He wouldn't remember her after today. He wouldn't see her. And he would truly believe, for many years, that someone else was his mother.

CHAPTER 4 — A RIDE WITH ARCHIE

Wanda sat in darkness, pulling the living room window's curtain aside a fraction of an inch every thirty seconds, monitoring the street for Archie's VW microbus. There normally wasn't a lot of traffic on the streets of Salem at this hour, but tonight seemed to be the exception. Now and then, a car would crawl down Derby Street, slow down in front of her place, then move on. Depending on the car's direction, she caught either the passenger or the driver stealing a furtive glance at her second-floor window. They were looking for her already. She'd expected this, of course, but was still amazed at how fast Solomon had gotten the word out and the troops mobilized.

An ounce of preparation is worth a pound of cure. They

were words to live by—literally. Wanda had discussed the scenario unfolding before her tonight, years ago, with Archie. No matter how many times you run a plan through your mind, it rarely survives the first few moments. Tonight was no exception.

Still, she was prepared. Archie knew to come down Derby with his lights off and to park in the rear of her apartment complex. As soon as she saw the dark shape of the VW turning onto Derby, she grabbed her keys, threw on her windbreaker, locked her door, and shuffled across the well-worn indoor/outdoor carpeting of the main hallway. The nasty after-odor of cabbage assaulted her nose. *Why*, she wondered, *do some people in apartment complexes insist on cooking the nastiest smelling stuff?*

The fire exit door had a large, red pushbutton on the wall next to the handle. Wanda slapped the button, cutting off the alarm. She shoved through the door and scurried down two flights, her footfalls echoing off the yellow brick walls. Wanda heard the Lollipop Guild singing *"Follow the Yellow-Brick Road"* in her head and was smiling when she pushed open the door leading to the alley behind her building.

Archie grinned and asked, "What's so funny?"

She climbed into the passenger's side he'd left open for her.

"Nothing. It's just every time I come out of the building through that exit—"

"The Wizard of Oz thing. I remember."

"You should. You're the one that started singing it that time."

"True enough. That was some good weed," Archie said, still smiling.

"Did you notice anything peculiar on your way over tonight?" asked Wanda.

"You mean the cars driving all around town trying, and failing miserably, to appear like normal Sunday drivers that just happen to be out at," he looked at his dash clock, "three forty-six a.m.?"

"Yes."

"Didn't notice."

Wanda smiled. "Keep the lights off until we're out of the neighborhood." She leaned the seat back as far as it would go. It was enough to conceal her from the prying eyes of her fellow motorists.

Archie put the bus in drive and eased out of the alley.

vinci-books.com/savingthewitch

ACKNOWLEDGMENTS

No one, as far as I know, writes a book alone. With that said, here are some props where props are due.

Thanks to my sister Susan, whose eagle eye catches the things I completely miss the first time through, and who is always my first reader when the first draft—aka dumpster fire—is finished.

I have to thank my wife, who puts up with my obsession and lets me get to work at night when we could be spending time together. Writing is a solo act, unfortunately. And also for the emotional support she gives me when I'm running around like a depressed chicken with its head cut off—usually when I start to think the book is going into the shitter.

Thanks to Jeff "Older Than Fire" Sims, who read my second draft and found the little things that slipped through the cracks. Said cracks have been sealed!

And finally, to you, the readers. None of this is even worth it without all of you. Thanks for reading my books!

ABOUT THE AUTHOR

Robert Sanborn lives in north central Massachusetts with his wife, Diana, their sweet-natured dog, Coco, the Brussels Griffon, their psychotic black cat Luna, the Devon Rex, Jason, the extremely talkative African-Grey Parrot, Angus, the cranky Quaker Parrot, Artemis, the cute-as-hell Java Finch, and two Parakeets named Sweetie and Sunny. He spends a lot on pet food.

Oh, yeah. And a Crested Gecko Lizard named Gretel. Sheesh!

He is a survivor of Hodgkin's Lymphoma, diagnosed in 1993.

He has been clean and sober since September 24, 1991.

His first book, *In Your Dreams*, was written and published in July, 2020, during the event which shall not be named, and between making deliveries to health care facilities as part of his day job. Not nerve-racking at all.

www.ingramcontent.com/pod-product-compliance
Lightning Source LLC
Chambersburg PA
CBHW011344010726
47493CB00011B/2945